Playing With Fire

I have come to bring fire on the earth

Luke 12:49

PLAYING WITH FIRE

▼

Scott Lazenby

Writers Club Press
San Jose New York Lincoln Shanghai

Playing With Fire

Writers Club Press
an imprint of iUniverse.com, Inc.

For information address:
iUniverse.com, Inc.
5220 S 16th, Ste. 200
Lincoln, NE 68512
www.iuniverse.com

ISBN: 0-595-19410-9

Printed in the United States of America

Acknowledgements

The author is indebted to the following individuals for their stories and inspiration. Any resemblance, however, between events and characters in this book and those in their own cities is purely coincidental.

John Greiner, city manager, Cornelius OR; Marilyn Holstrom, city manager, Fairview OR; Bill Pupo, city manager, Surprise AZ; Bob Jean, city manager, Fircrest WA; Jill Monley, assistant city manager, Richland WA; Charlie Leeson, city manager, Oregon City; Larry Lehman, city manager, Pendleton OR; Dick Zais, city manager, Yakima WA; Suzanne Barker, planning and development director, Sandy OR; Dale Scobert, police chief and Fred Punzel, former police chief, Sandy OR; Mark Adcock, city administrator, Canby OR; Beth Kellar, deputy director, International City Management Association; Michael Garvey, city manager, San Carlos CA; Steve Bryant, city manager, Albany OR; and Wes Hare, city manager, LaGrande, OR.

I

One of the fantasies that I indulged myself in was that I was in control. For years, I had told myself that I could manage anything, that all difficult events were merely tests to be conquered. It may have been my upbringing in a home that saw no major crises or conflicts, or the years at universities where professors in their insulated classrooms taught that there are rational solutions to all problems.

Looking back at it, I should have recognized that the series of events was placed there as a test for me to overcome before I could move to some higher plane of understanding. At the time, they seemed to start as mere nuisances, buzzing like mosquitoes at the edge of a relatively uncomplicated life. Whether I passed the test I will probably never know. But this I can say for certain: when I next find myself struggling against such a harsh current, I will be much more willing to let go of the tiller and let events steer themselves.

*   *   *

It started, I suppose, on a gray day around the spring equinox, which in Oregon means three more months of rain. I was feeling pleased with myself, having emptied my in-box and cleared most of the files off my desk. The city was running smoothly: there were no staffing emergencies, no city council elections to worry about, no serious police cases in the works. Whether they were satisfied or merely apathetic, the citizens had pretty much left me alone. Until, that is, Scarlet showed up.

The commotion in the reception area broke into my consciousness. One of the voices belonged to Terri Knox, my secretary, and the other was louder and shriller. I was thinking about getting up to check it out when a woman burst through the door carrying a white bucket. She marched up and dumped the contents on my desk—dirty diapers and bitter smelling water. I managed, barely, to jump back in time to avoid the splash of baby urine and bleach.

The woman stood defiantly, gripping the empty pail. "Now you can deal with this, since I can't," she shrieked.

Water ran off the edge of the desk and began to form a pool on the carpet. Out of the corner of my eye I saw Terri at the doorway, looking dumbstruck. Then she disappeared. I gently pried the mostly empty bucket from the woman's hands and gingerly started picking up the soggy diapers and dumping them in it. I didn't say anything—partly because I was at a loss for words, and partly because I was picturing her driving down to city hall, anticipating the reaction she would get from her dramatic gesture. I didn't want to give her the pleasure.

Terri reappeared with an armful of paper towels. "Do you want me to call the janitors?" she asked.

"No, I'll handle it," I said. Terri shrugged and dropped a wad of the paper towels on the floor to soak up the vile soup on the carpet, and handed me some to use on the desk. A memo I had been reading had plastered itself to the glass. I picked it up by a corner and dropped it into the trash can.

We got the mess cleaned up, and Terri left, glancing at the woman on her way out. I leaned against a credenza and looked at her. Even though it couldn't have been more than fifty degrees outside, she wore a stained tank top that wasn't quite long enough to cover a roll of fat that bulged over the sides of her jeans. Her toenails were painted orange—not a good match with the pink rubber sandals, I thought. Half her dirty blond hair was pulled back in a ponytail and the rest floated around her face. Her mouth was clamped in a thin line, and an ember of hate was still smoldering in her eyes. I waited.

"I got two full buckets and no clean ones," she said. "You shut the water off without telling me. What did you think I was supposed to do?"

I tried to keep my voice down. "It must have been an emergency water line repair. The crew usually knocks on people's doors if they know they're going to have to shut the water off. Where do you live?"

"Why do you want to know?"

"So I can find out what's going on with your water service."

"Twelve forty five Jorgensen Street. But that's not going to do me much good now, is it? I want to know *before* they do stupid things like that, not after. I don't care about no flimsy excuses. I have three kids and two of them are in diapers. And I'm a single mom."

I'm not surprised, I started to say, and caught myself. I guessed a question about artificial insemination wouldn't be appropriate either. My wallet was in my suit coat pocket, hanging behind the door. I pulled a five dollar bill out and handed it to her.

"What's this?" she asked.

"Pick up some disposable diapers on your way home. I'll bet your water is back on anyway, but at least you'll have a backup. What's your name?"

I saw her hesitate and I added, "So we can call you if the outage is going to last longer."

"Scarlet. And I don't have a phone." She stared at me for a moment, then wheeled around to leave. Halfway out the door she remembered her diaper pail, and stomped back in to grab it. She avoided my eyes and bent her shoulders as if she needed to plow her way out of the office.

I watched from my window until she reached her car in the parking lot below and then, without touching anything, made my way to the restroom in the hall. I stood, testing the water with a finger until it was nearly scalding, and plunged my hands in.

*   *   *

Trillium was a city of 42,500 people. It was far enough from Portland to have its own identity and business base, but close enough to reap the rewards of Portland's bustling economy. The trillium was, of course, the official city flower, but the plant didn't seem to grow naturally anywhere except in a few secluded parks. There had been a legend—unconfirmed—that the name came from an Indian phrase—Chee 'Ellum—meaning "tall trees."

In any case, the Indians were long gone, and so were most of the Douglas fir, cedar, and hemlock that once blanketed the rolling hills of the town. Old records showed a dozen active saw mills in the city around the turn of the century. Modern developers, when digging the foundations for their houses, were often surprised by the remains of mill ponds and buried heaps of sawdust.

Over the decades, the residents of Trillium had toiled to recapture the splendor of the old forest by planting a mixture of oaks, fruit trees, and the native soft woods. From a rooftop view, the town was covered by a green canopy, punctuated by the towering spires of the firs and cedars. Instead of wood chips, the city now produced computer chips, and the industry's executives were drawn by the natural beauty of the area.

Some felt it was too much of a good thing. The city—which forty years ago had numbered only 4,500—faced issues of traffic congestion and school crowding. And the city government itself had passed the peak of the natural economy of scale, and was facing big-city problems ranging from gang wannabes to centralized purchasing.

I had been city manager of Trillium for ten years—twice the national average for city manager tenure. It was long enough to feel comfortable with the quirks of the community and its leaders, but not long enough to take job security for granted. All it took was three votes in any city council meeting and I was out on the street. The council was mostly supportive, though, and one of the council members I could always count on was Seth Rosenberg.

He had called me to say he had something he wanted to talk about, but didn't have much time. He had to catch a commuter flight to Seattle to meet with some lumber brokers, he said, and was running behind. I offered to drive him to the airport and he quickly agreed.

Seth didn't waste much time on small talk. He was the manager of the last remaining lumber mill in the area, specializing in the export of dowels, broom handles, and banister spindles. His full black beard and the wrinkles around his eyes reminded me of Abraham Lincoln and made him look older than his thirty-eight years. He was wearing a conservative gray suit and maroon striped tie.

"So what did you want to talk about," I asked as we threaded through the mid-morning traffic on I-5.

"Just some rumblings I've been hearing from some of my colleagues in the so-called business community. Do you know a guy named Todd Pritchard?"

"Nope. The name's familiar, I think, but I don't know him. Why?"

"He runs a construction company. Fairly small, I think—just a couple of Cats and backhoes. He's upset at the city for some reason or another. Something about his fire sprinkler system going off in his equipment shed, and I guess he thinks it's the city's fault because the pressure is too high."

"But they set those things for—"

"I know, I know, but it doesn't matter. The point is, he's mad at the city and I hear he's been going around trying to stir some of the other businesses up."

"Did he talk to you?"

Seth glanced at me, amused. "No, that wouldn't happen. I wouldn't even know about it, except one of our suppliers got an earful, and shared it with me. I don't really care—my job on the council doesn't make me the defender of the city's reputation."

"That's *my* job."

He laughed. "Well, you might want to check it out."

"Sure."

*   *   *

My office still had a slight bitter odor, even though it had been a few days since Scarlet's appearance. I had told Terri that we should start burning incense; maybe she took me seriously because I noticed she seemed to be putting on the perfume a little thicker than usual.

I looked up the number for Todd Pritchard's business and called his office. After the inevitable "Can I tell him who's calling?" I was told that he was on a job site. I left a message, feeling pessimistic about the chance of the call being returned.

The feeling was justified. Over the next few days, I tried calling a half dozen times and always got an evasive story: "he's in a meeting," or "he's with a customer." It was like chasing a shadow. Ironically, other business owners told me that Pritchard was claiming that he had tried to contact me, but that I wouldn't return his calls. After a while I gave up, and let it go.

Two weeks later the *Oregonian* carried a story about a new political action committee that had formed in anticipation of the May special election. Citing the unresponsiveness of city hall and "a lack of fiscal stewardship," the committee was pushing a ballot measure that would cause an immediate rollback in the City of Trillium's property taxes. The committee's chairman was Todd Pritchard.

2

"So, what're we going to do?"

One of the council members tapped his pencil. Another reached for a donut. I watched, then got up to refill my coffee mug. This was going to take a while.

"Well, the choices aren't easy, but we might as well put them on the table," Seth Rosenberg said. It·was a Saturday morning, and he was wearing blue jeans and a Trailblazers sweatshirt. "We're either going to have to cut some services, or increase taxes. We're not the federal government—we can't just go out and borrow more money."

Without any appreciable campaigning, the property tax rollback had sailed through with a seventy two percent approval vote. It caught the city council members—and me—completely off guard. We had been lulled into complacency by a series of editorials in the local newspaper that urged voters to turn down the measure as an irresponsible and foolish vendetta against the city government. It gave me some small satisfaction to realize that the paper had no influence over elections, but I kicked myself for realizing it too late.

"Yeah, but I'm not sure we even have both of those choices," boomed Rob Titus, a lawyer in his other life. He was a pudgy bear of a man in a yellow golf shirt and pleated pants. "Even if we wanted to raise taxes, the State's taken away most of our options. The property tax is all we have left. We're just going to have to pull out the ax."

There was a rare silence. I couldn't tell if it was because they were trying to figure out what Titus meant by his cliche, or if they had come to the same conclusion.

Mayor Diane McTavish glanced at me out of the corner of her eye. She was a tall, no-nonsense woman with short black hair. She had little patience for Titus, and often refuted his speeches, but now she seemed to be waiting for me to do it. I didn't take the bait. The silence continued to hang.

Looking uncomfortable, Maggie Henderson finally blurted out, "The message from the voters is that they want government to be more efficient. We need to first cut any unnecessary expenses and waste." She was a recently retired schoolteacher with a thick head of blond curls that I figured had to be a wig. Talk about unnecessary expense and waste.

"You're right, Maggie," Seth said in his measured voice. "We do need to take a hard look at each budget. But we've been doing this for the past six years, since the first state tax limitation measure passed. We haven't left too many dollars lying around on the floor. There may be some opportunities to save money by looking at radically different ways of getting things done, but the choices aren't easy. They raise the same kinds of emotions and reactions that school vouchers and charter schools do."

Ouch. Seth looked serene, but he must have pushed Maggie's teachers' union button intentionally. She seemed not to have noticed; she probably hadn't been listening.

The mayor glanced at the council members in turn, acknowledging them. "You know, I'm not sure what the voters said they wanted. I think they mostly wanted to pay less tax. They're used to voting for presidents and congressmen who promise they will cut taxes, increase services, and end the deficit. They like living in that fairyland…. But Maggie's point is well taken. We need to shave costs where we can. And if we have to stir up a few hornet nests by talking about different ways of doing things, so be it. That's why we get the big bucks."

Her colleagues chuckled. They were all volunteers.

Rob Titus cut in. "I for one am not opposed to some major service cuts, in areas that are very visible. The voters need to get the message that there are consequences to irresponsible decisions. We can't just go on pulling rabbits out of the hat. Its time to show some tough love."

Seth leaned forward. "You know, it isn't our job to teach voters a lesson." He stroked his beard thoughtfully. "And it can backfire. For years, every time Multnomah County hit a budget shortfall, they would close libraries, and then ask the voters for more money to re-open them. And guess which county service is used by more residents than any other? The library patrons felt they were being held hostage. Like it or not, I think we have to do the best job we can to keep the impact on services as small as possible. The voters may well say, 'Hey, that was easy—let's hit 'em with another tax cut.' That's just the way it is. To do any thing else on our part would be shirking our duty."

More silence. Outside the glass and cedar walls of the Champoeg Retreat Center it was drizzling, typical of a June day. The sun had found a hole in the clouds. Drops of water collected on the branches of the fir trees next to the window and fell randomly, catching the sun and flashing like diamonds.

Maggie raised her hand. "How about if we cut—say—ten percent across the board? That way no single program would be hit hard, and we would spread the pain over all the areas, and maybe—"

"That's the chicken way out," Mayor McTavish said, her impatience starting to show. "If it was as easy as that, a computer could do our job. The fact is that some programs are more important than others to our constituents. And some departments can more easily take budget cuts than others. We're here to exercise some judgement, not make knee-jerk decisions."

Maggie's face reddened.

Seth quickly jumped in, "Its not that bad an approach—a lot of governments and businesses use it. But it does have its problems. One is that what looks like an across-the-board cut really isn't." He looked at the ceiling. "Uh, let's see. Take the senior citizens area as an example. We get a lot of grant money for meals, van rides, social services. And we use our own tax money as a match for the state and federal funds. So every dollar we cut there means we lose, maybe, three or four dollars of grant support. Another operation, say police, depends mostly on local taxes. So an across-the-board cut of ten percent would cut ten percent of the police department's budget, but maybe forty percent of the senior services budget. I doubt we'd want to see that happen."

Maggie nodded. "I hadn't thought of that. It was just a suggestion anyhow."

I leaned on an elbow and listened as the discussion continued. Seth and the mayor tossed some ideas back and forth, and the others started to tune out. McTavish eventually looked at me.

"Ben, what kind of a percentage cut do we need to make to be in balance?"

"Well, the ballot measure is pretty convoluted, and each property gets a different reduction—"

"I know that. Just give us a ballpark."

That's the way she liked it—short and to the point. If a staff report was more than three paragraphs long, she would make the department head verbally condense it to one sentence. "My guess is that we're looking at about fifteen percent," I said, "assuming our revenue assumptions are right. But if you follow Seth's suggestion, we should ask departments for larger reductions—say twenty five or thirty percent—because you know you're going to want to pick and choose between them."

"Yeah, we'll end up with a Chinese menu," McTavish said with a snort. "Give me combination dinner number five: pork fried rice, two less police officers, selling a park, with a side order of egg rolls."

Seth grinned. "Right, but I don't think this will be a meal we'll have much of an appetite for. Ben, how long would it take you and the staff to come up with some options for us?"

"Maybe two or three months. But if you want to look at some fairly radical ways of doing things, then it would take longer—say, six months."

"Six months? Why wait that long?" Titus snapped. "We're only postponing the inevitable. I still say we should make the tough choices now and get it over with. We don't have to analyze this to death."

Up to this point, council member Hank Arnold had quietly watched the conversation, nodding when he agreed with a comment. Now he shook his head and peered at Titus through thick glasses. "So Rob, what's your agenda? Do you have some cuts in mind? Is it really as easy as you're making it out to be?"

"No, I don't have any cuts in mind. But let's all put a few ideas on the table right now."

He looked expectantly at his colleagues. Silence. He shrugged and leaned far back in his chair. I thought it would tip over.

McTavish said, "OK, let's follow Seth's suggestion. Ben, go ahead and work up some options for us to consider. And while the staff is doing that, we should each think hard about our priorities. Ask the people you come in contact with for their opinions about city services. Which ones do they use the most? Which ones could they live without?"

*   *   *

When I met with my department heads after the council's retreat, I gave the usual speech about being creative and coming up with innovative ways to cut costs. They responded with a combination of weary resignation and gallows humor. But the issue was still abstract—until the council and I made the final cuts, life would go on as usual.

We quickly gravitated to other business. The Chamber of Commerce was having a spat with the Fourth of July Committee, and wanted the city to intervene. Our workers' comp agent wanted to do a walkthrough of city facilities to check our safety procedures. The school district planned to expand their ball fields and wanted to get free city water for irrigation. Employee performance evaluations were due again. A local dentist was in a feud with his neighbor over a barking dog. The usual stuff.

Jake Wildavsky, the public works director, held back after the meeting and said he needed some advice. "This is just a heads up in case you get a call. There's a guy on Clearview who's been reading us the riot act because he's had a temporary water service for 10 months. He threatened to go to the city council."

Wildavsky was an engineer by background and training, but didn't conform to the pocket-protector and horn-rim glasses stereotype. In a heated public meeting about neighborhood traffic or a sewer line project,

he would unfold his six foot four frame and use his wild curly hair, moustache, glasses, and slightly oversize nose to disarm the crowd with a perfect Groucho Marx imitation. His devil-may-care attitude about public works, and life in general, helped us keep our daily crises in perspective, and got us through dozens of sticky public relations challenges. He was one of the three department heads that I relied on for advice and counseling on any issue—sort of an inner cabinet. But that same strength of character exasperated me at times. Deadlines? Return phone calls? Organize files? Ha!

"So how come he doesn't have a permanent service line?" I asked.

"Well, he had one before, but he was fooling around with his backhoe and cut right through the pipe, about 5 feet from the tap to the 16" main up there. Water was shooting into the sky like Old Faithful. It took us half a day to patch it. The guy—Van Oort—thinks we're holding out because we're mad at him for cutting through our pipe."

"Are you?"

"I'm shocked you would ask that! Of course not. Well, maybe we are, a little. But the thing is, to make the permanent connection, we would have to close the 16" main. The whole south end of town would be without water, including Clearview School. The school gets pissed whenever they don't have water to flush toilets or cook lunches. Anyway, we just haven't found a good time to do it."

"What's the problem with the temporary connection?"

"Well, we filled the trench with gravel and won't let Van Oort landscape over it until we get around to putting in the permanent pipe. But he's got plenty of water. The patch has a small leak, but it's on our side of the meter, and we're not charging him for it."

"Is the leak making his yard wet or something?"

"No, it's too small for that—it just disappears into the ground. Actually, his lilacs are looking healthier than ever. We're doing him a favor."

"Okay, thanks for the warning, Jake." I thought about it. One guy with a backhoe costs us probably $2,000 in labor and staff time…and then has the audacity to demand his customer rights. Sort of like the guy who takes

his smelly, worn out shoes into Nordstrom's and demands a replacement because he wasn't satisfied with them.

*   *   *

On a rare day without evening meetings I had the luxury of walking home from work. I passed the storefronts on the east side of town, and headed into our neighborhood on Skookumchuk Drive. Our house was built in 1908 by one of Trillium's pioneer families, and it had stayed with the family for a couple of generations. It had small bathrooms and old plumbing, and as Mary said, plenty of character. The street side was dominated by two huge Douglas firs and the shade of a maple.

My daughter, Trixie, was huddled over something on the driveway. "Give me more tape," she said. Nathan, the neighbor boy, pulled some duct tape off a roll and sank to his knees. From my vantage point behind the tree I could see what looked like a toy car. It was the convertible that Trixie used to have Barbie and Ken drive. I held back to watch.

After a minute, they stood up. Nathan unwound a coil of wire and moved toward the edge of the driveway.

"Let me have the end," Trixie commanded, and hooked the wire to a battery. They spun around to watch the car. A model rocket engine, taped to the side of the car, hissed into life. The car lurched forward an inch, then rolled onto its side. The rocket engine squirmed and broke loose of the tape. It shot out, six inches above the concrete. Trixie leaped into the air as the rocket flew under her sandals and buried itself in the grass.

"Yow!" Trixie and Nathan tentatively approached the smoking rocket tube, and bent down to see what kind of a hole it had made in the yard. I resumed my stride along the sidewalk.

"Oh, hi Dad." Trixie looked sheepish. Nathan warily watched her, then me.

"You know, when I was a kid, I glued a piece of wood to the car to keep the rocket from coming off. And it's a good idea to stick the rocket on the

hood instead of the side to keep the car from spinning. And give yourself plenty of room—it takes a while for the car to start moving, but once it does, it can really fly."

"Oh. Okay." Trixie and Nathan looked at each other with a mixture of relief and embarrassment, and then broke into a fit of giggling. "I told you we needed more tape— did you see that thing fly?"

"Yeah, but you sure jumped fast, like you saw a snake or something. Hee hee."

Mary was working at the computer—paying bills—as I headed in to put on a pair of jeans. "I caught Trixie out there in the process of corrupting the neighbor boy," I said. Mary looked apprehensive. "Don't worry, she was just taking a page from my own childhood."

"Ha ha. Like that's supposed to make me feel better."

*   *   *

The phone startled me from a dreamless sleep. Two-thirty in the morning. A call that late usually meant some disaster was unfolding.

"Is this the city manager?" a woman's voice asked.

"Yes?"

"My street light has been out for a month. Don't your cops drive on these streets at night? Surely they must have noticed this by now. It's unsafe! Why hasn't anybody taken care of it?"

"Uh, yes ma'am. Have you called the power company about it?"

"No, why should I, it's not my problem, it's yours. It's not my street. I shouldn't even have to be calling you."

"OK, I'll have it taken care of. But I'll need your phone number and street address."

*   *   *

When I went into Jake Wildavsky's office to pass on the street light call, he and the police chief, Simon Garrett, were bent over in laughter. I asked them what was up.

"The taxpayers are getting their money's worth out of the police department's training budget," the public works director said, grinning.

I must have given them a blank look. Simon quickly explained. "We got a grant to do some crosswalk enforcement—"

"That's where they stick someone out in the traffic and see if anyone stops," Jake said helpfully.

"Anyway, there was a training session in Salem. We sent Howlett down for it. They spent some time in a room, going over the law and the procedures and whatever, then they went outside for some field training. There was about a dozen of 'em, half in uniform. They're all standing there watching as they send this guy into a crosswalk. It's a two-lane one-way street, see, so the first car stops like it's supposed to do. The guy keeps walking and gets to the middle of the crosswalk. A pickup comes barreling down the lane, but instead of stopping for the guy, the driver rolls down his window, flips him the bird, and lets loose an expletive having something to do with his mother."

"And the cops standing there hear it all?"

"Yep. As part of the training, a motor officer is sitting on his bike at the end of the block. He pulls out and nabs the guy. Turns out the schmuck was driving suspended and had a handful of warrants out on him."

"Oops."

"You got that right. He's surrounded by a dozen cops who can hardly keep from cracking up. They hauled his butt off to jail and towed his truck. Talk about hands-on training, huh?"

I shook my head and returned to my office, trying to remember what I had gone to talk to the public works director about in the first place.

          *   *   *

Back in my office I started digging through the mail. Most of it quickly went into the recycling basket, but a handwritten letter caught my eye. It was from a local resident whose wife had been involved in a car accident and had been seriously injured. Great, I thought, another guy who wanted to sue us for a poorly designed road or some other act of negligence. But it turned out he was writing in praise of the response by our public safety personnel, particularly the fire department. They had responded within minutes of the accident, and the ER doctor had credited our paramedics with saving the woman's life. The husband worked a couple of blocks from where the crash occurred, and a friend who had passed by called him on his cell phone. When he showed up at the accident scene, the Victim Assistance Specialist had been calm and reassuring, and had gone out of her way to drive the man to the hospital behind the ambulance, even making arrangements for having his car delivered back to his house. "I can't express how much this service meant to my wife and me," the man had written.

I sat for a while, indulging myself in the warm glow of praise. It was rare enough that the moment had to be savored.

"Got a minute, Ben?" Betty Sue Castle, my assistant city manager leaned against the office door.

"Sure," I said, putting the letter back on the stack. "What's up?"

She moved hesitantly into the side chair by my desk. She had brown hair that curled down to her shoulders and round glasses perched on the end of her nose. She pursed her lips, considering her words.

"You told the department heads to think outside the box, and see if they could figure out new ways to do things. It got me to thinking… When I applied for the assistant job in Kirkland, they gave us a test. They wanted us to review their new fire master plan and to critique it. Well, I noticed something that's bothered me ever since."

"What's that?"

"It was schizophrenic."

"Huh?"

"Here's what I saw. They—or their consultant or whoever wrote the plan—started off with a lot of background information. You know, number of calls to the fire department, response times, population growth, that sort of stuff. But the thing is, what dominated their statistics was medical calls, not fire calls. Over ninety-five percent of their responses were for medical calls, and that's where they forecast the greatest growth in demand for service."

"OK, makes sense."

"But then they described how they were going to meet the increased demand, and they suddenly switched to talking about fire. How they needed at least a three man crew—to protect the guy in the burning building—and four would be better, how many fire trucks they needed per thousand population, how many ladder trucks they would need for new office buildings."

Betty Sue leaned forward. She had an easy grace that was at least partly due to the two evenings a week she spent in her Aikido class. "I didn't think much about it at first," she said, "since I always figured that first aid calls were what firefighters did in their spare time. And maybe that's how it got started—the guys were just sitting around in the fire station playing checkers, and they might as well head out and rescue a cat from a tree or treat an accident victim. But looking at the Kirkland stats, it isn't a time-filler anymore. These guys are really paramedics first, and firefighters second."

"So?" I thought about the stack of work that was still waiting for me, and hoped she would get to her point. She looked excited, and I forced myself to be patient.

"So here's what I wondered. If the main job is responding to medical calls, what if they designed their programs around that? What kind of vehicles would they use? How many paramedics would they need in a crew? If they used 8-hour shifts instead of 24-hour shifts, could they match their manpower to the demands of each shift, like the cops do? I wasn't sure about the answers, but my intuition said that it wouldn't necessarily look like a fire department anymore."

"But what would they do about the fire calls?"

"At the time, I didn't have a good answer for that either. Maybe that's why I didn't get the job there—not that I mind, since in hindsight, I'd much rather be here." She smiled. I didn't take her brown-nosing seriously. "But that's what I thought was schizophrenic about it: they thought they were a fire department, but they really were a medical response team. That idea stuck with me."

"Uh oh."

"Yeah." She pushed her glasses back. "I kept my eyes open for more information about it. I read an article—by a fire chief, of all people—that gave some hard data on response times. It turns out that response times are much more important for medical calls, like heart attacks or strokes, than for fire calls. So many homes have smoke detectors that people get out in time. Saving lives is easier than it used to be. So then it just comes down to property loss, and again, response time from the fire station isn't that critical. If the call comes in after the fire has hit flash point, there isn't much the fire department can do except protect the neighboring houses. If the call comes in while the fire is just smoldering, there's probably someone around to throw some water on it."

"So when the guys jump into their turnout gear and slide down the fire pole, they're over-reacting?"

"It does help maintain the image. But remember, most of those calls are medical calls, and time can matter more. The first minutes after a stroke can be the key to recovery, or so I hear. Obviously, time matters a lot if you need to get a heart re-started."

"So you still need to pay attention to response times when you design your service…."

"Sure, when you're deciding where to park your paramedics, but you don't have to use the same response time criteria when you're building fire stations. We mix up the two just because we've been conditioned by years of using firefighters to respond to medical calls."

My phone rang. Betty Sue watched as I started to reach for it, then I changed my mind and let the voice mail machine take the call. "OK, suppose you're right. But does it change the situation much if you look at it as paramedics responding to fire calls in their spare time, instead of the other way around? You still need basically the same kinds of equipment and training."

"Are you playing devil's advocate or something?"

"Hardly. The public sees the folks you're talking about as angels, not devils." I thought about the letter in my in-basket. "They really do provide a valuable service. And some of them are fairly intelligent. Haven't they asked themselves the same questions?"

"I suppose. But maybe they haven't had to. And why mess up a good thing?"

"Well, whatever. But back to your point—what happens if you separate the medical service from the fire service? Do you necessarily save money?"

"My intuition tells me you should. Do you really need a $260,000 pumper barreling down city streets to respond to a broken leg? Do you need three or four people to operate a defibrillator or haul a gurney, or would two do? I'm not sure, but I do think we need to check into it. That's why I wanted to talk to you about this. I don't know where to go next, and besides, it's your call. If the fire department is a sacred cow and off limits in this budget mess, this is definitely a moot point. But if we're really going to leave no stone unturned, or whatever the cliche is, then I think we need to think about it."

I leaned back in my chair. Betty Sue only had a few years experience in city government, but she was sharp as a tack. And she needed major challenges to stay motivated. At the same time, there were a lot of other projects that I needed her to work on, and a snipe hunt like this would just be a distraction.

"I appreciate your thinking on this, Betty Sue. You may have something here—in fact, you probably do—but the chance of us getting anywhere with it is pretty close to zero." I could see a shadow fall across her face. "I've been through this kind of thing before," I said. "There are some things that just won't work, whether we like it or not. I'm afraid this is one of them. And I really need your help in so many other areas—"

"But you're the one who is always telling us that we need to be creative, and to challenge the old ways of doing things." There was an edge to her voice.

"I know. So maybe I'm chicken. But it won't do either of us any good to go poking around in the fire department. Just let it drop and move on to something else. See if you can come up with the same kind of ideas in, say, the planning department, or streets."

She tilted her head back and looked at me through the bottom of her glasses. "All right," she said. "But I—"

My intercom interrupted. "Ben, we need you at the front desk." The message had a note of urgency, and Betty Sue stood up and stepped aside as I headed out for the stairs. I told myself I needed to work out a code with the receptionist. Whenever she said, "There's someone here to see you," there was an equal chance that it was a friend, someone merely looking for information, or someone mad at the city. I figured this summons fell in the latter category.

Lenny Fiala, local resident and pool hall owner, had worked himself into a lather. Marie, the receptionist, was trying to hold her temper, but her face was flushed and I reckoned that Lenny was outstaying his welcome. I also knew what he was there for.

"They had no right to take it. It's an illegal confiscation of private property, and I'm going to get a lawyer on you." He added a few colorful descriptions of city employees, and I subconsciously checked the lobby to see if there were any children present.

"Lenny, are you talking about the basketball hoop?" I asked.

"Damn straight. All she tells me is to go to the police station. I want this taken care of NOW." He puffed out his chest and stood at his full five feet four inches, making me think of a dachshund with distemper.

"I'm afraid Marie's right." I started maneuvering him toward the door. "The police have your hoop, but I told them it was OK to pick it up. We warned you about all the complaints we've gotten from your neighbors. Apparently your kids wouldn't even interrupt their games long enough to let people drive past. You know, it's technically illegal to have a basketball hoop on the street."

"Oh yeah? I can show you hundreds, all over town. How come you're not stealing *them*?"

"Well, we let them stay up if they aren't causing any problems. Most kids get out of the way of traffic." By now we were on the plaza in front of city hall. "The last straw was when your kids got the can of spray paint and made a key and foul line on the asphalt. That even got our public works guys upset."

"It wasn't my kids. At least you can't prove it. You have no right to take my pole and hoop for something that someone else did."

"OK, talk to Sgt. Ramos about it. All I know is that our code enforcement folks felt the warnings were being ignored, and they had to let you know they were serious. Maybe you can work something out with them, but you've got to get those kids under control."

He cursed and headed across the street for the police station. I used Marie's phone to warn the police department, and to urge them to try to work it out.

"I wish he would just move out of town," Marie said.

"No kidding."

*   *   *

I was at my desk, editing a letter to our State Representative, when my phone rang. A woman's voice purred, "I was just thinking of you. How about sneaking out for a little fun. I reserved a hotel room. Come get me while I'm hot."

I laughed. "Hold that thought, Mary. I'm on my way."

3

The Oregon coast in early summer usually disappoints those who seek a warm beach experience. The Pacific currents bring cold water from Alaska, and the winds off the ocean serve up a random assortment of fog, clouds, drizzle, and—occasionally— sunshine.

In the winter, a continuous series of fronts pounds the coast. We had friends who kept standing reservations at beachfront hotels during major storms. Awed by the power and beauty of the waves and wind, they would sit with hot chocolate and Irish coffee and watch, warm in the shelter of their room while Mother Nature hurled sheets of rain at the thick plate glass windows.

The summers are milder, but the trees at the edge of the beach are permanently bent from the force of the winter winds. Mary had found us a room in the Sand Dollar Motel in Cannon Beach, a block from the ocean. We awoke on Saturday morning to a bank of clouds trapped on the sea side of the coastal range, with a fresh breeze off the water. Trixie had brought a friend named Abbie and the two of them took turns flying a kite, using the dual control lines to chase seagulls and to swoop down on dogs.

We had lunch of chowder and coffee and bought salt-water taffy in one of the tourist shops. The tide was out, and Trixie and Abbie tugged us back to the water. They sat a few yards from the waves and scooped up handfuls of wet sand. If the slurry was the right consistency, they let it slowly drop into blobs on the beach, building up layer after layer. Mary and I helped build their drift castles, and enjoyed the luxury of aimless conversation.

I watched as Mary sprinkled her castle with fine white sand to give it a finishing touch. "Hey, put some of that stuff on my castle too," I said. "It looks good." She leaned over on her elbow and let the powder slip through her fingers. The breeze caught a wisp of blond hair by her eyes, and I thought about how pretty she was.

Abbie started scooping out a channel from her drip castle to the ocean, to catch the incoming tide. Farther out, children squatted by tide pools at the base of Haystack Rock.

After dinner Mary and I left the girls in the motel room, watching a movie. We pulled on sweatshirts and returned to the beach. The sea breeze had pushed the clouds inland, letting the sun light the spray off the waves. Boats moved up the coast with their catch of salmon, and at the north end of the bay, fishermen retrieved their crab pots.

We sat on a driftwood log and watched the sun set. The north coast of Oregon is closer to the North Pole than to the Equator, and in June the sun hangs in the sky until ten o'clock. Far out over the ocean, lines of clouds turned pink, then crimson.

I held Mary close, feeling her warmth against the fresh breeze. We talked about our jobs, Trixie and school, the church activities we had in common, and the strange quirks of our friends and extended family. As the sun's fire was swallowed by the sea, we stood in a long embrace that reminded me of our courting days, eighteen years earlier. We would have to be satisfied with a passionate kiss—the downside to sharing a motel room with a pair of ten-year-olds.

*   *   *

Ten days later Betty Sue Castle and I sat in Ken Longstreet's office. The Finance Director had covered his walls with framed certificates for "Excellence in Financial Reporting"—the equivalent of the Pulitzer Prize for accountants. A strange concept, if you thought about it.

Betty Sue was animated, and behind her round glasses her eyes sparkled. She had placed in front of each of us a stack of spreadsheet print-outs and graphs.

"I've gone through this over and over again," she began. "Maybe there's something I'm missing, but this is really starting to look good to me. Let me try to convince you."

"Is this about the fire department again?" I asked.

"Uh, yeah."

"I thought I asked you to drop it." It came out harsher than I wanted.

Her shoulders sank. "I know. I did all of this on my own time. I even came in last weekend and worked on it. It didn't take away anything from my other work, Ben."

I looked at Ken. He shrugged, his narrow shoulders moving almost imperceptibly under his wrinkled white button-down shirt.

"All right. Show me what you've got."

Betty Sue looked at me warily. She probably guessed I would be looking for mistakes or bad assumptions, but she was bright enough that I would need all my concentration to catch any.

"Here are the basic costs we have now," she began tentatively, pushing her glasses back on her nose and holding up the top sheet on her stack. "There are three stations. Station One has two three-man crews, and the other two have a single crew each. The firefighters work twenty four-hour shifts and are off forty-eight hours, so there are three shifts, each with its own battalion chief. That adds up to thirty-six firefighters and three battalion chiefs. Each shift also has two spare firefighters, to fill in for vacations and other absences, bringing the total up to forty-two. Using the current averages for salaries, overtime, and fringe benefits, the annual cost is $3.5 million. This doesn't even count the overhead for the fire bureaucracy—the captains, assistant chiefs, fire marshal, and all that."

Ken watched Betty Sue and me, and hardly glanced at the spreadsheet. He'd already heard the presentation, I guessed.

"Now for the hardware," Betty Sue said, warming up to her speech. "Each station has a pumper, and Station Two has a smaller rescue rig. Station One has a ladder truck. Just looking at the operating cost, we spend around $400,000 a year on fuel, parts, insurance, and so on. Add in another hundred grand for uniforms, tools, repairs, training, and so on."

Ken added, "The cost of the trucks themselves is hi;
ing for most of them through bonds, so they don't
fund budget."

I nodded.

"So the basic cost to respond to fire and medical calls totals around $4
million a year," Betty Sue said. "This was the easy part. From here on, it
gets more speculative, but I think the numbers are close. I talked to
Oregon Ambulance Service—"

"You did??" I asked, feeling my shoulders tense. "Didn't you think the
word would get right back to our own fire department?"

"Yeah, I thought about that," she said calmly. "They promised to treat
the conversation as a confidential inquiry, and not to share it with anyone.
But about all I got out of them is that they run two-man crews on eight-
hour shifts. The OAS guy was pretty evasive when I asked him about his
costs, so I dug up their franchise agreement with Multnomah County.
The basic cost to provide a crew and ambulance is about $80/hour, for
twenty four hour coverage."

"That's not so bad," I said, trying to sound a little more encouraging.
"How come you hear about these astronomical bills when someone has to
get carted to a hospital?"

Ken answered for her. "That's between them and the insurance companies. Besides, the hourly rate is based on a contract cost for round-the-
clock service, so the overhead costs are spread out. When they charge
private parties, they have to recover all their costs through a relatively
small number of billable trips."

Betty Sue nodded and continued. "I dug out some of the call data from
our own fire department—I had to get the records out of the city hall
archives, so they aren't real current, but I figured it was a starting point.
Anyway, based on the call stats, I guessed that for medical calls, we could
easily get by with four two-man crews during the day shift and swing shift,
and three crews during the graveyard shift. I even used queuing theory to

take into account the fact that the calls don't spread themselves evenly through the day, but instead come in bunches."

Queuing theory? I vaguely remembered something about it from graduate school. It was good to have an egghead on staff. "So what's the bottom line?" I asked.

"Be patient, I'm getting there. Using the OAS hourly rate, it would cost around $2.2 million a year to provide medical response. But we still need to put out some fires. I think that a cop with a fire extinguisher in the trunk of his car could put out most of the fires, but we can leave that for later. Even looking at all the fire calls, two three-man crews, both housed out of Station One, could handle them and still have plenty of time for playing checkers and volleyball."

Ken noted, "There is still the problem with some calls bunching up, and major fires that take more than two pumpers to deal with. We could contract with a neighboring jurisdiction for additional coverage, and Betty Sue has included a cost for this. But another option would be to train other city staff as volunteer firefighters. A colleague of mine is the chief accountant for Scottsdale, and he volunteers for Rural Metro there. It works because he is only called out on major fires, which don't happen all that often."

A welcome relief from bean counting?

Betty Sue said, "You wanted the bottom line; so here it is. If you look at the difference between what it costs now, and what it might cost if we realigned the service, we could save as much as a half million bucks a year." She put her papers down and gave me a triumphant look.

I rubbed my eyes, then shuffled through the printouts. I was stuck in a corner. Betty Sue's work looked good, and she knew that with a total general fund budget of $9 million, I couldn't ignore a half million dollars in potential savings. I looked for a way out.

"This hinges on contracting with some outfit like OAS. What if that doesn't work out?"

"We anticipated that," Betty Sue said, her curls swirling around her neck as She shook her head. "Suppose we staff our own two-man ambulances. Even if we assume a ten percent pay boost as an incentive to switch to an eight-hour work shift, the net savings is still around three hundred and fifty to four hundred thousand. There would be a lot of start-up costs, like buying the ambulances, but we could cover most of this by selling some of the surplus fire equipment. I'm convinced the dollars are there."

I continued to leaf through the printouts. Betty Sue and Ken sat silently.

"I don't know," I said. "We're treading on sacred ground here. If it were any other city service—recreation, public works, library—we could get away with stirring things up. But here we're talking about motherhood and apple pie. I think you're probably right about the savings. But I just can't see how we could get from here to there. There are too many forces in the fire organization and in the community to let it happen."

"I have an idea on that," Ken said.

I listened to his plan.

＊   ＊   ＊

My first challenge was Max Oakley. If life were fiction, I would have pursued Betty Sue's idea with single-minded determination, and I would have dealt with the fire chief straight away. But I was bombarded with a thousand distractions. One of them was my planning director, Bess Wilson, who had an amazing ability to complicate my life. Before I could prevent it, I was roped into a meeting with Bess, city attorney Pete Koenig, and Jake Wildavsky, the public works director.

"We have an opportunity to close this deal, but we need support from you and the city council," Bess said. She was tall and wore her long gray hair in a simple ponytail. In addition to her planning director role, Bess Wilson was a master at economic development. Most developers and business owners found her flamboyant, almost reckless style a refreshing change from the bureaucrats they were used to dealing with. I appreciated the fact that they liked her, but she gave me a constant feeling of impending doom.

The deal that Bess was working on involved a high-tech ceramics plant that made components for the electronics industry. The company, Nova Ceramics, was jointly owned by American and Japanese corporations. It had closed the purchase for some industrially zoned property at the west edge of town, and was on a tight schedule to open the plant in nine months. It was a major coup for the City of Trillium, since the factory was slated to employ up to 1,000 employees, all fairly well paid compared to the service jobs that were typical of Portland's satellite cities.

We had managed to get a low-interest loan, backed by the Oregon State lottery, for the water, sewer, and street improvements that would serve the plant. Nova had signed an agreement to make the loan payments, secured by a lien on their property.

"They already have their contractor out there doing site prep," Bess said. "They want to go ahead and get the public improvements done at the same time. They don't want to wait around while we go through the friggin' bid process."

I looked at Pete Koenig, the attorney, dapper in a red bow tie and matching suspenders. "Developers do their own work for public improvements in subdivisions. So why is this any different?" I asked.

Pete slid over a memo on flimsy paper. As an act of defiance toward the computer age, he pounded out all his legal opinions on an old Remington. When he typed "cc:" on the bottom, it literally meant "carbon copy." He went through a box of carbon paper a week. I was surprised he could still buy the stuff.

"The complication here is the state loan," Pete said. "Technically, that makes it a city project, even if Nova is paying for it. So it falls under the state bidding laws. But the statutes allow the city council to grant exceptions under certain circumstances—I outlined them in my opinion. One of those is a case where overriding the bid process will save money. We could make the argument that the City would have to pay a premium to get the work done in time for Nova's schedule, when the time for the bid process itself is taken into account."

Jake said, "We figure the premium could add up to a hundred and fifty grand, assuming that the contractor would have to pay overtime for around four hours per day. The bid process would take at least two months, and Nova's contractor is already there."

"How do we set the cost for the contract, if we don't get a bid on it? Couldn't Nova inflate the cost just to get a line on the State's loan money?" I asked.

"Good idea—why didn't I think of that?" Jake scratched his head. "Seriously though, our engineers will make an independent estimate of the cost, and we'll hold them to that. As long as it's reasonable, it doesn't matter too much, since it's all their money anyway."

Under the table, Bess' leg was rocking like a sewing machine. It made ripples in my coffee. She said, "Other cities use their own funds for the infrastructure to attract good jobs. Here they're not even asking for any-one else to pay for it—they just want to be able to get on with the project. It's not much to ask."

"OK," I said. "Go ahead and put it on the next council agenda. Tell me, though—how did you find out we might have a problem with the bid laws?" It wasn't the sort of thing that Bess Wilson would normally think about.

"It came to her after her second pitcher of beer with the Nova guys at the Chinook Pub," Jake said, snickering.

"Show's what you know, Wildavsky," Bess said. "After the second pitcher we were wondering if we could find an upstairs room to close the deal. Seriously, though, the building inspector was on the site, looking at the grading plan, and the contractor mentioned that they were going to run the water line in soon. The inspector asked one of Jake's engineers if the project had gone out to bid. See, it's his fault for even bringing it up."

Jake shrugged.

*   *   *

After work I picked up Trixie and the gear bag and drove over to Trillium Grade School. Coaching a softball team made up of fourth and fifth grade girls was a healthy diversion from work, but at times the two didn't seem much different. The girls had the usual mix of personalities— and personality conflicts—and their parents could be as demanding as any city taxpayer. The league had its own set of arbitrary rules and power struggles. But at least we were working outdoors.

The outfield was still soggy from months of rain, but the girls didn't seem to mind. In fact, they were oblivious to just about everything. School had been out for a few weeks, so the practice was a great time to catch up on news and gossip. My attempts at coaching seemed to be an annoying intrusion in their social life. I was philosophical about it—it was a recreational league, and they were just supposed to have fun.

We did some batting practice and ran a few sprints, then played a short practice game with a few of the parents filling in for the outfield. The girls were disorganized and tentative, but I figured I had time to work on team dynamics. We ended the practice with plenty of daylight left, and had a late dinner.

That evening, I set my alarm for 2:30. When it went off, I turned on the light and called a number on a piece of paper on the bed stand. Mary buried her head under her pillow.

"Hello ma'am. This is Ben Cromarty, the city manager. You called me a couple of weeks ago about a street light that was out. Our staff contacted Pacific Electric to have it fixed, and I'm calling to make sure it got taken care of. Could you check if the light is on?"

"Huh? Oh." A yawn and a long pause. "Okay. Just a minute." I waited. "Yeah it's on."

"All right. Glad we could be of service, ma'am. Good night."

Mary squinted at me from under the pillow. "You're twisted," she said, and rolled back over to sleep.

*   *   *

Fire Chief Max Oakley's office was furnished in dark mahogany, an appropriate backdrop for the framed picture of his Ferrari. Your average public servant doesn't usually drive a car like that, but Max had retired from a California city with a full pension. He was probably drawing $60,000 from California, so with his Trillium paycheck I figured he was pulling down a hundred and forty thousand a year. No wonder state legislators and judges tried to get into the public safety retirement system, with its low retirement age. Job stress was probably a good reason for street cops and firefighters to bail out after 25 years, but how could you justify it for jailers and paper-pushers? There was a time when the pension system made up for low salaries, but the unions had finally fixed that, and the dreaded threat of "salary compression" pushed up the whole wage scale. Okay, so I was envious.

And on top of that, Max's mother-in-law had died a couple of years ago, and left them with something like a million and a half dollars. I could never hold the threat of firing over him—he wasn't working for the money.

Oakley wore a white uniform shirt and a badge. His gray hair, trimmed gray moustache and tan face gave him a distinguished look that he used to full advantage. It must have taken some work—a tan in Oregon in June was probably artificially induced. From my seat I could see Mt. Hood to the east, still white with snow.

Betty Sue Castle organized her notes, and began to go over her observations about fire and medical services. She spoke naturally and with a calm self-confidence. Nice job. I could see her pulse in the light that reflected off her neck, and she wasn't as calm as she looked.

Max kept a poker face, occasionally nodding or stroking his moustache. When Betty Sue finished, he raised his eyebrows and glanced at me.

"So what do you think?" I asked.

He paused. "I'm open to any ideas. There may be parts of this worth pursuing. But it's not as simple as you think," he said, turning to Betty Sue. His voice was deep and controlled . "Many of our calls require a fire and medical response. A good percentage of our medical calls are related to vehicle accidents, where there is typically a danger of fire due to gasoline and other combustibles. Conversely, many structure fires have a potential for injury, not only to the public but to our own personnel."

"That may be true," Betty Sue countered, "but there's a risk of injury when our utility crews go into a trench to fix a water line, and we don't send firefighters to those calls, do we? And how many of the traffic accidents really involve a fire danger? Even our supporters complain when they see a police car, fire truck, and ambulance all respond to a fender-bender. But I do respect your experience in this. Just let me go through a year's worth of hard data on your calls and see what kinds of trends pop up."

"I have no problem with that," Oakley said. "In fact, I'll ask my staff assistant to assemble the reports and bring them over to you. Some of my men might get anxious about someone from city hall poking through our files."

Eight of Oakley's "men" were women, but Betty Sue let the comment pass. She glanced at me. "There's one more thing I need. I've had to make some assumptions about the cost of providing medical service. Oregon Ambulance Service should have good numbers, since that's what they do. But I can't find the right person to talk to. Who would you suggest I call? Just to get an idea of some of the cost of providing medical service, not to talk about contracting out."

Oakley's jaw tensed. "I cannot help you there. You will not get much out of them. They are a private, for-profit business and they would not be willing to share operational data. And don't forget that our paramedics have a higher level of training and certification, so you run the risk of comparing apples to oranges. That wouldn't be fruitful." Max didn't crack a smile. Didn't he catch his own pun?

Betty Sue gave Max a level gaze. "I'll keep that in mind," she said.

Max paused for a moment, then turned to me, "If we're done with this, I have a personnel issue I need to discuss with you."

If Betty Sue resented the implied dismissal, she didn't show it. She silently got up and left the office. I watched her go.

"What is it?" I asked.

"I was forced to dismiss one of my firefighters."

"Oh? On what grounds?"

Max leaned back in his chair, relishing his role as hard-nosed administrator. "Unsuitable behavior in public. Apparently the individual in question—and this has been backed by several witnesses—went to some kind of party at a house in the woods near the Coast Range. He became intoxicated and unruly to the point that when he left the house, they locked the door behind him. He tried to return and was upset about the locked door. So he took a shotgun out of his pickup truck and blew it open."

I tried to picture it. "I imagine that had a sobering effect on the party."

"Yes, they called 9-1-1, but being out in the country, it took some time to get a response from a deputy, so one of the people at the house finally had to wrestle him to the ground to get the gun away from him."

"And you fired him?"

"Yes, today, after I completed my investigation."

"The union will probably protest, saying that we can't control what a person does on their own time."

Max shrugged. "Possibly. But I will not allow that kind of behavior by someone in my department, whether or not they are on duty at the time. We are in the business of protecting lives, not threatening them."

"Well, it sounds like you did the right thing."

Max added, before I could leave, "By the way, I don't very much appreciate a kid two years out of college presuming that she knows how to operate a public safety department. I think you will find that a radical restructuring of the fire service is unacceptable."

I bristled. Betty Sue was five years out of graduate school, but more than that, I didn't like the idea of a department head telling the city manager that anything was unacceptable. Especially a department head who leaned on the chain-of-command whenever he needed to justify his own decisions.

"Don't be too defensive, Max. You'll make me think you're trying to hide something. At this point, we're just exploring options. But I do think that Betty Sue is on to something here. All I'm asking is that you keep an open mind. To tell the truth, I want more than that. I want you to help me make it work. And I want you to put your PR skills into this, and help me deal with roadblocks we're bound to run into. Will you do it?"

"I don't know. I don't believe the savings are there, and even if they are, I don't think it would be worth the hassle. Besides, the fire chiefs association would excommunicate me."

He cracked a smile. Amazing.

"Yeah, I know this doesn't sound like the path to professional stardom," I said. "But hey, maybe you'll become famous."

"Great, I might as well go on the lecture tour—with just a skeleton fire crew and a few paramedics, what would there be to do around here?"

"Don't knock it. You wouldn't have to spend all your time watching your back with the union, since they wouldn't have all that free time to sit around and stew about their salary and working conditions and your management style."

Max was stone faced. I had hit a nerve. In another part of the buildings, the equipment bay doors opened. Max looked down at his pager.

"You know," I said, "Simon will probably retire at the end of next year. If you really do have extra time on your hands, we could look at some options there. Instead of hiring another police chief, I could create a public safety director position, over both police and fire. It's been done in other cities."

"And it never seemed to work very well," Max said.

"I don't know about that. And besides, maybe it's harder when you try to run a combined department that's really just a traditional fire department and police department. But if we can pull this scheme off, we'll end up with a medical response team that looks a lot more like a police force, with eight-hour shifts and vehicles that are free to wander around in the city. Before you know, we'll have to buy them donuts. It may really make sense to manage it like a combined department with three or four divisions."

Max looked noncommittal, but this was the kind of bait that he couldn't ignore.

"Anyway, give it some thought," I said.

"All right. I still believe that there are flaws in the concept, though. Nevertheless, I will support you on whichever direction you choose to go. That's my professional duty."

The battalion chief stuck his head in the doorway. "Do you want to join us on this one, Max? It looks like it's a real fire."

"Yes. Ben?"

"Sure, let's go."

Max drove his own car. We caught up with one of the pumpers and followed it. The dispatcher said the fire was at the edge of the city, in an area with large lots and relatively little development. It seemed to be a house fire that was called in by a neighbor.

We flew down a gravel driveway. Max parked on a grass field to get his car out of the way of the rest of the equipment. It looked like the front of the house was a sheet of flames. Firefighters had hooked the first pumper to a tanker truck, and as we got out of the car, a blast of water shot into the ground.

We skirted around the fire trucks to get a better view. As we got closer, it seemed that it wasn't the house that was on fire, but something close to it. Max found the battalion chief.

"Do you know what it is?" Max had to raise his voice over the noise of the engines.

"No. Looks like there's something in a pit there, but we can't see much."

"Is the owner around?"

"Nope. The guys said they saw someone running down the road, barefoot. Don't know what that's all about. I wish we could find someone who knows what's burning in there."

I could feel the heat of the flames on my face. The firefighters played out a line from the second pumper and shot a stream at the house.

"Is the house burning too?" I asked.

"No," Max said. "They're just keeping it cool to make sure it doesn't ignite."

The flames seemed unaffected by the attack. The firefighters dragged the hose around to hit the fire from a different direction.

I pulled out my mobile phone and hit the speed dial for the police department.

"Hi, Karen? This is Ben Cromarty. Listen, could you do me a favor? Have you been monitoring the fire call out here on Cougar Drive? Could you look up the address and get me the owner's name? And while you're at it, the fire guys saw someone running down Cougar—said he was barefoot or something. Can you check to see if any of your patrol officers have seen him, or know anything about it?"

I gave her my phone number and thanked her.

Slowly, the flames were being beaten back. The firefighter on the end of the hose was relieved by one of his colleagues. He walked over to join us, and pulled off his helmet. His face and neck were drenched in perspiration, and his turnout coat was gray with soot.

"It's a hot one, but at think we've got it now," he said.

"Good work, Phil," Max said. "Do you have any idea what's in there?"

"Not sure, but it sort of looks like a camper trailer. Doesn't make any sense though." I watched as he walked over to one of the pumpers and got a bottle of water out of the cab, then sat on the ground.

Suddenly the flames retreated. All we could see through the steam was the blackened top of some kind of frame. We walked over for a closer look.

Inside the huge hole were the charred remains of what looked like a 30-foot-long travel trailer. Glass splinters from the windows were still stuck in the frame. Sheet metal flapped slowly in the heated air currents. The hoses had filled the pit with a couple of feet of water, and two of the firefighters set up a gas-powered utility pump. The motor coughed into life, and black water gushed onto the lawn. The water level in the hole slowly fell.

The battalion chief was talking on the radio in his vehicle. I felt fairly useless, and I had a lot of work waiting back at the office, but I didn't want to drag Max away until he was ready. I felt the cell phone vibrate in my pocket.

"Cromarty here."

"Ben, this is Karen at PD. We found the owner's name, Ronald Boake. And guess what? One of the guys picked up the man you described, and it turned out to be this Boake. What do you want us to do with him?"

"How about bringing him out here? I think the fire marshal wants to talk to him."

"You're at Boake's house?"

"Yes."

"Okay, will do."

The firefighters opened their coats and pulled off the helmets and leaned against the side of the fire engine to catch their breath. One of them wandered over to the pit to check the water level.

"Hey, look at this."

"What is it?"

"I don't know. Looks like a bunch of propane tanks."

The entire group moved to the edge of the hole and peered over.

"Well I'll be. Must be a dozen of them."

"What should we do with them, chief?"

The battalion chief said, "Well, I don't know. We could leave them there until everything cools down, or we could try to fish them out to make sure they're well away from the hot stuff. Think it's cool enough to go in there?"

"Sure, I'll go," one of the firefighters said. Someone slid a ladder down into the pit. The firefighter put his helmet back on and descended. He approached the tanks cautiously, and pushed the closest one with his boot. Satisfied, he lifted it, and said something.

"What?"

He lifted his face mask. "Feels like it's full."

He hoisted the tank on his shoulder and climbed the first step on the ladder. Another firefighter gripped the top of the container and pulled it out of the hole. It was hard work—each tank must have weighed around 50 pounds.

By the tenth tank, both men were getting tired, and their gloves were wet. As the tank was being passed up, it slipped out of their hands. The firefighter in the hole fell on his back, putting his arms up to protect himself from the falling tank. It missed him, but hit the ground hard. An invisible stream of propane shot out, hissing furiously.

"Holy shit!"

Instinctively, we all jumped back.

Suddenly, one of the firefighters leaped into the hole. I crept to the edge, ready to run, and saw the firefighter dive toward the tank. He twisted the valve and the hissing stopped.

"You're crazy, Sven," one of the firefighters yelled.

"Hey, I didn't want this thing lighting up in here," he shouted back. "It could have toasted Sully." He looked at his comrade, who was picking himself up off the ground. "You okay?"

"Yeah, I think so. Hey, thanks man."

"No problem."

The battalion chief shook his head. Max nodded approvingly. "You won't find a finer group of men in any agency in this country," he told me, and he was right.

The rest of the tanks came out without incident. As the cleanup process continued, a black and white patrol car pulled into the driveway. The officer got out and opened the door for his passenger, a sheepish looking unshaven man in his early thirties. Sure enough, he wasn't wearing shoes.

The battalion chief walked over to them, accompanied by Bernice Jenkins, the fire marshal. Max and I followed.

"Who's this?"

"Ronald Boake, the homeowner," the officer said.

"Okay, Mr. Boake, my name is Bernice Jenkins, and I'm the Trillium Fire Marshal. So, what can you tell about this?"

"Well, uh, it's like this. I was welding a cover to put over the hole, and I guess a spark fell down there and caught the trailer on fire. So I panicked and ran—thought the whole thing was going to blow. Uh, sorry about that."

"You know, the thing I'm having trouble figuring out is what a travel trailer is doing down in the bottom of a pit. Can you help me with this?"

"Oh, sure. See, there's the Armageddon computer virus that's going to wipe out the world's computers in the next three months. If you've read about that, you know that the experts are saying that there will be real mayhem, lots of looting and stuff like that, when civilization ends as we know it. So I was building me a bunker to ride it out. I was packing it with plenty of food and water and fuel to get through anything. You never know what kind of crazies are out there."

Bernice and the bat chief shared a glance.

"So when we go through the debris, all we're going to find is the remains of the trailer and maybe some cans of beans, stuff like that?"

"Yeah."

"Nothing else?"

"No! Well, like what, weapons? Cause I hadn't put them in yet, needed to get it secured with a roof and proper entrance first. They're all..." Boake glanced at the police officer.

"They're what?" Bernice asked.

"They're all locked up in the house. But they're all legal, bought them all through the proper authorities, you know."

"Well, I'll leave that for Officer Sandler here. What I'm trying to sort out is this fire. So you were welding? Where's the welding gear? Was it an arc welder or oxy-acetylene?"

"An electric welder. I guess I left it there when I ran for it, and it must have fallen in the bunker. I can have a look if you want."

"That can wait. I doubt there's much of it left."

"Oh. Do you reckon my insurance will cover it?"

Bernice laughed. "If you had waited for Armageddon, then it might have been an act of God, but now..."

Boake raised his eyebrows.

"Sorry sir, it was just a joke. You'll have to take that up with your insurance agent. I imagine if you have some kind of homeowner's policy, it might cover some of this. Come on, let's have a look at what's left with your bunker."

Max turned to the battalion chief. "Tell your men thanks for the good work. I'll be heading out now."

"All right. See you Ben, Max."

On the drive back to the station, I asked Max, "What was Bernice getting at, with those questions about what that bozo was storing in his trailer?"

"I'm sure she's thinking it was a meth lab or grow operation. The computer virus story just sounds too farfetched. But even if that was it, he probably hadn't moved any equipment in—he wouldn't want to do that until he got the thing covered up."

"Hmm. But we've got enough survivalists who are paranoid about computers and other things they don't understand. Remember all the hoopla over the Y2K bug? Maybe he was telling the truth."

"Could be. But it doesn't really matter to us. I become concerned whenever anyone stores large quantities of propane in holes next to flammable materials, regardless of what crazy reason they have for doing it."

*　　　　　　　　　*　　　　　　　　　*

When I got back to the city hall, Terri Knox gave me a look of supplication. I paused before going on into my office. She was surrounded by files and stacks of papers, and her normally neat black hair looked like it had been caught in a windstorm.

"What's going on?" I asked.

"Oh, Todd Pritchard came in while you were gone. He filed a Freedom of Information Act request for copies of a bunch of documents. I told him we would have to charge fifteen cents a page. He said, 'fine,' but it's still a pain."

"What documents does he want?"

"All reports, correspondence, and records of phone conversations involving the Nova Ceramics company. There's a bunch of it, spread through a bunch of files here and in Planning."

"Hmm," I thought, with a sinking feeling. Now what?

4

I needed to talk to the council about Betty Sue's fire department idea, but the Open Meetings Law prevented me from talking to more than three of the council members at a time without calling a public meeting. And where to begin? Mayor McTavish was an obvious choice. She relished challenges and change, and wasn't afraid to put her political career—if that's what you called an unpaid, part-time position—on the line if the cause was something she believed in.

But I chose Seth Rosenberg.

"Okay, I see the advantages," he said. "Tell me what you see as the drawbacks."

We stood on a catwalk above the main saws. The huge blade of the band saw was being removed for sharpening, and the mill was quiet.

"Well, there is only one, but it's a huge one," I said. "If the firefighters don't buy into it, we may be dead in the water. They have an incredible base of support in the community."

"Could that be overcome if the community knows what the trade-offs are?"

"I'm not sure," I said. "Relatively few residents ever use the services of the fire department, but when they do, they become immediate fans. And the word spreads. Did you know that they carry an envelope with $100 in each fire engine? If they respond to a burned-out house, or to a bad accident, the incident commander is free to use his judgement on using the money to help the family out—for emergency motel stay or meals or whatever they need. Can you imagine the impact this has on folks?"

I tagged along as Seth crossed the catwalk to the other side of the plant.

"Besides," I said, "most of the firefighters I know are super folks. They really do believe in helping people, and they are decent, hardworking individuals. I know it sounds corny, but some of my best friends have been firefighters."

Seth leaned on the rail. "Sounds like maybe your heart's not in this either."

"You could be right." Below us, the mill workers were checking their machinery. A couple of guys swept up sawdust. "But while I do have a lot of respect for them as individuals, I think as a profession—well, maybe more as an institution—there are some problems. Ask any city manager which union is the hardest to work with, and fire will always come out at the top of the list. And staff in other city departments see them as prima donnas who get their way on everything just because they provide a popular service. The reputation may not be deserved, but it's there."

"And you're sure you're not seeing this as a way to get revenge for run-ins you've had in the past with the union?"

Sometimes Seth was too perceptive. "I've asked myself the same question, but I think I really am innocent here. Our labor/management relationship has been pretty decent over the past few years, even though the union is starting to chafe with the belt-tightening we've been doing. I'm not carrying any baggage from previous cities—well, not much anyway—so I don't think that's coloring my judgement. In fact, if I had my druthers, I would just as soon not rock the boat with the union."

Seth nodded, and after a pause, dropped down the stairs to the mill floor. I hustled to keep up. He approached a man I assumed to be the mill foreman.

"Are you going to be able to run the second shift?" Seth asked.

"Yeah, I think so. A couple of the guys on the green chain said they couldn't stay back, but I think we can cover for them."

"Good. Let me know if you run into any problems."

We passed through Seth's office—which was cramped and piled with books and files—and sat down in an adjoining glass-walled conference room. He pulled a pipe out of his coat pocket and tapped in some tobacco from a pouch.

"You're right about one thing," he said. "The fire department's an impressive public relations machine. It seems like every week we read about a daring rescue or a fire prevention program at a grade school, or some award for bravery that's being given to a firefighter or citizen. And

during slow times, they still manage to get in the paper with some program to give toys to children or food baskets to poor families."

"Uh huh. The motive is pure, I think, but the press coverage isn't any
accident either," I said.

"Right, and I don't fault them for it. Matter of fact, it makes our job
easier when it comes time to pass bond elections. I can't think of a time
when the voters turned down a fire bond."

I watched as he lit his pipe.

"What about the fire chief?" Seth asked.

"He says he'll back me, but I know he isn't convinced. He probably
reckoned he was done with headaches like this when he retired from the
last job." I filled him in on some of my conversation with Max.

"Now let me ask you a question," I said. "How do you think the business community would react?"

He thought about it. "They'd probably be supportive. What you're
talking about is a business-like decision—realigning your operations for
increased efficiency. For companies like mine, the main benefit of the fire
department is to keep our insurance cost down. We don't tend to worry
about cats in trees."

Over the course of a week, I managed to meet privately with each of the
council members. Sometimes they were hard to read. Maggie, especially,
would tell me she liked an idea, and then privately complain about it to
one of her colleagues. But in this case, they all seemed to understand the
implications of tinkering with the fire department. I emphasized that it
was only a concept, and that it would get plenty of public discussion
before we made any decisions. But without their moral support, it wasn't
even worth taking it public.

The next element of the strategy that Ken Longstreet, the finance director, had laid out involved the union leadership. But it didn't work out the
way we had hoped. John Lennon wrote that life is what happens while

you're making other plans, and this seemed to be the guiding principle in city management.

*   *   *

The city council met twice each month, on Tuesday evenings. The council members sat at a U-shaped desk, raised about six inches above the floor. The city attorney, recording clerk, and I sat at a long table across from the speakers' lectern. The audience was to our side. The meeting agenda was fairly light, typical for mid-summer meetings where everyone wanted to get out while there was still daylight.

While people were taking their seats, I organized my agenda file and collected my thoughts. The mayor ran the meeting, but I had to make sure that the staff members were ready to make their presentations and respond to any questions. I sensed that more people were filing into the room than I expected. I looked up.

In full dress uniform, the top brass of the fire department were wordlessly taking seats at the back of the room. Following them came a dozen firefighters, led by union president Brian Gallagher.

Who leaked the story?

I looked at Max, sitting in the front row with the other department heads. He shrugged. Great.

Mayor McTavish beckoned me up to the council table.

"What's up?" she asked.

"I don't have a clue. I haven't had a chance to meet with the union yet, but it looks like they got word anyway. Maybe it's a preemptive strike. Or maybe they're here on something totally unrelated."

"Oh, sure," she said, and rolled her eyes.

The mayor gaveled the meeting open and asked for the roll call. The first item on the agenda was public comment, where anyone could speak to the council on any subject that wasn't already on the agenda. Mayor

McTavish asked if there was anyone in the room who wanted to address the council.

Silence. I stole a glance at the firefighters. They simply sat with their arms crossed.

The mayor quickly moved on to the next agenda item. The council dealt with some routine business. Their questions and comments were shorter than usual.

Near the end of the agenda, under "new business," Bess Wilson moved up to the seat next to me and gave her staff presentation on exempting the Nova Ceramics work from the bidding process. Pete Koenig weighed in on the legal implications.

"Why does it matter if the project takes a couple of extra months?" Maggie Henderson asked.

Bess said, "Nova is in a hurry—"

"—to get their plant open," mayor McTavish finished. "It's all in the staff report." I looked at Maggie, but she seemed oblivious to the slap.

"Oh. But why is that so important?" she said.

"Don't you want to see those jobs come on line as soon as possible?" the mayor asked. "Besides, it's all their money, so if they want to move quickly, it seems to me we ought to accommodate them."

If other council members had questions, they held them. The massed presence of the fire department continued to weigh on them. The voice vote was unanimous in favor of exempting the Nova work from the bidding process. I looked out in the audience for Todd Pritchard, but I wasn't sure I would recognize him if I saw him anyway.

When the gavel dropped to end the meeting, the fire officers and staff filed out without a word. Sabrina Chan, the reporter for the *Oregonian*, followed them out the door. In less than a minute she was back in the room looking for me.

"What were all the firefighters here for?" she asked.

"I really don't know. They didn't tell you?"

"No—all they said was they wanted to attend a meeting to stay current with city issues. Sounds fishy to me, though." Sabrina didn't have a lot of years of experience, but she did have a knack for hooking a story. "So you're sure you don't know why they were here?"

"No," I said, technically telling the truth. She searched my eyes.

"Okay. If you find out, though, I want to be the first to know."

"Sure, Sabrina."

*   *   *

People said that Brian Gallagher was a good poker player, and it didn't surprise me. He was a thorn in my side most of the time, but I had to admire his skill at sizing up the odds and turning them to his advantage. In a perverse way, I actually enjoyed sparring with him.

We sat in a corner booth in the Fir Away Cafe. Gallagher was theoretically on duty, but it seemed like the guys cut him plenty of slack when he was doing union business. Like a lot of the firefighters, he started out in the construction business, and still did some house framing on the side. His face was weathered from working outdoors, and his black hair was streaked with gray.

Gallagher ordered a fruit plate and coffee and I asked for a double espresso. We engaged in the ritual of small talk while the waitress fetched our food.

"So what did you think of the council meeting last night?" I asked.

"Pretty dull. How do you sit through them?"

"Coffee. And I hide a copy of *Sports Illustrated* in my agenda folder." Gallagher laughed.

I said, "So why were you there?"

He held his spoon a second before digging it into a slice of pineapple. "Just wanted to stay up on city issues."

"Okay." I didn't expect much of an answer anyway. "Look," I said, "I don't know who you've talked to, or what about, but it doesn't really matter. You deserve to know what's going on, and frankly, I need your help."

He leaned back and took a sip of coffee, looking at me without expression.

I plunged ahead, sketching out the concept of separating the fire from the medical responses, but not mentioning the possibility of contracting with an ambulance company. No sense playing that card yet. I took ownership for the plan, not to slight Betty Sue, but to protect her. And I didn't pretend the idea was Max's—Gallagher would have seen through that, even if Max had really kept it confidential.

"So why do you think I would help you with this scheme? And what kind of help do you have in mind?" he asked.

"I think you know why I need your help. Firefighters don't often welcome change. Uh, what was your other question?"

"What makes you think I would want to help you?" he said.

"Here's what I'm thinking," I said. "A change to an 8-hour shift is about the only thing that is bargainable in this plan. Everything else—change in assignments and duties and reassignments to different fire stations—is a management right and outside the contract—"

"What? You don't really believe that—"

"Hear me out," I said. "Even though I think most of this is a management right, I'm willing—in fact, I want—the staff to be involved in all the decisions about it."

"I've heard that before—we get involved and make suggestions, and the response we get is, 'Thank you for your input.' That doesn't cut it."

"Okay. We can discuss how decisions get made later, but the point is, I'm willing to give you real power over them. I can't pretend to be an expert on the day-to-day operations of fire and medical services. Even Max has been away from the front line long enough that he told me he recognizes the need for a labor/management approach here."

I made the last part up—Max had said no such thing. But he couldn't deny saying it without sounding like an obstructionist.

"And Brian, my intention in all this is *not* to screw the union. As a city, we absolutely have to reduce our costs, and the fire department is too big a piece of the budget to keep off limits. But the important thing is to get long-term savings. In the short term, I'm willing to give you a lot. An immediate ten percent pay increase for any firefighters switching to an eight-hour shift, giving them parity with police officers. A promise of no layoffs, using attrition only to reduce positions. No demands for concessions in other parts of the contract, like a cap on medical insurance costs or reductions in other fringes—and you're going to see a lot of that kind of thing in other cities as they come to grips with tax limitations like we've had to."

He shrugged.

I said, "I'm just telling you my bottom line. We can go through a process where you win all these things through tough negotiations, so you can come out as a hero to your membership. That's fine with me. I want us to both win on this."

Gallagher pulled out a can of Skoal and stuck a pinch in his cheek.

"Why didn't you talk to us first?" he said. "You say you want it to be a win-win situation, and then you cut us out of the decision."

Interesting—was he revealing that he knew the council had been briefed, or was he just fishing? I said, "The only people who know about it are the council members. I understand your concern, but look at it from my point of view. I had to sound them out to see if it was even worth moving ahead with. And believe me, they haven't made any final decisions. But they did make it clear that they didn't consider the fire department to be off limits in solutions to the budget problem, and that's really what I needed to hear." And what I wanted Gallagher to hear, too.

"So what's next?" he asked.

"I want to meet directly with the firefighters," I said. "Go over the concept, and get their feedback. So I need you to tell me how you want them to be involved in decision making. It would be too cumbersome to have all forty of them making each decision, but they all need to have a say in some way."

"Stay out of that part, Ben. We have a good track record of dealing with issues. We don't need your help in telling us how to do it…but I don't think it will even go that far."

"How come?"

"I've been a firefighter for eighteen years. Been a paramedic for eighteen years. They're the same thing. You try to tell us that we can be one but not the other…it ain't going to work. Sort of like telling a duck he can fly but he can't swim anymore. Or telling a pilot he can take off but he can't land. Or telling—"

"—telling a medieval barber he can't perform surgery anymore," I said. "Okay, I get the point. But a lot of professions have gone through changes. Matter of fact, most professions that I can think of have, in some way or another. Having firefighters be paramedics is itself a change that happened less than 50 years ago. It doesn't have to stay that way forever. Doctors don't insist on putting out fires, and the Forest Service fire jumpers aren't paramedics—at least not for the Forest Service. Keep an open mind, Brian."

"I always do," he said.

"I'll give you some time to think it over," I said. "But I don't want to go public with it until I have a chance to talk to your fellow employees. I would appreciate it if you would keep it confidential until then. I don't want them reading about it in the paper first."

"Okay," he said.

*   *   *

That afternoon I climbed into Jake Wildavsky's massive city-issued pickup truck and joined him on an inspection of a new filter unit at our sewage treatment plant. Not that I knew anything about sewer engineering or biology, but I wanted the excuse to get out of the office. Besides, I was proud of this new addition—the engineers said it took us from secondary to tertiary treatment, which didn't mean much to me. But the bottom line was that during most of the year, the treated water going into the Willamette River from our plant was cleaner than the river itself, with its upstream farm fields and towns.

We bumped over a grate at the plant entrance and slowed in front of Bo French's camp. Jake leaned out the window.

"Hey Bo, what's happening?"

"It's a glorious day, Jake. A good time to ponder the meaning of life and cook a few weenies."

"Well, you hang in there. Let me know when you find the answer."

Bo had moved onto the sewer plant property over a decade ago. It seemed an odd place to take refuge, but it was secluded and had running water. In the live-and-let-live philosophy of the Northwest, the treatment plant operators tolerated Bo's presence, even though he must have been violating a few city ordinances. He did, after all, keep an eye on the place after hours.

Once a month Bo would make the hike up to town to collect his railroad pension and social security check, and pick up provisions. I got a call from a concerned resident who felt it was unconscionable for the city to allow the man to live like that. I told her that Bo had been offered public housing, but had refused it. She said this just showed he was incapable of making rational decisions, and that he should be institutionalized. She was genuinely concerned about his well being, I think, but didn't have much grasp of the concept of free will.

Bo kept a fire going in a fifty-five gallon drum. He gathered sticks in the woods at the plant entrance, and driftwood on the bank of the river near the outfall pipe. At one point he had started a collection of stray dogs that wandered near the plant, but the staff finally vetoed that idea. The ducks and geese that lived on the settling pond, and the occasional deer that wandered up the edge of the river, were enough in the animal department.

Jake found the senior plant operator in the lab. He was pouring a light brown liquid out of a flask into a mug. Before I could say anything, he took a sip.

"Don't worry—it's just a custom brew of tea," he said. "Coffee was starting to give me a buzz."

"How do you keep from mixing that stuff up with your treatment samples?"

"Good question. But they probably taste the same anyway."

We hiked over to the filtration unit. I listened to the two of them talking about the procedures for cleaning the filters for a while, then wandered over to the rail and watched a couple of sailboats tack up the river. The sky was deep blue, and Mt. Hood and the Cascades dominated the horizon. Bo was right—life was good.

5

Kate Anderson and her two boys, Luke and Joshua, met us at the gate at the Denver airport. Kate and Mary had been close friends since high school, and our two families had kept in contact through the intervening years. Luke was a year older than Trixie, Josh a year younger. They chattered behind us as we made our way to the baggage claim area.

"How's Gordon's work going?" I asked.

"Good—maybe too good," Kate said. "He's putting in pretty long hours. Today he's with a client in Aurora—putting in a new network or something. He can do some of the work out of our home office, but a lot of his clients need hand holding. Tell you the truth, I don't know why people buy computers if they're too stupid to use them."

"Don't knock it—Gordon would be out of work without them," Mary said.

"Yeah, but don't worry—there's an endless supply of stupid people around here. I run into them every day at the shop. I ask them if they want their copies on twenty pound paper, and they just give me a blank look. Or they bitch when you tell them that color copies cost more than black ones. Or they come in to have something typeset, and they don't have a clue what they want it to look like. Sometimes when they do that, I make it come out as ugly as I can—and they still don't say anything."

"Still enjoying your job, huh?" I said.

"Yeah, as the boys say, it sucks."

Trixie had packed roller blades, her baseball glove and flute, four library books, five pairs of shoes, and enough clothes to last a month. The back of Kate's Explorer sank as we lifted the bags in.

Gordon made it home in time for a beer before dinner. He and Kate had met in college, and were married soon after. The crowning achievement of his life was hitting a hole-in-one, completely by accident, at the Glen Abbot golf course.

"So what's new?" Gordon asked.

"Trixie made a double play a couple of days ago," I said. "She caught a line drive at second and tagged the bag before the runner knew what was happening. I was pretty proud, but I think she was mostly surprised. She had put her glove up to guard her face and the ball just kind of stuck in it. But hey, the play looked good."

"The same sort of thing happened to Luke this soccer season," Gordon said. He was playing forward, a teammate chipped the ball in, and it bounced off Luke's head into the goal—"

"He didn't know it had gone in," Kate said. "He was spinning around looking for the ball and couldn't figure out why his team was cheering. Our star athlete."

"Give them credit," Mary said. "Trixie at least had the presence of mind to get the runner out, and it sounds like Luke was at the right place at the right time. I'm not sure I would have been able to pull it off."

Kate laughed. "No, you would have had the sense to keep a muddy soccer ball out of your hair."

*   *   *

The vacation went by in a blur. A day of trail riding at a dude ranch high in the Rockies. Rafting down the Poudre River and having water fights in the calm spots. Watching the kids show off at the neighborhood skate park. Card games and laughter. But it wasn't a complete escape from work.

In the middle of the week Ken Longstreet called. "Thought you might want to see the article in this morning's paper. Do you have a fax machine there?"

"Hold on…Kate, do you have a fax machine by any chance?"

"Sure—Gordon uses the fax modem on the computer."

She set it up while I got the rest of the news from Ken before he hung up. I had left Betty Sue in charge, and things were running smoothly.

The fax came in a minute later. Kate leaned against me as the message appeared on the screen. I could feel the heat of her body. I breathed in her scent. What was it-lilac? Some kind of natural pheromone?

Trillium Firefighters Offer to Hold the Line

TRILLIUM—Fire union president Brian Gallagher announced that the firefighters have made a unilateral offer of no pay increase for the coming year. The two-year contract expires on December 31. Negotiations between the union and city management were scheduled to begin in July. Gallagher said, "The firefighters unanimously voted to offer a wage freeze to save other city positions. We realize that the tax limitation measure will hurt the city's budget, and we don't want to push for a pay increase if this would cost other city jobs." Ken Longstreet, the chief negotiator for the city, could not be reached for comment.

Kate looked at me.

"It's a brilliant move," I said. "They probably guessed they were looking at a wage freeze anyway. But now they come out as heroes. And look—they're making this sacrifice to save *other* city positions. The possibility of losing fire positions is inconceivable, not even worth mentioning. They're setting the agenda here."

"What does it do to your reorganization idea?" Kate asked.

"I'm not sure. But if they want to fight it, this will give them a stronger base of public support."

"How do you put up with this kind of crap? I would just tell them the facts of life, and let them take a hike if they didn't like it. You know?"

I laughed. "Well, here's my secret. I was listening to a psychologist on a radio program. She said they used to think that the people who were the most balanced—who coped best with life—were the people who had a firm grip on reality. But then they discovered that people who were the most mentally stable actually lived in a fantasy world. They looked at life through rose colored glasses. But it was more than that. They actually believed that people were better than they really were, and that good things happened even though the fantasies didn't bear much relationship to reality. So that's what I try to practice. I try to keep as far removed from reality as I can. You know what I mean?"

Kate grinned and straddled a chair. She pulled her hair back, a dark mane that set off the sapphire of her eyes.

"And I suppose it was probably easier a few decades ago," I said. "Most of the city managers then were engineers. They built things—roads, bridges, water systems, buildings. The city councils were made up of the good old boys from the business community. They didn't spend a lot of time on touchy-feely stuff like citizen surveys and focus groups—they knew what they wanted. And for the most part, I think, the residents were okay with that. The city got things done, and they could go on with their lives without thinking about it much."

"Ah, those were the days, huh?"

"No kidding. Instead of the good old boys, now we have a moving collection of special interest groups—unions, environmentalists, anti-tax zealots, handicapped advocates, concerned citizens for this and that, flat taxers, home schoolers, right-to-lifers, pro-choicers, smoke-free crusaders, women's libbers, animal protectors, civil libertarians, trade associations, hyphenated-Americans, neighborhood activists, pacifists, rifle association lobbyists, gang wannabes, anti-growth nimbies—

"Huh?"

"Not in my backyard, NIMBY. You get the picture. It's hard to do anything without offending one group or another, and so many of them enjoy skirmishing. So a city manager is sort of like a coach in a game where the teams and rules keep changing. But, like they say, it makes life interesting."

Kate stood and stretched with feline luxury.

"Too bad everyone isn't like me," she said, "perfectly balanced and with the right views on everything."

I thought about her as our plane climbed over the mountains on the way back to Portland.

* * *

I spent a few hours in the office on Sunday afternoon. Betty Sue had weeded out some of the junk mail, and responded to the most urgent messages, but my in-basket stack was still six inches high. A survey from the League of Cities on our financial condition. Invitations to meetings and seminars. A copy of a letter from a developer requesting a credit against his fees. A copy of a memo from the payroll clerk to Jake Wildavsky nagging him to get his public works department timesheets in on time. A grant announcement with a four-week due date. The third draft, for my review, of an intergovernmental agreement setting up a green belt between Trillium and the Portland urban growth boundary. Personnel Action Forms to sign.

A letter caught my eye. It was on plain paper and appeared to be done with an old dot matrix printer. It was full of misspellings and grammatical errors, so I figured it had to be from a local resident.

To the City Council:

Subject: Nova Ceramics Project

On behalf of the TBLC-Trillium Business Leaders Committee, Inc. its directors and a concerned community. In the opinion of the TBLC and for the public record all issues in this testimony should be addressed in a continued public hearing process for the protection of Trillium citizens, property owners rights, values and the existing employment base in our community.

There is an issue with the public record and the Mayor stating that they are on a time line for opening the Nova plant. There is the issue of the propriety of the city manager apparently attempting to influence the outcome of the council decision by talking to members before the meeting.

The question still remains to who is managing the city. Why is the city manager spending so much time and money for the benefit of a private developer. Why has the planning and development director been seen socializing with Nova employees?

The insistence that the housing project be part of the proposal for the Nova plant when it is increasingly apparent that so many different people are against it.

Especially the decision to violate the bidding process and give the job to Nova this doesn't make any sense.

The directors request an explanation, were is the independent review by the City Councilors in this process. The staff reports and planners leave a great amount of public concern unanswered.

Director members in the industrial area are absolutely opposed to the use of any reimbursement agreements which could result in additional costs to support this special project.

This community can't afford to loose areas which will continue to create a job base for our community. The special treatment and approach by our city staff and manager is reflecting a disregard for public communication and openness to public concern. Trillium Business Leaders Committee is asking for the support of the City Council which will act for the benefit of our community and not for the interests of individuals or special projects of our city employees.

Todd Pritchard
On behalf of TBLC Directors

cc: The Oregonian

At our management team meeting the next morning, I asked about the letter. I had never heard of a Trillium Business Leaders Committee.

"Never heard of them before, either," Bess Wilson said. "Must be some underground society. But I recognize most of the so-called directors. Mostly whiners and curmudgeons. I don't know why they've got their undies in a bundle over the Nova deal. I'd say it would be good for their business."

"What about Pritchard?" I said.

"Don't worry about him," Bess said. "He couldn't find his ass with both hands in the dark. You know, the wheel's turning but the hamster's dead."

"But he got the tax measure passed. We can't ignore him."

"Aw, he only got lucky with that because he had the anarchists out of Grant's Pass coaching him every step of the way. Believe me, he just isn't that smart."

"Yeah, I couldn't help noticing that his letter would have been rejected from an eighth grade English class. How can it help his case to send that piece of work to the *Oregonian*?"

"Actually, that might not hurt him," Jake Wildavsky said. "Have you noticed how the newspapers have been using literal quotes for the people they interview? You know: 'We was just minding our own business and I don't got no idea how the case of beer got in my coat.' It makes them sound more real, more believable, I guess."

"Sure," Betty Sue said, "most of America's heroes are pretty light in the brains department. Football players. Test pilots. Action movie guys. Homer Simpson. Roseanne. Cops—"

"Hey!" the police chief said.

"Just kidding, Simon."

"So, what do we do?" I asked.

"Why don't you call Pritchard and see if he wants to talk about it?" Ken Longstreet said. "Who knows what's bothering them? It's hard to figure out from the letter. Maybe it isn't a big deal after all."

"Probably a good idea, but it may be futile. He refused to talk to me before his ballot measure stunt. Do you want to join me in this?" I asked Bess.

"No, it's OK, I'll leave that pleasure to you."

*　　　　　　*　　　　　　*

I heard a commotion as I headed back to my office. Terri Knox was holding a yellow legal pad at arm's length.

"Just write it down, Mrs. Dunwoody."

"I am sure the airborne vehicles are emanating some sort of ray. It is making young girls pregnant, and keeping others from getting pregnant. You don't believe me, but I have the facts. And I say airborne vehicles because they aren't just airplanes, no, the helicopters are doing it too. It must be stopped. It must be stopped now before any harm is done."

"Yes, I know ma'am. But it would help me if you could write it down so we have all the facts."

Mrs. Dunwoody snatched the yellow pad and shuffled over to a chair. She began to sit down, then snapped, "I need a pen." Terri quickly obliged.

When I saw that my path was clear, I walked between them. Terri smiled and shrugged. We had both run into Mrs. Dunwoody before.

I pulled eight messages off my voice mail, returned six of them, and actually reached two human beings. My seventh call was to Todd Pritchard.

"Say Todd, this is Ben Cromarty at the City of Trillium. I read your letter to the city council, and wondered if you wanted to talk about it."

"Yes, I'd be glad to." His nasal voice had a tone of smug satisfaction.

"Well?…"

"We have some real concerns about the whole thing involving Nova Ceramics," Pritchard said.

"Like what, specifically?"

"The whole thing."

"Okay—"

"Like for one," he said, "the idea to include low income housing as part of the project. That seems to us like very bad planning."

"I don't know if I would call it low income. The rents will between $750 and $1,000 a month. Not all of the workers at Nova will be able to afford a $250,000 home in Trillium. It seems to make sense to let them live near their job. It's not like they'll be living next to a steel mill—Nova's factories usually look like college campuses."

"But we don't think families with children should be near trucks coming from an industrial park. And we understand that these plants tend to attract Orientals. Whatever. We just don't think you should mix housing and industry."

"Well, you're entitled to your opinion. But it's not a new idea. Have you seen pictures of Trillium when it was a mill town? Homes were scattered all around the saw mills. People could actually walk from their home to their job, or to the grade school, bank, cafe, or grocery store. It may seem like a novel concept, but it isn't."

"We just think it's bad planning. And we're concerned about the costs that the other property owners are going to have to pick up."

"What do you mean? Nova is using their money up front for all the water, sewer, and street extensions. When the other property owners are ready to develop, they won't have to lift a finger—everything will be in place for them."

"Tell me this, then. Won't they be asked to pay to hook up?"

"Of course. They would pay their share based on how much they use. That seems only fair. But they wouldn't have to pay anything until they developed their own property."

"So how is it calculated? Based on size of properties, or what?" Todd asked.

"The engineers use different methods—frontage or trip generation for streets, square footage or meter size for water, it depends. I don't know the details; Jake Wildavsky's handling that. But it's done in a public process—there will be plenty of opportunities for the property owners to give us feedback on that."

"So what if they don't want to participate at all? Why should the city be allowed to force them to?"

Huh? This conversation didn't seem to be helping much.

"So you're saying that Nova should take on the full burden for everything in the area, even if those other guys will benefit from it?"

"Well, Nova's the one asking for it. Let them put their money where their mouth is."

"Todd, you wouldn't accept that if you were in their shoes. Be realistic."

"They really have bought you off, haven't they? How did they do it?"

I held my tongue. The line was silent for a few seconds.

"I mean, it's obvious you guys are pushing this deal," Pritchard said. "Like how you violated the bid process. That was—"

"Hold on. No one has violated the bid process. State law specifically allows exemptions, and this qualifies for the exemption."

"Our attorney doesn't think so."

So that's how it was going to be.

"Okay Todd. Let me know when you have something constructive to contribute to this issue. You know how to reach me."

Terri leaned around the door. She pointed toward her desk.

"I have to leave, but she's still here."

"That's all right Terri, I'll take care of her. Have a good evening."

I got some more work done, and then went into the reception area.

"Well, Mrs. Dunwoody, would you like to join me in a cup of tea?"

She shrugged. I brewed up two cups in the conference room. When I offered it, she stared into the cup and frowned. She took a sip and said, "Darjeeling. Good." She returned to her writing.

I sat at Terri's desk and sipped my tea. There were probably at least a dozen people still working, but the main doors were locked. The hum of traffic from the evening commute broke through the whoosh of air from the building's ventilation system. The only other sound was the scratching of Mrs. Dunwoody's pen. I watched her write. She had filled around ten pages of the yellow pad with a small, probably unreadable scratch. What were Todd Pritchard and his followers up to? If they were going to mount a legal challenge to the Nova project, why hadn't they shown up at the meeting? And who would pay an attorney? The people listed as the "directors" of the Trillium Business Leadership Committee were, in my experience, too cheap to pay for a two-egg breakfast. And why couldn't I stop thinking about Kate?

The minutes passed.

"Okay, my friend, it's time for me to lock up here. I can take what you've written, and you can finish tomorrow if you want."

"Well, fine."

I turned off the lights and locked the office doors behind us.

*   *   *

I pulled up outside council member Hank Arnold's house. He and I were to have the pleasure of sharing a dinner of cold sandwiches with the Metro Area Storm Water Task Force. The topic was important enough—figuring out how to treat all the grit and grime that got washed into the region's streams and rivers—and we had to stay at the table to make sure Trillium's interests were represented. But I felt that if I really counted the precious hours of life on earth, this wouldn't be high on my list of ways to spend them.

Hank's thin frame weaved between a couple of fifteen-year-old Chevy sedans in various stages of reassembly. He folded himself into the passenger seat of my car and fumbled with the seatbelt. Hank was a 60-year-old journeyman plumber who mostly worked on new commercial buildings. He had risen through the ranks of the union, and served a term as president of the union local.

Twenty years ago, Hank and his wife Gretchen, along with a few friends, had founded the Trillium Community Services Center. He still spent weekends there, distributing cheese to poor families, refurbishing furniture and other cast-offs for the store, and delivering free firewood. He had started a program that paired up migrant farm workers with long-time residents of the community, teaching them English and Spanish together. Of the five city council members, Hank was the first to volunteer for any task, whether it was cleaning out creek beds or representing the city at the Veteran's Day ceremony.

I was grateful to be driving. It must have been decades since Hank had taken the vision test for his license. He may not have been legally blind, but that was only because the legal system hadn't caught up with him yet.

"Picked up a new fuel pump from the junk yard today," he announced. "At first I couldn't find the one I needed, but I kept digging, and there it was. I was glad I found it. Stopped first at Bellah's Chevy Dealership. The kid in the parts department wasn't much help, but he finally found it in his computer and they wanted to charge me two hundred bucks. Heck, I didn't pay much more than that for the whole car. So a half hour in the junk yard saved me a hundred and fifty bucks. Not a bad wage, huh? By the way, that reminds me, Sparky Bellah caught me at the dealership and said something about the city getting swindled by the Nova Ceramics deal. I couldn't figure out what he was talking about…"

Sam "Sparky" Bellah owned the Chevrolet dealership and was listed as one of the directors of the Trillium Business Leadership Committee. Except for that connection, I couldn't see why he would have a problem with it. The Nova execs would be good for a few Blazers and Suburbans, and Sparky could make a killing on a fleet deal for their motor pool.

"Hey, look at that place," Hank said. "How can someone let a yard get looking like that?"

I tried not to show my reaction. A while back, Hank had had so much junk in his own unfenced back yard that one of our code enforcement officers was forced to issue a formal warning.

He seemed to sense the irony. "At least I keep my appliances neatly stacked," he said.

I made it home around ten. Mary curled up with me on the couch and shared a glass of wine. The days were already getting shorter and there was only a trace of light to the west. Trixie was in bed after a hard workout at a softball day camp.

Mary worked half time in the high school office. It kept the rest of her time free to be with Trixie, and to do some volunteer work in the church office. Things were quiet in the middle of summer, but class registration was coming up in a week, and she had plenty to do.

"The hard part," she said, "is not knowing how many kids we're going to have. We can make our best guess, but in the first few weeks we'll have to scramble around and try to balance out the classrooms."

"Don't you have a pretty good idea from the kids who were in each grade last year?"

"That just gives us a starting point. People move so much, you lose and gain a lot each year. And the newcomers don't always get the word about registration, and a lot of the rest just never bother to show up. You would think we could sort it all out on the first day of school, but even then there are kids missing because they're still on vacation. And that's when we start getting the complaints from parents because little Johnny doesn't have the teacher he wanted or he doesn't have enough time to walk from Spanish to biology."

"That's what makes your job fun, hmm?"

"That's not half of it. Sharon's so anal she needs everything set in stone months ahead, and gets on our case when we can't give her the final class lists. Mike's the opposite—so laid back about it, he just tells us that we'll work it all out in the end, so he waits until the last minute—"

"Sort of like me?"

"Yeah, just like you," Mary said. "But at least there's Gina Olmos to help us keep our sanity. She deals with it so well that she ends up doing most of the work. She works up tentative schedules but she's cheerful about all the changes. I really admire her."

"Well, you're a lot like her, plus you have a cuter butt."

"I'm glad you appreciate my finer points."

"I appreciate them every chance I get."

*   *   *

I met with the A Shift in the training room of Station One. Max Oakley and Betty Sue Castle joined me at the front of the room. Brian Gallagher stood at the back with his arms folded. I enjoyed most meetings with the firefighters—handing out awards, welcoming new members to the ranks, participating in promotion ceremonies. I felt a strong rapport with at least some of them. But from the tension in the room, I knew this one would be different.

Max stood. "You all know the kind of budget challenge we're facing—I don't need to go into that again. We've had some ups and downs, but the Fire Department has done moderately well over the past few years."

There was some stirring in the crowd. They had settled for smaller pay increases than some of them wanted, and the equipment budget had been frozen for a year.

"We haven't lost any positions," Max said. "In fact, we were able to add two firefighters to cover for absences. Most other local government agencies haven't been as lucky. But now with the tax rollback, we may not be able to dodge the bullet any longer. The cuts are going to be deep, and they will affect all departments, including fire. There does not appear to be a way to avoid it. Our challenge is how to make these cuts with the least impact on the public."

A firefighter in the third row interrupted. "What about us? The public knew there were going to be consequences when they passed the ballot measure. Screw 'em."

Max sat on the edge of a table. "Yes, I know it is difficult. But we all made a commitment that the public comes first when we entered the fire service. That's just the way it is. So as I was saying, we have been exploring a way to become more efficient by taking a hard look at the way we handle medical calls compared to fire calls. Betty Sue, please share your analysis with my men."

This wasn't part of the script. Max was trying to distance himself from the issue. Betty Sue gamely summarized the concept without adding too much technical detail. But she couldn't gloss over the fact that most of the savings came from a cut in firefighter positions.

"So what are you talking about, a RIF?"

"Not necessarily," I said, trying to shield Betty Sue from unfriendly fire. The union contract laid out the procedures for a reduction in force, but it still involved layoffs. "Normal attrition might work. But I want to discuss those issues with Brian Gallagher and your other representatives before making any decisions on it. I need to emphasize that no decisions have been made yet—we're talking to you now so you know the kinds of things we're looking at. And I want to set up a process where you have a say in whatever decisions end up being made."

Someone in the back muttered something that provoked a few snickers. A new recruit raised his hand. "What would this do for our careers? I don't think Portland would hire us if we didn't have experience in both medical and fire."

"I don't know," I said. "But it seems that people from the ambulance companies do pretty well with fire departments. Lack of firefighting experience doesn't seem to hurt them." In fact, several of our own firefighters had come from Oregon Ambulance Service.

"Max, you talk about service to the public," an older firefighter said. "But here you're talking about lousy response times to fire calls. Is it good service if we let someone's house burn down? Is it good service if someone gets killed from smoke inhalation because we didn't get there in time? You need to get real."

"We would have to double our efforts in prevention," Max said. "If every home and business had working smoke alarms, we wouldn't have the kind of scenarios you're describing."

"Those aren't scenarios, they're real life," someone else shouted.

"I say this sucks," one of the firefighters in the back said. "Essential services should be the last to be touched. Why don't you go after the frills and luxuries, like recreation and seniors and planning? Why don't you cut overhead, like assistant city managers and other useless positions? Why don't you stop management from taking trips out of state? It's ridiculous to jeopardize the safety of the public when you could cut the fat out of the rest of the city."

"I'm sure your fellow city employees appreciate your concern," I said before I could stop myself. I saw another hand raised and quickly acknowledged it.

"How come this is the first we've heard of this?"

"I've talked privately to council members, and to Brian. But except for them, you're the first to know. You haven't seen anything in the papers, have you?"

"No, but it still looks like a done deal to me. We already offered to take a wage freeze to save other city positions. We've done our part. Look somewhere else to balance your budget."

We took a few more questions and comments, but it looked like the crowd was getting restless. Max ended the meeting with a pledge to keep them involved. I watched their faces as the firefighters filed out of the room. There was a mixture of disgust and apathy. Some had a look of smug amusement, which worried me. The officers—captains, lieutenants, and the battalion chief—hid their emotions. I would meet with the B and C shifts over the next two days, but the news of this meeting would spread fast.

When I got back to the office, I called Sabrina Chan and got her voice mail. "Sabrina, this is Ben Cromarty. We're working on some budget issues that you might be interested in. Give me a call."

I did some desk work and logged onto my e-mail account. Just the usual spam. I hit the Create Message button.

To: kanderson@rockynet.com
Subject:A Message

Hi Kate. How are you doing? Since we got back I got an attack out of the blue from some mysterious business group, and talked to some hostile firefighters. But I can still hear your laugh and see your blue eyes, and that helps. Keep in touch. —bc

---

I sat for a minute, then hit the "Send" button.

6

A few days later Pete Koenig came into my office. "I just got a copy of this."

He handed me a document from the Washington County district court. It was typed in the usual double space with legalese at the top. Basically, it looked like the lawyer for the Trillium Business Leadership Council—who happened to be the son of a local gas station owner—was requesting a writ of review of the city's bid exemption for Nova Ceramics.

"What's a writ of review?" I asked.

"It's sort of a second opinion on the council's decision. You don't see them very often, and to tell you the truth, I'm not that familiar with the process." He was wearing a bow tie, dark blue with large yellow dots. It reminded me of a tropical fish.

"Are they asking for any damages or penalties?" I asked. "I don't see any mention of it here."

"No, in a writ of review, you don't have to show that anyone was harmed."

"So what's the remedy if they prove their case? Nova's contractor is a quarter of the way into the project. We can't undo that."

"I suppose it could invalidate the contract award," Pete said, "but I don't know exactly what happens. I figure they just want to make the city look bad."

"Great."

"Now, I don't think they have much of a case. The Courts have generally deferred to the local governing body in cases like this, as long as they're within the overall guidelines in the law. And there's no question in my mind that the council was within its rights."

"Okay. Thanks Pete. We'll have to brief the council in Executive Session after Tuesday's meeting."

*   *   *

Sometimes I needed a sage to consult in times of trouble, and the person I turned to most was the police chief, Simon Garrett. He had been with the police department for 30 years, and chief for over 20 of them. Simon was a wiry man with a presence that commanded the respect of both his officers and his law breaking clientele. In spite of the differences in our backgrounds, we had become good friends over the past ten years.

"You want to hear a story?" Simon asked.

"Sure," I said. We sat at Simon's customary table at the Fir Away Cafe. The food wasn't great, but the place was across the street from police station and the noise from the kitchen was a good mask for private conversations.

"We got a complaint about odor at the Sunrise apartments. Stohoski and Chambers went on the call. You know where the Sunrise apartments are?"

I nodded.

"They're really pretty decent as those rat cages go. Stohoski knocked on the door and a gal let them in. The inside of their place looked pretty decent too."

"It did?" The last odor complaint involved a woman who had kept thirty cats—all indoors and without a single litter box. The officers could hardly keep from retching when they finally got in the place.

"Yep. That was the funny thing about it. But they could smell something bad, too. Chambers said, 'Ma'am, we got a complaint about odor here.' She said, 'Come here,' and took them to a room at the back of the apartment. They opened it, and it was filled to the ceiling with bags of garbage. Some of it must have been there a long time, 'cause they said it was rotting pretty good. They just looked at the gal. Know what she said?"

"What?"

"Taking out the garbage is *his* job!" Simon burst into laughter. It was contagious.

"Is that true?" I asked.

"Swear to God."

"People are strange sometimes, huh?"

"You better believe it. I wouldn't have a job if there weren't so many nut cases running around."

Simon lit a cigarette. He pushed the ashtray to the end of the table so the smoke would go up the flue for the gas fireplace. "So, did you ever talk to Pritchard?" he asked.

"Yeah. Didn't learn much though. I don't know if he's miffed because his company didn't get to bid on the project, or what. He says they don't like the plan, but they've never weighed in on any other development. Don't know why they're hot on this one."

"Maybe because Nova Ceramics is from the outside, and Pritchard and his buddies don't like outsiders. Or maybe because they're part owned by the Japanese. Hard to tell."

"Anyway," I said, "they filed a writ of review to overturn the council's contract award. It won't slow the project down, but it's a hassle for us to go through. I can see the headlines—Trillium Business Group Sues City Over Contract. Even when we win in court, they'll have done their damage."

"Don't worry." Simon leaned forward. "Todd Pritchard's an asshole. We nearly had him on cocaine charges a couple years ago. Got off on a technicality. Ever notice that sometimes he doesn't seem like he's all there? He's a jerk who would be living on the street if it weren't for his wife and her daddy."

Pritchard's construction business had been founded by his father-in-law. Pritchard himself had a degree in accounting from a correspondence school and as far as I knew, never had any real construction experience.

"Yeah, he's hardly the American success story himself," I said. "Or maybe he is, if you think about it. But even if he's a few bricks shy of a load, that doesn't make him any less dangerous. He could be a real loose canon."

Simon leaned back. He wore his usual uniform—blue jeans, cowboy boots, a white shirt, and an old windbreaker with an Oregon Trout logo instead of a badge. He looked around at the room.

"This place here has been around a long time," he said. "I remember when I first got hired. I was the only guy on the graveyard shift. In fact, the whole department only had eight people. Anyway, I got a call on a fight in the lounge here. Came in and two big guys were mixing it up pretty good. I thought, shit, what do I do now? They could've sent me through the wall. One of the city council members was sitting in the corner, drinking a beer. They didn't have a city manager in those days; the council and the city recorder pretty much ran things. He motions me over and says, 'Simon, sit down.'"

"The fight's still going on?"

"Damn right. The council member—I don't even remember his name any more—he says, 'Just give 'em some time. They'll wear themselves out after a while.' So that's what I did. And don't you know, they hit each other enough that after a while I could just go over and grab them by the collar. I escorted them into the back of my cruiser and they came along, peaceful as lambs."

"Wild West days in Trillium, huh?"

"It was. And it really wasn't that long ago, either."

"Maybe not much has changed," I said. "But instead of using fists in a bar, they use lawyers now. Hard to tell which is more civilized."

*　　　　*　　　　*

"We thought it would be a good idea to keep our lines of communication open here." John Collins was a vice president responsible for Nova's operations in Oregon, and he would manage the Trillium plant when it was built. He had already moved into a $400,000 home on the bluff over the Willamette River, and one of his daughters, Renee, was on the softball team I coached.

The Nova executives looked like they would be equally comfortable on a golf course as on a factory floor. We sat under umbrellas on the sidewalk deck of the Hokkaido Express Grill, surrounded by the sounds of birds and passing cars. Ken Ishido, the facilities development manager for the parent company, punched some buttons on a palm computer.

"Our schedule is holding up well. We appreciate the assistance we have received from the City of Trillium. We still project an opening date of May 1. This is important to meet the new orders we typically receive in the spring."

"What effect will this legal challenge have on the infrastructure project?" Ramon Diego was the owner of Northwest Construction, Inc. He lived in Trillium, but his company was based in Tualatin, a Portland suburb. "We don't have a lot of slack in our timeline."

"Our city attorney says there's no effect, since they didn't ask for an injunction."

"Why didn't they?"

"Apparently, they can't. They don't have standing. And maybe they really don't want to kill the project—they might just want to make the city look bad."

"So we're in the clear, then?"

"As far as we know," I said. "But we could use your help on the defense for this case. Pete doesn't shy away from a fight, but he's really not a trial lawyer."

"That's not a problem," Ramon said. "I'll have someone from Dewey and Howe get in touch with him."

"There is something that has me a little concerned," Bess Wilson said. She wore something that looked like a cross between a dress and a sweatshirt. She never was a slave to fashion. "You're going to need some right-of-way from Bruce Poulet to get your road access off 73rd Avenue. He had said he was open to that, but I saw his name listed as one of the directors of this Trillium Business Leadership Committee. They may use him as leverage to screw things up."

"Can't you use eminent domain?" John asked.

"Only as a last resort," I said. "If we started talking about condemning private property for Nova, the critics would have a field day. I think in the long run, Poulet will work with us—the road will benefit him as much as you folks. He'll probably drive a hard bargain, though."

"So what's the problem? If he doesn't give us the right-of-way, we don't build the road. We can still get access off Chief Joseph Boulevard."

"The problem is the fire marshal has a bug up her ass about two accesses to the project," Bess said. "It's not like the place is going to burn down, with all the sprinkler equipment she's making you install, but they need another way in if one of them gets blocked. That's why the planning commission required the 73rd Avenue access as a condition of approval. No way around it now."

"So how will this affect the schedule?" John Collins asked.

"Normally, we wouldn't even issue a building permit for the plant until all the infrastructure is in," Bess said. "But I'll be damned if I want to give Poulet that trump card. I suppose we could let you go ahead and pull your permits—we just couldn't allow occupancy until the road is finished. We've done it before. What do you think, Ben?"

Why not? In for a penny, in for a pound. "Sure," I said.

"Community support is important," Ken Ishido said. "If it looks like opposition will cause delays, we will have to switch to another location. I say this not as a threat, but as an accurate statement about our industry. If we are not able to meet the demand of our customers, our competitors will quickly move in, and we will lose market share. So I want to know, is the City of Trillium behind us?"

"Of course," I said. "We'll make sure you can meet your deadlines. And I have a question for you. The food here tastes pretty good to me, but what do I know? So what did you think of the tempura?"

*   *   *

I was in the office at 7:30 the next morning. I logged onto my Internet account and quickly scanned the new mail list, half hoping for a message from Kate. I replied to a few of the messages, but I couldn't stop thinking about her.

To: kanderson@rockynet.com
Subject:Another Message

Dear Kate,
 It's been a week but I'm thinking about our trail ride, and watching your pony tail bounce while I followed you. Write me.
 Love, Ben

Later that morning, Jake Wildavsky and I were finishing a discussion on a water plant grant application when Ken Longstreet, the finance director, came into the office.

"I just got the current year property tax numbers from the county, and thought you would want to know. Actually, you don't want to know this, but I suppose you have to." He slumped into a chair and pulled at his collar.

"That bad, huh?"

"Yes. No one knew exactly how Measure 5-47 was going to work—the formula is too complicated—and it depends on property data from every parcel of property in the city. So they put all the figures in their black box, and just now came out with the results."

"And?"

"And the bottom line is, we're going to take a 30 percent hit."

"Really? Why so big?"

"A lot of reasons. We've had strong growth in values and new construction over the last three years, and the measure wiped that out. The amount of the tax set aside for payments on our fire and library bonds is fixed by contract law, so that leaves less for the general fund. Like I said, no one knew how the final numbers would shake out, the ballot measure was such a convoluted piece of work."

"Crank up the bake sales...." Jake said.

"I wonder if Pritchard knew it would work out this way," I said.

"No, he's not that smart. Maybe his backers had an idea based on how it's played out in other cities, but I'm sure Pritchard was just throwing a hand grenade into the system, and he didn't care what it would hit."

"So, what are we going to do?"

"We have enough cash reserves to get us through this fiscal year," Ken said. "But we're definitely going to have to do something drastic to make next year's budget balance. It's going to be a mess."

"What's going to be a mess?" Diane McTavish blew into the office and joined us at my conference table. Ken repeated the news. The mayor sat in silence for a few seconds—a rare enough event that I could tell she was shaken.

"With so much of the budget tied up in personnel cost, it's pretty obvious what this is going to mean, isn't it?"

I wasn't sure exactly what she was thinking, but I nodded anyway. Layoffs would be unavoidable; I knew that.

"And your fire department idea is looking like a lot more than an academic exercise," she said.

"Looks that way," Ken said.

"Well, I just left a meeting of the Governor's Revenue Reform task force," McTavish said. "Once more, they're talking about a state sales tax. I think the effort is doomed, but where else can we go?"

"Yeah, the message from the voters seems to be that they won't allow a sales tax until the state does away with property tax," Jake said. "So we would build a three-legged stool and immediately kick the third leg out again. I had an uncle who built furniture that way, too. Not very successful."

"Ha. The task force is tied up in knots trying to figure out how to make a sales tax sellable," McTavish said. "A big criticism is that the tax is regressive, especially when you tax food. But if you exempt food, you let a lot of middle- and high-income folks off the hook—sort of throwing the baby out with the bath water. So then what do they do? They start looking at each grocery item, trying to decide which one is essential, and should be tax-free, and which ones are discretionary, and should be taxed. What a paternalistic way to go about things."

"Sure, and it would end up being even more regressive," Jake said. "Think about it—you would be taxing Twinkies, Ding Dongs, Dorritos, TV dinners, beer, cigarettes—the very staples of the low-income family's diet. What's Joe Sixpack to do?"

"Don't ever run for political office, okay Jake?" the mayor said.

"You know, though, there's some truth to it," Ken said. "When people complain about a tax being regressive, they usually aren't worried about low income folks—they're worried about themselves, the middle class. That's who a sales tax exemption on food is really for—and the home mortgage deduction, and the standard deduction, and IRAs.... Only problem is, when you exempt the middle class, the tax is pretty useless as a revenue source."

"Yeah, the trick is to make it look like a break for the middle class, but not have it actually be one," Jake said. "The middle class conservatives think that getting rid of capital gains tax and going to a flat tax would be great—it would fix the IRS, wouldn't it?—but they would be the ones getting screwed. They buy into the myth that social security is a government sponsored pension system for their benefit, when it's really a massive income transfer from the working middle class to people who as a group are the wealthiest in America—"

"Don't get started on that," McTavish said. "It isn't worth wasting time talking about—there will never be any real changes to the tax structure anyway."

"Afraid so."

Jake and Ken excused themselves. The mayor stayed to catch up on business.

"Not going to be a fun year, is it?" she said.

"Doesn't seem that way."

"How close are you to giving the council some options?"

"Pretty close. We have some ideas for tweaking some fees—building permits, that kind of thing—and cutting some costs. But the next step will be to get some feedback from the council on priorities."

"Mmm. You ought to know our priorities by now. Just give us what you think is best." Diane McTavish and her husband owned an insurance office. She had served a few terms on the budget committee and then the city council, and had been elected mayor two years ago. The public seemed to respect her even though she was outspoken and sometimes headstrong—or maybe because of it.

"So, how does Sean like West Point?" I asked.

"So far, so good. But they don't let him call much, so I really don't know. It just hit me that we won't be seeing him much for the next four years, and then who knows where they'll station him. They grow up too fast."

McTavish put on a pair of reading glasses and flipped through a stack of correspondence she had picked up in her in-box. The mayor had her own office in city hall—we called it the Ceremony Room. With its mahogany furniture and relative lack of clutter, it was the best place to greet visiting dignitaries or have pictures taken. McTavish kept a few working files there, but she was good at delegating most of the paperwork to staff.

"Saw in the newspaper that you've had some interesting meetings with the firefighters," she said. "They going to work with you, or not?"

"I don't know yet. I followed Ken's advice and offered a bunch of concessions—sort of a pre-emptive strike. Immediate pay increases for switching to an eight-hour shift. No layoffs. Direct involvement in decision making. I thought Gallagher might take the bait, but I can't tell…"

McTavish looked over the top of her glasses. "Think about what you're up against. What's the top of the pay range for a firefighter—about $50,000? Add on overtime, and you're at $60,000. But with the 24 hours on/48 hours off shifts, that leaves you with, what, about 240 days off out of 360. So you figure in a part time job as a framer or roofer or plumber. What's that, another $40,000 a year? Then factor in plenty of time at home with the family, or for fishing or hunting. So you've got an annual income in the six figures, a job where you're paid for sleeping, and plenty of leisure time. Then Ben Cromarty comes along and offers a 10 percent pay increase to give all of that up and switch to a regular job like the rest of us have."

I laughed. "Thanks for the encouragement. So you don't think they're going to buy it?"

"Nope. But keep trying"

She signed some letters we had prepared, and the official copies of the ordinances and resolutions that the city council had adopted last Tuesday.

"This Trillium Business Leadership outfit is threatening legal action on the Nova contract award," I said.

"Not surprised. I saw the letter from Pritchard. Anything to it?"

"Pete reckons we're on solid legal ground, and it won't hold up the project timeline. He'll brief the council at the next meeting. But it will be a nuisance—the press will eat it up if it smells like a scandal. It always seems like the accusation gets the headlines. You know, Contractor Accuses City of Shenanigans, and the final resolution of the case months later gets a half an inch at the back of the Metro section—Court Finds in City's Favor. If our federal counterparts are any example, the primary role of government is to entertain the public and provide fodder for the press."

"Now, now. You can take it."

I smiled. "You're right. I won't last long in this if I indulge myself in self-pity."

"Well. I've got to get back to my paying job. You and Mary doing anything this weekend? Maybe we can all go to a show or something."

"Sure."

        *   *   *

The conference room in Station One was fully equipped with comfortable chairs, a heavy oak table, a white marking board, and a coffee maker.

Three of the walls were covered with pictures of blazing buildings and soot-covered firefighters holding babies and house pets.

Brian Gallagher sat on one side of the table with another firefighter, Doug Osborn. They were joined by Red Rogalsky, a hired gun from the International Association of Firefighters. His presence didn't do much to encourage me. Max Oakley, Ken Longstreet and I sat on the other side. This technically wasn't a contract negotiating session, but it sure looked like one.

Brian and Red politely engaged in small talk with us as we filled coffee cups and organized our papers. Doug sat silently.

"Well, it's your meeting—what do you want to talk about?" Brian said.

I had of course told him what we wanted to talk about when I called him a few days earlier. But I didn't blame him for keeping the ball in our court.

"Basically, we want to set up a process for involving the firefighters in the process of re-engineering our service delivery. Like I told you, the bottom line is that we need to save a lot of money, but I'm flexible on exactly how we do that. The news from the State is even worse than we first thought, and there is no possible way to avoid an impact on the fire department. So I want to establish some form of a labor-management task force to look at our options, and figure out the best way to target our resources separately to fire and medical calls."

"You're making one big assumption," Brian said.

"Which is?"

"That we'll go along with this scheme in the first place. We've seen this before—you try to co-opt us in a decision by making it look like we're a part of it."

"Okay, maybe I am making an assumption," I said. "So let me put it another way—do you want to be part of the decision-making process, or not? I think the choice is simple."

Doug burst out, "So you're threatening to push this on us whether we like it or not?"

"Ben's not making any kind of threat," Ken said. "He's offering things that go way beyond the provisions of the employment contract. He's offering a chance to set up a process that gives real power to the line staff, to let them call the shots, in areas that have always been reserved as management rights. But the choice is yours. Like they say, you need to decide whether to lead, follow, or get out of the way."

I wasn't sure that quoting Lee Iacoca was going to win points with the union, but I appreciated Ken jumping in.

"But the bottom line is, you will never let us call the shots," Brian said. "What do you pay Max here for? And what if we decide on some other way of saving money besides splitting fire and medical?"

"Like what?" I said, immediately regretting it.

"Like closing a fire station."

I played out the scenario in my mind. The city announces the closure of a fire station in response to Measure 5-47. The firefighters carefully leave the decision as to which station is closed to management. Then when the decision is made, the firefighters quietly—or overtly, if the past was any indication—rally the neighborhood surrounding the station against the city council. A barrage of letters to the editor and packed public meetings ends up forcing the city to keep the station open and manned. This happens late enough in the process that there's no time to find any other significant savings in the fire department. I'd seen this happen in enough other cities to know that it was a hopeless situation.

"Would you and your colleagues rally public support for such an option?" Max asked.

"We can't guarantee that. We don't have any influence over how the residents think," Brian said, with a straight face. "But we see this as a much better plan. Sure, there would be a reduction in service, but the voters had to anticipate that when they passed the ballot measures."

"But they also expect us to find more efficient ways of doing things," I said. "Closing a fire station is an option, but I still want to pursue re-engineering our service. So I suppose I agree with you on one point: I'm retaining the right to set the overall direction the city goes, subject to city council direction. But within that, we're offering a chance for real participation by the line staff."

"Let me offer another option," Red Rogalsky said. "The Association is mounting a major campaign to lobby Salem for more funds for firefighting. We think this will be successful, based on similar lobbying work by the Oregon Teachers Association. So there won't be any significant reduction in the resources available for fire. This will give you the chance to avoid all the headaches associated with fire and medical cuts."

Sure, and most of those headaches were caused by his association.

"So far," Ken said, "the word from Salem is that if the legislature does increase funding for fire, they will take it from the small amount of income tax they already share with cities. So we wouldn't see any net increase in revenues. How does that help us balance the budget?"

"How they fund it is up to the legislature," Red said. "But if it's dedicated to fire, you can't spend it somewhere else."

"But we still have discretion over the amount of property tax that we use for fire," Ken said.

"Then we may need to make sure the legislation restricts state funding assistance to only the cities that keep fire whole," Red said.

I let that statement hang for a while.

"So you're telling me that you are promoting legislation that doesn't help cities at all, but instead provides for further revenue cuts for cities that reduce fire budgets. In what way do you see this as an option that helps me?"

"I didn't say that," Red replied. "We're looking at ways to keep revenues available for fire departments at sufficient levels to protect the public. Hopefully there won't be an impact on any other city revenues, but we can't dictate how the legislature makes its budget decisions. You may still have some funding challenges in other areas, but we are offering a way to avoid the problems associated with reductions in the fire service."

"Okay, fine," I said. "But the legislature won't act soon. In the meantime, we have to balance next year's budget. So we're back to where we started. Brian, let me ask one more time. How do you want to see the firefighters involved in decisions that affect the way we provide responses to fire calls and to medical calls?"

"The only way they want to be involved is to fight it."

*   *   *

The team warmed up in ninety degree heat. I had put Trixie in at short stop and was trying a new pitcher. For slow pitch softball and ten-year-old batters, I wasn't looking for strike-outs. What I needed was someone who was fast on her feet, who could think quickly, and who would set up the plays for the infield. Sarah Preston seemed like a good prospect, and as the visiting team came up to bat, it looked like my decision was a good one. The first batter hit a hard line drive, and Sarah leaped up and caught it in the end of her glove. The second batter popped a fly ball into a hole in center field for an easy single. The third batter bounced a ball just inside the right foul line—the first baseman ran in to scoop it up and lobbed it to Sarah, who had run over to cover first. She had moved so quickly that the runner stayed planted to the bag. The fourth batter hit a pop fly. Trixie back pedaled into the outfield and made the catch for the third out. Sarah had instinctively moved over to back up the second baseman. The team ran in, sweating and grinning.

Our first batter sliced the air with her first two swings, then pulled a beautiful line drive between the short stop and third baseman. The second batter struck out. John Collins' daughter, Renee, let fly with a hit into right field, driving in our first run. The girls were pumped.

I motioned one of them over.

"Jenny, you're doing great out there. I saw how you backed up Trixie when she went for that fly ball."

"Thanks."

"Now, remember, when a left-handed batter comes up to the plate, go ahead and move over to your left a little, okay? They tend to pull it that way, right?"

"Sure."

"That a girl. All right, you're up next."

A breeze moved up from the river valley. The heat felt good. We got another run thanks to a fielding error, then got out on a fly ball and a tag play at second.

The visitors were another Trillium Team, the Bad News Beavers. As my team took to the field, one of the parents ambled over from the visitors' bleachers. I recognized him, but didn't know his last name. He was one of our firefighters.

"Hi, Phil," I said.

"Howdy, coach."

He leaned on the fence next to me and watched the game.

"Your girls are doing real good. That pitcher of yours is a pistol. You must be doing something right in practice."

"No, I just got lucky. Sarah's never played that position before."

Sarah walked a runner for the first time. "Okay ladies, the play's at second," I yelled. They ignored me.

"Which one's your girl, Phil?"

"Beth, the one with the ponytail over there. Looks like she's on deck."

Sarah fielded a short pop fly, and Beth moved up to the plate. Phil gave her a cheer. She ground her left foot in the dirt and cocked her bat. Sarah put the ball over the plate in a high arch, and Beth sent it just out of reach of Marcia at second base. She gave her dad a quick glance as she sprinted toward first. She rounded the base, but the center fielder had scooped up the ball and was heading for second.

"I know the guys are giving you a hard time about your idea for setting up a medical response team," Phil said.

"Looks that way."

"Well, I just wanted to let you know I don't think it's that bad an idea. I wondered about the same thing when I first started on, then sort of forgot about it after a while."

"Really?"

"Yep. I wouldn't want the union guys to know I said it, though." He laughed.

The next batter hit into left field. Lupe picked it up and Marcia ran out to catch the relay. I noticed that Trixie automatically covered second. Good. The throw was wild and Beth rounded third. Phil hooted as she ran for the plate. He started jogging back to the visitors' dugout.

"Hey Phil," I called.

"Yeah?"

"Thanks."

"Sure. Hang in there, Ben."

We ended up winning, eight to four. I gathered the girls for a post-game wrap-up, but they were too excited to listen to much, so I let them go home. I swung the gear bag over my shoulder and Trixie and I left.

"You looked great out there, buddy. You made some nice plays, and were using your head."

"Thanks, Dad."

She took my hand. I wished she would never grow too old for that.

*   *   *

Jake Wildavsky came into my office early the next morning.

"Remember the problem I was having with one of the customer service reps, Rich Martinsen?"

"Yes. Ever get it resolved?"

"I thought we did, at least for a while. But yesterday he told a customer to go to hell, then hung up on him. So I fired him."

"Oh, man. How did he take it."

"Okay, at the time," Jake said. "But I just got a call from a guy claiming to be Martinsen's attorney. He made a lot of noise about it being a wrongful dismissal. Said that Martinsen suffers from multiple personality syndrome, and since it's a disease, he's protected under the Americans with Disabilities Act."

I laughed, then noticed that, for a change, Jake was serious.

"You're kidding, right?"

"Nope. This lawyer says we need to make reasonable accommodation for Martinsen's disorder, and can't fire him."

"Reasonable accommodation? What does that mean here?"

"I guess we would have him do book work or something else that doesn't involve human interaction when his bad personality takes over. The job description for his position lists physical requirements—ADA requires that—but apparently we failed to mention that applicants need to refrain from abusing other people. Can you believe it?"

"But you went out of your way to help the guy. Didn't you put him through counseling under the employee assistance program?"

"Yeah. It came to a head with his last outburst and he signed a last chance agreement where he accepted counseling as an alternative to dismissal. The employee assistance program staff confirmed that he was showing up for the counseling sessions, but they never said anything about a multiple personality disorder. Even if they had, I'm not sure I would have done anything different. You sort of assume that people who act up enough to get fired are a little crazy anyway."

"Have you talked to Pete?"

"Not yet. Wanted to let you know first."

"Well, assuming that Pete agrees that you took the right steps in the discipline process, tell him I want to call their bluff. It's absurd."

*   *   *

My phone rang just after Jake left.

"Hi Ben."

"Kate?"

"Yeah. How're you doing?"

"Great! It's good to hear you."

"You too."

"Did you get my e-mails?"

"Uh huh," she said, then paused. "That's why I called. I, umm, I enjoyed reading them, but maybe I was reading too much into them. I wanted to send a message back, but finally I decided I couldn't..."

"Why?"

"Well, I was worried about where it might take us. Most of all, I don't want to do anything that would mess up my relationship with Mary. She's been my best friend for most of my life. I didn't want to do anything that I felt I would have to hide from her. You know? We really haven't had any secrets. I don't want to start now, okay? I don't know if this makes any sense—it's hard for me to talk about."

"No, you're making sense. I don't think you read too much into my notes, but I did feel like a kid in 7th grade sending them. Sorry to catch you off guard."

"Oh, that's okay. But are you all right with this?"

"Sure."

"Well, what else is new?"

My mind went blank. Sitting there in my office with the phone in my hand and Kate on the other end, all I could think was that my days were filled with nothing but trivial minutiae.

"Not much," I said. "Trixie's team won their game yesterday, Mary and I had a great night out at the Portland Symphony a few days ago, I'm still playing cat and mouse with the fire union, and a business group is suing us on a contract issue. Pretty normal stuff, I guess. How about you?"

"Same. Things have quieted down some at the print shop. Gordon is as busy as ever. The boys are going to a camp for a week."

We were silent for a few moments.

"A customer just came in," Kate said. "I guess I better get off the phone."

"Yeah. It was good talking to you. I'm glad you called, Kate."

"Me too. Bye, Ben."

"See you."

I sat at my desk and tried to read the letter on the top of my in-box, but gave up. I left the office and climbed the stairs, then used my master key to open the roof door. The morning air was still cool, but the heat of the sun reflected off the building. I leaned against the parapet and watched the traffic below. The cars seemed to wander aimlessly.

7

The Crown Victoria climbed up into the Penumqua Heights gated community, its engine barely registering the effort. Inside the gate, the road leveled off. We ran the gauntlet of imposing three-car garages and newly planted saplings. Officer Mike Howlett waved to a couple strolling down the sidewalk.

"Surprised to see anyone walking in here," he said. "The whole point of the gate is to keep the outside world out. Seems like folks mostly drive straight into their garage and close the door behind them. If they're real adventurous, they'll duck into the backyard to barbecue a steak. And if a person has the nerve to walk in front of someone else's house, we get a call from the block watch captain. They drive their kids to the neighborhood park two blocks away, for Pete's sake—it's outside the gate, you know."

Every once in a while I went on a ride-along with one of the patrol officers. If nothing else, it was a good way to keep up with the changes in the city.

"They always want us to catch speeders on the main drag, but they complain if we actually ticket one of the residents. Who else do they think drives in here?"

I laughed. "You have much trouble with burglaries? Seems like there'd be some pretty lucrative jobs here."

"Nope. But domestic violence…you'd be surprised."

"Money can't buy me love, huh?"

"What's that, a Beatles song? Before my time, anyway. And I bet if we dug into a few of the teenagers' bedrooms, we'd have us some pretty good drug charges."

Mike circled out of Penumqua Heights and pointed his cruiser toward a new subdivision. We slowly passed by houses in various stages of construction. It was seven p.m., but most of the workers were still there, finishing up a 14-hour day. The builders counted on the long days and dry weather of July and August, and homes seem to go up overnight. A roofer in shorts and a tank top saluted us with his nail gun.

We dropped down the hill back into the main part of town, turning onto Chief Joseph Boulevard, a major arterial that connected Trillium with Portland. The traffic was still heavy with the last of the evening commuters. Mike eased the car into the parking lot of an insurance office and calibrated his radar gun. Within minutes a white BMW shot by, twenty miles over the speed limit. Mike reacted quickly, and the sudden acceleration caught me by surprise. He switched on his lights as he merged with the traffic. It only took a couple of blocks to catch up with the BMW. As we pulled over, Mike punched the license number into his mobile digital terminal. A radio modem linked up with the state and national crime information centers, scanning for outstanding wants or warrants. The search came back empty. Mike grabbed his ticket book and walked up to the driver's window. I could tell that the driver was a woman—probably the registered driver listed on the screen of Mike's MDT—but couldn't see much else. Her bumper had a sticker that said REALITY IS FOR PEOPLE WHO LACK IMAGINATION. It took Mike ten minutes to check her license and insurance forms and write the ticket.

"That'll help our revenue picture a little," he said.

"How much was the ticket?"

"Eighty bucks. She wasn't happy about it, of course. Said she was in a hurry to pick up her kids from day care."

After we took out the state's share of the fine and our court system's cost for processing the ticket, there wouldn't be much left to cover Mike's salary. But the traffic stops were intended more to keep speeds down than to make money, anyway.

Mike wrote up a few more speeding tickets. The fourth car that he hit with the radar gun was an old Ford pickup, going 55 in a 35mph zone. He whistled when he entered the license number into his terminal.

"What's that mean?" I asked.

"The Portland Police Bureau has an arrest warrant out for him. He's wanted on a few assault and battery charges, it looks like." Mike squeezed the button on his radio's handset. "Three Charlie Six."

"Three Charlie Six, go ahead."

"I'm on a traffic stop, on Chief Joseph just south of the T Marketplace. Got a possible wanted. Could you roll cover?"

"Okay, Three Charlie Six, rolling cover."

Mike picked up his ticket book and loosened the Velcro flap on his service revolver. He went out and spent a few minutes talking to the driver, then got back into the car.

"What's up?"

"I told him to pull up to the parking lot there so we can get his truck off the road. He's going to take a little trip with us."

"Is he the guy with the warrant?"

"Well, wouldn't you know, he gave me a different name, but he just doesn't seem to be able to find his license, or anything else with his name on it. He matches the description, though, so we'll take him on down to the jail and let them sort it out."

Mike stayed on the truck's bumper as it moved down the shoulder and pulled into a supermarket's parking lot. The cruiser's red and blue lights painted the parked cars in the growing darkness. Mike got out and talked to the driver, then motioned him out of the car. Another black and white sedan pulled into the parking lot. Officer Tony Sanchez got out of his car and walked over to Mike. I got out to join them.

"Hi Ben. You want to be one of the Reserves?"

"Sure, Tony. Don't know if I could pass the test, though."

They laughed.

"Everything under control?" Tony asked.

"Yep, so far," Mike said.

"Looks like it's turning into a busy night. Must be the full moon. We already have a couple of drunks cooling off back at the station." We had caught some of that through the radio traffic. "Well, take it easy."

"Yeah, thanks."

Mike escorted the pickup truck's driver into the back seat of the patrol car. Tony stayed in the parking lot until we were underway. The twenty minute drive to the Multnomah County jail was relatively uneventful.

Back in Trillium, Mike parked at the fire station. The food and coffee were better there than at the police station, and there were more people around in the evening. The firefighters were either watching TV or cleaning up after dinner, depending on seniority. They were surprised to see me there after hours, but they were cordial enough. Mike probably felt a little awkward with me hanging around, but the officers did enough ride-alongs with citizens and council members that he handled it well. We were in the middle of a discussion on the Mariners' prospects for the playoffs when Mike's portable radio summoned him to another call. It was a burglar alarm at a local art gallery.

"Probably a false alarm," Mike said.

He was right. The gallery was dark and the doors and windows seemed secure.

"Happens all the time. A blowing curtain or something sets off the motion detector."

"Frustrating for you, huh?"

"Sometimes, but we're on patrol anyway. Might as well check out this place as anywhere else."

Around midnight we cruised through a neighborhood at the edge of town. A girl—must have been around 12 or 13—was walking alone, apparently in a hurry. Mike called out his window, "Excuse me, miss. Can I help you?"

She stopped. "No, I'm okay. I'm fine. I'm just going home."

Mike got out of the patrol car and talked to her quietly, for several minutes. At one point, she seemed to hesitate, then showed him her arm. I couldn't make out much in the street lights. After a minute, he opened the car door for her.

"She was babysitting for her uncle. Seems he was out drinking, and came home and started hitting her and the kids around. Says she lives on the other end of town, but doesn't want to go there."

Mike gave the house description to the dispatcher and headed for the police station. All four interrogation rooms were full. We no longer maintained any jail cells or even holding rooms. The civil rights laws made our old cells obsolete—we just used them for records storage—and we couldn't afford the medical and other costs associated with holding prisoners. So we relied on the county jail, and used our interrogation rooms for temporary secure space when the officers were too busy to make the trip into Portland. State law allowed us to hold suspects for a few hours before officially booking them.

"Listen, do you mind staying with Stacy here while I try to sort out what's going on in the home front? I'd rather not leave her alone."

"Sure, Mike."

Stacy wasn't very talkative, but we managed to find some common ground.

"Where do you go to school?"

"Nowhere, yet. We just moved here this summer. I guess I'm going to Snook Middle School, or something like that."

"Chinook. It's named after a kind of fish. Some of my daughter's friends are going there next year. Where did you live before?"

"California. Yreka. My stepdad got a job up here. He's in construction."

"He must be pretty busy now."

"Yeah. I don't see him much."

Tony Sanchez let himself in from the sallyport. "Man, what a night. I got to get some of these characters out of here to free up some room." We heard him unlock one of the interrogation rooms. It sounded to me like he must have trapped a rabid longshoreman in there. Stacy had heard that language before, I guessed.

"Crazy place, huh?" I said.

"Yeah. What do you do here? You don't look like a cop."

"No, I work at city hall. I'm just riding around with Officer Howlett to see what it's like."

"Oh. So do you want to be a policeman?"

I smiled. "Maybe some day."

*   *   *

Every other week we held a development coordinating meeting to make sure nothing slipped through the cracks on major projects. The team members included Bess Wilson, and Jake Wildavsky, as well as our city engineer, the chief building inspector, and the fire marshal. Bess' secretary handed out a status sheet.

"What's going on with the Trillium Village subdivision?" Bess asked.

"Search me," Jake said. "We red-lined the plans and got them back to their engineer about a month ago. Haven't heard anything since."

"There's a rumor out there that Heinz Hesse is trying to sell the thing," the building official said.

"Well, that would explain it," Bess said. "Nothing much we can do now. Wasn't there some issue with a sewer easement?"

"Yes, there is," the city engineer said. "They need to run the line through the Boatwright's property. We met with Dick Boatwright, and he seemed open to it, but he wanted to deal with the city instead of with Hesse. Ben, we may need your help on this one."

"Sure, just let me know."

The next project on the list was Nova Estates. The company was proposing a mix of six-plex apartments and townhouses as part of their project. Combining housing with an industrial plant broke with several decades of exclusionary zoning practice. That was fine with me—it was exclusionary zoning that gave us urban sprawl, increasing commute times, lifeless suburbs and dysfunctional communities.

"Nova is set for a public hearing on the housing project next month," Bess said. It may be a little rough—apparently the Hemlock Creek neighborhood has formed a group to oppose it. They're calling themselves Citizens for Good Planning."

"What are they, your typical Nimbies?" the fire marshal asked.

"No, they're Bananas…Build Absolutely Nothing Anywhere Near Anything," Jake said.

"More like Nopes," Bess said.

"What's that?"

"Not On Planet Earth."

"Ha ha. Really, what's their beef?" the fire marshal asked.

"Not sure," Bess said. "I got hold of a flier they've been circulating—full of bullshit about how residential and industrial traffic can't mix and how the environment will be destroyed. I think they're mainly worried that poor folks will move in there."

"At least they'll be poor folks with decent jobs," I said. "Besides, Hemlock Creek is separated by a major arterial from Nova's property—I really don't see how it will affect them. How does the project look from a planning perspective?"

"They need to keep a few more trees on the northeast corner," Bess said. "And the state will probably restrict them to right turns onto Chief Joseph. Other than that, it looks pretty good. They're keeping plenty of separation from the creek, and the design for the apartments looks better than your typical barracks."

"Well, good luck with the hearing."

We dealt with a gas station remodel, a car wash, a five-story downtown office building, a row-house development, an assisted living center, four subdivisions in various stages of planning, a manufactured home park, a warehouse building and a mini-storage lot. After two and a half hours of that I was ready to retreat to my office, even though it inevitably held a dozen voice messages. Pete Koenig caught me in the hall.

"You know Pete, I'm not sure I'm glad to see you. Seems like all you've been giving me is bad news."

He chuckled. "Well, here's some more, then. I got a call from Todd Pritchard's lawyer. They want to take a deposition from you and Bess."

"Great. Maybe I can schedule some root canal work instead."

"You'll do fine. Besides, I don't think the deposition is admissible in court. The writ of review isn't a regular trial—the judge has to limit his review to the record of the city council proceedings."

"So why do we have to go through with it?"

"Well, you still do—it will have to be up to the judge to decide if it's admissible. But really, you'll do fine. I think Bess actually enjoys these things. She told me she wouldn't pass up an opportunity to get screwed by an attorney."

*   *   *

The offices of Snodgrass, Sandlefart and Bump were on the twenty-second floor of the New World Bank Building in downtown Portland. The decor, from the glass-walled reception area to the mahogany paneling of the conference room, was designed to impress clients and intimidate adversaries. The firm made its money on contingency contracts in lawsuits—mostly product liability and civil rights claims—and the opulent offices were intended to convey the message that they were successful at it.

At the corner of the table sat the court reporter, an anachronism in the days of speech-recognition software, but in keeping with the Byzantine procedures of the judicial system. Todd Pritchard had short brown hair and a goatee, and he wore a navy sport coat and navy slacks. The colors didn't quite match. It was the first time that I had had face-to-face contact with him, and I wasn't impressed. In fact, I was amazed that he had been able to work his way into a leadership position with his good old boy network.

Terry Judd, his lawyer and a junior partner at Snodgrass and Sandlefart, was dressed in a dark pin stripe suit and wore a gold watch. He was leaning forward and staring at Bess Wilson.

"So you're telling us that you didn't know from the start that Northwest Construction was going to do the work on the Nova project?"

"That's what I said. I spent most of my time trying to make sure that Nova would locate in Trillium. Why would I care which contractor they used?"

"All right. You say your job was to persuade Nova to choose Trillium. How did you do that? Tax incentives, special treatment, or what?"

"We don't have any tax incentives to offer—you should know that. About all we can do is sell the benefits of our community—workforce, available land, freeway access, high quality of life—"

"But wasn't the financing from the State part of the deal?"

"Think about it before you ask stupid questions, Judd." I saw a hint of a sparkle in Pete Koenig's eyes. He was enjoying Bess' feistiness. "First, we couldn't guarantee the State funding, all we could do is tell them we would apply for it. Second, any town in Oregon could have made the same offer. Third, do you really think a million bucks in grants and loans makes that big a difference in a fifty million dollar project?"

Judd looked through his notes.

"What about special treatment in the planning process? Did you tell them you would fast-track their development application, or anything like that?"

"We told them we would process it as quickly as possible, but we still put them through all the hoops that anyone would have had to go through."

"Does that mean that you gave their project a higher priority than, say, an application from a local business?"

"No local business had a project that big. We handled the building plan review concurrently with the development application to speed things up, but we've done that for other businesses...including Pritchard's here, come to think of it."

I watched, but not with complete detachment, knowing that my turn was coming up next. Bess seemed completely at ease. She wore a simple maroon v-neck top and gray pants, and had either made a calculated decision to dress casually to avoid giving too much dignity to the occasion, or—more likely—she hadn't thought about it at all. She leaned back in her chair and ignored the notebook in front of her.

Terry Judd was barely thirty years old. His shirt collar was a little too big for his neck and it looked like he used some kind of mousse in his hair. He kept his attention on Bess and his yellow legal pad, but I got the feeling that his primary goal was to impress Todd Pritchard.

Pritchard, for his part watched with a smug, sanctimonious look as if he had already trapped Bess in some grave misdeed. It was just a spectator sport for him since he wouldn't have to take the hot seat. "So you made promises of special treatment," Judd said, "and you offered a special financing deal to Nova, a company you had never heard of before, is that right?"

"Listen, it seems you're trying to imply that we did something wrong or out of the ordinary, and that's just bullshit."

"Miss Wilson, I need to remind you that the court reporter will make a transcript of this deposition for the judge."

"Oh, I'm sorry. That's spelled b-u-l-l-s-h-i-t, Marilyn."

Marilyn gave a slight smile and continued tapping her keys.

"So whose decision was it to exempt Northwest contracting from the bidding process," Judd asked.

Bess paused. "The city council's, ultimately."

"But they based it on staff's recommendation. Was it your recommendation?"

"Yes."

"Why did you recommend that?"

"Because it was in the city's best interest."

"Or was it in your own personal interest, too? Did you receive any fees or special consideration from Nova for your cooperation?"

"No, of course not. You watch too many movies, Judd. I've never even been offered a kickback on anything, let alone sought one out. Your client may be more familiar with that kind of thing, but it's not part of my professional experience."

Judd spent a minute flipping through his notepad. Finally he looked up.

"Okay, Bess, that's enough for now."

For an hour Judd questioned me about the financial arrangements behind the Nova and Northwest Construction contracts. He seemed to take special interest in the fact that Nova was making all the loan payments, although the city was acting as the conduit for the State financial package. During a break Pete, Bess and I got coffee at a Starbucks shop in the building lobby.

"Why is he so hung up about the fact that Nova is paying for the road, water, and sewer work?" Bess asked. "What's so unusual about that?"

"I suppose he's trying to make a case that the city shouldn't have used cost savings as a criterion in bypassing the bid process," I said. "Since Nova was ultimately paying all the costs, a few hundred thousand more wouldn't have affected the city."

"Maybe you're right, but the statute allows a bid exemption based on cost, regardless of the source of the city's funds for a project," Pete said. "If you think about it, almost none of our construction projects are financed with city taxes. Most are paid for by developers or property owners one way or another, through local improvement districts or development impact fees. They're still city projects if the money goes through us, though."

"Sure, if you follow Judd's reasoning, it isn't a city project at all, since Nova is paying for the work," I said. "If that's the case, then it isn't bound by the bidding process in the first place, and we're wasting our time here."

They laughed. Pete said, "I doubt he really thinks he has a case. I still believe the purpose of the deposition is just to rattle your cage a little. Do you want a refill on your coffee?'

"No, I'd have to take a pee break in the middle of the deposition. But maybe that isn't such a bad idea."

For the next hour and a half, Terry Judd probed around on the circumstances leading to Nova's decision to locate in Trillium.

"Early on in the process, didn't you and the mayor join John Collins and some of the other Nova executives on a trip to San Jose?" Judd asked.

"Yes."

"What was the purpose of that trip?"

"Nova has a plant there. We wanted to see what we were getting into."

"The minutes of the April 20 council meeting indicate that Nova paid for that trip. How much did it cost?"

"They offered to pay," I said, "but the mayor and I paid our own way."

"What, out of your own pocket?"

"No, with city funds."

"Why did you do that?"

"We wanted to avoid any conflict of interest."

"So what did the trip cost?"

"Oh, I don't know. Around sixteen hundred, total, I suppose."

"So you used city tax money to accept Nova's invitation to check our their plant. Why did you decide to do that?"

"I told you. We wanted to see what the city was getting into. We wanted to see what kind of impact the plant had on the environment, working conditions, the range of wages and salaries they had…"

"What, they let you look at their payroll records?"

"No, we could get an idea by the kinds of jobs they had."

Judd looked at his notes.

"How long were you in San Jose?"

"Around two days."

"Aren't you sure?"

"No, it was last spring. I can't remember the details."

"So you spent at least one night there. Did the Nova people entertain you or take you to dinner?"

"They joined us for dinner one night, and then we all went out to a jazz night club. But the other night we didn't do anything since we had an early flight back to Portland."

"Who paid for all that? The dinner, drinks, club cover charge and that sort of thing?"

"Mayor McTavish and I paid for our own dinner—"

"City funds?"

"Yes. We paid for drinks out of our own pocket. Nova may have picked up some of that. But it was fairly minor."

"Now Ben, you said earlier that you wanted to avoid the appearance of a conflict of interest. But here you were in closed meetings with members of a for-profit corporation, socializing with them, letting them entertain you. Doesn't that seem to you to present a conflict of interest?"

"No."

"Why do you think that?"

"A lot of reasons. We were visiting a factory in San Jose. That's not exactly a political junket. We went with the city council's approval. Everything was above board."

"But if nothing else, you established a friendship with John Collins. Isn't his daughter on a team you coach?"

How did Judd know that? I looked at Pritchard. He tried to suppress a grin.

"Yeah, so what? The players are assigned by the softball league, they aren't drafted by the coaches."

"I just want to get that on the record. What other social activities do you engage in that involve Collins, Ramon Diego, or any of the other executives of Nova or Northwest Construction?"

This was getting tedious. There was no way any of this would have a bearing on their lawsuit—if they wanted to pursue a conflict of interest case, they would have to go after city council members, not me, since the council made the final decision on the bid exemption. And with the possible exception of Rob Titus, I knew the council would come out clean on that score. I wished I had Bess' ability to dish it back to Judd.

"Trillium's a small city. We bump into each other occasionally. Ramon is a member of my church. Except for Collins, Nova doesn't have much of a presence in Trillium yet, but I see John at chamber functions. But you can say that about most people involved in business in Trillium. You grew up there, you ought to know that."

"Okay. Let me return to the financing issue. First you said the work was a city project. Then you said that Nova was paying for it. Which answer to you want to go with?"

Nice try.

"They're both accurate," I said. "It's a city project, but we have a development agreement that states that Nova will pay us an amount equal to the state loan payments. What's so complicated about that?"

"Fine. Thank you for your time, Mr. Cromarty."

We left the conference room without speaking.

8

The City of Trillium marked the end of summer with a labor day concert in Town Square Park. Mary and I stretched out on a blanket and watched the crowd swaying to a blues band. Trixie had been with us for a while, until she got assimilated by a group of pre-teen friends. The smell of charcoal drifted up from the concession stand. I closed my eyes to take in the sounds and scents and the feel of the breeze, heated by the streets that bordered the park. Mary scooted closer to me.

The town square formed a physical link between the members of the community, sort of a family room for the city. A group of young girls in long dresses danced by the stage. A line of octogenarians sat in folding chairs under the shade of a cedar, tapping their feet. A man with an "I Brake for Slugs" T-shirt sneaked a beer from a cooler. Children played in the fountain in the center of the park. Trixie and her group laughed about something, completely oblivious to the music.

The band played a tight rendition of a John Mayall song and took a break. Out of the corner of my eye I saw a pale bear lumbering toward us. It was council member Rob Titus. When he sat down beside us I noticed the sides of our cooler bulged a little.

"Great turnout," he said.

"Yep. I'm surprised more people aren't on vacation."

"No, the campgrounds are too crowded," Mary said, "and they have to have their kids in school tomorrow anyway."

"How about you and Linda?" I asked. "Are you taking a final fling while the weather's good?"

"Naw. Too busy. We spent a few days on the coast this month—that was enough."

"Want a can of pop? We've got a few extra." At least that would get him off my cooler.

"No, but thanks anyway."

Trixie stopped by long enough to get money for an ice cream cone. I watched her disappear into the crowd.

"So how did you feel the work session went last week?" I asked.

"Pretty good. I think we'll be able to take care of this budget thing."

"Uh huh."

"I'm not sure about the fire department deal, though."

Strange. He had been one of the strongest supporters of the idea when the council reviewed their options. He knew we couldn't pass a budget without it.

"How's that?" I said.

"Max isn't convinced it'll work, you know."

"He sounded pretty positive at the work session. I know he had some reservations at first, but I think he's come around."

"I talked to him last week," Rob said. "He thinks the union will sink the deal."

"Well, he may be right, but only if we let them. Are you having second thoughts?"

"No, I backed it based on your recommendation, and I'll stand by that."

Mary pulled a blade of grass and wound it around her finger. The sun was starting to sink below the tops of the trees, but the air was still warm.

"Has Diane said anything to you about running for re-election?" Rob asked.

"No. I doubt she's really thought about it yet. Why?"

"Just curious."

Rob scanned the crowd, probably looking for important clients or fellow Rotary members. "Guess I better get going," he said.

"Okay. See you tomorrow night, if not before."

Mary waited until Rob was out of earshot. "What was that all about?"

"Which part?" I asked.

"The part about 'Is Diane running?' He isn't going to run for mayor, is he?"

"That would be something, wouldn't it? But the election is more than a year away. Anything can happen."

"It's frustrating knowing you can't get involved, isn't it?"

"Yeah. Sort of like watching the dice roll on a craps table. But hey, that's what makes life interesting."

"Isn't that a Chinese curse? 'May you live in interesting times'?"

I laughed.

After a while the band started up again. Hearing the blues made me think of Kate. I hadn't heard from her since she called me at the office a few weeks ago. I tried to keep her out of my mind—at least I told myself that—but it didn't work. I looked at Mary, beautiful in the glow of the setting sun. We didn't have many secrets, but I figured there were a few things that were better if I just kept them to myself.

*   *   *

The Boatwright brothers owned 40 acres of farmland on Chief Joseph Boulevard, the same road as the Nova project, but closer to town. It was in our urban growth boundary, and our comprehensive plan designated it as commercial property. Their mother had lived on the property up until the day she died a year and a half ago.

The Trillium Village development was a 400-home subdivision just to the west of the Boatwright's property. The land sloped to the east, and the gravity sewer line would need to follow a swale, with a lift station at the low point to tie it into the trunk line in Chief Joseph. Heinz Hesse needed the sewer line for his development, but having the pipe and the lift station there would be a huge benefit to the Boatwrights, if they ever got around to developing.

Dick Boatwright owned a dairy farm a few miles out of town. He had run, unsuccessfully, for county commissioner a few years ago. He was a wealthy man, not so much from his dairy operation, but from profits on farm land that happened to fall inside the urban growth boundary. The dairy farm, too, was in an area called "urban reserve," a fact that didn't particularly bother him. In twenty years or so, the growth boundary would probably move out there, so he could sell the land for a hundred times what he paid for it, and either retire or move the farm a few more miles out.

His brother Tom ran what was left of the family farm, and did work on the side driving tractors and backhoes for local contractors. In contrast to Dick's easy-going common sense attitude, Tom was intense with a hair-trigger temper.

Normally, one of Jake Wildavsky's engineers would have worked out the easement issue. It seemed to me to be a fairly routine deal. Most times, property owners donated the easement just to have access to the sewer system. But the Boatwrights, especially Tom, had a strong distrust of government, and insisted on dealing directly with me on it. So I had walked the property with them and exchanged a few versions of the easement document. It looked like we were finally ready to close, and I had set up a meeting in the city hall conference room.

"The language looks okay to me," Dick said. I never saw him in anything other than jeans and a cowboy hat. He reminded me a little of Dennis Weaver in the old McCloud mystery series.

"Well, I have a question," Tom said. "We're getting a credit of $54,000 against our future hookup costs. What if it costs less than that? Will we get money back?"

"No, but you would end up with essentially a free hookup. That's worth a lot these days, especially if you get some buyers for the property that use a lot of sewer service, like restaurants or a laundromat. But we don't know what the final costs are going to be until Hesse finishes his work, and we draw up a reimbursement agreement—"

"So we may end up having to pay, even with giving away our land?"

"Maybe, but $54,000 is a healthy credit for that easement."

Tom stared at me a moment, then went back to reading the document. Dick flipped to the last page and pulled a pen out of his shirt pocket. "I'm ready to sign it," he said.

"Well, there's one more thing I'd like to see in here," Tom said. "We're going to be moving some dirt around on the property. Want to cut the slope down a little before we try to sell it. Says in here that we can't change the depth of the pipe without permission from the city—"

"Which pipe are you worried about?" I asked. "The gravity line is pretty close to the creek. The city code doesn't let you move dirt around down there. Or is it the force main?"

"What's that?"

"The pressure pipe that goes from the pump station up to Chief Joseph Boulevard."

"Yeah, that's the one," Dick said. "See, the property by the street has the most commercial value. You can't blame us for wanting to get that as level as we can."

"And that's going to be a problem with that pipe in the ground," Tom said.

"I don't know about that," I said. "Jake may not really care how deep it is. Or if worse comes to worst, you can move the pipe after you're done with your earth work—it's just plastic pipe like you use in your house, only on a little bigger scale. All the easement says is that you get our permission first."

"Well, here's what I'm thinking," Tom said. "We've got some angle iron lying around in the barn. Couldn't a guy make up supports with that angle iron and just hang the pipe, say, about ten or twelve feet up? Then a guy could just drive his tractor around there until he got the final grade right, and then bury the damned pipe. Could we make that change to this agreement?"

His brother Dick was studying the end of his pen.

"I'm not an engineer," I said. "I'm not even sure that's possible."

"But don't you have the authority—if we pencil in that change here— don't you have the authority to just sign it?"

"I don't know, Tom. You sure you want to do that? You really want to be driving a tractor under a pipe full of raw sewage under pressure? It really isn't such a big deal to move the pipe later if you have to. And who knows? You may be able to get your grading done before Hesse is ready to lay that pipe anyway."

Tom stared at me again. Dick said, "How soon is Hesse ready to move?"

"Well, he says he needs this stuff right away, but he's taking his time on the design. That's pretty typical—the developers want immediate turnaround on their plans, and then they sit on them."

They sat in silence a few moments. Tom tapped a pencil on the table.

"Say, Tom, isn't your son a senior this year?" I asked.

"Yep."

"I reckon the football team's going to have an outstanding season," I said. "With your son and a few of the other kids that are returning this year, we ought to make state easily." Tyson Boatwright had been the starting quarterback last year as a junior. He had had the highest passing record in Trillium High's history.

"Sure. Old Ty has been working out pretty hard this summer," Dick said. "And his brother Timmy will be a freshman this year, and I bet he'll make the varsity team."

Tom grinned. "You bet. We finally found him a coach he can work with. He went through a few to begin with. I guess Timmy can be a handful sometimes."

Quietly, Dick signed the easement, and slid it in front of his brother.

"Both Ty and Timmy do a lot of hay baling on the farm," Tom said. He looked absently at the document in front of him, and signed it. "That's what gets 'em in such good shape for football. Well, anyway, it's been a pleasure doing business with you, Ben."

*   *   *

The League of Oregon Cities existed mainly to see that towns like ours didn't get shafted too bad in Salem. Even though most of the state's population lived in the cities along the Willamette valley, the state constitution was pretty much an anti-government document, and the legislature was disproportionately tilted toward rural interests with a strong distrust of the Portland area. I had gotten roped into one of the League's legislative committees that met in Salem every few months. It included a mix of mayors, city council members, and city managers.

We dealt with a lot of topics—affordable housing, mandatory sentencing guidelines, water rights, energy deregulation, development fees, storm water regulations, pension funding, building codes, airport controls, street and highway funding, annexation laws, endangered species listings, juvenile crime, drinking water standards, cell phone towers, urban renewal, manufactured home regulations, school funding, groundwater limitations, highway signs, business licenses, and records retention laws. We even had a two-hour discussion on tsunami zones in coastal communities.

But today, the main topic of discussion was what we euphemistically called state tax reform—or more accurately, how to find new taxes to make up for the hits the cities had taken in property tax revenue. It was a problem we all had in common, so in that sense it gave us a strong feeling of unity. On the other hand, we were no different than the state population as a whole—the members of the committee came with a wide range of political ideologies—and it was hard to come up with solutions that met any sort of consensus.

Part of the challenge we faced was that the state tax system was a two-legged stool, supported only by property and income taxes. Not surprisingly, the tax rates were higher than in states that had property, income, and sales taxes. But the Oregon voters had rejected a sales tax so often that it was political suicide to talk about it directly. So we talked about tax reform instead.

A recently elected city council member from Umatilla had earnestly put forth a proposal for legislation that would combine a modest sales tax with cuts in both the property tax and income tax rates. It sounded logical.

"Only one problem with it," boomed a voice from the other side of the room. It was Al Hobbes, the city manager of Klamath Falls. "It won't work."

"Why's that?" the councilor from Umatilla asked.

"The state is structurally unable to make decisions on tax reform, or anything else that makes a real difference."

"Huh?"

"It's like this," Al said. "Ever hear the story about the scientist and the frog? The scientist, see, is doing an experiment. He says, 'Jump, frog.' The frog jumps three feet. So he writes in his notebook, 'Frog jumps three feet.' Then he cuts off one of the frog's legs. He says, 'Jump, frog,' and the frog jumps two feet. He writes in his book, 'Cut off one leg, frog jumps two feet.' He's making real scientific progress here. Then he cuts off another leg and says, Jump, frog.' The frog jumps a foot. So he writes in his book—"

"—frog jumps a foot," someone said.

"Don't interrupt me, I'm telling this story. So he writes in his book, 'Cut off second leg, frog jumps a foot.' Then he cuts off another leg and says, 'Jump, frog.' The frog jumps six inches. He writes in his book, 'Cut off third leg, frog jumps six inches.' You still with me?"

"Yes Al, we're with you."

"Okay. So the scientist cuts off the last leg. He says, 'Jump frog.' The frog doesn't do anything. He says, 'JUMP FROG.' The frog still doesn't do anything. So he takes out his notebook and writes, 'Cut off last leg. Frog goes deaf.'"

"Ha ha. So what does that have to do with the legislature?" the councilor from Umatilla asked.

"Nothing, I just thought it was a good story," Al said.

"Great."

"No really, here's the parallel," Al said. "We keep yammering that the legislature isn't listening to us, that it's not doing anything about our screwed up tax system. The voters think the legislature's gone deaf. But really, we've cut all the legs off the legislature."

He waited for the obvious question, but didn't get it.

"It's like this, see. First, we elect a democrat governor and a republican legislature. We make it hard for them to agree on anything to begin with.

That's the first leg we cut off. Second, we have a state constitution that's the size of a phone book. It completely ties the hands of the legislators. That's something we've done to ourselves, since a lot of the garbage that ended up in the constitution got put there through voter initiatives. That's the second leg we cut off. Third, one of the useless features of the state constitution is a bicameral legislature—both a house and a senate. That was put in the U.S. constitution as a compromise between representation based on population and equal representation for the states. We don't have that situation here—the sixty house members and thirty senators are all elected based on population. With the urban vs. rural, east of the Cascades vs. west of the Cascades splits that we have, it's hard enough to get one house to agree on anything, let alone two—"

"But look, Hobbes, do you really want to make it easy for those guys to pass laws?" the mayor of Eagle Point asked.

"That's my point. As far as getting work done goes, we've designed the system to be f... uh, we've designed it for failure. So where was I? The two-house legislature is the third leg we cut off. And the fourth one is the threat of a voter referendum, and those are a dime a dozen these days. If we can have ballot measures on what kinds of traps to use for bears and cougars, or whether trucks can have three trailers, or how chiropractors are regulated, we sure as hell will get a referendum on *anything* the legislature tries to do with tax reform. And now, buying elections through the initiative process is a lot easier and cheaper than buying candidates. You can bet that the owner of the Sinklow Inns will put up the money to kill any new tax measure, whether or not it's revenue-neutral. So the point is, we can yell at the legislature as much as we want, but they're not going to give us tax reform, for the simple reason that they can't."

"Thanks, Al, for that upbeat view of the world." Carol Lewis, the mayor of Lake Oswego gave him a piercing look. "So what do you think the solution is?"

"Time to haul out the bludgeon," Al said. "Forget the legislature. Go straight to the voters with an initiative that, say, requires the state to share a third of the income tax with cities—"

"And what makes you think *that* will pass?"

"Simple. When you stack up our services—police, fire, parks, libraries, the senior centers—against the state services, the choice will be easy. The average resident probably doesn't even know what the state does. Public utilities commission? Who cares? Prisons? Make the prisoners pay their own way. The Oregon Health Plan? Get those people off welfare in the first place. No, the election would be easy—the trick is buying the signatures to get it on the ballot. But I bet the unions would put their money where their mouth is, and some of the suppliers and contractors would, too."

"Seems irresponsible," a council member from Neskowin said. "That would just shift the problem to the state. It would hit school funding, universities, state parks, you name it. Do we really want that?"

"No, that's why it's a meat axe approach," Al said. "But look, that's just what all these property tax measures have been, too. We need something like this to shake things up, get us some real tax reform. Like I said, we can't wait around for the legislature to do it."

"Well, your bludgeon won't work, either," Carol Lewis said. "You're right that the trick is to get it on the ballot. But the unions are going to have their hands tied, since the teachers would fight it out of fear of losing their state funding, and businesses wouldn't risk getting crosswise with the legislature. So we won't be able to buy the signatures. Ain't going to happen."

A woman to the right of me asked, "What about recruiting residents to just go door to door and get the signatures? It would be for a good cause."

"No, there hasn't been a grassroots initiative in years—people aren't that motivated." Carol popped the top of a Coke can. "Besides, people may vote for a measure like this, but they wouldn't spend much time getting it on the ballot. By and large, the voters don't have a clue how the state taxation system works. I really don't know what's worse, apathy or ignorance."

"I don't know and I don't care!" Al shot back.

Carol made a choking sound.

"Cool," Al said. "I want to see if that pop comes out your nose."

I enjoyed listening to the bantering, and occasionally chipped in myself. But we didn't seem closer to solutions, and I wondered if I could make it back to Trillium before rush hour. Some of the committee members agreed to do some research and make a few phone calls before the next meeting, but we all knew that, with the crush of day-to-day work, not much would actually get done. We wrapped up the meeting by 3:30 and I headed for I-5. After a few minutes, I switched my car radio from a talk show to music. Talk was the last thing I wanted to listen to now.

Traffic wasn't too bad, and when I hit my exit, I avoided the highway connection to Trillium, and instead pulled onto a local road. As I started the climb up from the Willamette, I saw Bo French, our sewer plant bum, trudging along the side of the road. I pulled over.

"Hey Bo. Need a ride?" It looked like he had used the shower at the treatment plant, and cleaned up a little.

"Sure. Thanks." He opened the door and slowly climbed in, laying a worn, empty backpack at his feet.

"You're kind of late to be running your errands, aren't you?"

"Not as long as the bank and post office are open. I caught a fish this morning, had to celebrate some. So busy, hard to keep to a schedule, don't you know it."

"Right." I didn't think he was serious. "River been warm enough to swim in much?" I asked.

"Yes sir, I've ventured out a few times. About got run over by one of those water motorcycles, what do they call 'em?"

"Jet skis?"

"Yep. Don't care for 'em much myself, make too much noise."

I had left my window open, but Bo didn't smell too bad. Mostly a mixture of smoke from cigars and his wood fire.

"What brings you to my part of town?" Bo asked.

"Had a meeting in Salem. We're getting ready for the next legislative session."

"Oh." Bo scratched his head. "If you need any help from Lynn Pennington, let me know."

"Why, do you know her?"

"Yep. I communicate with her fairly regularly."

Bo must have been pulling my leg. I doubted he used the phone at the treatment plant, and it was equally unlikely for a state representative to spend much time there.

"Just out of curiosity, how do you do that?" I asked.

"Easy. Just use one of the Internet stations at the library."

Well I'll be darned. Bo had a P.O. Box, so there was no way for Pennington to know that Bo's actual residence was a lean-to camp in a corner of our sewer treatment plant. I pictured her and her staff assistant dutifully responding to e-mails and keeping Bo apprised of the latest issues, and had to smile. But it probably helped them more than I first thought. Bo talked to half the town when he made his rounds, and was really a fairly reliable information conduit. I guessed he voted, too.

"Say Bo, what did you list your residence as when you registered to vote?"

"Uh, you're not going to get me in trouble, now, are you?"

"No, I'm just curious."

"Well…I used the street address for the plant. Figured no one else was registered there—pretty good, eh? But they send my ballots to the post office, and that's what really matters. I just got to make sure I get up there when elections are going on."

We joined the traffic in downtown Trillium.

"So where are you headed?"

"The bank will do."

"Uh, which one?"

"Trillium Community Bank. Been a customer there for years."

It was on my way, just a couple of blocks from city hall. I pulled over to the curb.

"Thanks," Bo said. It took him a few moments to get his seatbelt unhooked. He swung his backpack over his shoulder. "Go with God, my friend."

"And you," I said.

When I got back to the office, Mrs. Dunwoody was scribbling furiously on her yellow pad, and Terri Knox was trying to placate someone on the phone. She put her hand over the mouth piece.

"Todd Pritchard wants you to call. He says it's urgent."

Great. I had a dozen voice mail messages, but I decided to get it over with and call Pritchard first.

"Hello Todd, I'm returning your call. What's up?"

"The TBLC is meeting tomorrow and we want you to join us."

Well, here was a strange turn of events. I had picked up a rumor that the Trillium Business Leadership Committee met early in the morning. I had considered attending one of their meetings. On one hand, I didn't want to give them any more credibility than I had to, and didn't want to treat them like a force that had to be reckoned with. On the other hand, as Seth Rosenberg pointed out, that's exactly what they were, whether I liked it or not. So I had called Todd Pritchard and offered to sit in on one of their meetings to answer questions about the Nova project, but he had always been evasive. I figured I knew why—it would cramp their style to have an outsider observe their bellyaching and strategizing. So what had changed his mind?

"I'll try to. When do you meet?"

"Seven in the morning, in the back room at Tall Jim's."

"Am I just sitting in, or do you want me to talk about anything?"

"We just have some questions," Pritchard said. "Some about the Nova deal, and about city management in general."

"Okay. I'll see you there."

I walked across the hall to Bess Wilson's office. I found her at the development services counter, standing across from Sparky Bellah with a plan unrolled between them. Bellah, it turned out, wanted to plant a seventy-foot sign on his car dealership, just in case someone missed the fifteen thousand watts of lights on the display lot, or the tangle of plastic flags flapping over the cars.

"Ben, make her be reasonable. All I'm asking for is a sign. I don't know why these mossbacks here have to get in the way of everything."

"I hear you, Sparky," I said. "Your sign would look great—for miles to the west, people would see your sign instead of Mt. Hood, and I'm sure they'd appreciate the change. But you know, if we allowed yours, we would have to let anyone put up a seventy foot sign, and then yours wouldn't stand out anymore."

Bellah just grunted. I used the break in the conversation to ask Bess to join me at the TBLC meeting. She wasn't very enthusiastic about it. Bellah didn't say anything.

"You're not tied in with that outfit, are you Sparky?" I asked.

"Naw, I just go for the breakfast."

*   *   *

The back room of Tall Jim's had cheap wood paneling and no windows. The walls were decorated with saw blades from old mills, which had been painted with scenes of lush forests. The irony was probably lost on the loggers who ate here twenty years ago. Bess and I had arrived at seven, but it was obvious that the meeting had started earlier. There had been an awkward pause in the discussion when we walked in, and after some silence, several side conversations broke out. They had saved a seat for me at the head of the U-shaped table. They clearly weren't expecting Bess, but she found an empty chair at the end of the table.

I ordered an omelet, which later turned out to be a mistake, since I didn't get any time to eat it. As soon as the waitress left, Todd cleared his throat and tapped his knife against a water glass.

"I invited Ben Cromarty to join us this morning because I know you have questions about things happening in the city that you haven't been able to get answers to— questions on the property, uh, probity, of certain decisions that have been made that I don't need to go into, that involve Nova, and questions about things that the city manager and city council have done in the past and how that relates to present situations at the local government level."

Todd sat back. The room was silent.

"I guess what Todd was trying to say is, if you have any questions for me, go ahead and ask them," I said.

"Okay." Neal Orso owned a couple of car wash operations. He spoke with the macho jock voice that professional wrestlers or football linebackers use in a press conference. "Here's one. Why did the city close down Willy's Grill?"

"The city didn't," I said. "It was the county Health Department. I don't know the details, you'd have to ask them."

"City, county, same difference," Orso said. "It seemed like a fine establishment to me, and it didn't need any government interference."

I didn't react to that.

"All right, what's this I hear about the city giving Sparky here a hard time about a sign?" Cliff Ashcraft, who happened to be sitting next to Sparky Bellah, owned a small industrial park. "Since when is it illegal for a man to advertise his business?"

"He wanted a sign so high that the FAA was worried about it knocking planes out of the sky."

"That's ridiculous!"

"I was joking, Cliff."

"Most cities have height limits for signs," Bess said. She talked about the philosophy behind sign codes, and got into some debate about it. It gave me a chance to take a mental note of the people in the room, and to wonder why they were there. I noticed that one of the painted saw blades that had been turned into a clock was stuck at 3:35. It had probably been like that for years.

Todd Pritchard leaned forward, looking for a break in the conversation.

"I want to get the discussion back on track," Pritchard said. "Ben, tell us why Nova doesn't have to go through the same hoops that all the rest of us do. Now there's a question I have."

"They do have to go through the same hoops. Give me something more specific."

"Aw, come on now. We have to put in street improvements and fill out all these application forms and put up maintenance bonds and all sorts of other stuff. I don't see Nova having to do all that."

"Bess," I said, "did we let Nova off from any of those requirements?"

"Nope."

"What may seem different to you," I said, "is that Nova agreed from the start to meet all our requirements, and didn't complain about it. They probably see some of them as an unnecessary burden, just like you do, but they've done enough work in other states that they weren't surprised by them."

"Well, I think the whole deal stinks," said Paul Happell. He was the manager of Trillium Screw & Fastener Company, which he liked to abbreviate to Trillium Screw.

I shrugged.

Happell said, "Why do you guys spend so much time chasing after an out-of-town company at the same time you make things tough for us business people who have been here for years?"

"Well—" I started.

"We didn't chase after them," Bess said. "They came to us. You bet your ass we worked with them—they were bringing 1,000 jobs, and we would do the same for any of you if you were looking at that kind of expansion. Matter of fact, we helped Phillip's Fruit get a grant for their new processing equipment, and we set up a local improvement district for Bruce Poulet here to take care of the streets and parking at his shopping center. Besides, Nova had to meet all our development code requirements, but most of you have gotten around that because your businesses got grandfathered in."

"Yeah, but—"

"I think we have some more questions for the city manager," Pritchard said. "So, about this zoning for the Nova's housing project, how do you justify that when—"

"Now that's right," Neal Orso said. "Didn't the city use zoning to keep Hillman from being able to use his property downtown?"

"We didn't stop him from using his property," I said. "There's a whole page of outright permitted uses in the downtown commercial zone. He could have done any of them."

"But his business is used parts. That's what he bought the land for."

"What he wanted to do just didn't fit with our downtown, or any city's downtown, for that matter. It should be in an industrial park or in a commercial area where it can be screened." Hillman had called his business "used parts," but he wanted outdoor storage for parts and the carcasses of old cars. It was a junk yard by any other name.

"So the city keeps an honest business man from using his own property, but it lets Nova make a zone change to put housing in an industrial area. How is that fair?"

"The zone change hasn't been decided yet. But having homes close to jobs fits with our comprehensive plan."

"And having jobs downtown doesn't?" Orso said, spitting his words out. "I don't know how you get off trying to run everybody's life!" He stood up, threw his napkin on the table, and stomped out of the room.

There was an awkward pause. Bess rolled her eyes. There were a few more questions, but the guys started looking at their watches as if they really wanted to get to work. The waitress put the bill next to my mostly full plate and I watched to see if Pritchard made any attempt to pick it up. He didn't.

Bess and I had parked at our usual spots at city hall and walked the two blocks to Tall Jim's. The morning traffic was a little heavier when we headed back, and we had to wait for a signal to get across the street. The air was cold—a sign that our Indian Summer was coming to an end.

"Did you notice anything unusual about the folks at that meeting?" I asked.

"No shit. They were all men. Talk about the good old boys club."

"Why do you think that is?"

We got our "walk" signal and Bess stepped out. I tried to match her pace.

"Well, I suppose life has probably gotten hard to understand for a guy like Orso," she said. "Look at the real leadership positions in the community—almost all of them are filled by women. The mayor, of course, but look at the president of the Chamber of Commerce, and even the president of the Rotary Club, Linda Bartell. Polly Andrews is the chairman of the board of the Trillium Bank, and the managers of the other bank branches in town are women too. Most of the active, positive business owners who have gotten anything done in the last five years have been women. What's a boy like Orso or Pritchard to do?"

I laughed. "And to make matters worse, their zoning and development issues are being managed by a woman, and the chair of the planning commission is a woman too."

"Ah, the conspiracy must be working," Bess said.

"There's something else. Did you notice that most of those guys got their businesses through their fathers, or maybe their fathers-in-law? Sparky married into the car business. Orso's business was started by his father, and he's been pretty much a caretaker since. Paul Happell's business was founded by his father-in-law, and so was Pritchard's. Bruce Poulet's Dad started him off in the fruit trucking business and it was almost by accident that he ended up owning so much land. Cliff Ashcraft has the industrial park because his father needed a place to put his metal fabricating business."

"Not exactly self-made men, huh?"

"No, and it may help explain the split you noticed." I held open the city hall door for her. "Most of the women who are running things around here built their businesses from scratch. They don't have time to sit around and stew about how the world is unfair to them. They're too busy making things happen, and they're smart enough to know how to work with city regulations—"

"Or work around them, maybe..."

"Yep."

"So what good does this tidbit of information do us?" Bess paused in front of the elevator door.

"Not much, except maybe to help figure out where they're coming from. As much technical training as we get, doesn't it always seem our biggest challenges are dealing with human psychology? And if you get very far into that, you wonder how the world functions at all..."

***

That evening Mary and I attended an open house at Trixie's new middle school. I wore jeans and a polo shirt, but the disguise didn't help—people still insisted on talking to me about their street that needed paving, or their neighbor's barking dog. On cue, Mary would interrupt to tell me that we needed to move on to the next classroom.

Trixie had already mastered the labyrinth of hallways and proudly showed us her locker. The sixth graders still had home rooms, sort of a way to phase them into junior high. Her home room teacher, Miss O'Malley, looked barely old enough to be out of college. But I could tell Trixie liked her, and she seemed to have a strong enough sense of self-assurance—and sense of humor—to be able to deal with middle school kids.

"Trixie told me you work for the city. What do you do there?" she asked.

"I'm the city manager."

"Oh! Then you probably know my fiancée, Jim Ripp."

"Hmm, not sure. Where does he work?"

"He was on the reserves for the fire department, and just got hired on full time. He's a good looking guy, with a moustache."

"You just described most of the department," Mary said.

"Yes, I sort of noticed that. Oh, but don't tell Jim I said the other guys were handsome—he gets kind of jealous."

Mary laughed.

Trixie joined a knot of her friends. They pretended to ignore their parents, but they would sneak glances to see what Mom or Dad were doing. There was already artwork on the wall—watercolor paintings of different species of salmon. They all looked the same to me, and some of the students' work was unrecognizable as fish. Modern art, no doubt. Mary pointed out Trixie's picture of a coho—she had carefully used a pen to add scales. I was impressed.

I stood back and watched the fish. I could picture them moving down the Snake River. Some of them made it past the huge turbine blades in Bonneville Dam. They swam under the hundreds of hooks dangling from boats in the Columbia, and reached the open ocean. They thrived on the cold Alaskan currents, but some fell victim to the orcas and sea lions, and others were scooped up in massive nets from American, Canadian and Japanese trawlers. Some were slowly poisoned to death from the runoff of farm fields or the tons of oil and chemicals pumped from the bilge of ships. A handful made it back up river to their spawning grounds, only to fall victim to the sport fisherman's bait, or to find that silt from a road building project had covered their stream's gravel bed. One—maybe Trixie's coho—was able to lay eggs.

It had always been a numbers game for them, where thousands of smolts had to be born to produce a few dozen healthy adults, but the odds weren't in their favor any more. I could see the photograph—it was that recent—of Indians at the rapids where Bonneville Dam now squats, spearing the salmon as they passed in a boiling torrent of fish. What was it that Spock said to Kirk when they visited twentieth century earth? "It is illogical to hunt a species to extinction." As individuals, we human beings prided ourselves on being rational creatures, but as a group, we seemed to have a hard time doing anything that was logical.

I felt a tug on my elbow, and the sounds of the classroom seeped back into my consciousness. "Come on Dad, I want to show you the band room." Trixie had broken free from her group of friends and was pulling me through the crowd.

*   *   *

The city council agenda had taken a while to prepare. We put most of the routine items— approval of the minutes, liquor license renewals, a bid award for a street sweeper, authorization to apply for a state grant for a bike path, reappointment of Norma Givens to the planning commission—on the consent agenda, where the council could pass all the items with one vote.

But we still had some tough policy issues left. Our citizen's urban forestry committee was recommending a strict policy that would require everyone—homeowners included—to get a permit for cutting any tree. A survey had shown that most residents wanted a strong tree ordinance, but they just wanted it to apply to everyone else. Jake Wildavsky had negotiated an agreement to buy future water from a city that had a treatment plant upstream. The provisions of the agreement seemed fair, but it would commit us to sharing a portion of the plant expansion cost no matter what our growth rate was. And Simon Garrett had a proposal to shift the jurisdiction of certain juvenile offenses from the county district court to our own municipal court, with community service being the primary form of punishment.

Pete Koenig slid his agenda in front of me. He had written "10:45" and circled it. He and the other department heads had an informal pool to guess the length of the council meeting. "I'm afraid you're right," I said.

As Diane McTavish started the meeting, Todd Pritchard came striding in like the emperor's messenger carrying a new edict. His armor-bearer, Neal Orso, trailed him. They stood at the back of the room. After the roll call and changes to the agenda, the mayor called for public comments. Pritchard marched up to the dais and dropped a thick bound document in front of each council member. The mayor watched him with suspicion as he took his position at the lectern.

"What you have before you is a transcript of a deposition taken, under oath, by the city manager." Pritchard gripped the sides of the lectern and leaned into the microphone. "I think you will find it very interesting. In this deposition, you can see that the city manager misled and lied to the city council. I have highlighted the relevant sections. I think you will be appalled at what you read, and I trust you will take the appropriate disciplinary measures." Pritchard strutted back down the aisle, and stood at the door to listen to the council's reaction. It occurred to me that in all the cartoon pictures, the devil had a goatee just like Pritchard's.

The council members sat in stunned silence. I whispered to Pete, "Have you seen that?"

"No."

Pete cleared his throat. "Mayor and council, this issue relates to a pending lawsuit, and we shouldn't comment on it or discuss it at this time. We have not yet received the transcript, and can't comment on that either."

"Okay," McTavish said, and quickly moved on to the next agenda item. Pritchard and Orso left the room. The council members studiously ignored the transcripts sitting in front of them, except for Maggie Henderson, who furtively reached out, slid the document closer to her, and leafed through the pages.

The meeting dragged on, and I had a hard time concentrating. By the end, most of the members of the public had left. Under the council comments portion of the agenda, Maggie Henderson raised her hand.

"You know, I heard about something at the National League of Cities meeting. It's about putting a quiche in the mall. I think we should have a quiche in the mall."

The council members stared at her. The mayor said, "What? A quiche in the mall? I don't get it."

Maggie snorted in exasperation. "I know you've heard of them. People can look up things about the city, you know, how to get a permit or where to get a dog license. All sorts of information."

"Maggie, do you mean a kiosk? An information kiosk?"

"Yes, whatever. I think it's a good idea."

"Oh. All right. Ben, could you have your staff look into it?"

Betty Sue looked at me and raised her eyebrows. She scribbled a note to herself: "Check into mall quiche!"

Finally, the mayor gaveled the meeting to a close. She looked up to make sure the live cable TV feed had been cut, then opened the transcript. I tried not to look too eager, but I couldn't stop myself from walking over.

"So what does it say?" I asked.

"Not sure," McTavish said. "It looks like he highlighted this part where you're explaining how the Nova work was financed. Take a look."

> Judd: So the city didn't incur any cost on the contract?
>
> Cromarty: Not any net cost. Nova agreed to pay us an amount equal to the state loan payments.
>
> Judd: If the contract cost more, would you have changed the agreement based on the higher cost?
>
> Cromarty: Sure, we would have tried to.
>
> Judd: The, uh, decision to exempt the contract from the bid process was based on the theory that less time for construction would have driven the cost up. But this is a cost the city didn't have to pay, right?
>
> Cromarty: We don't know that. The state loan and the agreement with Nova were both based on the cost estimates we had. We couldn't guarantee that either the state or Nova would change the agreements.
>
> Judd: But why would the state care? Don't they just sell bonds?
>
> Cromarty: Have you ever filled out the paperwork for a state bond bank loan? Once all that stuff gets written up, people don't like to change it much.
>
> Judd: So did you ask them if you could amend it?

Cromarty: No.

Judd: Why not?

Cromarty: We, uh, we didn't need to. We were pretty confident the project would get done within the initial estimates.

I slid the transcript back to McTavish. "So what's new about that?"

"Nothing, as far as I can tell," she said.

The council members and department heads were gathering their papers and leaving, too tired to hang around and talk. I took the stairs to my office. How did Pritchard reckon I had misled the council? Maybe he was fully aware that I hadn't misled them, but he also knew we couldn't discuss it in a public session, so the damage would be done for the viewing audience and the press, without me being able to respond. But I didn't think that was the case. It could be that the loan agreement was news to him—he hadn't been paying much attention to the issue when it first came up—and he figured it must have been news to the council. But in any case, he made the impact that he wanted.

I unlocked the door and sensed the comfort of the silent rooms. I sat in my office in the dark.

9

Will Samuels, the parks and recreation director, stopped the van at a gate. I got out and fished around in my coat pocket for the key. The steel hinges were rusty but the gate swung easily. The van eased by, and I watched the cartoon faces of the children painted on the side, followed by the *Trillium Parks Department* logo. I closed the gate and looped the chain through it, then got back in the van. Drizzle had collected on the windshield.

We followed the dirt track until it reached a graveled parking area. Will pulled up beside an old John Deere tractor. I held the door open as Diane McTavish and Seth Rosenberg got out. "So this is it?" McTavish asked.

"This is it," Will said. "There's almost two hundred acres, so you can't see it all from here. But you can get a pretty good sense of it. If it wasn't so cloudy, you could see Mt. Hood somewhere over there."

"You can even see some of downtown Trillium," McTavish said.

"Such as it is," Seth said.

"Well, so it isn't Portland. But I like it anyway," she said.

"The clubhouse would be about where we're standing," Will said. "I think from the second floor you could see both Trillium and Portland. They're talking about a driving range somewhere over there, and the first hole would be just to the left of that. The rest of the holes would be between here and the power lines over that hill."

The land was gently rolling, and colored with every shade of green. Fir and cedars were left in the steeper portions; the flatter areas were carpeted in pasture grass that had greened up with the fall rains. A small walnut orchard bordered the property on the west edge, and the leaves hadn't begun to turn. The parts of the landscape seemed to be assembled randomly, but they fit together more perfectly than anything an architect could have designed. A hawk circled over a ridge top, never moving its wings.

"It would be nice, but I kind of like it this way," McTavish said.

"True," Seth said, "but a golf course would look better than a subdivision or strip mall. Will, do you think they could keep many of the trees?"

"That's what they're saying. They would have to clear some space for some of the fairways, but there's enough open pasture land to build most of the course without cutting a lot of trees."

"Aren't they pretty tough on the environment?" McTavish asked. "Don't they use a lot of fertilizer to keep the greens green?"

"That depends," Will said. "Here, check this out." He plodded down the hill in his heavy rubber boots. The rest of us picked our way more carefully. We stopped about fifty feet from the bottom. A creek fed a small man-made pond that had a bright cover of algae. Cattle used the pond for drinking water, and the banks of the pond and creek were a trampled soup of mud and moss.

"This feeds into Banjo Creek," Will said, "and apparently they're getting pretty high readings of…what's it called?"

"Fecal coliform," I said.

"Right. And the farmers have been using their share of herbicides to keep the weeds down, and some kind of spray on the walnut trees. So it's hard to say a golf course will be much worse, especially if we use some sense in how we maintain it."

"So does this pond become a water trap?" Seth asked.

Will shook some rain off his forehead. "You got it. Even though it's man-made, it qualifies as a wetland now, and the state wouldn't let us drain it. The way I golf, this is where most of my balls will end up."

We made our way back up the hill. A row of starlings watched us from a fence.

"How's this deal going to work?" McTavish asked.

"Well, it's a little complicated," I said.

"Great. Everything you've gotten us into lately has been a little complicated." Seth said it with a smile.

"How about if we get back into the van?" Will said. "At least we'll be a little drier."

Seth took a last look at the panorama. The mist made his beard look grayer. He joined me in the middle seat of the van. McTavish sat sideways in front. "Okay, shoot," she said.

"Where to begin?" I said. "First, this is a long way from being a done deal. The person trying to put it together is a guy named Tuck Williams. He's had a fair amount of experience in the golf business, but not in land development. He's got some investors, apparently, who are willing to put up the money, and are at least asking the right questions. Their first hurdle is the land. Matterson is willing to sell this piece—it's about eighty acres, but the other hundred plus acres is in three separate ownerships. Williams hasn't even contacted them yet. He doesn't want to drive the price up, but he needs their land. Two of them live in old farm houses on the property—part of the deal he can offer is not only paying for the land, but giving them a new house right on the golf course."

"But don't they depend on the land for their living?" McTavish asked.

"They may have at one time, but the pieces have gotten divided too small to support a family. They keep some horses, and do get some income off farming, but it's more of a hobby than a profession now."

The moisture and heat from our bodies had fogged the inside of the van's windows. Will started the engine and found the switch for the defroster. "You know," he said, "I don't miss Louisiana, but I'm still not used to all this rain. One of these days I'm going to lose my tan."

We laughed. Will was still as black as the day he arrived in Oregon, around five years before.

"The second hurdle is a little easier," I said. "We're outside the urban growth boundary here, but inside the urban reserve. Normally the state wouldn't let us expand the boundary without a compelling reason. But there just isn't this much acreage in one place inside the UGB, and the state has come to the realization that it's a good thing for golf courses to be inside cities."

"Why is that?" Seth asked. "They're mostly grass—you would reckon they would fit fine in a rural or agricultural area."

"The golf course does," McTavish said before I could answer, "but the housing around the course doesn't."

"Right," I said. "For a lot of reasons, you don't see isolated golf courses anymore. You also get houses, condos, a clubhouse, you name it. For an extreme example, think of Sun River outside of Bend. That's grown to be bigger than most Oregon cities."

"Besides," Will said, "It doesn't hurt to have some open space inside a city. I like it that way, truth to tell."

"Okay," Seth said. "You know, I hate to cut this short, but I've got to get back to work. We're getting ready for a visit from a buyer from Singapore."

"You and your international deals," McTavish said. "I never thought cutting wood was so exotic."

"Right. Me and the other business tycoons, we have to keep up with things."

Will turned the van around and maneuvered it down the dirt lane.

"So anyhow," I said, "we have to extend the urban growth boundary and then annex the property. But like I said, I don't think that will get much opposition—at least from the state or county—but it'll take some time. As big as the project is, most of the land use stuff is still pretty straightforward, since our comp plan talks about something like this out here. It's the financing that gets interesting."

McTavish rolled her eyes. "Okay..."

"So here's the deal. Tuck Williams and his investors buy all the land. They keep the land for the housing, and give the rest to the city for the golf course. We help finance their water, sewer, and streets with a local improvement district—"

"But they have to make the payments?" McTavish said.

"Sure. But they can take advantage of our lower interest rates. And we secure the bonds through a first position on their land. That part of it is really pretty common. Then we use revenue bonds, paid back through green fees and other golf course revenue, to build the course. Hold on..."

I jumped out and locked the gate after the van passed through. The sun had broken through and steam was rising from the wet grass.

"Just out of curiosity, how did you get that key?" McTavish asked when I climbed back in.

"I got Williams to make me a copy. When I told him I wanted to take you dignitaries out here, he was more than happy to oblige. In fact, he wanted to come and roll out the red carpet."

"So why didn't he?" McTavish asked.

"You didn't want us to have to disclose the ex parte contact in the hearing, right?" Seth said.

"Exactly. The less direct contact you have with the developers, the better. Everything we're looking at is above board, but you know how folks twist things around."

McTavish was silent. A couple of years ago, she had been closely involved in an affordable housing project, targeted at former migrant farm workers who had transitioned into full time jobs. Her intentions were honorable, but she ran into a buzz saw of controversy from neighbors and rednecks. Channel Eight smelled blood and sent a reporter out to tape an interview. The reporter didn't know anything about Oregon land use laws or city government in general, but he had picked up on the rhetoric from the opposition groups. They had seized on an obscure statement buried in the comprehensive plan document that talked about goals for a mix of housing types. The reporter had hammered the mayor on that point, and she had simply said she wasn't familiar with every sentence of the document—it was, after all, over two hundred pages thick. The reporter had replied, "Well, as mayor, don't you think you should be?" and left the question hanging. The broadcast framed the mayor as an uninformed politician who had been suckered in by the developers. McTavish was furious, and several of her friends wrote, without result, to the station manager. Since that day she had avoided, wherever possible, interviews with television reporters.

"Anyhow," I said, "we use revenue bonds to pay for the golf course. Then we turn around and enter into a concessionaire agreement with Tuck Williams to operate the golf course. The first part of the green fees goes to pay back the revenue bonds, we take a cut, and Williams gets the rest, plus profits from the pro shop. It makes it worth Williams' effort in doing all the leg work for the project—"

"And we get a source of funds to help support the rest of the recreation program," Will said, raising his voice to be heard over the engine noise. "That's the whole point of the exercise, as far as I'm concerned."

"You don't think we could use a golf course?" McTavish asked.

"Oh sure, it would be a good addition to Trillium," Will said. "I wouldn't mind the convenience myself—it's hard enough finding the time to play nine or eighteen holes without having to drive a ways to do it. But it could just as well be a privately owned course. The only advantage to having it be a municipal course is that we get some extra fees out of it— Portland gets a good share of its support for their rec program that way."

"You have some control over the fees too," Seth said. "Some of these courses claim they're open to the public, but their fees are so high it's hard for most of us to play."

"What about a club house?" McTavish asked.

"Good question," I said. "We haven't figured that one out. It may be a good idea to own the building and lease it to a restaurant operator on a concession basis. But we don't have much of a track record in the restaurant business—if you don't count the senior center's hot meals program— so we may just be better off to let the club house be privately owned and operated, on the housing developer's land. What do you think?"

"Not sure. My instinct says we should own it, but I'd have to think about it."

"It may be a moot point anyway," Seth said. "From what Ben says, this Williams guy still has a lot of land to assemble. I'd say the chances are good this will all fizzle out before it gets very far."

"Always the optimist…" McTavish said.

Seth laughed. "No, just a realist. Here's how I see it. As long as the land is outside the urban growth boundary, all it can be used for is farming, so what's it worth? Maybe $10,000 an acre or so? Forty thousand tops? And ordinarily, it would be years before the boundary would get pushed out there—twenty years at least. But once they catch wind that somebody wants it for a golf course, all bets are off. Suddenly they're talking a hundred thousand or so an acre, since they know that would let them put houses instead of horses on it. But if the land costs that much, I suspect it will kill the deal."

"Yeah, but if that happens, they're stuck, since there aren't many ways to get land inside the UGB," McTavish said. "The golf course is their ticket to getting in. It's a catch-22 for them—if they ask too much, their land is only worth $10,000 an acre again, 'cause all it will be good for is growing hay."

"Well, greed has a way of working that way."

"They may just be patient, too," I said. "They may be willing to wait twenty or forty years for the UGB to come to them, and in the meantime enjoy their rural living."

"I wouldn't blame them," McTavish said. "And if that's the way it turns out, it's just fine with me. We've got enough on our plate now anyway."

The break in the clouds had closed again, and Will had to turn the wipers on. McTavish turned in her seat to watch the homes pass by. On this end of town, most were fairly new—built in the last twenty years or so—and they were generally well maintained. We stopped for a traffic light in front of a white house, built in a copy of the Portland craftsman-style homes of the streetcar suburb era. A row of elms was planted between the curb and sidewalk, not yet tall enough to form a canopy. A four-foot bank, planted with dark blue lobelia and natural basalt and granite rocks, was bisected with a set of concrete stairs leading up to the yard. Marigolds, still in full bloom lined the path to the front porch.

"Isn't this house beautiful?" McTavish asked. "I have to admire it every time I pass by."

"It's owned by the Fredricksons," I said. "Ned Fredrickson works for Muller Nurseries, so I guess that does give him an advantage in the green thumb department."

"So Ben, do you know everyone in Trillium, or what?" McTavish asked.

"Sure, it's my job," I said, chuckling.

"Okay, who lives next to them in the yellow house?"

"Beats me," I said.

"Good."

***

Ken Longstreet headed up our union contract negotiating team. As much as he complained about it, the challenge of negotiations was probably the real reason he had been our finance director so long. He approached each contract renewal like a chess game, planning his strategy several moves in advance, and studying the strengths and weaknesses of the negotiators on the other side of the table. Newcomers to the process usually misjudged him. They saw a quiet, almost meek accountant with thinning hair and a few extra pounds, and thought they saw softness. His razor-sharp intelligence and ruthlessness came as a shock.

I stayed out of the direct negotiations, so I could act as an added buffer between the city council and the negotiators. Ken had called me to come down to his office. They were reaching the final stage of the process with the police union. To our relief, the union local had brought in a professional negotiator who handled a lot of the contracts in the Portland area. They had fairly quickly cleared aside most of the small, diversionary issues—uniform allowances, training time, shift differentials, fitness incentives—and had concentrated on pay. I had hoped that the fire union's unilateral offer of a wage freeze would have taken the wind out of their sails, but the police union had demanded a nine percent increase— twice the inflation rate, and a one-year contract renewal term. Ken had pushed for a three-year contract tied to the Consumer Price Index. The two sides had reached an impasse. Police officers—like firefighters—were barred by state law from striking, and disputes were ultimately settled through binding arbitration. We were at the step just before that, and a state-appointed mediator was shuttling between the two camps, searching for a resolution.

They were sitting around a small table. Ken had his tie loosened and his shirt sleeves rolled up. Simon Garrett, the police chief, was slumped in his chair, with a coffee mug in his hand. Betty Sue Castle smiled when I came in. "Beware. Those who enter may never leave."

"Still dragging along, huh?" I said.

"Sure. Part of the strategy is to see who gets worn out first," Ken said.

Simon rubbed his eyes. "It's working."

"But we may have a way out, and I wanted to run it by you," Ken said.

"Okay."

"I was fiddling around with the model, and something occurred to me." Ken, with Betty Sue's help, had programmed his laptop computer with a full simulation model for the police department pay and benefits package. He could—almost instantly—reduce any combination of contract terms into a single number representing the cumulative cost to the city.

"What's that?"

"Well, we could offer a $1,000 signing bonus, paid immediately to every member of the union, if they approve a three-year contract tied to the CPI."

"You're kidding," I said. "We would pay them to accept something that they're lucky to get anyway, with our tax situation the way it is?"

"Yes. We really don't want to go into binding arbitration. It seems the arbitrators never take into account the financial resources of the organization. Instead, they'd probably pick up on the wage comparisons that the union has been pushing."

"But they compared us with the county and Portland. Those aren't comparable organizations at all."

"Yeah, but they're in the same labor market. In any case, we really don't want to roll the dice with an arbitrator—they can be too arbitrary. Watch this. Suppose binding arbitration leaves us with a seven percent increase, about halfway between our two positions…" Ken typed some numbers into his computer. "Even if we hold them to CPI for the two years after that, the total annual cost by the third year—with benefits—is this." He entered a few more numbers and turned the laptop around so I could read the screen.

"About two point eight million," I said. "So its a big number."

"Right, but look at this. If you assume CPI for all three years, this is what you get." He typed for a few seconds, then spun the computer around.

"Okay, it's about a hundred thousand less."

"Exactly. The signing bonus is around $50,000, but that's a one time cost. This hundred thousand difference is something we would be paying *each year*. So look at it like an investment. It's the premium we pay for buying some certainty—and reasonableness—in the pay and benefit package."

"Sort of like a futures market, huh? I wonder if we could develop a secondary market, and let someone else do all this negotiating. We could put out bids for future union contracts, and only buy when it seemed worth the risk."

"Yes, but it would only work if the commodity was portable, like pork bellies."

"What the hell are you guys talking about?" Simon asked.

"I was wondering, myself," Betty Sue said.

Ken laughed. "Well, anyway, what do you think?"

"What's this going to do to the fire contract? Will they back down on their wage freeze?"

"Well, we can make a good argument that they're already paid closer to the market rate than the cops. But I can guarantee you that the wage freeze was just a PR ploy—they know dozens of ways to get increases in benefits that have the same effect as a pay increase. So I don't think it'll have much effect on them."

I thought for a moment. "I guess it seems all right. Go ahead and give it a try."

Betty Sue looked at Ken, who began to doodle on a pad of paper. "We sort of already have," she said.

"Oh? How's that?"

"Well, we sent Cabot down there with that proposal," Betty Sue said. Cabot Corning was the state-appointed mediator. "But don't worry. Cabot said he would let it seem like they came up with the idea, and then bring it back up here to try to talk us into it. That would still give us an out if you didn't think it would fly with the council."

"Hmm." Why did we keep having to go through this song and dance? City employees had, for the most part, reached parity with their private sector counterparts years ago. Whenever we opened up hiring for a new police officer, we got hundreds of applicants. But we were all trapped in this process, since it was the only one we knew. And it was self-perpetuating. The union environment enforced an us-versus-them mentality that made it difficult for any other alternatives to be explored. So we were locked in the dance forever.

"You're upset with us."

"Huh? No, I was just thinking. I need you guys to take the initiative on this stuff—you know my philosophy on that."

"Which one? The one that goes, 'It's better to ask forgiveness than permission'?" Betty Sue asked.

"That's it. So how long has Cabot been down there?"

"About an hour and a half."

We talked about the process if the negotiations were successful, how much time it would take to get it ratified by the union members and approved by the city council, and whether we would be setting a precedent for a signing bonus with the firefighters and public works unions, which were still in negotiations. A few minutes later Cabot Corning knocked on the door. I had taken his seat, so he pulled a chair in from the reception area.

"How did it go?" Ken asked.

"It worked. They're willing to recommend it to the members, and they asked me to talk you into it."

"Bingo." Ken leaned back in his seat and took off his glasses. "One down and two to go."

"Speaking of which," I asked, "have the firefighters asked to put the medical response team on the bargaining table?"

"Nope," Ken said. "They've got everything else there. I've never seen so much trivia in a list of issues. How many pairs of boots they're issued and the right to wear their boots when they're hunting. The maximum slope for parking their apparatus so the doors don't close on them. The number of satellite channels on the cable TV in the fire stations. What magazines the city will subscribe to for them. A limit on the number of business inspections they have to do. An increased budget for exercise equipment, and city-paid memberships to private health clubs. You name it, it's there, but they refuse to talk about the firefighting/paramedic issue—it's like they're assuming it'll never happen."

"Well, they could be right. They won't bargain over it if they think its dead on arrival." Unlike the police, the firefighters were negotiating the contract themselves. Gallagher had enough experience at it, but the fact was that he didn't have anything else to do, and could take as much time at it as he wanted. He would drag out the discussions on the small stuff until the last minute, and avoid the big pay and benefit issues until the state mediator got pulled in.

Cabot Corning asked us about new restaurants in town, and shared a few fly fishing stories. He wore a plaid shirt and green work pants. His hands were callused and he looked like he'd be comfortable in a hard hat, like a good shop foreman—exactly the image he wanted to convey to both the labor and management sides. When it came to union issues, the cops liked to act like coal miners or dock workers, which was odd, since the tools they used consisted mostly of pens, radios, and radar guns, and they avoided walking beats like the plague. Instead of working like laborers, the best of them had more in common with trained psychologists and scientists, and they got fulfillment from their jobs when they were using their minds, not their hands.

After a while I excused myself, thanking the negotiating team and Cabot for their work. Betty Sue joined me.

"Cabot takes his time about things, doesn't he?" she said as we climbed the stairs.

"Yeah, you were wondering why he didn't hustle back down to wrap up the agreement, right?"

"It crossed my mind."

"The cops thought the signing bonus was their idea. If it looked like we agreed too quickly, they'd think they didn't push hard enough. Cabot had to make it seem like we were wringing our hands over the decision. You know, let them think we were in heated debate over accepting their proposal, not sitting back telling fishing stories. They would get suspicious if they won victory too easily."

Betty Sue paused in front of her office door. "But if you knew what Cabot was up to, wouldn't they guess that too?"

"Maybe their hired gun would. But he wants to get this over with as much as we do. As long as we follow the script, he'll have a hard-won agreement to take back to the members for a vote."

"So he plays along? Geez, this gets complicated. You know what it reminds me of? One of those complicated mating rituals in a nature show about birds or insects. I start to think, quit the theatrics and just get it over with."

I laughed. "Well, that's not a bad analogy. It's probably closest to mating with a black widow spider. We can complete the agreement, but even when it's done, we have to be wary, since the conflict over the contract poisons our whole relationship."

Betty Sue shook her head. "Speaking of tangled webs, do you have a second? I need to update you on the OAS deal."

We used the meeting table in my office. Betty Sue looked out the door to make sure no one was in hearing distance.

"You were talking about making things look too easy. Well, the folks at Oregon Ambulance seem to be going out of their way to be accommodating. I added a bunch of new things to the draft contract, and they said, fine without batting an eye."

"Like what?"

"Oh, response time guarantees, backup crews during peak periods, extra coverage when one of the units needs to transport a patient…and a pledge to hold the hourly rate flat for three years. I feel like I'm at a car dealer and keep offering a lower price, and the salesman keeps saying, okay. Makes me wonder if I'm buying a lemon."

I thought about it. "Could be they see this as a way to get their foot in the door with this kind of service. Trillium is one thing, but what if they could do the same thing in Beaverton or Gresham, or Vancouver?"

"Maybe. Or it could be that they're worried that we'll start negotiating with someone else. They seem to have a monopoly on the private ambulance business around here, but what's to stop someone like Tualatin Valley Fire from offering the same service?"

"Yeah, except for the fact that we don't want to open that can of worms now. Maybe they just want to get the agreement signed before we change our mind."

"Well, they don't want to actually sign it."

"Huh? But it doesn't bind either of us to doing anything, right? It just sets out the conditions if we do decide to offer them the work, and if they decide to accept it."

"I emphasized that—"

"You said 'I,' not 'we.' Wasn't Max with you?"

"Uh, no."

"I asked you to keep him involved."

"I know." She ran both hands through her hair. "But I still don't trust him. I didn't want to give him another way to derail this whole thing. All he would have to do is let it slip to Brian Gallagher that we were talking to

OAS, and all hell would break loose. This is just a backup anyway, and with any luck it will be a moot point."

"Look, Betty Sue, if Max wants to derail this, he will anyway. It's not going to fly without him. What if we do end up having to contract out? He isn't going to be comfortable with terms that he didn't have a hand in writing—you wouldn't be either, if you were in his shoes."

"I guess you're right. But this will make such a difference in being able to balance next year's budget, I don't want to do anything to mess it up."

"Yes, I appreciate that. But don't cut Max out."

Betty Sue was silent. There was more to her reluctance in working with Max than she was saying. I didn't blame her.

"Here's what you can do," I said. "Give Max a copy of the draft, and fill him in. Make sure he understands that you, me, and the OAS guy are the only ones that know about it. That way he'll know that if there's a leak, we can track it to him. But I really think he's got more integrity than that."

She shrugged.

"So what were you saying before?" I asked. "Something about Oregon Ambulance liking the agreement but not wanting to sign it?"

"That's about it. They say we can't keep it confidential—it becomes an official agreement of the city, even if you sign it and it doesn't go to the city council. So the Freedom of Information Act would let anyone get access to it."

"Hmm. You know, they may have a point. Chances are, no one would know the agreement exists, but I wouldn't put it past Gallagher to start nosing around for one."

"But the odd thing is, the issue of secrecy is more important for us than them. They're not the ones dealing with the political and union issues. Still, they refuse to sign it on the basis that it isn't in *our* best interest. I don't normally see businesses going out of their way to protect us. Seems like there's something else going on."

"This is such a hot potato, maybe we're all over-reacting." I rubbed my eyes and thought about rafting down the Poudre River with Kate and her family. We steered when we could, but most of the time we were at the mercy of the current. When the rapids were long, we could only guess where the rocks might be, and we paddled to stay in the main channel so the river would naturally carry us around them. I knew Betty Sue liked to feel in control of situations, but here we didn't have that luxury. As much as we mortals liked the concept of free will, most of the events that swept us along were outside our control. We could only do so much, and had to trust fate or God to carry us along. Perversely, on the river, the only way we could maintain headway for steering was to paddle *toward* the rapids.

"Well, just keep plugging away at it," I said. "At least you have the framework in place. That's something, even if we never have to use it."

*   *   *

For security reasons, the grand marble entrance to the Multnomah County Courthouse was locked to the public. We stood in line in the rain at a side entrance, waiting to get through the metal detector that had been squeezed into the hallway. Our justice system had achieved true equality: it treated everyone like criminals. Hank Arnold had a tiny Swiss army knife hooked to his key ring. The security guards wouldn't let him through with it, so he had to put it in my car. I pictured him stomping back to where my car was parked, probably muttering comments about the threat to society he posed with his one-inch letter opener.

We stood in the second floor hallway, outside Judge Moose's courtroom. Pete Koenig was already there, and Diane McTavish, council member Maggie Henderson, and I joined him. A few feet away, Todd Pritchard and Neal Orso were huddled with their attorney, Terry Judd. After a few moments, Maggie ambled over to join them. Strange. A court fight was just that: a fight. What was Maggie doing going into their corner?

Hank Arnold came up the stairs, damp and slightly out of breath. He stood with us, squinting around and trying to figure out who else was there. I watched Maggie out of the corner of my eye. Judd suddenly asked her a question, and she took a step back. Pritchard's eyes narrowed. Judd marched over and interrupted Pete in mid-sentence.

"Why didn't you tell us about the videotape?"

"What videotape?"

"The tape of the meeting of July 12. Why did you withhold that from us?" A group of people waiting for another court session turned to watch.

"You didn't ask for it."

"Yes, we asked for everything in your possession that was pertinent to this case. I certainly think a videotape of the meeting is pertinent."

"We gave you the minutes. That's the official record of the meeting—the videotape is only used for replaying on the cable TV channel. If the minutes weren't good enough for you, you should have said something earlier."

"But you let other people watch the tape," Judd said. Maggie was standing a few feet away, looking sheepish.

"Look," Pete said, "if you want to make an issue of this, let's just let the judge decide, okay?"

"Yes, I do want to make an issue of it. You intentionally withheld evidence."

Judd was like a kid stirring a wasp nest with a stick. Pete kept his cool, but I had known him long enough to realize that he was making a quiet internal resolution to skewer Terry Judd whenever the opportunity presented itself. "Okay, Terry, you've made your point. Leave it for the judge."

Judd backed off. Pete shook his head. A minute later, the courtroom door opened and a group of people filed out, looking tired. Pete found the court clerk and talked to her for a moment. He signaled to Judd, and they disappeared out a side door. I sat with the council members at the back of the courtroom. There were only three rows of seats—most trials didn't get many spectators.

"I got called for jury duty once," Mayor McTavish said. "It was for a federal court. I ended up being an alternate for a jury on a bank robbery case."

Hank said, "So, did you hang 'em?"

McTavish chuckled. "Well, it restored my faith in the intelligence of the common crook. The prosecuting attorney was young—looked like she had just got out of law school. She had the video from the bank's surveillance camera, and it showed the guy with something hidden under a sweatshirt he had over his arm. She brought in the teller as a witness. The teller read the note the guy passed, but she was a little embarrassed to do it. The note said 'I have a gun give me the money,' but it had a few expletives thrown in for good measure. The defense attorney was young too— probably doing the work as a public service—and he made a brave attempt to get the guy off. Said that since the teller never actually saw a gun, the guy didn't technically threaten her. I knew we were supposed to be impartial, but it was hard for us to keep a straight face."

"An open and shut case, huh?" I said.

"Seemed like it to me, but none of the jurors got sick or anything, so I got dismissed just before they went into deliberation. But here's the best part. When the teller got the note, she pushed the alarm button. Turns out the FBI office was only two blocks away. It was lunchtime or something and there weren't many agents around, so the office chief himself decides to go check it out. As he's walking toward the bank, the crook rounds a corner and literally bumps into him. He dropped the bag of cash, but the FBI guy just grabbed him and made the arrest. Can you believe it?"

Seth and Maggie shook their heads. The court clerk organized some papers at her desk, then left the room through a back door.

"You know, though, that kind of thing happens more often than we think," I said. "Simon told me about a bank robbery in Eugene. It was at the Central Bank, a big glass building in the middle of town. The guy passes the teller a note. But she's cool. She stares at the note for a while and says to him, 'Hey, I can't read this. I don't know what it says. Go re-write it.' Just like Woody Allen in that movie where he writes, 'I have a gub.' So anyway, the putz gets out of line and goes over to the counter where the deposit slips are and starts writing—"

"You're kidding." Seth said.

"No, this is a true story. So you know what the teller does—she hits the alarm button. A couple of Eugene plainclothes cops come in and the teller motions to the doofus who's still writing away. Finally he gets back in line and the cops file in behind him. He gets to the window and passes the note and the cops grab him."

They laughed. Pritchard's group looked over at us. Probably thought we were talking about them.

Seth said, "When I was on a ride-along with one of our police officers, he told me about a man who robbed a bank—full mask, machine gun, the whole nine yards—and then disappeared. An hour later he's sitting in his kitchen counting the money when a whole army of cops converges on him. They march in and nab him. He says, 'Okay, you got me—but how did you find me so fast?' The cops said, 'It was easy. You wrote your note on the back of your water bill—it had your name and address right on it.' Go figure!"

McTavish wiped tears of laughter from her eyes. "Simon calls that job security. There's an endless supply of incompetent crooks."

Finally the attorneys came through the side door. Pete motioned to me, and I sat next to him in front of the judge's seat. Pritchard and Judd sat at the desk to our left.

"So?" I whispered.

"The judge wasn't interested in the tape," Pete said, "and the deposition isn't admissible. Moose agreed with me that the writ of review just deals with the procedural issues under the state bid laws, and has to be based on the record of the council's decision. Judd pushed it, but I think all he did was piss off the judge."

The court clerk swept in and barked, "All rise." She was followed by Judge John Moose. The judge sat down, opened a file and put on a pair of reading glasses. After a few moments he took off his glasses and looked up.

"This is a writ of review of the Trillium city council's decision pertaining to the state contract law. I have read your briefs, so keep your comments short. Mr. Judd, why don't you go ahead."

Judd began a dramatic speech on how he was going to prove his case. Moose interrupted him. "We don't have a jury here. Just make your point."

Judd flipped a few pages in his notes. Predictably, he dragged out the issue of cost, and the fact that Nova was reimbursing the city for the work. He also went into a long discourse on the provision in the bid law that stated that the bid process couldn't be exempted if doing so would limit competition. It had always seemed an odd provision to me, since it appeared to invalidate any exemption. Judge Moose watched Judd for a while, then put on his reading glasses and began sifting through the file. Judd spoke faster.

Pete scribbled a few notes on his pad in his private code. When I first met him, I was impressed by the fact that he had learned shorthand, and that he knew how to type. Most attorneys I had come across felt that manual labor was beneath them, and used secretaries and paralegals to get their work done. But while Pete liked his old Remington typewritter, he wouldn't touch a computer, and what I took for shorthand was simply unreadable handwriting.

Finally Judd wrapped up his comments. Moose kept his head buried in his file for a long moment, then looked up, almost in surprise. He peered over his reading glasses. "Uh, thank you, Mr. Judd," he said. "What do you have for us today, Mr. Koenig?"

Pete was deferential, in the quiet style of a southern country lawyer. He summarily dismissed most of Judd's arguments as being irrelevant to the case, and touched on recent Oregon case law to plug any of the remaining gaps. He concluded by quoting from the majority opinion in an Oregon Supreme Court case, which stated that the court's job wasn't to rule on the merits of the decision made by the contract board—the city council, in our case—but instead to decide if the process spelled out in the law had been followed.

The judge took off his glasses and scratched his head. "Well, I've heard a few of these cases in the last few years. I appreciate your comments and arguments, but the issue seems pretty simple. The court must defer to the decision made by the local governing body, unless there is some overwhelming evidence that the law has been violated. I can't comment on the wisdom of the Trillium city council in this issue; the council is ultimately accountable to its constituents, which have the power to make that judgement at the ballot box. But it does appear that the procedures prescribed by the bid law have, in fact, been followed, and I must find that the council acted in accordance with the law."

We all stood up. Both lawyers thanked the judge. We filed out, and McTavish worked hard to suppress a grin. "Good work, Pete," she said.

I O

November and December seemed filled with the kind of tedious tasks that take time with too little to tell for it. There were personnel rule amendments, grant audit reports, meetings with state legislative candidates, responses to citizen complaints, staff meetings and employee brown bag gatherings, and slow progress on a dozen projects.

Mary and Trixie's winter break started a week before Christmas, and I was ready for some time off too. Mary had driven to the airport to pick up the Andersons, who were flying in from Colorado to spend the holidays with us, and I tried to clear my desk so I could get out by five.

Ken and Betty Sue had put together budget forms for the departments to fill out over the next four weeks. They had included instructions on how to prepare the material, but they wanted a cover memo from me. It was a dismal task. I tried to hold out optimism that things would turn around in the long run, and challenged the staff to be innovative, but the message was still a negative one. I struggled to find words for a closing paragraph.

Jake Wildavsky came in and slumped down in the chair on the side of my desk. He waited until I was finished writing.

"We finally got the Rich Martinsen case wrapped up," he said.

"Oh. Good job—that means you avoided a messy court battle, huh?"

"Yeah. It wasn't a bowl of peaches, though. His attorney dragged in the Bureau of Labor and Industries and some snot-nosed bureaucrat hounded me for weeks. He got high and mighty about good management practices, but I doubt he could manage to tie his shoes. For those guys, good management really means covering your ass, but I can't live my life that way."

"No, I don't see that as one of your weaknesses."

Jake looked at me with an eyebrow raised. He said, "At one point, the BOLI guy asked me where I kept the recordings of phone conversations that Rich and the other customer service staff had. Recordings? He said we couldn't show that Rich was rude if we didn't hear both sides of the conversation. I kind of felt that having two other staff members overhear Rich telling a customer to go to hell was proof enough—I didn't give a shit what the other half of the conversation was. I told the ferret faced bureaucrat that—

"In so many words?"

"Well, sure, I suppose so."

I laughed.

"Anyway," Jake said, "it seemed like he was from some other planet. But the guy was such a moron that Pete called the Labor Commissioner herself to complain about him. They assigned somebody else and I didn't hear much more from them."

"So what happened? Did the whole case go away? You said before that the insurance company was getting a little soft."

"Yep, they caved. Settled for $19,000."

"Huh? They couldn't have bought that multiple personality disorder story."

"No, they didn't, but they just didn't want the time and expense of a court trial. Figured it was cheaper this way."

"But all the insurance company would have had to do was get their attorney to start pushing Rich's buttons on the witness stand. He would have blown up in front of the jury and it would have been all over for him."

"Well, I don't think the trial would have had a jury, but we did talk about that. They figured Rich's lawyer would have coached him on it, and he would be on his best behavior."

"So he can pick which personality inhabits his body, eh?"

"Funny thing about that, isn't it?" Jake leaned back and put his hands behind his head. "After the settlement, he shows up in a new red Corvette. He was using his happy personality then. And in spite of his disorder, he didn't even have a handicapped tag on his license plate. Must have been an oversight."

"Ha." I sneaked a peek at the clock on the corner of my computer monitor, but the screen saver had taken over. It was pitch black outside, but that didn't mean anything. Night came pretty early in northern

Oregon at the winter solstice. I guessed that Kate and her family would be at our house by now.

"How's Megan doing?" I asked.

"All right, considering. She had her first chemo session on Monday. But you hate to see your kid have to go through this."

Jake's four year old daughter had been diagnosed with leukemia a week ago. I tried to put myself in his shoes, but it was hard. We had been lucky with Trixie. She had had her share of bumps and bruises, but outside of that, she rarely had as much as a cold.

"How are your boys taking it?"

"Well you know, they're sort of spooked. They're old enough to know that this is serious, and it's definitely put a damper on their holiday spirit. But the side benefit is that they've been real good to Megan—we haven't seen a fight all week."

"Well, if there's anything I can do, let me know. And take any time off work you need to."

"Thanks. But I can't do that—somebody might stumble across my 'Escape to Argentina' fund that I've been accumulating. Can't have that."

I laughed. Jake had to go to his office manager just to get a pencil to write with. Financial manipulation wasn't his strong suit.

I finally turned back to the budget message. I thought about a quote to end with, but the only thing that came to mind were the words of Solomon: "This too is meaningless, a chasing after the wind." Not exactly the inspiration I was looking for. All I could come up with in the end were a few sentences thanking the staff for their hard work and positive spirit. I consoled myself with the fact that few of them bothered to read the message anyway.

I carried my briefcase and an umbrella, but it wasn't raining when I got outside. Our downtown was glowing in the lights from the buildings and cars and on the Christmas wreaths that were hung on the telephone poles. My footsteps made an even rhythm on the sidewalk, falling in time with the song that was playing in my head—"Good night, America, how are ya?

Don't you know me, I'm your native son…I'm the train they call the City of New Orleans…I'll be gone five hundred miles before the day is done…" The cold air frosted my breath, making me a two-legged steam engine.

The homes in our neighborhood sparkled with lights, and the Christmas trees inside cast soft spots of color on the drawn curtains. My pace slowed as I got to our house.

I opened the front door and stepped into a pool of brightness and warmth and the music of laughter and chatter. They were all crammed in the kitchen, where Mary was stirring a pot of clam chowder. I shook Gordon's hand and made some inane comment about the balmy Oregon climate. Kate's eyes twinkled and she gave me a quick hug.

*   *   *

The next morning we loaded our ski gear in the cars and headed for Mt. Hood. Gordon rode with me, and we talked about our work, and about the prospects for the Seahawks and the Broncos. We pulled over for donuts and a pee break at a small town halfway to Mt. Hood. Gordon and Kate switched places.

Kate leaned over the seat and asked Trixie about school. The answers were cryptic—typical of a junior high kid. I put in a tape—Crosby, Stills, & Nash—and Luke and Trixie complained about my selection. Luke said he preferred Barenaked Ladies. I heartily told him that I did too. Kate noticed that amidst the natural beauty of the trees and mountain streams, people had scattered cheap houses surrounded by rusted cars on blocks, broken fences, and piles of junk. Typical of the western frontier attitude that land was free and plentiful and ours for the taking. Snow started falling as we drove between the towering cedars of the Mt. Hood National Forest.

At the ski resort, the three kids strapped on snowboards and disappeared. Gordon and Kate got plenty of skiing in at Breckenridge and Keystone, and I wondered if I would have trouble keeping up with them, but they seemed content with our pace. The snow was light and dry—unusual for the Cascades, especially that early in the season. We floated down the side of a canyon, hooting as the sides got steeper and the valley floor rushed toward us.

A two-seater lift took us out of the canyon. Gordon and Mary went ahead. I got on with Kate. We sat in silence for a few moments, catching our breath. Kate leaned back to catch a snowflake on her tongue.

"So how are you doing?" she said.

I looked at her, but her eyes were hard to read under the tinted goggles.

"Fine. Sort of rusty on the skiing, but having a great time." In my mind I was answering a different question. How am I doing? I love hearing your laugh, I love seeing your eyes, and I love watching your body move. But I can drink deeply from that cup without asking for more, so I guess I'm just doing fine.

Kate swung her skis and the chair rocked. Below us some teenagers carried their boards up a ridge so they could track up the fresh powder under the lift. Kate put her mittened paw on my arm. "Life is complicated, isn't?"

"Yeah," I muttered, not knowing exactly what she was referring to. "Speaking of which, we've got a gal in the police records office in her late fifties who's had all sorts of boy trouble. She goes out dancing with a guy and the next thing you know, they're married. Then a month later they split up and she goes on a binge and we don't hear from her for two weeks. She's fine for a while, and then the pattern starts over."

"I'd fire her ass."

"Man, you're cold, Katie. I'm only telling you this story to…uh, what was the point I was trying to make?" My heart rate was still up—probably from the unaccustomed exertion of Heather Canyon.

"I don't have a clue."

We laughed. A gray jay glided down into a tree well in the snow.

"Where are we going now?" she asked.

I thought about that for a minute.

"How about going over to see if the Cascade Express is open?"

She turned her goggles toward me. "All right," she said.

Later we came across the kids, sitting in the snow with other boarders. They all wore baggy clothes in dark shades of brown, green, and gray. They reminded me of a group of walruses lying on the rocks of an offshore island. Occasionally one would get up and scoot to the edge of the half-pipe, then plunge in. The others would lean back on their elbows and bark approval.

Back home we took showers and made a feast of cheese fondue, fresh French bread, slices of apple, white wine and hot tea. We talked the Andersons into joining us for the candlelight Christmas Eve service at our church, which was a hit for Josh and Luke since they got to play with fire.

Later, after we finally got the kids to bed, we stretched out on the rug in front of the old stonework hearth with a bottle of red wine. The embers bathed us in warmth, Christmas carols played softly on the stereo, and I felt a comfortable drowsiness.

Mary leaned against me. "I wonder when the kids are going to get us up in the morning," she said.

"Too soon," Kate said. "Let's just ignore them. We'll just say, 'Go ahead without us—tell us when you've got all the presents open...'"

"Well, it's worth losing a little sleep to watch them," Gordon said. "I really think I like seeing them open presents more than I like getting them. Of course, the ones I like don't fit under trees any more."

"Like what?" I asked.

"Oh, you know—cars, a new house, maybe a small plane—"

"Speak for yourself," Kate said.

"How's that?"

"Well, a diamond would fit just fine under that tree."

"Dream on," Gordon said.

"So would one of the Chippendales," Mary said. "But the box would have to be pretty big, with air holes."

"Why would you need air holes for furniture, or whatever it is you're talking about?" Gordon said.

"Ha ha."

I closed my eyes. I tried to pick out the words to a Celtic carol that was playing on the radio, but couldn't.

Mary asked how they liked the candlelight service. I doubted that Kate and Gordon had been inside a church much since their wedding.

"It was good," Kate said. "No long sermon. That's how they should all be."

Gordon leaned over and slid another log on the fire. A cloud of sparks swirled and flew up the chimney. Kate uncurled and stretched her legs over mine. Her cheeks glowed in the reflection from the fire—maybe it was windburn.

"It's good to think about things like that sometimes," Gordon said. "But I have a hard time picturing God as a baby in a barn."

"Hmm. Then how *do* you picture God?" Mary asked.

"I don't know. Not so much like a person. Maybe more like fire. Something that's powerful, even with the potential for destruction, but usually good. But definitely different from us, and too hot for us to touch."

"Uh huh. That metaphor isn't bad—it's used in the Old Testament a few times," Mary said. "But I don't think it's the complete picture."

Kate yawned. "At least it answers my concern about how we're going to toast marshmallows in heaven."

"But I have to admit," Gordon said, "as screwed up as the world is, sometimes I have to wonder if there really is a God. I just don't know."

"Well, fire itself is a good enough argument," I said.

"Huh?"

"Well, here's how I see it. We're surrounded by stuff that burns really well. Wood, paper, plastic, cans of gasoline. And we depend on it. Where would we be without fire?"

"Vegetarians," Kate said.

"Yeah, I suppose. Except for nuclear or solar power, we need it for everything we do. But the temperature of the earth is balanced at the precise point where things don't quite burn by themselves, but they'll burst into flame with a little nudge. Any hotter, and all this fuel we're living around would take off in a chain reaction. Any colder, and it would be too hard to do the things we take for granted, like lighting candles or smoking cigarettes."

"God created the earth so we can smoke cigarettes?" Gordon said.

"No, but you get my point. Do you really think the earth reaching this perfect temperature balance just by itself, by random chance? What are the chances of having all this fuel lying around—wood in the forests, and oil in the ground—at just the right temperature so it won't quite burn without us adding a flame to start it? It just seems to be too good to be true. To God, we probably seem clueless if we can't see this."

"Well, thank you professor Cromarty," Gordon said. "But I don't know if I buy your argument. Absolute zero is only around minus 260 degrees Celsius, so we're about halfway between absolute zero and the temperature where paper burns. And the climate varies by around fifty degrees Celsius in there. It isn't that big a trick."

"Still, it seems too convenient to be pure coincidence," I said.

"Well, you could be right. But you started this, Mary. What's your version of the great Fire Maker in the Sky?"

"Well," Mary said, and paused for a moment. "I see God as someone who will take care of and protect me. Someone who will hold me in his lap when I need it, but also someone who will give me a push and make me grow, too. I like that image. Before he was arrested, Jesus was praying and said, *Abba,* Father, take this cup from me. I think 'Abba' means something like 'daddy.' Isn't that a great way to see him—daddy?"

"A little more personal than fire, huh?" Kate said. I could feel her legs move a little when she talked.

I tried to put together a coherent thought. "Lao Tzu said, the Tao that can be told of is not the absolute Tao. I think there's a lot of truth to that."

"So you're a Taoist too, huh?" Gordon said.

"No." A gust of wind rattled the windows and sucked at the flue. "The Bible says the same thing: 'Can you fathom the mysteries of God? Can you probe the limits of the Almighty?'"

"I'm not sure I agree," Mary said. "Maybe we can't understand everything, but that doesn't mean God is unknowable. Here's another metaphor I like; it's one that C.S. Lewis used. God is a lion, strong and powerful, and like Gordon's fire image, sometimes fierce. But the lion says, Climb on. And when I get on its back, I have to hold its mane with both hands, because it takes me places I would never have the courage to go on my own, and at speeds that take my breath away. He doesn't try to knock me off, but I still have to use a lot of energy to stay on. And I fall off a lot, but when I do, the lion paces and pushes until I get on again. But the effort's worth it, because together we experience things that I couldn't even fantasize about. And when I'm on that ride, my senses are much stronger—colors are brighter, everyday sounds seem like music, I savor the spice in food, and simple pleasures make me laugh inside. So I guess to me, God isn't some kind of mystical creature to contemplate, or even just to worship—that's too passive. I don't see God as an indifferent, unapproachable entity at all. But peace and comfort aren't the first adjectives that come to mind when I think about a relationship with God. Maybe security—in the same way that an F-16 pilot can feel secure in the cockpit of his plane. And maybe peace too, in the sense of being at peace with yourself and not feeling agitated. But not peace like floating in a calm lake—it's more like riding a waterfall in a raft. And…well, I'm not sure any of this makes any sense…"

The others were silent. I put my arm over Mary's shoulder and rubbed her neck. She looked at Kate and said, "So, what's your opinion?"

Kate laughed. "I can't keep up with you philosophers. My opinion is that I need more wine." She rolled over languidly and crawled over to the wine bottle. I felt the warmth on my legs where hers had rested, and watched her silhouette in the firelight. Her hair was dark with a hint of red, like the Merlot in her glass. Outside, the storm picked up force, but it didn't bother me. Not much could, then.

*   *   *

As our week together drew to a close, I realized I had been kidding myself when I thought that I had gotten over my infatuation with Kate. If anything, it was only getting worse.

One evening, Gordon and Mary took the kids to the mall and left me alone in the house with her. We played a few hands of double solitaire to pass the time. I wondered if Kate knew what was on my mind, and I struggled to keep my voice normal. She seemed especially cheerful and talkative, as if she knew she had to fill the void with something. The problem was, I could hardly concentrate on my cards, and my heart was pounding so hard I was sure it was making my hand shake.

After a half hour we attempted some small talk, then just sat in the living room within three feet of each other reading our books. At least I assumed Kate was reading. I could hardly see the words, and I ended up slowly turning pages, pretending to read.

After what seemed like an eternity, I couldn't take it any longer, and sneaked a long gaze at Kate, half hoping she would look up. She read with her hand on her chin, and occasionally her eyelids dropped in sleep. How could she be so calm? Couldn't she hear my heartbeat, as loud as it was pounding in my ears? It began to occur to me that the attraction was probably one-sided, which only caused depression to mix with frustration in my cauldron of emotions.

But I kept it all corked up, and tried to stick to my internal commitment not to burden her with any of it.

*   *   *

The next morning, I sat with Mary over breakfast, reading the newspaper. We had taken Kate and her family to the airport the night before, and my soul was filled with a dull ache. I replayed in my mind the moments we had spent together, and wished they had lasted longer.

"I bet you miss Kate," Mary said.

"How's that?" I asked, startled.

"The crossword," Mary said. "She helped you with the crossword puzzle every morning. Now you're on your own again."

"Oh. Yeah, she's pretty good at puzzles."

11

When I got back in the office, one of the first calls was from Simon Garrett.

"Just thought you should know. We had to arrest Lenny Fiala on New Year's Eve."

"Oh no. How come?"

"I guess he had done a little too much partying, and started beating on his wife. Made such a ruckus the neighbors had to call. So we let him cool off in the drunk tank, and then booked him for domestic violence. Course, he claims we're picking on him and that the town was full of people drinking that night. Says he's going to get a lawyer on us."

"He always threatens that. Any validity to it?"

"Nope. Just letting you know in case you hear about it somewhere else."

"Thanks. Anything else going on?"

"Not much. I've got a couple of guys out with the flu, but we're covering. Somebody's been paying for their holiday shopping spree with stolen checks, but the bozo agreed to give a thumbprint to one of the stores. We'll have 'em pretty quick."

I took a break at lunchtime to join Will Samuels, the parks director, for a couple of games of racquetball at the downtown health club. He had a few years on me—he and his wife Ruby were already grandparents—but he still beat me most of the time. Between games we leaned on the wall to catch our breath.

"So, did you and Mary have a good holiday?"

"Yes, but it was too short, as usual. Some friends from Colorado joined us. How about you—how was the trip to Louisiana?" Will and Ruby had spent Christmas in Lafayette with Will's mother and extended family.

"Good, good. Didn't mind getting out of the rain for a while. We had a nice visit, but I'm not sorry I don't live there any more. Too much baggage from my youth—civil rights rallies and all that scene. Good seeing the folks, though."

"How are the parks in that part of the country?"

"Don't have as many big trees, but they aren't bad either. Most of ours look so much newer, which I guess isn't a surprise, since they are. I hope we'll be able to keep them up as time goes on."

"Think the budget's going to make that hard?"

Will used the sleeve of his T-shirt to wipe the sweat off his forehead. "Probably. But we'll manage. We're getting pretty good at designing them."

He was right. The grass areas in the parks were all sized so the public works staff could unload a gang mower off the back of a truck and cut the grass in just a few passes. All the tight spots were converted to bark dust and shrubs. One of Will's proudest moments was when he took the city council and me to a new covered picnic area. He said, "Look up and tell me if you see anything unusual." It looked like a normal metal-framed shelter to us. "Give up? It doesn't have any cross bars for birds to sit on and decorate the picnic tables." They had come up with a roof design that put all the weight on a rectangular frame. Attention to details like that had made it possible to add parks without increasing the maintenance budget, but that could only go on so long. Grass still had to be mowed, trash cans had to be emptied, and no matter how we designed them, restrooms took a beating. We had finally taken the step of locking them up at night, but a group of young miscreants had gotten up on a roof of one of the restrooms and dropped so many rocks down the vent pipe that we had to tear out all the plumbing.

"You know Will, I like your optimism. It seems that whenever there's a budget crisis, the things that really make a positive difference in our lives—parks, recreation, libraries—are the first to go. But you don't seem to let that bother you too much."

"Thanks. But don't be deceived. I take all my frustrations out here."

Will served and the ball exploded out of his racquet. I jumped out of the way, and let the back and side walls absorb some of the ball's fury, then

whipped my racquet out to tap the ball into the far corner. Will was going
to make me work for every point.

*   *   *

The conference table was littered with spreadsheets and printouts.
Betty Sue punched some numbers in a calculator.

"We're still off by a hundred thousand." We had given each department
a target to shoot for in preparing their budgets. That meant that we could
work on balancing the general fund without waiting for the line item
details to come in. We had already mapped out a set of options for cuts in
each service area, to give the city council as many choices as possible. But
I had to pick among them to present the council with a balanced budget,
and the decisions weren't easy.

"Are you sure we're not forgetting any revenues?" I asked. "Can we
squeeze anything more out of business licenses or franchise fees?"

"Well, even if we doubled the business license amounts, it would only
bring in $30,000."

"Probably isn't worth getting the businesses all riled up, I suppose."

"And the franchise fees are all at their maximum rates," Betty Sue said.
"The only way to get more money out of them is to over-estimate the revenues, 'cause I don't think we're being too conservative now."

"Hey, it worked for Ronald Reagan."

"What? Do you mean cooking the estimates? That was before my time,
and anyway, we can't get away with deficit financing."

We stared at the numbers.

"How about this," I said. "Charlene Wolf told me that her city tacks on
a five percent city administrative fee on all building permits. Let's see what
that would get us."

"All building fees, even utility hookup fees?"

"Yeah, I think so."

"Hold on." Betty Sue leafed through the revenue pages and wrote a series of numbers on a scratch pad. When she was satisfied that she had them all, she began punching them into her calculator. She had what looked like an engagement ring on her finger. When did that get there? She was guarded about her personal life, but even I should have caught the clues about a relationship that serious.

I did some math in my head. If the total building fees for a typical house were $8,000, then five percent would be $400. The builders would squawk, but they would pass it on to the homebuyer, and tack on another $400 for themselves and the realtors. An extra $800 in the mortgage would come out to less than $80 a year in house payments. That was small compared to the homeowner's property tax savings from ballot measure 5-47. So it would probably fly. Besides, it would only hit new home buyers, and the existing residents didn't have much sympathy for them.

"Okay, that would bring in around $60,000," Betty Sue said.

"Great. What do you think?"

"I think we should go for it."

"All right, put it down."

Maybe the ring was from Lavar Washington in engineering. They had gone out for lunch a couple of times over the last few months.

"What about the expenditure side?" I said. "Any frills we can cut out?"

"How about the summer concerts in the park?"

"Ouch. That's one of the few things that we do that makes life worth living for."

"You mean you don't get excited about sewer service or traffic enforcement?"

"Exactly. Have I told you my motorcycle story?"

"Uh, I don't think so."

"Well, one summer in college I worked part time on a crew for a motorcycle racing team. Didn't pay much, but that didn't matter then. Anyway, we spent a lot of time getting the bikes as light as possible. We experimented with different alloys for the frame, and even drilled holes in the rotors for the disk brakes. The only area that was allowed to get much weight was the engine—each cylinder had it's own carburetor, that sort of thing."

Betty Sue gave me a quizzical look.

"You wonder where I'm going with this, huh? Well, I think as a society, we have our priorities screwed up. We're putting all the weight in the brakes, the suspension and the frame—things like police, fire, medicine. Did you know that half of all medical expenses in this country are spent in the last six months of a person's life?"

"Is that true?"

"Well, I'm not sure. I think I heard that somewhere. I do know that sixty-six point seven percent of all statistics are made up on the spot."

Betty Sue thought for a second, then laughed. "Including that one, no doubt."

"Yep. But back to my story. We're obsessed with hygiene, with safety, and it's sucking away all our resources. We're so preoccupied with basic services that we don't set enough aside for the things that actually add to quality of life, like the arts, exploration, spiritual growth—"

"But we seem to put a lot of money into Hollywood and professional sports."

"I said *quality* of life. See, our motorcycle has huge brakes and a heavy frame and almost no engine, and it can hardly move. And if we could turn our priorities around, and get people living more fulfilling, healthy lives, I have to believe we would need less of the so-called basics, like police and medicine. I would choose an Alfa Romeo over a Volvo any day—it may not be built like a tank, but it can maneuver me out of tight spots."

"So why do you drive a sport utility?"

"Mary made me get it."

"Sure, blame it on her."

"Well, here you are, wanting to take away my summer concerts."

She rested her head on her hand and was quiet for a few moments. "It doesn't have to be all or nothing. Maybe the Chamber can round up sponsors for the concerts, or maybe we can charge an entrance fee."

"You could be right, but it seems like admitting defeat to me."

I looked through our option list one more time. "Is that a new ring?" I asked.

Was she blushing? "Yes. A guy gave it to me. Actually, it was Lavar. It isn't an engagement ring or anything—he just gave it to me for my birthday."

"Well, that was nice of him. Seems like a good guy."

"Yes."

She wasn't going to volunteer any more information, but it really wasn't my business anyway. She didn't have any supervisory authority over public works, so an office romance wasn't going to cause problems.

"Okay, add the summer concert to your list."

"All right. That puts us within $20,000."

"That's close enough. Just stretch a revenue estimate somewhere. These numbers are going to change a lot more than that before the budget committee gets done with it."

She nodded and started gathering the papers.

"So, do you and Max have all the details worked out?" I asked.

She paused. "Sure, pretty much. I think we can get a lot more savings than Max does. But we're ready to go ahead with it."

"Good."

*　　　　*　　　　*

Time in city hall was driven by cycles, like the gears of a clock. We had the budget cycle, council meeting agendas, state legislative sessions, sunset clauses in ordinances, citizen newsletter deadlines, election filing dates, and the annual financial audit. The cycles overlapped, and hit us in a series of uneven waves. It seemed like we would meet one milestone, only to plunge immediately into a dozen more urgent tasks. In the middle of all this, the union contracts had to be negotiated, with their own sets of expiration dates and timelines.

"Are you getting any closer to a settlement?" I asked Ken Longstreet when he stopped by my office.

"No. Every time we think we can declare an impasse, the firefighters make some minor concession, and then pull out some new issue to debate. It looks like they're intentionally dragging it out."

"Sure. They're waiting for us to make a move."

"Probably. At least they're finally putting some of the compensation issues on the table. Of course, they want parity with the police."

"Won't that make them look bad after their public statement about a wage freeze?"

Ken shrugged. "Nobody will know about it for a long time—one of the ground rules we agreed upon was that the negotiations would be kept confidential. And they will say it's not a wage increase by disguising it as something else. They're talking about certification pay for anyone who has gone through Advanced Life Support, which pretty much covers all of them."

I nodded and walked over to the window. Fog filled the Willamette valley like a thick white river.

"Do you think they'll find our contingency accounts?" I asked. Since we had to go public with the budget, we had to set aside money for an eventual contract settlement. Ken and Betty Sue had figured an overall increase equivalent to the change in the Consumer Price Index, and tucked it away in a few obscure line items like property and liability insurance.

"They might. But they've never paid much attention to our budget or ability to pay when making their demands."

"Yes, but an arbitrator could, if it comes to that."

"Then it might help us. It could establish the parameters for a settlement."

I shook my head. "Why are we kidding ourselves? An arbitrator would be even less inclined to spend time digging around in the budget. The best place to hide secrets is in financial reports—no one reads them."

Ken feigned shock. "Well thanks a lot. Go ahead and burst my bubble."

"Okay, your annual report is an exception. People hang on to every word of it, especially all those footnotes, and the pages that say, 'This page intentionally left blank.' Have you ever noticed that that's a contradictory statement?"

"Yes. I know I should write, This page intentionally left blank, except for this sentence, and that page number down there, and the page heading. Like, 'I'm leaving, and I'm not taking anything with me. Except this thermos. And this lamp. And this—'"

"But that would make you a jerk, huh?" We laughed together

*   *   *

I called Max Oakley's office, but he was out, visiting with the president of the Chamber of Commerce. I left a message. A stack of paperwork was waiting for me, but I had a hard time mustering any enthusiasm for dealing with it.

Hank Arnold walked in. I was saved.

"Got my new computer up and running," he said. "I hooked up a scanner and a printer, so I can use it like a fax machine and a copier. It's pretty neat. Had some trouble connecting back into my Internet service, but I called them and got a new password, and now everything's working fine. If you want to send me the council packet material through the Internet, instead of the mail, that would be fine with me."

"You know, I've thought about that, but a lot of the stuff on the agenda doesn't come to us in electronic form—you know, zoning maps and consultant reports, liquor license renewal forms, Pete Koenig's typed memos…"

"Uh huh. You'd have to scan that in—probably not worth the time."

"Sure, and once we did, the packet would be a few dozen megabytes. Even with a fast modem, it would take all night for you to download it. Someday we might be there, but in the meantime we'll have to keeping cutting down the forests."

"What's that?"

"We'll have to keep using paper."

"Oh. Yes. Well, I got one of my cars towed away to give me more room to work on my plane in the garage. Too wet to work outside much. I had to build a wood support to hold the wings up while I hook 'em on. Took me a while to figure that one out."

In the middle of all his other hobbies and activities, Hank was building a lightweight replica of a World War II fighter plane. "Are you going to be able to fly it this summer?"

"Yep, should have it finished by this summer, actually." Hank gave me the complete details of his construction progress, his most recent golf score, the challenges his car racing club faced in finding a new track, and the venues where his bluegrass band was playing. If he had asked if he was taking too much of my time, I was going to tell him that the city manager's job is to talk to council members. But he didn't ask.

"...So with all that, and dealing with city issues, I'm keeping pretty busy. But the reason I stopped by was to see if there's anything going on that I should know about"

"Yes, as a matter of fact, there is something involving planes," I said. "You know the fixed base operator at the Trillium Airport, Olaf Larson? He reckons there's a need for more hangar space, says that people don't want to leave their planes out in the weather."

"Hangars? Yes, I can see that. Wouldn't use one myself. Unless I had to, of course, if I needed to work on my plane. But there are a lot of fellows who don't care so much about the cost."

"Yeah, well Larson wants the city to be a partner in this. He wants us to pay for the hangars. He'll lease space for his operation, and contract with us to be the property manager for the rest of it."

"He wants us to build them? Can't he do that himself?"

"Well, he says he's deep enough in debt from starting his business. He can't get another loan."

"Oh. I see. Will the rent be enough to cover the cost?"

"More than enough, based on the numbers we have so far. It would help cover some of our cost of owning the airport."

"Well, then, it sounds like a good idea to me. Let's do it."

"Okay. I'll put it on one of the next agendas. The council has to take formal action on it."

"Yes. Well, I better get going. Keep up the good work."

"Sure"

*   *   *

That afternoon, Max Oakley called back.

"Max, Betty Sue has worked up some graphics—have you gone over those with her?"

"Yes. I think they will be helpful. I made some suggestions on improving them, but it was a good start."

"So you're ready?"

"Yes."

"Good. I appreciate the work you've done on this."

"All right." He paused. "Tell me Ben, has Simon made any plans about retirement yet?"

"Uh, no. He's talked about it in general, but nothing specific. And I'm not going to push it—I'm not in a hurry for him to leave."

"I see."

"Why—have you given more thought to the idea of a combined public safety department?"

"Yes. I've come to the conclusion that it could be beneficial."

"Okay, good."

"But I don't want to wait forever to see it happen."

"Umm." What did he expect me to do? "I wouldn't worry. With the cushy public safety pension system you guys have, it's going to cost Simon more to work than to retire pretty soon."

The line was silent. Jake Wildavsky was standing in my doorway.

"Well, Max," I said. "Thanks again for all your help on this. I'll talk to you later."

I nodded to Jake and he sat down next to my desk. "Working on your budget presentation, eh?" he said.

"Yeah, we're getting close. So, what's up?"

"I need a raise."

"Oh?"

"Yep, I think I need a raise."

I looked at him and waited.

"You see," Jake said, "I'm not just a public works director, I'm a detective too. Don't you think that's worth something?" He grinned.

"Sure," I said.

"Here's the story. Remember the family whose sewer backed up just before Thanksgiving?"

"Vaguely."

"Well, we didn't admit liability or anything, but we put them up in a motel. Didn't want the bad press of a family spending Thanksgiving surrounded by sewage."

"Right."

"They put all sorts of charges on their motel bill—meals, movies, you name it. I couldn't believe the final bill when we got it. But anyway, we were stuck with figuring out the cause of the backup. None of the neighbors had a problem, but the blockage didn't seem to be in the lateral to the home, either. They have a five-foot sewer easement in their backyard where the sewer trunk runs, so we ran a TV down there to see what was going on. Found a metal post sticking in the pipe."

"How did it get there?"

"I'm coming to that. We got around that one, and found four more posts further down, all in a row. Here's what happened. When the guy's pea crop or whatever was finished, he tried to pull the posts out of the ground, but couldn't. So he decided to punch 'em into the dirt. He got them most of the way in, but then he hit what he thought was a rock. So he took out his sledge hammer and just hit 'em harder—right through our concrete sewer pipe. Did it with all five of them."

"What a goof ball. So did you bill him for the pipe replacement?"

"Yeah. But he said his insurance wouldn't cover it, and claimed that he didn't have anything to do with the posts, that they must have been put there by the previous owner. So Simon helped us out—we had the posts sent to the state forensic lab, and they determined the posts had been in the ground for less than a year. The guy bought the house two and a half years ago. And the neighbors confirmed that he had some kind of garden, and one even thought that they had heard him pounding something back there in late October or so."

"Good work, Sherlock. So the case is closed?"

"Not quite. We agreed to pick up the motel tab. But we still want him to pay for the pipe repair—it wound up costing around $4,500. So it looks like we have to take him to court."

"Okay. Do what you have to do."

*   *   *

Oregon law included a bizarre provision that required local governments to form a "budget committee" that would set the upper limit each year for spending and for the property tax levy. The committee was made up of five additional residents, appointed by the council, who would join the five city council members in making budget decisions, as if having ten—instead of five—citizens setting the budget in a city of over forty thousand people somehow made it more legitimate. And it made even less sense when the property tax levy was fixed by the ballot measure, and no longer set by the city council. But we went through the motions anyway.

The budget committee members included an accountant, the information services manager for a hospital, a retired teacher, a retired secretary, and the owner of a small manufacturing company. They straggled in and took their seats at the conference table, making awkward jokes and small talk to bridge the time since their last meeting a year ago. The city council members joined in for a while, and then broke off into quiet side conversations, waiting for the mayor to show up.

Betty Sue Castle and Ken Longstreet sat with me. The other department heads sat in chairs that lined the walls. Brian Gallagher and a handful of firefighters were off to the side, arms folded.

Sabrina Chan from *The Oregonian* sat with the staff and leafed through the draft budget document. She could have picked it up a few days earlier, but didn't, to my relief. I didn't want it showing up in the paper before I had a chance to brief the council.

Diane McTavish swept in and dropped her papers and files at her place at the table. "Okay, let's get started," she said, slightly out of breath. "For the benefit of the non-council members here, we asked Ben to give us a range of options for balancing the budget under ballot measure 5-47. Since it's going to affect the final budget, we thought it would be a good idea if you were in on it. I have to be up front about one thing, though. Some of these options involve changes in the organization or in the programs that the city offers. The council members and I are interested in your comments and ideas on those, but the council has final responsibility for them, and we reserve the right to make the final decisions. Any problems with that?" The business owner raised his eyebrows, but the rest nodded assent. "Good. All right Ben, it's your show."

"Thanks. As Diane said, our charge was to give you some options, and that's what we've done. We're also giving you a recommendation on how to balance the budget, but this is clearly a policy decision that is up to the council—you can take or leave our recommendations, and we understand that."

I flipped the switch on a video projector that was connected to Ken's notebook computer. Betty Sue dimmed the lights.

"Here's where we are with the property tax," I said. A bright yellow line sliced through the deep blue background, climbing steadily, flattening, then dropping. "This is our levy over the past fifteen years. Years ago, a state constitutional change limited the levy to a six percent increase per year, plus the value of any property that annexed to the city. Then the voters approved a ballot measure that capped the tax rate itself. That apparently wasn't good enough, so the Trillium citizens passed measure 5-47, that actually cut the rate, and then capped the rate of increase of assessed value, regardless of increases in the real market value of property. So our property tax revenue has dropped sharply, compared to every measure that we could think of."

I clicked on the mouse. The property tax line was joined by others, all showing steady increases.

"Our population has gone up. Property values have gone up. County-wide personal income has gone up—a lot. And check this one out—the state income tax has gone up more than all, in percentage terms. While we're dealing with a combination of state- and locally-imposed tax limitations, the state government itself is rolling in dough."

The screen wiped to a different set of graphs. "We can't measure it as well, but it seems the demand for our services has gone up, too. Here are the trends in the number of crimes reported, library books circulated, senior meals served, recreation class participants, water customers, emergency medical calls. They're all up.

"Here's a pie chart showing all our revenues. Property tax makes up less than a tenth of it. And here are our total expenses, split into different services. The public works areas—water, sewer, streets, storm drainage—make up the majority of the pie. But check this out—when you take out all the services that have their own revenue sources, like water rates or building permit fees, look what you're left with. The areas that depend on the property tax are police, fire, the library, recreation, and senior services. So even though it's a relatively small part of the total budget, it affects services that mean a lot to people."

The budget committee members and Maggie Henderson were watching intently, but the rest of the city council members were starting to fidget. They knew this part of the story and wanted to get to the meat.

"And this means our options are relatively limited, too. We either need to find cost savings in these areas, or find some other general revenue sources. In other words, saving money in the water department is good for our customers, but it won't help us offset the property tax loss.

"So where does this leave us? We've prepared a series of options you can look at—here's a list of them, with our estimates for savings or additional revenue. The ones in red are the ones we used to balance the budget, but you can pick any combination you want."

The mayor leaned forward to read the screen. Seth wrote some figures down.

"The largest area of savings is in the area labeled fire and medical re-deployment. It's a major issue, and we need to spend some time with it. By way of introduction, we first approached this as a way to save money. And there's no doubt about it, we have an opportunity for some substantial savings. But the more we looked at it, the more it seemed a better way to provide service. In a way, this is the holy grail of any business or well-run government: a way to provide *better* service at *less* cost. I'd like to ask Fire Chief Max Oakley to give you the details."

Max stood and addressed the committee.

"Yes. What we are proposing to do is to re-deploy our forces to specifically target the differing needs of fire suppression and emergency medical services. Rather than using a one-size-fits-all approach, we would target manpower and apparatus to fire fighting as necessary, and do the same for emergency medical service. Let me explain how this would work."

Max shot a laser pointer at a chart showing the current staffing and shifts at the three fire stations.

"Our workforce deployment is currently aligned in accordance with traditional fire fighting patterns. The fact is, however, that majority of our calls fall in the area of emergency medical services."

Out of the corner of my eye, I saw Sabrina scribbling furiously. Gallagher looked bored. He undoubtedly had the current staffing level committed to memory—he threatened union action any time we talked about reducing it.

"Our proposal is to provide comprehensive fire suppression service, with the primary response from Station One. This will provide a solid base line response for the protection of property. A critical component of this deployment, however, is continued emphasis on fire prevention, building plans review for fire and life safety, and especially smoke alarms. Early detection of a fire is the single most important element for both property safety and life safety."

Betty Sue was making a visible effort to keep from speaking. But most of Max's listeners were nodding sagely—if they didn't know what he was talking about, they didn't want to show it.

Rob Titus interrupted. "If the primary response is out of Station One, won't there be a negative impact on response times to the more remote edges of the city?" Rob had— weeks earlier—asked this question privately, and I thought he had been satisfied with the answer.

"For the fire apparatus, yes," Max said. "But again, the critical time factor in a fire is detecting it, and getting a report called in so that we can respond to it. Studies have shown the response time in rolling to a fire is less important. We don't feel there will be an affect on property loss. And under this proposal, we will be able to respond more quickly to medical emergencies and other threats to life safety."

Max nodded at Betty Sue and a map of the city filled the screen. "We propose to deploy mobile two-man emergency medical teams. We will be able to configure the number and location of the teams according to our documented patterns for medical calls. During times of the day when the call volume is typically low, we will have three teams. They will—"

"What if someone has a heart attack then?" Rob Titus asked. Another question he knew the answer to. "People don't always schedule their medical emergencies according to our staffing patterns."

"If you think about it," Max said, "this is no different than our current situation. With the fixed staffing level that we now employ, the closest unit may be in service when you have your heart attack. So the response may come from a more remote station, or possibly from a station in a neighboring jurisdiction. Individual situations will still exist, but on average, we will be able to provide a better response if we can tailor our manpower levels to the variations in our call patterns. Let me show you. Betty Sue, bring up the chart with the call pattern."

This was a diversion from their prepared script, but Betty Sue reacted calmly. In a moment a scattergram filled the screen.

"Here are the number of medical calls by hour of the day, taken over 150 days last year. As you can see, there are day-to-day fluctuations, but there is a general trend to the pattern. And the pattern isn't flat. So during these shifts—" He used his pointer. "—we can deploy four units, and during these shifts, three units will be sufficient. This is no different than the way we staff our police patrol shifts. And of course, most private sector organizations use a similar technique to match staffing levels with demand. Does this answer your question, councilor?"

"Yes, very well," Rob said.

Max looked at his notes.

"All right. This map shows the approximate location of the medical response units, but note that they can be mobile. For example, they may move closer to schools during the day and closer to retirement homes at night. You may ask about the call that falls outside this pattern. Again, this happens now, since not all medical emergencies conveniently happen next to our fire stations, and it is very expensive to move fire stations in response to different patterns of physical development. So having mobile emergency response units is a better approach."

I couldn't tell if the budget committee was buying this. They seemed to be nodding at the right times, but that could have just been out of respect for the fire chief. The presentation was going well, and Betty Sue's graphics gave it a professional touch. I doubted the committee members were thinking about the political implications of what we were proposing, but they were insulated from that anyway. No one would walk up to them in a grocery store and say, "Hey, wasn't that you on the city budget committee that voted for this fire deal?"

Whatever they were thinking, I felt a weight beginning to lift. It was out of my hands now. I wanted the committee members to give the council some encouragement, and I wanted the council to back our proposal, but it was still their decision. And I had to admit to myself that if they decided not to, my life would be simpler.

"Max, would you be recommending this if we weren't facing a budget crisis?" The question came from Seth as the chief wrapped up his comments.

"No," he said immediately. I couldn't believe my ears.

"Oh? Seth said. "Why is that?"

"I do believe that what we are proposing is a more efficient deployment of personnel. But I believe it will be much more difficult to hire and retain staff. The fire service has established a tradition of 24-hour shifts and responding to emergency medical calls. A non-traditional approach will not be consistent with the expected career path of the fire service—"

"What does that mean?" McTavish asked. "Do you think the city government exists to provide career paths for firefighters? Do we collect taxes so that we can provide jobs that keep to *traditions?*"

"No," Max said. "I'm just responding to council member Rosenberg's question. Recruiting and retaining staff is a practical concern, and as a manager, I'm also concerned about staff morale."

"So you don't want to rock the boat, even if you believe that you can provide more efficient and more effective service to our citizens?"

"Don't misunderstand me. I support Ben in this proposal. I don't see many alternatives to it under the budget limitations we have. But there are good reasons why we didn't pursue it before."

Betty Sue leaned over to me and whispered, "So it's your proposal now."

One of the budget committee members looked up from his papers. "You're showing fairly significant savings here. How are you going to achieve that without layoffs?"

"You're right," Ken Longstreet said. "We won't see the full savings in the first few years. We plan to let the personnel reduction happen through normal attrition. We've still got enough cash in the bank to let us make the transition without layoffs."

I had talked about this with Ken before. The "attrition" of staff would be anything but normal. If the firefighters followed through on their threats, there would be a mass exodus. Some would bail out with early retirement, and others would go to the Portland Fire Bureau or Tualatin Valley Fire. It was a mixed blessing. We would get our salary and fringe savings sooner, and some of the hot heads would be the first to leave. But many of our best staff would quietly resign and find a place where they could do their jobs without as much conflict. We would be left with resentful mediocrity.

The questions continued for a while. The teacher and the business owner said the proposal made a lot of sense. The accountant noted that we could see additional savings if we leased out one of the fire stations as office space. The retiree wondered how our mutual aid agreement with neighboring jurisdictions would work if we had such a non-traditional approach. It was a good question.

After a while, the mayor pointed out that they didn't need to make a decision now. I introduced the presentations from the other departments, and then sat back and watched with a mixture of amusement and admiration as the department heads pulled out their budget tricks.

Will Samuels made a case for the replacement of some beat up old furniture in the parks department conference room. It sounded good, but the fact was that he had never had the furniture in his budget in the first place. It was all scrounged from other departments when Will converted a spare office into a meeting room.

Simon Garrett argued for the addition of a traffic enforcement officer. The money from fines, he said, would not only cover the officer's salary, but it would help close the budget gap. I remembered that he had made the same argument six years ago. When Simon had gotten the officer trained and on the street, the revenue from citations did jump up, enough to cover the cost, but it dropped back down a few years later. With the growth in the city's population, the officer was too busy responding to calls to write many tickets.

Bess Wilson somberly described the setback to our long range planning work that would result from our proposed cuts to consultant contracts for inventories of trees and historic properties, and for the establishment of airport overlay zones. These were all state mandates, and Bess had never wanted to do them in the first place. They had carried forward in her budget for the past three years, unspent. I had asked Bess if there would be repercussions from the state if we didn't do the work. She had replied, "Screw 'em. Let them pay for it."

Jake Wildavsky focused the budget committee's attention on proposed reductions in landscaping in the street medians and in the planting strips between the curbs and sidewalks. The strategy worked—they didn't seem to notice the huge water and sewer budgets, which included several new trucks, a backhoe, twenty thousand dollars worth of personal computers and drafting software, and fifteen million dollars worth of new pipes and improvements to the treatment plants.

Diane McTavish and Seth Rosenberg—and probably Hank Arnold— knew what the department heads were up to. They didn't resent it. They knew that the staff needed to get the resources to do their jobs, and this was just part of the song and dance. Sort of like the rules for haggling with a merchant in a Hong Kong alley. You knew what the outcome was going to be, but custom and courtesy called for playing out the script.

By 11:00 everyone was exhausted, and the mayor adjourned the meeting

*   *   *

A week later we were back at the same place. The *Oregonian* had run an article with the headline, "Trillium City Manager Calls for Restructuring Fire Service." Sabrina Chan had done a good job in summarizing the proposal, and the very fact that it was a careful, objective report guaranteed that few readers would pay any attention to it. Halfway through the article, Brian Gallagher was quoted as saying that the firefighters supported improved efficiency, but that a top-down approach wasn't the way to achieve it. Sabrina hadn't followed up with the question of exactly how the firefighters proposed to save money in a bottom-up approach—or maybe her editor had cut it out to save space.

"I don't know about the fire proposal," Rob Titus said, and wiped some spit off his lip. "I have considered all the options, and the needs of our constituents, and I am convinced we need to reduce services in all areas, not just in fire. So I am going to vote for that—an across the board reduction."

McTavish squinted at him. "But if Ben and Max are right, we're not looking at a reduction of service in fire."

"Maybe not in EMS, but you can't convince me that concentrating our firefighting personnel in just one station isn't going to reduce our fire protection. I just don't see it."

"I have the same concern," the teacher said. "I'm worried about the safety of our residents—to me, that's the most important thing."

Betty Sue leaned over to me. "What made her change her mind?"

It was easy for me to imagine. The firefighters association called on the school union leadership in Salem, who put pressure on the local, who had a little chat with our budget committee member. It probably all took place within twelve hours of last week's meeting. The curious thing was why they hadn't gotten to her sooner. But I kept my opinion to myself, and shrugged.

"I don't know about that," Hank Arnold said. "I think Max laid it out pretty well. But if we have concerns about it, we can try it out for a while, and if it doesn't work, go back to the old way. It's not like the fire stations are going to go away."

Ken Longstreet raised his eyebrows. He was trying to picture what the firefighters would do if we approached it as an experiment. There were a hundred creative ways they could come up with to make sure it failed. It reminded me of a midwest town that once thought it would be a neat idea if their police officers drove Checker cabs. The vehicles were built to last a few hundred thousand miles, and to be driven day and night. The experiment, of course, failed. The cars had a surprisingly high tendency to be totaled in accidents, including a mysterious incident where one of the Checkers ended up in a lake.

"Uh, I think we have to make a decision to back this, or not," Seth said quietly. "We can't go half way."

"Yes, I agree," Hank said.

The hospital IT manager said, "Why don't we start listing the cuts we all agree with? Once we do that, we can see what kind of a gap we're left with."

"Great idea," McTavish said.

Betty Sue kept a running tally on a flip chart. In a few cases, it took a while to get consensus. If there was a hold out on a decision, the mayor would keep the discussion going until the dissenter was worn down. But after an hour they were done, and the gap was about what I expected it to be—roughly equal to the savings from the fire proposal.

They sat and stared at Betty Sue's flip chart, hoping for some other alternative to appear.

The business owner finally spoke. "The solution seems fairly obvious. We can cut services to Trillium residents and businesses, or we can make the delivery of fire and EMS service more efficient. I recognize that doing so would cause some turmoil in the fire department, but the city doesn't exist for the benefit of the employees."

"I agree," said the computer manager.

"Okay. Let's go around the table and see where we stand on this," McTavish said. "Should we follow through on the fire proposal? Seth?"

"Yes."

"Hank?"

"Yes, I think it's in—"

"No," Rob said,

They continued around the table. All voted yes, except the teacher.

"Maggie?"

"Oh, I don't know. It's hard. Yes, I guess."

*   *   *

In our staff meeting the next morning, the department heads were more animated than usual. They had escaped serious cuts, and the budget process was over. Even Max seemed cheerful. It occurred to me that they all liked change, and except for Ken, they thrived on chaos. I figured that they would really enjoy the next few months.

For the first time, I began to think there was a good chance we could pull this off. A lot of my colleagues had talked about doing something different with their fire departments, but none had been able to follow through. I let my mind wander to thoughts of giving a presentation at the next International City Management Association conference, or writing an article for *Governing* magazine.

*   *   *

Later, I got on the Internet to check out the latest developments from the League of Oregon Cities in Salem. A new message caught my eye.

From: kanderson@rockynet.com
Subject:Depressed in Denver

Hi Ben. I've been thinking about you. Talk to me.
—love, Kate

12

We moved quickly to start the fire department on its new course. Max and his assistant chief set up a process for splitting his staff between fire and EMS service. I insisted that he poll his firefighters to find their preferences, but Max didn't hold out much hope that they would respond. Betty Sue drafted an insert for our city newsletter to explain the plan to the residents. I set up meetings with the chamber of commerce board and a few other groups to assure them that their fire protection wouldn't be diminished. This was the fun part of the job: creating new things. I felt energized and looked forward to going to work, and woke up early in the morning with my mind full of ideas.

After the court victory, Nova's contractor had moved several pieces of equipment on their site, but not much else was going on. I reached for the phone to call Bess Wilson, but changed my mind and walked across to the planning department.

In the open office area behind the counter, Bess was holding a three-hole paper punch over a trash can. She let go, and it landed with a metallic clunk. One of her staff assistants was watching, her expression frozen in disbelief.

"Okay, now go get yourself something that will do the job," Bess said She turned to look at me. "Did you want to see me, Ben?"

"Uh, yeah." I followed Bess into her office. "What was wrong with the punch?"

"Nothing. It was perfectly good. But it only handles twenty pages at a time. Our planning commission packets are running up to two hundred pages, and it was taking her forever to put them together. For months I've been telling her to get something that would drill through the whole damn thing, but she didn't want to spend the money. So I had to make my point."

"Oh."

"You don't approve?"

"No, it's not that," I said. "In fact, I wish I had your flair for the dramatic. Anyhow, what I came over for was to see what was holding up

Nova's plant. They haven't even broken ground yet. Do you know what's going on?"

"Well, the last I knew, they were still having problems with Bruce Poulet on the right-of-way for their road connection to 73rd. ODOT is making them use that road for construction, to keep their trucks from slowing traffic on Chief Joseph. So they're kind of stuck."

"What's Bruce's cell phone number?"

Poulet answered on the third ring. It sounded like he was on the road. I had once passed him on the freeway, and recognized him by his long gray beard and denim jacket. He had had a newspaper opened over the steering wheel of his pickup truck, and he was absorbed in some article while driving at 60 miles an hour.

"Hi Bruce. This is Ben Cromarty. Is this a bad time to catch you?"

"No. Go ahead."

"I'm in Bess Wilson's office. We're talking about the Nova Ceramics plant, and the access road off 73rd. What's the status of that?"

There was a pause.

"Well, we're still talking," Poulet said. "I am willing to deal with them, but I want due consideration for the land."

"So how close are you to working something out?" I asked.

"I don't know. Hold on."

I heard an engine being gunned. He was probably merging onto a highway somewhere.

"Okay. Ben, you still there?"

"Yep."

"You see, there's one other thing. I'm getting a lot of pressure from the TBLC not to enter into a deal at all. So I'm not sure yet what I'm going to do."

"What kind of pressure can they put on you?" I asked. "It's your land, not theirs."

"See, it's not that simple. I do business with a lot of those guys. I'm in Trillium for the long run...I can't afford to be making enemies."

"Hmm. Well, if there's anything I can do to help, let me know."

"Yeah." The sound of a horn, and then another one, closer.

"I don't know if this would make things easier," I said. "I told Nova I wasn't interested in using eminent domain, and you might as well know that. But if it could help you with the TLBC, we could start talking about condemning the right of way. It would give you an out, if you really wanted to work with us."

"Well, let's not go there. At least not yet. Talk of condemnation always raises my hackles, you know what I mean."

"Sure. But let me know. I want to see that project move ahead, and your right-of-way seems to be a key part of it. Go ahead and get a fair deal for the value of the land, but do me a favor and try not to take too long. Okay?"

"All right, we'll see. Well, I've got to go. Catch you later, Ben."

Bess raised her eyebrows. "Well?"

"Says he's still dickering, but the Trillium Business Leadership Committee is trying to keep him from making a deal. How about that?"

"Assholes. Doesn't surprise me, though. I heard your condemnation idea. How about if I get Pete to start working up the paperwork?"

"No, let's hold off. I don't want to make life hard for Bruce—he's really a pretty decent guy."

"Whatever."

"While we're on the subject, when is the Nova Estates project going to come to the city council?"

The mixed use housing project had gone through a few hearings in front of the planning commission. The commission had finally—in the face of public opposition—approved the subdivision plan with a list of over twenty conditions. The Hemlock Creek neighborhood association had promptly filed an appeal to the city council. I didn't know where they were getting their funding, but I had a guess. Their attorney was Terry Judd.

"If I get my butt in gear, it'll be on the next council agenda," Bess said. "We're getting close to running into the 120 day rule."

"Now that would be ironic, wouldn't it?" Under Oregon land use law, if a land use application didn't get a decision in 120 days, it was automatically approved.

"Yeah, I thought about letting the clock run out, but even I don't want to piss off the neighborhood that much."

I laughed. "Okay. Well, call me the next time you decide to trash some more city office equipment. I want to watch."

          *   *   *

Will Samuels and I sat in the reception area of the county administrator's office. Will had told me that he had hit an unexpected snag in the golf course project, and needed my help. To build homes around the golf course we needed to expand our urban growth boundary, and to do that, we needed to amend our urban growth management agreement with Multnomah County. Normally, it was a fairly routine procedure, but for some reason, we had run into resistance.

While we waited, Will gave me an update on his department. The senior trip fund was bringing in enough money to re-finish the dance floor, a neighborhood group was fighting the construction of a skateboard park, a peace-loving resident was up in arms because the newest offering in the recreation program catalog was a paintball war game, and the staff had a good lead on a grant that would convert an old railroad right of way into a bike path, but some of the residents along the trail didn't want the public anywhere near their homes.

Will laughed. "When I got started in this business, I thought my job would mostly be a lot of fun and games. Recreation, you know? But I end up spending most of my time dealing with conflicts between adults."

He was right, and it worried me. I didn't want him to get burned out—he was the best parks director I had worked with, and a good friend. But I didn't know what I could do about it.

"Does it get to you?" I asked.

"No, not really. It's not that much different from sorting out playground squabbles or refereeing a little league game, right?"

I chuckled. "Well, hang in there."

After a while, we were ushered into the office. Shantee Angelou, the county administrator, had an impossible job. The three county commissioners supposedly had part-time positions, but they spent most of their days in the county offices, and gave executive authority to the administrator only when it suited them. In practice, that meant that Shantee was left with either the most unpleasant, or the most boring, tasks. And to make matters worse, most of the department heads were elected directly by the voters, and felt that they didn't have to answer to anyone, least of all to Shantee, who was merely appointed by the commissioners. It was a form of government that was designed for failure.

But at least Shantee knew most of the ins and outs of county politics, even if she was relatively powerless.

"Hey, you're looking pretty sharp, Will," Shantee said.

Will's olive green suit set off his dark skin. I was wearing gray, in keeping with the weather.

"What about me?" I said.

"Sorry Ben, didn't mean to overlook you there."

"Oh, it's okay. I don't look good in green, especially this time of year. Do you know what the native Oregonian said to the Pillsbury dough boy?"

"No, what?"

"Nice tan!"

They laughed, but then I wondered if the joke was politically correct.

"I guess I should ask—are you a native, Shantee?"

"Yep, as it turns out. My Dad worked at the Kaiser shipyards during the war—he moved out from Detroit. The folks even got caught in the Vanport flood, but that was before I was born. The family's been here ever since."

"Well, what do you know."

"So, you really came here to talk to me about your urban growth boundary change, didn't you?"

"Yes. What's the deal?" I asked. "Do the commissioners want to do a golf course development themselves?"

"No, it isn't that at all," she said quietly. "It's the Fly Creek Fire District."

"How's that?" Will asked.

"Well, it's a long story. Do you know much about them?"

Will shook his head; I shrugged.

"Okay, it's like this," she said. "The fire district, they're like a separate country unto themselves. The chairman of their board, Ed Mann, thinks he's the mayor. He runs a lawnmower repair business out of his garage, but being the big kahuna at the fire department is what his life's all about. He and his colleagues on the board think they call all the shots for that end of the county."

"But Fly Creek isn't even an incorporated city," I said. "It's just a cross-roads in the middle of cow pastures."

"That may be true," Shantee said, "but the fire board has delusions about getting all sorts of commercial and industrial development out there—I know it goes against the state planning laws—but that's the way they think. Do you know what their tax rate is?"

"No, what?"

"Around two eighty per thousand."

I whistled. "That's more than half the rate for our whole city. But I thought they were an all-volunteer department."

"Sure, that's what they'll tell you, and they do have a lot of volunteers."

"Didn't I read about some of them not too long ago?" Will asked.

"You mean the recognition banquet? Yep. Every year they throw a big bash for the volunteers, with lots of prizes—wide screen TVs, stereo systems, all terrain vehicles and a bunch of other toys like that. No one in the community ever raised their eyebrows at that. Who knows, maybe they thought it was worth it on account of all the money they were saving by using volunteers."

"But then they made the mistake of bringing in strippers, huh?"

"Yes, that's it. The wives weren't too thrilled with that and got on the fire board's case, and by some accident the whole thing finally made it onto the radar screens of the local press."

"So what do they need such a high tax rate for?" I asked. "Is their assessed value that low?"

"No. You'd be surprised. I would wager their tax base is as big as your city's. They don't have much density, but the homes they do have are pretty big, and their district is huge. No, the reality is they just like to spend money. They pay cash every couple of years for another $500,000 fire truck, and they have more full time staff than you can shake a stick at. They've got battalion chiefs and lieutenants for training, for polishing the equipment, for writing emergency plans that sit on shelves, you name it."

"And the taxpayers are okay with all that?"

"Sure, the firefighters and their department are so popular, they pretty much do whatever they want."

"So what does this have to do with our golf course project?" Will asked.

"It threatens their little fiefdom, doesn't it?" I said.

"Yes," Shantee nodded. "Anything you annex automatically leaves their tax base and gets added to yours. They're obsessive when it comes to protecting their turf. Around eight years ago, Nottingham, at the other end of their district, tried to annex 100 acres for an industrial park. Ed Mann was going around to neighborhood meetings saying that it would be over his dead body before they gave up a square foot of land. They printed up bumper stickers with a thumbs-down sign, saying, Annexation-NO. We suspected they used tax money to do it."

"That's illegal."

"Sure, but like I said, they get away with a lot. Even though the fire district is hugely popular with their residents, nobody really knows who the board members are. Few citizens ever show up at their board meetings, and the election turnout is always low. The board members are mostly former fire volunteers themselves—it's sort of a closed system. Nobody pays any attention."

"Except for the county commissioners, I gather."

"You got it, Ben. When Ed Mann and his buddies got wind of your golf course and the urban growth boundary amendment, they went ballistic. They met privately with each of the commissioners. I wasn't in the meetings, but apparently they threatened all sorts of political repercussions if the county approved the UGB change. It was fairly ugly, I think. And my board has enough to contend with right now. They just don't want that headache."

"Okay. What can we do about it?" Will said.

"Nothing, far as I can see."

"So you don't think a meeting between the city council and the county commissioners would do much good?" I asked.

"No. We could try it, but it would have to be a public meeting, and I wouldn't be surprised if Ed Mann and his entire board showed up. Even if they didn't, they would get to the commissioners soon enough, or organize some kind of 'grassroots' campaign against annexation."

We were silent for a few moments. Shantee said, "We could work with you on developing the golf course, but leave it outside your city limits."

Will scratched his head. I said, "The thing doesn't pencil out without the housing around the golf course. That's basically how you pay for the golf course land and development."

"Well, we could look at a change in our zoning to allow that," Shantee said.

"I doubt that would get past the state. At least I hope not." Unmanaged development in unincorporated areas had already made a mess of a lot of the county, but I didn't want to bring that up now.

Shantee didn't say anything.

"What about this," Will said. "Could we come up with some sort of agreement with the Fly Creek folks so that the area stays part of their fire district even if we annex it?"

"You know, that's a good idea," Shantee said.

"Well, it's theoretically possible," I said. "But it would set a precedent that I don't think our fire department—or city council, for that matter—would be comfortable with. Maybe we'll just have to be patient, and wait until Ed Mann isn't in office anymore."

"Good luck. He's been there 26 years so far and hasn't shown any signs of wanting to retire."

"Sounds like they need term limits," Will said.

"Hmm. It might be possible," I said. "They could just do it the old-fashioned way: get someone to run against him, and vote him out of office."

"Easier said than done," Shantee said. "Even though nobody cares much about the board, Mann does have name recognition, and the volunteers would get the vote out to keep him in office."

"And besides, I can't get involved in local elections," I said.

"How come?" Shantee asked.

"Part of the city management code of ethics," I said. "Thou shalt refrain from all partisan political activities, or something like that."

"But that doesn't apply to your council members, does it?"

"True. Good point."

"How about Dick Boatwright?" Will asked. "Does he live in that part of the county?"

"Yes, I think so," I said. "But why would he want to waste his time with a fire board position?"

"Hmm. Right."

We sat in silence for a few moments.

Will looked at Shantee. "This is driving Ben crazy. He doesn't accept it when there aren't any good solutions to a problem."

I laughed. "Yeah, and I can't think of anything now. Can you? And I don't think this is worth using up much political scrip with the commissioners anyway."

Will's shoulders sagged a little, and he frowned. "No, I guess not."

*   *   *

I had a six o'clock meeting with the Trillium Historic Society, and had enough time in the quiet of my office to log onto the Internet. I had sent a reply to Kate's message, but hadn't seen anything else for a few days. I watched the new mail pop onto the screen as the server downloaded the messages.

From: kanderson@rockynet.com
Subject:Reply to Reply to Depressed in Denver

Hi Ben. Thanks for writing back. I haven't had much time to get back on line, but that isn't the whole reason for the delay. If we were together, I wouldn't know what to say, and it doesn't help to sit here in front of the computer—I still don't know what to write. I know this isn't making any sense. So I guess I'll just start somewhere and see what words appear here.

Last summer when you sent those messages, I knew it could get us into trouble. But a part of me—a big part of me, really—wanted to write back and see where it would take us. When I called you, I half hoped you would talk me out of what I was saying, and that you would keep sending messages anyway.

Part of the reason I was torn was I didn't trust myself. I still don't. To tell the truth, I've been attracted to you for years. Anyway, it always made me uncomfortable, because I always felt I was being disloyal to Mary thinking that way. But at the same time, I have to admit I enjoyed it. Whenever I was around you I felt like a school girl with a crush. I didn't know how to tell you, or even if I should. You know?

So, there it is. These last few weeks have been pretty rotten. The boys are in basketball and my free time is spent carting them to practices and games. I don't mind, I guess, but it gets old. And Gordon has put hours into his work—one of his clients has some kind of virus in his network and it seems like it's hard to kill it. I sometimes wonder if Gordon is the only network programmer in Denver, his clients are so demanding. But we can use the money. The print shop has been pretty slow and I keep catching myself standing over the machines and thinking about you. We had such a good time over Christmas and I miss you.

So I finally told myself there's no real harm in some e-mail. It's not like we're being unfaithful. But I need to hear from you—write back quick. Sorry if this is making your life complicated, and if you just want to tell me news, that's fine. Just stay in touch.

Love, Kate

I got to the historic society meeting on time. Someone made a presentation on the plans for a new addition to the museum, but I couldn't pay attention.

13

A few days later, over breakfast, I opened the metro section of the *Oregonian*.

Hi Tech Company Sues Trillium Business Group

TRILLIUM—Nova Ceramics on Monday filed a $50 million lawsuit against the Trillium Business Leadership Committee. Nova, a manufacturer of precision ceramics components, claimed in the lawsuit that the business group was illegally obstructing the opening of Nova's new factory in Trillium. Alleged actions by the Trillium Business Leadership Committee hindered Nova from securing an access road to the plant, causing delays in the plant opening.

Nova vice president John Collins said, "We have enjoyed good relations with the community of Trillium, and our plant has been welcomed by the city. It is unfortunate that a small group like this has embarked upon a crusade against us." The Trillium factory is projected to employ up to a thousand residents of Trillium and the surrounding communities.

Nova's project has not been without controversy. A housing project proposed as part of the development has divided the community. According to Collins, the company plans to move ahead with the mixed-use housing component, called Nova Estates. "It was approved by the planning commission, and I am confident the city council will support it," he said.

The Trillium Business Leadership Committee was formed last year, partly in response to concerns over the Nova project. The group's president, Todd Pritchard, said that he had been advised by his attorney not to comment on Nova's court filing.

I chuckled. Mary asked what was so funny.

"Oh, it looks like the TBLC is finding themselves on the receiving end for a change." I passed the paper over to her. She had her hair in a pony tail and hadn't put on her makeup yet. She was still as pretty as the day we first met.

After a minute Mary looked up. "Is this the thing with Bruce Poulet's land?"

"Yeah, looks like it."

"So do they really think they can make a lawsuit stick?"

"Good question. I doubt it, but maybe they're just trying to make Pritchard squirm a little. If nothing else, they're going to have to shell out some dough to Terry Judd to fight this off, and those guys are cheap enough that it may take some of the wind out of their sails."

"How did Nova find out about it?"

"I don't know," I said.

*   *   *

Later, I sat in Pete Koenig's office. Oriental tapestries hung on the walls, and the room lights were muted. A green desk lamp lit up the clutter of papers and files, and the row of pipes in a holder. He had quit smoking them years ago. Just as well—some of his tobacco used to smell like cow dung, not the sweet scented mix I remembered from my father's pipe-smoking days.

We talked about the Nova lawsuit. Pete kept a professional distance from it, but I could tell he was amused.

"That's not the only headache Judd has, either," Pete said.

"Oh? How's that?"

"It seems someone has filed an ethics complaint against him with the Oregon Bar."

"Really? I wonder why someone would do that."

"Well, I know why, since that someone is me."

"So what's the story?" I asked.

Pete rummaged around in his desk. "My daughter Martha and her husband were having a late dinner last week in Finnigan's Bar and Grill. Terry Judd, Todd Pritchard, Neal Orso, and another person apparently had just had a meeting, and stopped in for some drinks. They were in the booth next to Matt and Martha. Matt, you know, was with the intelligence unit when he did his military service. They heard my name being mentioned, and started listening in—"

"Didn't the other guys know they were there?"

"I suppose so, but Matt was pretty crafty. He and Martha pretended to be huddled in a deep conversation, and at one point he started bantering with the waitress. The place was pretty crowded, I guess, and a lot of conversations were going on. They finished their dinner, and then went straight to their car, and Matt wrote down a couple pages of notes. They called me when they got home, and I asked them to write it down for me." He lifted a pile of papers on the corner of his desk. "Aha. Here it is."

Pete handed me a typewritten paper. I skimmed the first paragraph, which summarized what Pete had already told me. It read like a police report.

…when subjects 3 and 4 entered and sat down, subject 1 stated, "Well Terry, you're really earning your money. You did a fantastic job tying up Nova's access road." Small talk took place for a few minutes, then the conversation again returned to the Nova project. It was stated they thought they were wearing Bess Wilson down, and she might be ready to give up on the whole deal.

The conversation then turned to Diane McTavish. Subject 3 stated, "The Mayor is turning into a real nuisance for us. We need to start hassling her the same way we did Ben Cromarty." Subject 1 then stated, "It would be very easy to stop her." He then directed his next question and statement to subject 4 (the attorney). "Can I call her and threaten her with lawsuits, with a recall, write her threatening letters and tell her she will have to pay our legal costs?" Subject 4 stated, "I will back you on anything you want to do to the bitch as long as you do not put anything in writing. I, well we, can not afford anything in writing or in person for that matter to be traced back to us."

Subjects 1 and 2 then started talking about a street project that subject 2 was doing in front of the Mayor's house. They said how easy in would be to "accidentally" stub her sewer service off, forcing a major back up onto her property. Also they discussed how they could call her late at night and threaten her. Subject 3 then stated, "Make sure you punch in the numbers so the call can't be traced back to you. Well, the best way to do this is like I do when I make calls to people that get in our way. I always make them from different pay phones. No chance of tracing."

During the course of the evening the four made continuous derogatory statements towards the council and employees of Trillium and several of its residents. This both my wife and I found very offensive.

I handed it back to Pete. "Why didn't you tell me about this sooner?"

"Martha was uncomfortable about raising too much of a fuss with it. She agreed to let me use it in the ethics complaint against Judd, because that's handled internally by the bar association, but she didn't want it to go any farther."

"Hmm. I don't blame her for that."

"Yes."

"But don't you think this was just a bunch of guys blowing smoke over a few beers?" I asked. "They were probably joking about the whole thing."

"Could be. But as an attorney, Judd shouldn't have even been joking about harassment or illegal acts."

"Are you going to show it to the mayor?" I asked.

"Not unless you want me to. Like you say, they were probably joking. There isn't any need to—"

The phone rang. Pete looked at it for a second. "Hold on," he said.

"Hello, Koenig......yes.....now, look here....no....no....do what you want, but I don't think that would be a good idea...now look...all right then."

Pete hung up and leaned back in his chair, rubbing his forehead. "Speak of the devil," he said.

"Judd?"

"Yes. He was just notified by the Bar Association about the ethics investigation. Claims I'm harassing him."

"If you can't stand the heat, stay out of the kitchen, eh?"

"I suppose. He threatened to take it to the newspapers."

"Really? Think he will?"

"No. The last thing he needs is publicity about an ethics complaint."

*   *   *

Judge Fritz Poppen wore a black robe, but I knew that under it he had on a flannel shirt and blue jeans. The robe was as much formality as he wanted in his Trillium Municipal Court. He sat at a high bench—a smart move, since he was barely five feet tall—but he didn't care if his clerk addressed him as "Fritz," instead of "your honor," even if his customers followed her example. He dispensed small town justice while dispensing with ceremony.

I sat near the back, and watched as a few sorry souls pleaded their case.

"Yes, judge, I might have been going that fast, but the speed sign was covered by a tree."

"Doesn't matter, young man. You should know the speed limit in urban areas—it was in your driver's manual when you took the test back...when was it?"

"Uh, two years ago. But it's hard to remember—"

"All right, if you've learned your lesson, I'll save you thirty bucks, but watch your speed in our fair city, you got that?"

Fritz had pestered me for years to sit in on one of his court sessions, but I just hadn't gotten around to it. There were always more important things to do, or so I told myself. But Fritz and his court staff ran an efficient operation, bringing in $600,000 in fine revenue to the city, and he did it without causing me any headaches. I owed him the visit.

After a few more traffic cases, Fritz took a break. I figured he had ducked into his office to review the next trial, and I took the opportunity to play back the voice mail messages that had been accumulating for me. I scribbled a few numbers to call if I had the chance, and saved the rest. Nothing really urgent anyway. I was just putting my phone back in my pocket when Fritz re-appeared.

"Okay, our next case involves a Mr. Sedgewick. Are you here?"

"Yes, I'm Dr. Jonathon Sedgewick."

"All right. This case involves a barking dog. Your neighbor, a Mr. Eckhart, has complained about it many times. Are you here, Eckhart?"

"Yes, your honor."

"And in turn, we have a complaint against you. It seems that you have a boat stored illegally in your side yard. Your neighbor, Mister, uh *Doctor* Sedgewick, has also complained to us about this numerous times. Do I have the facts about right so far?"

"Yes, but—"

"Good. Okay, let's start with the boat, that's going to be the easier one to deal with. Mr. Eckhart, why don't you take a seat over here and tell me why you think this boat isn't a violation of our municipal code."

Eckhart hesitated, then moved up to a chair next to the court clerk. "Well, yes, I do have a boat, but it isn't on the street. From what I can read, parking it on the street is a violation of your city code. But my boat isn't on the street, it's parked out of sight by the side of my house. And it's been there for years. The previous neighbors, they never said anything about it. Neither did Sedgewick, until I talked to him about his dog—"

"Objection, your honor!"

"Mr. Sedgewick? Are you an attorney?"

"No, your honor. I'm a dentist."

"All right, then. I'm a lawyer, but as far as I can see, I'm the only one in this room. And I really don't have much patience for legal theatrics, as much as we all enjoy them on TV. So why don't we settle down and let Mr. Eckhart finish his story? If you have something to say to me, just raise your hand, but I would prefer it if you would just sit still there for a while. Comprendez?"

"Yes, your honor."

"Okay. Go ahead Mr. Eckhart."

"Well, that's about all there is. My boat is on private property, out of sight like I said, and it isn't bothering anyone. I keep it under a cover, and use it during the summer. Where else am I supposed to park it if I can't put it on my own property?"

"Point of law, your honor!"

"What's that I hear? I don't see your hand raised, Mr. Sedgewick *esquire*."

"Excuse me, but the municipal code is specific in prohibiting the storage of boats and recreational vehicles where they can be seen from the street. It's in section—"

"I'm well aware of that, sir. But I believe in a live-and-let-live attitude. Now, exactly how is this boat harming you, aside from this technical violation of the city code?"

"If a boat is allowed, what about other things? The next thing you know, our neighborhood will be full of abandoned cars and sporting goods. It affects my property value, too. I moved out of Lake Oswego to get away from this kind of lax code enforcement."

Fritz stared at Sedgewick. It looked like his eyes would pop out of their sockets. He eventually turned back to Eckhart.

"You seem like an educated man, Mr. Eckhart."

"Yes, I am a financial advisor and have degrees in—"

"Then in that case, let me suggest a simple solution that will allow you to keep your boat, and comply with the city code at the same time. Wouldn't that be a smart thing to do?"

"Yes, I suppose so."

"All right. Then here's what you do. You just put a fence around this boat. I assume you already have one on your side property line, between you and Mr. Sedgewick here?"

"Yes."

"Okay. Now just put the fence in front of the boat too. I know, you have to put a gate in somehow to get the boat out, but an educated man like you can figure that out, right?"

"Yes."

"And check with our building and zoning folks before you do it. Can you tell me how soon you can have this done?"

"Uh. A month, maybe two."

"All right. Polly, could you write that down for me? If Mr. Eckhart doesn't have his boat behind a fence in three months, he's getting a citation. You can take your seat now, sir."

Eckhart went back to the third row, avoiding eye contact with his neighbor.

"All right, Dr. Sedgewick, come on and join us at the table here, and tell us about your pooch."

"If it pleases the court—"

"Whoa! No legalese here. Just plain English, remember."

Sedgewick frowned. "What I'm trying to say is that I believe this case is moot.

"And why is that?"

"Dog died."

"Pardon me?"

"My dog died. There isn't a case if there isn't a dog."

"Well, I'm sorry to hear that, but why did you let this thing go to a trial? Why didn't you just tell the clerk when you got your citation?"

"I didn't plan it. Harley just died two days ago. It seems he was poisoned."

"Poisoned? How do you know? Do they do autopsies on dogs these days?"

"No, I didn't take him to the vet. He just keeled over after dinner. I buried him in the back yard. He wasn't that old—maybe twelve."

Fritz sat back and rubbed his eyes. "Well, you're right, this does simplify this case—and I'm not going to touch this poison business, that's for the animal coroner or whatever. But if you get another dog, try to make sure it doesn't bark when you're at work fixing peoples' teeth. And another thing. It seems the real crime here is that you two fellows don't seem to get along, but you live next to each other and you have to deal with that. So do me a favor."

"What's that?"

"The next time one of these things come up, just pick up the phone and call our neighborhood mediation folks. It's their job to patch things up between people. They're really good at it. Will you do that for me?"

"Yes, your honor."

"Did you catch that, Mr. Eckhart?"

"Yes, sir."

Sedgewick and Eckhart left the courtroom. Fritz climbed down from the bench and joined Polly as she gathered her papers.

"So what did you think?" he asked me.

"You did a nice job," I said.

He chuckled. "Pretty weighty legal matters, huh? I don't think any of these are going to make their way to the Supreme Court."

"No. But you know, for the last two guys, this is probably the most important encounter they're going to have with the City of Trillium. We can pick up their garbage, sweep their streets, deliver them water, and treat their sewage, and they take that for granted. But a barking dog or their neighbor's boat just gets under their skin, and it's a big deal for them. Compared to that, city hall is pretty remote and insignificant. So I don't know, Fritz, I think what you're doing here makes a lot more difference to them than esoteric points of law at the Supreme Court."

"Ha, I know you're just saying that to flatter me. But I'll take it. Come on, I'll buy you a cup of coffee."

*   *   *

Terri Knox handed me a message when I got back to my office. Mrs. Dunwoody was sitting in the reception area, wearing a yellow raincoat and scribbling furiously on a legal pad. Terri looked at her and shrugged.

The note said "Max wants you to come to his office." No voice mail for Max—he had made his secretary call Terri.

I returned a few phone calls and then walked over to the fire station. A couple of firefighters were scrubbing down a red and chrome pumper. They greeted me, but without much enthusiasm. I let myself into the office door.

"Any results yet on the firefighter sign-ups?" I asked Max.

Max looked up from a magazine. "No, not a single one. There is too much peer pressure."

"They can't look like they're buying into the plan, huh?"

"That's right. But I will tell you that a few of the guys have talked to us privately about their preferences."

"They want to make sure they stay on the fire side?"

"No." Max turned his back to me and opened a drawer in his mahogany file cabinet. "Interestingly enough, they want the medical assignment."

"You're kidding. They want to give up the 24-hour shift and cushy job?"

"Yes. They want to stay busy. Give us some credit, we're not all like Gallagher."

"How about that," I said.

"Of course, they swore us to secrecy and said they would deny they had talked to us if anyone asked." Max pulled a bright red piece of paper from a folder and sat back at his desk. "But enough of that, this is what I wanted to talk to you about."

He laid the paper on his desk. In the top corner, in black, was a large Trillium Firefighters Association emblem.

WHAT'S A LIFE WORTH?
DON'T LOSE <u>YOUR</u> FIRE PROTECTION!
**On the basis of "saving money" the City Council has voted to
ELIMINATE FIRE PROTECTION SERVICE at TWO OF THE
THREE TRILLIUM FIRE STATIONS
<u>ACT NOW</u> TO PROTECT THE SAFETY OF YOUR FAMILY
AND YOUR NEIGHBORHOOD.
<u>CALL</u> the City Council members at the numbers below.
<u>WRITE</u> to the Mayor and City Council.
<u>ATTEND</u> a City Council meeting and voice your concern. After all,
WHAT IS A LIFE WORTH?**

I groaned. "Where did this come from?"

"A friend of mine found it on his porch. Apparently the guys are going door to door passing them out. It appears to be a fairly well-organized campaign."

"Well, this will sure elevate the level of public discussion."

"How do you mean?"

"I'm using irony, Max." He frowned. I said, "Any ideas on what we should do about it?"

"No. I believe we should just leave it alone. People haven't paid too much attention to the issue so far. Perhaps they will just see this as a union issue."

"Maybe. But it's one that folks will probably be sympathetic to. So you don't think we should do a mailing to residents, that sort of thing?"

"No, with the possible exception of something in the regular city newsletter. It would be difficult to fight emotion with logic."

"Yeah, you've got a point."

       *   *   *

It was 5:45 by the time I got back to my office. The place was quiet, and even Mrs. Dunwoody was gone. I sent an e-mail to Kate. The messages were coming almost daily now, and I couldn't help myself from looking for them when I got to the office every morning. We shared news and trivia, and Kate revealed more of her feelings. This was a side to her I had never really known—it had been hidden under her cynicism and devil-may-care attitude—and I wasn't exactly sure how to respond to it. I did the best I could, for above all I didn't want to break the bond that was forming between us.

I had coffee with Maggie Henderson the next day. She was only in her mid-fifties, and was filling her time with a variety of volunteer activities. One of them was the retired teachers association. I first thought the organization was aimed at supporting education, but I later realized that their primary mission was to fight for pension benefits in Salem and Washington. She did have a variety of altruistic causes, including handicapped rights and at-risk youth, and I suspected she ran for council because she thought that it would be a way to help the needy and downtrodden. She was shocked to discover that the city provided few social services, and that she would instead spend her time on the council making tough policy decisions on issues as diverse as debt management, intergovernmental agreements, and land use planning. She may have been in over her head, and her waffling was frustrating to me and her fellow council members, but her heart was in the right place, and I admired her for having the courage to work for the things she believed in.

Maggie had one of the bright red flyers. The firefighters had actually knocked on the door and handed it to her. They didn't recognize her, and Maggie said they had been very polite.

"But when they left, I read this, and I have to say I was disturbed," she said. "It seems very one-sided and misleading. It says here we voted to reduce fire protection. But that's not what we did, is it?"

"No, of course not. The fire equipment will roll from Station One and not the other two, and we think the medical response time will actually improve. But people see fire and medical response as the same thing these days. So when the firefighters say that fire protection will be reduced, people automatically picture themselves standing by the phone waiting for the paramedics to show up while Uncle Benny is rolling on the floor and turning blue from choking on a chunk of steak."

"Well, this behavior by the firemen is not good, not good at all. Some city residents have already called me about this, and I have had a hard time explaining it to them. They think I'm being evasive or something, but it's so complicated…"

Maggie shook her head and stirred some cream into her coffee. Her blond wig made her look like a poodle that needed shearing. She said, "I'm wondering now if the people should have been more involved in this decision."

"Uh, which people in particular?"

"The *people*."

"Uh huh. Well, they did get involved by voting for Measure 5-47. And if we had made major cuts in services, that's one thing. But here, we're really just making an existing service more efficient. It seems to me that the people elect a city council to make those kinds of decisions."

"I don't know."

"Besides," I said, "the budget discussions were open to the public. The newspaper printed an article on it, so if the public wanted to comment, they could have."

"Oh. That's true."

"By the way, when residents called you about it, what did they say?"

"Mostly that they don't want to see any change in the fire department. I've only gotten four—no, three—calls. One of them was from Bill Lyons—you know him, don't you? The other two didn't give their names. They gave me a lot of statistics about how long it takes to drive a fire engine to a fire, things like that. I tried to write it down, but I couldn't really follow it."

"Hmm. That's what I expected."

"Yes. Uh, what do you mean?"

"Sorry. I meant that I'm not surprised they used a lot of statistics. Were the two anonymous callers men or women."

"Women. Both were women."

"I see. Well, I suspect that the other council members will get the same calls. And you'll get more."

"But what do I tell them?"

"Just listen, ask questions if they say anything that you don't understand, and thank them for their comments."

"Yes, but what do I say if they ask me to change my mind?"

"You could tell them the decision has already been made by the council and the budget committee, and that the meeting was open to the public. If they have any actual questions about it, have them call me or Max. And if that isn't enough, they can always come to a council meeting and speak under the public comment part of the agenda. I'm not sure what good that will do, but at least it's there."

"Okay." Maggie pulled a small notebook out of her purse. "There was something else I wanted to ask you, but I can't remember it." She flipped through the pages. "Oh yes. Bill Lyons said he had heard that the city was going to close down our well station in Trillium Heights because the water in the ground was polluted. I didn't know what to tell him. Is it true?"

"No, absolutely not." This was a new one to me. How do these rumors get started? "In the first place, we only use that well station as a backup source in the summer, and we have never had any problems with the water quality. But more important, if we ever did do something like that, you would know about it. It would involve some kind of city council decision. If you hear rumors like that, just flat tell them they're not true."

"Well, I wanted to say that, but I wasn't sure if I missed something along the way."

*   *   *

After dinner that night, Mary and I went to the supermarket for our weekly grocery shopping. The parking lot was still fairly full. Two firefighters were standing at the doors, handing out the red flyers. One was a relatively recent recruit with short black hair and a moustache. The other was older—George Richards, if I remembered right. Everyone entering the store took one of the flyers, and a man stopped to talk. As we approached, the younger firefighter held out a flyer, and Mary took it. I was wearing jeans and a sweatshirt, but his partner must have recognized me. He interrupted their conversation and glared at me.

"I'm not sure you want one of these," he said.

"Hey, George, I'm a resident just like everybody else. I'm as affected by this stuff as much as anybody." More than some, in fact—over half of the firefighters lived outside the city, on acreage where they could store their fishing boats, snowmobiles, and campers. They were protected by the Fly Creek rural fire district, whose response times were up to ten times longer than ours.

But he didn't offer me a flyer, and we kept on walking into the store.

"Isn't it against some policy for them to do that?" Mary asked.

"What, stand outside a supermarket?"

"No, I mean handing out propaganda while they're in uniform. It makes them look like they're on duty." She pulled a shopping cart out of the rack.

"Well, you're right, that's definitely a violation of department policy."

"So are you going to do anything about it?"

"Not sure we really can. Can't you see the headlines? Firefighters disciplined for protesting management decision. It would make martyrs of them."

I pulled a loaf of French bread off the shelf. It was still warm.

Mary said, "I don't know how you put up with that kind of thing." Kate had written something similar, but with stronger words.

"Hey, you work in a school. Compared to the teachers union politics, ours seems tame."

She laughed. "Yeah, but I don't have to deal with it."

*   *   *

Maybe I was paranoid, but the firefighters' attack seemed to include some non-traditional tactics. I was sitting at my desk, working up a letter to our U.S. Congressman on telecommunications regulation when I heard a commotion in the reception area. Betty Sue and Terri were looking out the window at the entrance to city hall, three stories below.

"What's going on?"

"It looks like something's burning on the steps," Terri said.

I tried to see, but the angle made it hard to get a good view. A small crowd was gathering, and a police car pulled up in front of the building.

"Guess I'll check it out," I said.

I took the stairs, with Betty Sue behind me. Out on the front landing of the building, orange flames were dancing above a clay pot. The air held a slight scent of kerosene. A woman—fairly young but with long gray hair—sat cross-legged next to the pot. She was wrapped in a brown shawl, and the flames reflected off a set of brass trinkets she wore around her neck. Several smaller pots and jugs were arrayed by her side. A uniformed officer was squatting next to her, talking firmly, but too quietly for me to hear well.

"Who's she?" I asked Marie, the receptionist.

"Beats me," she said. "She just showed up and started burning something. So I called the cops."

A car pulled into the visitor's parking lot, and after a moment Sabrina Chan got out. Either she had a police scanner, or had come for another story and just got lucky. She saw the crowd and made her way toward me.

"What's going on?" she asked.

"I really don't know. It looks like Officer Howlett has it under control, though."

The flames were starting to die. I was thinking that Sabrina probably wished she had a photographer with her. But then she whipped out a small push-and-shoot camera and stepped closer for a clear shot. The woman with the pot gave her a scornful look.

The officer stood up, and then helped the woman to her feet. She bent down and poured something from a jug onto the fire. Steam hissed into the air. Talking to herself, she began to place the smaller pots into a wood crate. The officer touched the side of the larger pot, then picked it up. The two made their way out of the crowd and put their load in the trunk of the patrol car. The officer held the back door open and waited for the woman to slide in, then closed the door and turned back toward us. I moved a few paces away, but Sabrina stayed close. A few of the other onlookers hovered near us.

"So what's the story, Mike?" I asked. The officer looked warily at the reporter, then shrugged.

"Says she's a witch. Says she came to put a curse on, well...."

"On who?"

"Well, on you actually. I don't know why, that's just what she said."

"And she needed a fire to do it?"

"Apparently. Now, I'm no expert on witchcraft, but I guess they do that sometimes. They write stuff on little slips of paper and burn 'em."

"What was in the jugs?"

"You name it. Some goat's blood, a few other concoctions, or so she says."

"Do you know why she has a beef with me?"

"No idea. But she did say you'll be dead within twenty four hours."

"Uh oh. I still feel fine now." They laughed.

"What are you going to charge her with?" Sabrina asked.

The officer rubbed the back of his neck. "Oh, I doubt we'll have any-thing the D.A. will want to mess with. I don't think she really violated any city ordinances, and I'm sure there's some sort of free speech issue here."

Sabrina cocked her head.

"I'm just going to take her over to the station and talk to her for a few minutes," the officer said. "Just to see if there's anything else we need to know about."

"What's her name?" Sabrina asked.

"Star of Sagittarius, or something like that. What do you bet we can't find that in the LEDS database, huh?"

Sabrina was trying to figure out how she could interview the witch. She would have to hang out at the police station for a couple of hours, and I doubted she would have the patience for that

                    *   *   *

I was wrong. The small article in the morning paper stood out, with it's bizarre picture. The good news, at least as far as I was concerned, was that I was still alive and reasonably healthy. Maybe Star of Sagittarius had used the wrong type of goat's blood. Mary didn't find the humor in it, though. She said her faith and her reasoning told her it didn't mean anything, but it still gave her shivers.

Sabrina hadn't had any better luck than Officer Howlett in discovering the reason for the curse. There were a few vague comments about how Ben Cromarty was putting the safety of the people in jeopardy, but that could mean anything. What was more disturbing to me was the separate article that focused on the firefighters. Sabrina Chan wrote that one too, and she didn't seek out many people who supported our position. In fairness, she did follow through with residents who objected to the change, asking what it was exactly that they objected to. Few of them were able to come up with anything concrete, but there was the usual refrain, "We didn't hear about this before," and "They should have informed us about this before making a decision." There were even a few letters to the editor that continued this theme.

I talked about it later with Betty Sue. She reckoned it was the American Way: if you don't have a good argument to use against the substance of a decision, then attack the process. It was certainly reinforced by the legal system, where criminals that were caught red-handed got off on technicalities. The problem, she said, was that people were so used to arguing against the process that they forgot it was a separate issue, and that policy decisions should stand or fall on their own merits. She was right, I thought, except that a few of the people who used the attack-the-process tactic were smart enough to know the difference, and they were shrewd enough to use any tools at their disposal.

I 4

To: kanderson@rockynet.com
From:bcromarty@ci.trillium.or.us
Subject:Missing you and wishing you were here

Hi Kate. I'm sitting here in my office. It's late but I'm too wound up to go home.

The city council just had their hearing on the appeal of the Nova housing project. It was a real spectacle. The first hour was taken up with Bess Wilson's staff report, and a logical—and dry—recitation of the benefits of the project by Nova's attorney and planner. But no one paid any attention. Someone once said that Congress is a strange place: a man gets up to speak and says nothing, no one listens, and then everyone gets into an argument. Maybe that holds true for any public hearing.

Anyway, the council was then treated to a parade of characters speaking on a variety of topics, few of which had anything to do with our criteria for allowing planned unit developments. First the Citizens for Good Planning (does anybody advocate *bad* planning?) wrung their hands over the fact that the development would include affordable rental housing, and how that would destroy their neighborhood and the value of their homes. An old guy with an Italian accent jumped on that bandwagon in a twenty-minute tirade, and somehow got in a comment about how he fought the gooks in the Philippines during WW2. I doubt Ken Ishido (Nova exec) was too thrilled with that statement.

The attorney for the Trillium Business Leadership Committee made a speech about how the city's own laws and policies "militated" against a positive decision in the case. A few tree-huggers complained that the project would mean some vine maples and a few evergreens would come down, even though none of it is old growth. Someone even managed to dredge up an Indian who claimed the place was an ancient hunting and meeting place. When the council asked him some follow-up questions, he was pretty vague. It turned out he lives in downtown Portland and has a grandfather who was a full-blooded Sioux. Not exactly a local native.

The strangest moment came when a gal who looks like Mama Cass got up and sang a few bars of Joni Mitchell's "Pave Paradise and Put Up a Parking Lot." The council just had to sit and watch. But maybe more music would have made the hearing more bearable. The save-the-trees group made such a dramatic speech that I was surprised they didn't back it up with a rendition of "Pomp and Circumstance."

All that took another three hours. If the council members weren't convinced, they were at least worn out. One of the council members—Seth Rosenberg—started the council discussion with the statement, "We've heard three hours of testimony, but there wasn't much more than fifteen minutes of substance in it." The standing-room-only crowd was shocked into silence. How dare an elected official tell the truth? Didn't he know he was supposed to suck up to the audience? But the silence lasted only a few seconds—the mayor had to use her gavel to get the meeting back to order.

Another councilor—Rob Titus—made up for Seth's honesty by praising the crowd for their intelligence, eloquence, and perseverance. He said the people had spoken, and it was clear how he should vote.

Maggie actually made a good summary, saying that the concerns about the environment were well-taken, but that if the folks didn't want any development at all, they should have forked over the $600,000 to buy the property themselves, and that as developments go, Nova's was pretty good. She also defended renters, pointing out that she rented a home herself. If truth be told, though, the Citizens for Good Planning wouldn't want either Maggie (prefers "native vegetation," i.e. weeds, to lawn) or Hank (prefers appliances and car bodies) living in their neighborhood.

Hank Arnold talked about the controls that were in place in the city code to address the concerns that had been stated, and the mayor didn't say much except that she was tired, and that she put a lot of faith in the planning commission's recommendation. So I could count the vote before they took it—four to one in favor. We still had a half dozen business items on the agenda, but the room emptied out, with a few loud comments that the council clearly hadn't listened to them. In fact, I think their problem was that the council *did* listen to them, and found their comments hysterical, inane, bigoted, self-serving, or irrelevant. But even Seth didn't put it in those terms—and you can't tell anyone I said that, either.

I know what you're thinking—I'm crazy to put up with this. But do you know what made it easier to sit through? Knowing I could write to you about it. The decision was the council's, not mine, and I could distance myself from the nonsense by taking the role as your faithful and secret correspondent.

You know that I do love you? I suppose that's easy to say/write, sitting here at my computer, but it's true. But part of loving you means I really do care about your happiness and welfare. So I have to ask you this: has our cyber romance had an effect on your relationship with Gordon?

In a strange way, it's actually made me feel closer to Mary, and I hope that's not just because she's here and you're not. It's even heated up our sex life, and yes, I'll spare you the details. So how about you and Gordon? I confess, I would be jealous if you had a relationship with anyone else, but I somehow I don't feel this way about Gordon, since his claim on you is right, and keeping that relationship strong is the only way you can be happy living there with him. OK, maybe a small part of me doesn't want to be writing this, but if I didn't, I wouldn't really love you—I would only be in love with a fantasy.

So let me know, OK?

Love, Ben

When I finally got home, Mary asked me where I'd been. I told her I had stayed after the meeting, talking.

*   *   *

The firefighters hadn't let up in their public relations campaign. They had even done a mailer to all the homes in Trillium—a tribute to the size of the union war chest they had built up over the years.

On a hunch, I pulled the red flyer out of my desk drawer and dialed the number on it.

"Hello, Trillium Firefighters Association." A woman's voice.

"Hello, could I talk to Brian please?"

"Uh, yes. Can I tell him who's calling?"

"Ben Cromarty"

A pause. "All right. Hold on."

I waited a minute. Outside my window the sky was low and dark, and it was raining again. Oregonians resented the Californians who moved up, but like the pioneers of a hundred and fifty years ago, they must have been desperate to come. The weather was so lousy that there must have been something else attracting them. I did notice that our friends who were California transplants were careful not to complain about the rain.

"Gallagher."

"Hello Brian. This is Ben Cromarty. I want to talk to you about this little war that's going on. Can I buy you a cup of coffee somewhere?"

"No, I don't think so."

"See, I don't understand the point of it. The council's already made its decision. I don't see what you have to gain by stirring the public up over a done deal."

"Oh, I wouldn't call it a done deal. Last I knew, we're still living in a democracy. It's supposed to be government of the people, by the people. We're just giving the people a chance to stand up for their rights."

"Come on Brian, don't give me that crap. It's a representative democracy—the people elect a council to make decisions like this. It's a budgetary and administrative decision anyway. You can't undo it through a referendum, if that's what you've got in mind."

"I know that. But the council is still accountable to the people, and if they refuse to listen, they can be replaced."

I squeezed the phone receiver and thought for a moment. "Look, it doesn't need to come to this—it isn't doing the community any good. You're raising questions about their safety when you know as well as I do that the issue isn't safety at all. I've given—"

"How can you sit in an office and lecture me about safety? We're the ones on the street and in the burning buildings. Don't you think that makes us a little more qualified to talk about public safety?"

"Not when you're just using it as a scare tactic. I've given your members every opportunity to be involved in this transition, and they could come out looking like heroes. Instead, once people figure out what's going on here, you're going to look like a bunch of sniveling whiners whose main priority is protecting jobs, not the public."

There was a pause. Another conversation that wasn't going the way I wanted it to.

"Well, you're entitled to your opinion," Gallagher said, "but I doubt many other people see it that way. Listen, I told you we weren't going to go for this, and I meant it. What you do is up to you, but that's the way it is."

"All right, Brian, but remember, you guys still work for the City of Trillium, not the other way around."

"So do you, Ben."

*   *   *

Betty Sue Castle and I were in my car, heading for Beaverton. I had reported the phone conversation to Ken Longstreet and Betty Sue, and they had looked at each other for a moment. Then Ken had asked, "time for Plan B?"

While we had been talking, Jake Wildavsky dropped in. I don't know how we got on the subject, but someone mentioned a summer job during college. Jake said he had worked in the woods, setting chokers and reading "Sometimes a Great Notion" at night. Ken said he had worked for his father in Seattle, putting out catalogs for his New Zealand wool products import business. I had pumped gas or worked in restaurants most of the time, except for the summer I worked on the motorcycle racing crew.

During the entire conversation, Betty Sue had been silent. Jake asked her what she did—she couldn't have forgotten, since it was relatively recent. Interestingly, Betty Sue's face had turned crimson, and she just muttered something about odd jobs. Jake made some crack about maybe seeing her dance at one of the bars on Sandy Boulevard. It did make me curious, but I knew I would never find out any more about it.

I pulled onto the freeway on-ramp and checked my side mirror. "So, has Lavar given you any more rings?" I asked.

"No, but he says he wants to take me to Reno," Betty Sue said. "What do you suppose that means?"

"Ah, maybe he wants to get lucky." Betty Sue gave me a sidelong glance. "At gambling, of course," I said. "I meant gambling."

She laughed.

The Oregon Ambulance Service office was in a nondescript business park, in a metal and glass building in a sea of asphalt. We sat in the waiting room for a few moments. The coffee table held a mixture of ambulance trade journals and hunting magazines; neither of them were of much interest to Betty Sue and me.

Joe Secomb was the president of OAS. He wore a navy sport coat and tan pants, and a moustache. He ushered us into his office and had us sit around a small round table.

"So, I hear things are heating up a little out in Trillium," he said.

"Yes, you could say that," I said. "I guess we could have anticipated it, but I had this naive idealistic idea that the firefighters would work with us. Or we could at least come to some reasonable accommodation."

"They haven't even been willing to talk with us about it," Betty Sue added.

"Yeah, but you can bet that they're getting a lot of pressure from the state and national organizations," Joe said. "If you could pull it off, they'll be facing the same thing in other communities, sort of like putting out brush fires all over. There's a lot at stake."

"I suppose." I was hoping that Joe would offer us some coffee. It was mid-morning, and I needed a caffeine fix. But he didn't—maybe he didn't intend for the meeting to last very long.

"They've made threats about a referendum, and recalling city council members," Betty Sue said. "The union contract negotiations are at a complete impasse, and we're pretty sure that if we change their shifts and assignments, they'll try to sabotage the whole thing every chance they get."

"And that's why we're here," I said. "I'm going to recommend to the city council that we enter into a contract with you for the medical side of the service."

"To save you the headache of dealing with the firefighters association?" Joe asked.

"Yes, partly," I said. "But to save money too. We'll still have to deal with them for the fire protection side, but on the medical side, I just can't see why we should pay more and have to deal with the strife too…"

"Uh huh." Joe nodded a few times, then bit his lip pensively. "Well, I'm glad you came out here first, before talking to your council."

"Yeah. Uh, what do you mean?"

"Look, here's the deal. I guessed you might be wanting to go this route, so I talked to my board about it again. Thing is, they just don't think it would be, well, prudent, to enter into this particular contract at this point in time."

"Oh? How come?"

"Well, primarily due to the negative publicity this has generated in the area. We enjoy good working relationships in the communities we're in, and we can't afford the controv—"

"But you negotiated with us in good faith, or so I thought," Betty Sue said. "How can you do this kind of double cross?" Her eyes drilled into Joe, and he looked away.

"Betty Sue's right," I said. "You're leaving us hanging here."

"Yes, I know. You have a right to be upset. And we did negotiate in good faith. It's just that this whole situation has gotten too hot for us to touch. You have to look at it from our point of view. We have our franchise in most of these communities due to our strong reputation, and we just can't jeopardize that."

Betty Sue looked at me, imploring me to do something to salvage the deal.

"You're sure about this?" I said. "I mean, what if you created a subsidiary corporation, with a totally different name and completely separate from OAS?"

Joe smiled. "What would we call it, 'Fire Union Busters'? No, I actually thought of that, but if it was a subsidiary, or at all connected with OAS, the word would get out, and the damage would be done. And if it was completely separate, what's the point for us?"

I kept silent for a while, in the hopes that the Joe would get uncomfortable and offer us something. Betty Sue held her tongue.

"Well, maybe we'll be able to work with you some way in the future," Joe finally said. "But now…it just isn't in the cards. Sorry about that." He pushed himself away from the table, as if preparing to stand. We paused for a few minutes, and then got up.

On the drive back, Betty Sue exploded. She called Joe Secomb a few names, some of which weren't exactly politically correct. I could understand her frustration. She had done all the earlier negotiations with Secomb, and her honor was at stake.

"It probably won't make you feel better," I said, "but I'll bet that from the beginning, they had no intention of entering into a contract."

"Why?"

"Well, in every community they're in, they have to suck up to the fire department. The ambulance company shows up at accidents like hyenas after the lion has made the kill. If they don't kiss up, the fire department will just take over their business. I've seen it happen before. The firefighters say, 'Hey, we're here anyway, we might as well make the transport.' Of course, that takes their rescue rig out of service, so pretty soon you get a request for more rescue units, and it ends up costing you more than it did before. But it *looks* more efficient to the public. So anyway, anything that would rile up the firefighters association would spell doom for them."

"But why did he lead me on, then?"

"Maybe he just wanted to appear helpful and accommodating. After all, there was a good chance that we would never have gone through with this, and maybe that's what he was banking on."

"Well, I say it sucks."

"Yeah, it does."

*   *   *

I hadn't heard from Kate in several days. I knew she had some kind of conference in Chicago, but figured she could plug in her laptop there. I remembered something Mary had said, a few years earlier. She had commented on the string of boyfriends that Kate had had in college. I said, that's not so unusual, but Mary had pointed out that Kate had most of the boyfriends simultaneously, and seemed to get a thrill from keeping them all around, like the way a juggler keeps a half dozen torches in the air. Mary had described an episode—amusing to me at the time—when Kate had an early evening date with one guy, then a later date with another, and in a moment of passion moaned out the wrong name.

So now I couldn't shake the image of Kate in a Chicago hotel room with some Xerox salesman. It was crazy, and hypocritical, for me to feel jealous, but there it was.

Will Samuels had drafted an update on the golf course project, and I was going over it when councilor Rob Titus marched into my office. He pulled up the side chair and sank into it.

"We've got to get off the pot on this Nova access road issue," he said, skipping any attempt at small talk.

"You're right, I've been concerned about how long it's been dragging out. I thought that Nova's lawsuit against the TBLC would shake things loose, but I haven't seen anything happen yet."

"Yes, well, we're not doing enough as a city."

"What do you have in mind?"

"It's time to condemn the son of a bitch."

"You mean the road right-of-way."

"Yes. Of course."

"But using eminent domain takes time, too," I said.

"Perhaps to set the price, but you get the land quick. Have Pete file it with the court tomorrow, and we'll have the right-of-way within a week. Nova will pay whatever it costs."

"Just out of curiosity, how come you're on Nova's side now? Didn't you vote against them on the housing project appeal?"

"The housing is a separate issue. The people had a valid concern that I had to acknowledge. Besides, I figured it had enough votes to pass, no matter what I did. But we need to get that plant open. Trillium needs the jobs."

Rob had once told me that his goal was to maximize his billable hours so that he could retire at 45. He did work long hours, and he hardly had time for his wife and his two-year-old son. I had wondered how useful that goal would be if he got hit by a truck some time in the next ten years. Once, when we were driving to a meeting, Rob sat in the passenger seat, opening his office mail. He would glance at a letter, throw it in the pile on his lap, and talk into a pocket recorder. "Margolis, fifteen minutes. Rodriguez, fifteen minutes. Trillium Auto Body, fifteen minutes."

"All right, if you want to go the condemnation route, I can schedule an executive session for next Tuesday's council meeting," I said. An executive session was closed to the public. The council members could only discuss certain issues—including pending legal action—and they couldn't make any formal decisions in the closed meeting.

"No, we can't wait that long. You have the authority to make this decision, and you know that the council wants to see this project move forward."

"Yes, but condemnation takes a council resolution."

"Well, go ahead and start the process, and we'll ratify it with the paperwork later. I don't want to drag this out in a council discussion—Maggie will be all over the place, fretting about what the people will think, and Hank Arnold won't have a clue what's going on."

"You know Rob, I appreciate your concern about this. I'll ask Pete to draft the resolution and a last offer letter to Bruce Poulet. But I've got to be up front with you—I can't take action on it until I get direction from the full council."

"Dammit, Ben, that's a chicken shit attitude. Sometimes you just need to do what needs to be done, and quit worrying about what people think."

I shrugged. The phone rang. Normally I let the answering machine take it when a council member was in my office, but this time I was glad of the interruption. It was Jake Wildavsky, on his car phone.

"Ben, I'm on my way to the sewer plant. There's been an, uh, incident that you may need to see."

"Okay. I'm on my way."

I turned back to Rob. "I've got to head down to the sewer plant. Something's going on there."

"What?"

"Jake didn't say. Look Rob, I'll get the condemnation process started, and we can have the resolution ready for the council meeting. It really won't add that much time."

"If that's your decision. I've got to get back to the office."

I couldn't figure Titus out. If Mayor McTavish had ordered me to start a condemnation process without the full council's direction, he would have been livid. I stewed over it as I drove, then pushed it to the back of my mind.

A shaft of thick black smoke rose into the air, and as I got closer, it did seem to be coming from the plant. I saw several cars—and something burning—at the far end of the plant, near the overflow basin. I parked next to Jake's truck. Silhouetted against the flames were five men.

"Looks like an unusual treatment method," I said.

"Yeah, but it works quick," Jake said.

A man wearing a hardhat with a Department of Environmental Quality sticker leaned forward. "Are you the city manager?"

"Yes."

"Hi, I'm Dan Beyer with DEQ. Well, this seemed like a good idea at the time."

The flames were dying, but reluctantly. Every few seconds the fire would muster itself on the clay floor of the basin and shoot into the air like a geyser. For several yards beyond the fence, the weeds were charred.

"So what happened?"

"You tell him, Finney," Jake said. Cap Finney was the senior plant operator.

"Well, we noticed this stream of stuff—looked like oil of some kind—coming into the plant. Luckily we caught it before it killed the bugs. We shunted the stuff into a spare cell in the aeration basin, but we didn't know what to do with it. We called Dan here, and got a guy from a septic tank service to bring his truck down. We figured we'd just pump it out and haul it off."

Finney's assistant nodded. "It was a mess. We didn't want it around here too long."

"So the guy with the truck gets it out," Finney said, "but then he tells us he's going to have to take it to Arlington, and dispose of it as hazardous waste. It would've cost a bundle. Maybe ten grand for this much stuff."

I took my eyes off the flames for a moment, and noticed that Finney's eyebrows were singed, and the hair on his right forearm had been fried into tight little curls.

"Anyway, we wondered if we could burn it off," Finney said. "Dan here said it would be all right." The DEQ man shrugged. "The overflow basin was empty, so we just spread it out over it. Took a while to get it lit. Matter of fact, we had to use a little gasoline. So when I tossed the match onto the gas, the whole thing just took off. We had to scramble to get the fork lift out of there, even though it was thirty yards away."

"Yep, it was pretty hot," Bo French said. "I didn't get in on the fun part, but even by the time I moseyed over here it still looked like the fires of hell. Quite a spectacle."

"For a while there, we wondered if the blower building was going to catch fire," Finney said.

"Did you call the fire department?" I asked.

In answer, I heard a siren, and turned to watch a pumper barreling through the plant entrance gate, followed by the fire command car.

"No," Finney said. "We had our hands too full, and besides, after the first flare up it looked like the building was safe."

The firefighters jumped out of the truck, wearing their full turnout gear. Max Oakley got out of his car, leaving the door open and the engine running.

"What's the story here?" Max asked.

Finney gave him a condensed version. As he talked, the fire was reduced to isolated flickers on the blackened clay. The firefighters walked around the area, looking for signs of embers.

"I am extremely disappointed that you didn't call us *before* you attempted this crazy stunt," Oakley said.

"Yeah, the firefighters wanted to do it themselves," Jake said. "Must be a guy thing."

"You're right," Oakley said. "Our crew would have said, 'cool, let's burn it.' Only they wouldn't have used gasoline to start it. We train them with more sophisticated methods."

The plant operators laughed nervously.

"Any idea what that stuff was, or where it came from?" I asked.

"No," Jake said. "They did keep a sample, so we can have it analyzed. Maybe a mechanic decided to dump a bunch of used oil down the sewer. As much of it as there was, it could have been that somebody backed a tanker up to a manhole cover and just poured it in. It was probably pretty close to the plant, or it would have mixed in with the sewage more. The only way we'll find out is if someone was watching and calls us."

"Well, do me a favor," Oakley said. "The next time you decide to play with fire, call us, okay? That's what we do."

"Sure."

*   *   *

The next day, the Trillium Business Leadership Committee announced that they were going to conduct a phone-in straw ballot over whether the city manager should be fired because of the Nova housing project. I tried not to take it seriously. A few well-meaning friends called to offer their condolences, as if I had some kind of terminal disease. Mary was furious about it, and I wished I would hear from Kate.

15

My pack was heavy—I was carrying most of the food, the stove, and the tent—and my skis sank deep into the snow. Trixie was able to keep up, sliding her skis along the track I made. On the west side of the Cascades it was probably still cloudy, but here the sky was a brilliant blue, and even with sunglasses, the white peaks of the Three Sisters were almost too bright to look at. The air temperature was well below freezing, but with the sun and exertion, I was building up a sweat.

"How are you doing, buddy?" I asked.

"Okay, Dad. Whose idea was this anyway?"

"If I remember right, it was yours. Didn't you say it looked like I needed a break?"

"Oh yeah. I guess I didn't think it would take so much work."

We stopped for a rest, sitting on our skis in the snow. I had put the water jug in the pack, next to my back to keep it from freezing. I pulled it out, and tossed a chocolate bar to Trixie. Far overhead, a jet drew a white trail across the sky, and I could hear a faint echo of the rumble of its engines.

"How much farther?" Trixie asked.

"Oh, I don't know. We're high enough already, and we have to get our camp set up before we run out of daylight. Maybe another mile or two."

"Can we climb one of those mountains?"

"I thought you said *this* was hard work!"

"Oh yeah. But they seem so close. Wouldn't it be cool to look around from up there?"

"Yes, it really would. Maybe if the weather holds out, we can climb up a ways tomorrow."

We set up our dome tent on a flat spot in the snowfield. It was well above the timberline, and the only thing that anchored the tent was the weight of our packs. We crawled into it to get out of the cold as the sun sank behind the Cascades.

"Here." I handed Trixie a small pot. "Reach out there and put some snow in it." I carefully poured some white gas into the camp stove through a small funnel, and dribbled a little extra on a piece of starter briquette. I struck a match on the zipper of my pack and lit the starter, checking to see if the blue flames had sneaked down the side of the stove to the tent floor. After a minute I figured the burner was hot enough. The thin air at our elevation sucked out the hot fuel, and the stove roared. The snow melted almost instantaneously. Trixie dumped in the contents of a couple of packets of freeze-dried soup.

The tent warmed up quickly. After the soup and a half baguette of French bread, we heated up some hot chocolate. I opened the tent flap and stuck my head out. The stars seemed close enough to touch.

"Take a look at this," I said.

Trixie slid up to the tent opening and rested her head on my arm. "How come there are so many more of them out here? Is it 'cause of the smog in the city?"

"Partly. Up here the air's thinner and cleaner. But I think it's mostly because there aren't as many lights to drown them out."

I kept my eyes wide, hoping to see a shooting star. The frost from our breath made the starlight shimmer.

"You know, a lot of those things that look like stars are really other galaxies, like the Milky Way. Pretty cool, huh?" Trixie said.

"Yep. Billions and billions of stars." I tried to sound like Carl Sagan, but for Trixie it wouldn't have meant anything.

"So Dad, do you think there are other people out there?"

"There's probably some lonely Russian in a space station."

"You know what I mean. On another planet."

"Like E.T., huh? Well, you know, I'm not sure. There have to be other planets, and there are so many suns out there that it hurts my head to try to think of it. But I read somewhere that you need exactly the right conditions for life. Just the right distance from the sun, just the right chemicals on the planet, just the right temperature, just the right amount of time for evolution to do its thing. And the chance of all that happening randomly is, like, one in a really big number. Some people think that really big number is bigger than the number of stars out there, so as big as it is, the universe isn't big enough to make life happen by random chance. Does this make sense?"

"Uh. Not really."

"Well, here's something else to confuse you. One of the things you need for life is to have just the right amount of stuff in the universe. If there wasn't enough, stars and galaxies would never clump together, and everything would be thin and cold. And if there was too much, there would be so much energy flying around that we would be nuked before we even started. So…maybe God needed to put all those billions and billions of stars out there just to keep everything in balance, and make it possible for life right here on earth. What do you think about that?"

"Hmm. I think it's kind of scary."

"How's that?"

"Well, what if we are all alone? And what if we mess up? People don't seem to be doing too good a job taking care of the place, with all the pollution and people killing each other. You know?"

"I suppose."

*   *   *

I awoke to a gray light and complete silence, except for my daughter's breathing. I bundled up and went outside to pee. The tent was coated with a couple of inches of snow, and all I could see in every direction was white. The forecast had been for clear weather, but the combination of storms off the coast and an east wind howling out of the Columbia gorge made accurate predictions almost impossible. Every time the jet stream shifted, we got served up a different batch of weather. I followed my boot tracks back to the tent, and lit the stove to cook a bowl of oatmeal and a cup of coffee.

Trixie stirred. "You hungry?" I asked. She just groaned and huddled deeper into her sleeping bag.

It was still snowing when we broke camp.

"Where are we gonna go?" Trixie asked.

"Well, since there's not much to see, I think we might as well make our way back down," I said. The problem was, I wasn't sure how we were going to do that. Our tracks from yesterday were completely obliterated, and in the whiteout, it was even hard to tell which way was down. I had had the foresight to bring a compass, but all that could do was keep us in the right general direction. At least there were no crevasses or steep canyons below us, as far as I knew.

"Stay in my tracks, and if I go too fast, let me know, okay?"

"Yeah."

The wind picked up and whipped the snow into a thick froth, making it hard to see my skis. In a moment of panic, I thought I had lost Trixie. I froze and called her name. She was over the back of my skis before I saw her.

"Are you having any trouble finding my tracks?" I asked.

"No, its easy. That's the only place my skis want to go."

"Good."

We continued in what I hoped was a straight line, checking the compass every few minutes. At one point my skis broke into thin air and I plunged six feet down a steep bank. I rolled into the powder at the bottom and called a warning to Trixie, but it was too late. She whooped when she hit the drop off and crashed into me, giggling. "Can we do that again?"

"No, that was exciting enough for me. Let's just take a break here. Want some water?"

"Sure. Got any of that trail mix stuff?"

The bank gave us some shelter from the snow as we rested. On an impulse I reached into my pack for the cell phone, and took my gloves off so I could work the buttons.

"Whatcha doing?" Trixie asked.

"I'm just going to call Mom and tell her we're okay."

The roaming light turned on, and the battery level barely registered. I got a dial tone and punched in the numbers, but the phone went dead before I could get a connection.

"No answer," I told Trixie. We were alone in the middle of the Three Sisters Wilderness with a cell phone that didn't work. The folks at the Survival School wouldn't have approved. My finger tips were numb even with my gloves back on. "Let's keep moving to stay warm," I said.

We struggled on for another two and a half hours. In places the snow had drifted so deep that I had to kick my skis through it. There was no way I was going to float on top with a heavy pack on my back. But the snow was so light that it was hard to tell where the surface ended and the atmosphere began. We didn't seem to be making much progress, and I had no idea where we were. I thought about Mary and about Kate, and said a silent prayer. At least the compass kept us from going in circles.

We stopped for a lunch break of apples and cheese and a few Snickers. "Are we close to the trail?" Trixie asked me.

"I think so. We ought to hit the trees before too long. Are you tired?"

"Not really. I think you're doing most of the work, Dad."

I decided to change direction and head due east, figuring that would take us to the tree line quicker. There was a change in the light pattern, and at times I thought I could see rock outcrops twenty or thirty feet away.

Finally we reached a few stunted trees, permanently bent over from the wind. Nothing looked familiar, though. We turned north, skirting the edge of the tree line and looking for some sign of the trail. The visibility continued to improve.

At one point we hit a large stand of trees, and I decided not to go uphill to get around them and instead picked a path between them, trying not to fall into the tree wells surrounding the trunks. We stopped for a water break and I looked around. "Hold on," I told Trixie. "I'm going to check something out."

I thought I could see a paint mark on a tree a hundred feet away. I made my way over to it, but I couldn't tell if it was a trail marker, or something that the foresters had put there for some reason of their own. I squinted to see any features that would line up with my green trails map. In the summer, a line cut in the ferns and undergrowth would have revealed the path, but now the ferns and huckleberry bushes were buried under ten feet of snow. Something drew me downhill slowly.

Another blue mark appeared on a trunk. There was a linear depression under the branches of a massive fir, and I slid my skis into it. They moved on their own, pulled straight down the fall line, following the track we had left the day before.

I called for Trixie. No answer. I re-traced my path, shouting her name. Where had she gone? At the point where I had left her, a pair of tracks led off into the trees. Uh oh. She couldn't have decided to look for the trail on her own, could she? She was impetuous enough to do it—like Kate in that way. I followed the tracks, holding down my panic. As the forest got thicker, I suddenly came on her skis, thrown into a snow bank, with a set of boot tracks leading away.

"I had to go to the bathroom," Trixie said, sinking to her knees in the soft powder as she worked her way back to the skis.

"You had me worried there."

"Sorry."

"Guess what?" I said.

"You found a McDonald's around the corner? I'm starving."

"No, you knucklehead. I found the trail."

"Oh, good. I thought it was around here somewhere."

She grinned at me, deep brown eyes twinkling under her red wool cap. I gave her a one-armed hug.

The time passed quickly as we went gliding along the path. The knot in my stomach eased, but other demons settled in to haunt my thoughts. Why wouldn't the TBLC ease off for a while? What was really going on with Rob Titus? What had I done to lose Kate—was it the part about Gordon? Maybe it was none of my business, I shouldn't have brought it up.

By the time we got to the car, the sky had cleared. The South Sister looked down at us smugly, surrounded by a placid crown of blue.

*   *   *

"Forget it. We're not going to jump into that." Diane McTavish spit the words out. When I had told her about my conversation with Rob Titus, her face had flushed. This was going to get sticky.

"Umm. I agree, it wouldn't be a smart thing to do, but as a councilor, Rob is free to bring it up for discussion. I promised him we would schedule an executive session on it. He wanted me to just go ahead and file the eminent domain paperwork, but at least I held him off from that. He was kind of peeved, though."

"He has absolutely no right to do that. Who does he think he is?" I just looked at McTavish. Technically, the mayor had no more authority than council members under our city charter—except for chairing the meetings—but I didn't reckon this was the time to point that out.

"No, we won't do it," McTavish said. "Even talking about it will leak out and we'll have those Business Leader Curmudgeons all over our case. Forget it—"

"But it puts me in kind of an awkward position. Rob already thinks I'm dragging my feet. You can try to talk him out of it if you want, but I sure didn't have any luck."

"Aw Ben, have some guts. Don't let him throw his weight around like that."

"All right, but what if the roles were reversed here? What if you felt as strong about it as he does?"

"I might feel that strong, but I wouldn't be that stupid."

Out in the reception area, Terri Knox was laughing with Betty Sue. Terri was wearing something that looked like a maternity blouse, but she hadn't said anything to me.

"Okay, I'll talk to Rob," McTavish said. "Just keep it off the agenda."

*　　　　　　　*　　　　　　　*

After an endless process of grievances and appeals, the firefighter that Max Oakley had fired for blowing the lock off a door in a drunken fit was down to his last hearing. We sat in the council conference room—I was flanked by Pete Koenig and Max Oakley, and the firefighter had in his corner Brian Gallagher and an attorney in a gray suit whose name I had forgotten.

I was impatient with the whole process, but this meeting promised to be interesting. Max had told me that he had heard through the grapevine that the firefighter had concocted a new story. The new version, apparently, was that the guy had gone outside to take a leak, and had stumbled across a cougar in the woods. In order to protect the partying crowd, he had grabbed his shotgun, and as he was running back to the house, he had tripped and the gun had gone off by accident when he hit the ground.

Gallagher began the meeting with a prepared speech about how it was his duty to protect his members from the arbitrary and capricious actions of management staff. While he did admit that some mild form of discipline would be acceptable, the alleged incident had occurred outside the workplace and the firefighter hadn't even been prosecuted by the local authorities.

I wasn't surprised by that. The young couple that had hosted the party wasn't about to file a complaint. I had read the police report, filed by the deputy who responded to the call. He had exercised a fair amount of discretion in ignoring the fact that a number of the guests seemed to be under the influence—and in possession—of a variety of controlled substances.

Gallagher had barely got through his speech when the firefighter blurted out that he was, in any case, innocent. We would understand if only he could share the truth about what had happened.

Come on, I thought, spill it. The police report showed clearly that the buck shot had sprayed into a close pattern on the floor, and there was no way he could have stumbled and made those holes. Lying in a disciplinary hearing was clear and uncontestable grounds for dismissal, and it would be the quickest way to wrap this up.

But the lawyer shot his client a stern look. The story never came out. We sent the firefighter out of the room, and negotiated a compromise where he would be reinstated, but without back pay, and with an agreement to participate in an alcoholism program. It didn't seem right to me, and Max listened to most of the negotiations in stony silence, but Pete had counseled me that it was about the best we could get without getting into an expensive legal battle.

*   *   *

I was trying to come up with some excuse to call Kate when I finally saw the message I had been waiting for.

From:kanderson@rockynet.com
Subject:I'm back....

Hi my electric lover. I got your messages—sorry to keep you waiting. I couldn't get my internet connection to work in Chicago and then when I got home this two bit rockynet gang of thieves was messing with their modems or something like that. Gordon offered to let me use his work account for e-mail, but I'm not quite crazy enough to send a message to you that way. I had visions of you hitting the Reply button to one of my hot messages, which would be a little hard to explain. I missed you, though.

Since you asked, the Chicago party, I mean conference, was OK. The business sessions were pretty boring, but I hung out with some friends I had met earlier and we had a good time. I really wished you were there—that would have been a GOOD time, nudge nudge wink wink—but then I wouldn't have learned about the latest full duplex color copiers or whatever it was they were trying to sell us. I say that with my tongue firmly in my cheek…but it would rather be in yours.

This e-mail intimacy is frustrating some times, but it is safe sex, I guess.

Sorry to hear about the jerks you have to deal with there. I don't know how you do it. I still think you should quit. But that's probably not the advice you want to hear from me. Ok, I admire you—keep up the good fight. Somebody has to do it. Oh, screw it, Mary is better at this sort of thing than me. Here's what I say—find a way to put prozac in their water. You control that, don't you? I'm a little punchy here, I know it, but it's late at night and I can't sleep.

There was something that came up at the conference that I really do need your advice on. Some of the print shops are branching into all sorts of business services. You know, like Kinkos, but some of the independents are doing it too. The people I talked to said they get a bigger profit margin on some of it, but the main thing is it increases their overall business.

So here's the deal. The rest of the space in my building is up for lease. I talked to the owner about it. He said, why don't you buy the whole thing and I got thinking about it. I would have enough space for the usual junk—faxes, Internet stations, maybe even some small-scale video conferencing. But I could easily fit an espresso bar and some good tables and chairs. This place is lousy with people who work out of their homes (yeah, like Gordon) who just need someplace to get away to for a while.

They already hang around the shop and waste my time when I'm trying to get work done. And if you want to talk about profit margin, wake up and smell the coffee, ha ha.

I sort of pencilled it out and it seems to work. But it's a big risk. I'd have to put up everything we have in the business to back a loan for the building and remodeling and extra equipment. Maybe I'm just bored with the way it's going now, and this is just a crazy idea. But I always thought you had a good business sense, and for a bureaucrat, you seem comfortable with risks. That's partly why I love you. So what do you think?

Anyhow, I eagerly wait your reply.

Love, me

p.s., you asked about how things were going between Gordon and me. Just peachy. Don't feel guilty about driving a wedge between us—there already was one, for a long time. But we're working on it. I don't have any delusions—fantasies maybe, but not delusions—about dumping him and living with you happily ever after, etc. Somewhere deep within me is a small voice of common sense that occasionally squeaks out (I want to strangle it) and I can still tell the difference between fantasy and reality. So believe it or not I do try to be a good wife and a good mother. I sound so old saying that, whack me with a Ladies Home Journal. Good night sweetheart, before I ramble on any longer...

I hit the Reply button.

To:kanderson@rockynet.com
Subject:Reply to: I'm back….

Kate, thanks for your message. It was a ray of sunshine in this cloudy weather. I don't have much time to write now, but you know what? You could actually call me about your business idea. That isn't anything that Gordon or Mary would find unusual, and it would give me an excuse to hear your voice. Do it this evening if you get this message in time. I should be home by 8 your time. Until then….
—love, bc

I hit the Send button and Bess Wilson burst in.

"Guess what?" she said.

"Ok, what?"

"Bruce Poulet just came in and said he would dedicate the right-of-way to us."

"Well all right! This will get things moving again." And get Rob Titus off my back. "What made him change his mind?"

"All he said was that Nova made him an offer he couldn't refuse. You know, I think he wanted to do it all along, but he was just getting leaned on by Pritchard and his crowd."

Bess plopped into the side chair by my desk. She picked up a paperweight—a chuck of smooth glass with a copper version of the city seal in the center—and twirled it around in her fingers. It looked like she might have actually put on nail polish in the recent past, but it was mostly worn off now.

"Just out of curiosity, did he mention the Nova lawsuit against TBLC?" I asked.

"Nope. It didn't come up. But maybe he knew that Pritchard couldn't push the issue with him with that hanging over their heads." She put the paperweight back on my desk. "Do you think Nova will drop the suit now?"

"Hmm. I don't know. You know, I bet they won't, just to make TBLC squirm a while longer, and make them pay Judd some more legal fees. But they'll probably drop it before the court date. They can still claim damages from the delay, but it will be sort of moot if the road is built by the time they show up in court."

Bess nodded. "You're probably right. By the way, did you know that Nova is talking about buying another forty acres, supposedly for future expansion of their plant?"

"No. Where, though? There isn't that kind of land left."

"Well, that's the problem. They're looking at a piece next to their property, but to the west, which puts it outside the urban growth boundary. Collins called to ask me what it would take to get inside the UGB. I said, like, hell freezing over, but it didn't seem to faze him."

I rubbed my eyes. "That's all we need, another controversial land use issue involving Nova."

"No kidding."

I always wondered about Japanese electronics plants surrounded by huge campuses. The land was for expansion, they said, but in fact they rarely expanded, and often scaled back their operations. If business was good, they built factories at other sites, arguing that they needed to tap into other labor markets. It seemed that the land was the important thing, and that the factories were a secondary issue; a plum to keep the locals happy.

"You know what they should do," I said.

"No, what?"

"They should go ahead and buy the land, or at least get an option on it. Then in the future, when they've maxed out their existing site, they would have a much better argument for expanding the urban growth boundary. All they'd have to do then is dangle another 500 jobs in front of our eyes."

"You're right. They say they don't like dealing with uncertainty. They want to be sure the land is buildable. But hey, that's life."

The phone rang. "Go ahead and take that. I gotta go," Bess said. She stood up and sauntered out of my office.

The caller was Matt Monroe, with City/County Fire Services in Las Vegas. He said he wanted to fly up to meet with me, and what would be a good time. Any time, I told him. I had been hoping to hear from him. I pencilled a date in my calendar for the following week.

*　　　　　*　　　　　*

Mary answered the phone when Kate called. They talked for about twenty minutes while I sat in the living room and tried to skim through the stack of professional journals in my briefcase.

"Kate has a question for you," Mary called from the kitchen. I went in and picked up the phone.

"Hi Kate."

"Hi ya."

"Well?"

"Okay, where should I begin? I'll spare you the details. So I'm looking at this business decision, whether to buy out the rest of my building. Here's what I've got so far." She summarized the costs she'd figured for the building mortgage, the loan costs for start-up equipment and tenant improvements, and extra part time staff. Then she went over revenues, down to the level of how many cups of coffee she would need to sell.

"Wow," I said. "You have given this some thought, haven't you? What do you need me for?"

"Hmm, now there's a loaded question."

I laughed. "All right, I walked into that. But here's a better one. I'm having a hard time picturing you sitting around yucking it up with cus-tomers who just come in to hang out. But that's what you're going to need to do to keep the place busy. You want to be the 'Cheers' for the Denver home-based business crowd, but how are you going to deal with the Cliffs and Norms of the world who just come in to buy coffee, shoot the breeze, and maybe buy a few office supplies?"

"Yeah, I've thought about that. Actually, I'm better in the customer service department than you might think. Plus, I was thinking of hiring a studly coffee hunk—uh oh, Gordon's giving me a strange look. Okay, make that a barista babe—who would handle most of the small talk department. So what do you think?"

"That sounds good," I said, "if you've got the wages figured into your calculations. And having some more staff around could help take some of the load off you, too."

"Uh huh. But it would give me more personnel headaches to deal with. There are so many trade-offs."

"Sure." I drank in the sound of her voice, wishing the conversation would never end. "You know Kate, I haven't heard you sound so fired up about your business for a while. Maybe you should just go where your heart takes you."

"Mmm. Speaking of which, do you want to know what I'm wearing?"

"Huh? Okay, what?"

"Just a bra and undies. Well, and socks, but they're coming off right now."

"Oh." My mind formed a picture, and I felt an almost forgotten sensation at the base of my stomach. "So what does Gordon think about this?"

"He's downstairs, watching the tail end of the Lakers game. Speaking of tail end, I'm sliding my undies off now. There. If I can keep from dropping this phone...okay, now my bra's coming off. Well what do you know? There's still a tan line from last summer. I'm completely naked, Ben, what do you think about that?"

I glanced at Mary. She was bent over a sheet of paper, writing a note to her parents. "I'm thinking this maybe isn't such a good idea."

"Really? But it's bedtime, and I've really been looking forward to undressing with you on the phone. It's actually kind of thrilling."

I fumbled for a response. "Um...you talked about some video phones in your new business? Now that opens up some possibilities..."

She laughed. "Well, I've got my fuzzy blue bathrobe on now...even though I'm too hot to want to wear anything. Look what you do to me."

"Always glad to help."

"Goodnight, Ben," she purred.

"Goodnight, Kate." I tried to keep my hand steady as I placed the phone back on the hook.

"So she's thinking of expanding her business?" Mary asked.

I paused, not sure I could trust my voice. "Yeah, that's what it looks like."

"Why don't you think it's a good idea?"

"How's that?" I asked.

"Isn't that what you said? Maybe it isn't such a good idea?"

"Oh, right. Well, it's pretty risky. They would have to invest a lot into it and wait it out for a few months before they really would know if it would work. But it sounds like she wants to go ahead with it."

I went to the sink and poured myself a glass of cold water.

16

It seemed like it had rained every day for the last three months. Most of the time it was a light drizzle—nothing to carry an umbrella for—but as always, the wet winter was overstaying its welcome. Although, come to think of it, I had been able to walk to and from work when I didn't have night meetings, and I never got really wet.

The firefighters' effort to stir up public opinion had kicked into high gear. There was an unending chain of letters to the editor in the local weekly paper, most of which I guessed were written by relatives and friends of firefighters or their union brethren. Firefighters, in uniform, started showing up at neighborhood association meetings, even though they had rarely attended in the past. They were ostensibly there to talk about fire prevention, and just happened to be available to answer questions about the imminent threat to public safety that would occur with fewer fire crews. A columnist for the *Oregonian* took up the cause, with a cynical piece that boiled down to the cliche, "if it ain't broke, don't fix it."

On the other side of the metro area, in Troutdale, someone died in an apartment fire, and the Trillium Firefighters Association jumped on the news like a pack of drooling hyenas, trumpeting the message, "IT COULD HAPPEN HERE." No one made any mention of the fact that the young single mother had died of smoke inhalation long before anyone called the fire department. Her ten-year-old son had pilfered the battery in the smoke alarm for his Game Boy, and the fire department's response time was never a factor.

I had a strategy session with Betty Sue Castle and Max Oakley. Betty Sue argued that we couldn't just sit still, that we had to respond to the allegations and misinformation. Max countered that almost anything we did would be seen as defensive and self-serving, and that we should trust in the common sense of the public.

"Common sense?!" Betty Sue squinted at Max. "PT Barnum was right when he said you can't underestimate the intelligence of the American public. If the public had any common sense, we wouldn't be in this tax rollback pickle in the first place."

"But you must admit that some of the staff's arguments are valid," Max said. "They do have some experience in this area."

"Yeah, and here's my opinion about that," Betty Sue retorted. "I was at a party last Saturday, and a friend of a friend was there with her husband, who happens to be a firefighter. He didn't recognize me, thank God. I sat there eating nachos and cheese and listening to this guy spout out drivel to all the assembled guests. He informed us that having fewer fire crews would clearly lead to more deaths, but that the public's top priority was public safety, and that the city council was coming around and would rein in the city manager any day now. He used big words, like 'utilize our apparatus more efficiently,' but it was obvious, at least to me, that he was spouting the party line from rote memory, and—"

"Now, how can you say that?" Max demanded.

"Easy. Look, here's a guy that probably barely made it through high school, maybe got good enough grades to pass, as long as it didn't interfere with his JV football team and going out in the woods killing animals with his old man. So he finds himself with a diploma and no skills, and falls into firefighting because it's a macho job and not too intellectually demanding. Sure, he's got to memorize a bunch of responses to situations, like an army private getting drilled on taking apart his rifle, but his knowledge of medicine and biology is at best superficial. And he starts to get a thrill when he shows up at accidents and people treat him like a hero, like an expert. This happens enough times that he gets an overblown opinion of his own knowledge and intelligence, and suddenly becomes an authority on fire and medical strategies and tactics. He can lecture people at parties on the right way to manage a forty-person department, and he comes off as a big expert, but the fact is he couldn't figure out how to pour piss out of a boot with instructions printed on the heel." She stopped to take a breath.

"Tell me, Betty Sue," I said, "how do you really feel about this?" She looked at me for a moment. Then her shoulders sagged and she laughed. So did Max.

"I don't agree with your characterization of firefighters," Max said, "but you are correct about one thing. There are belief systems involved here, not just cold hard facts and analysis. And it is hard to use data and logic to change belief systems. For centuries, the Catholics believed it was a sin to eat meat on Friday. Suddenly the Pope tells them they can eat meat on Friday, but it was hard for a lot of people to do it. They thought, 'What if he's wrong and I go to hell?' Now, you can dig into the Bible and make logical arguments one way or another on what people should eat, but it is simply a hard thing to change beliefs. And I think you will find that this is true of many professions, not just ours."

"So exactly what belief is it that we're up against here?" Betty Sue asked.

"Well, it resists simple definition. But one of them is that it is the firefighter's job to rescue people, period. They are the ones who are supposed to come to the rescue. That means fires, accidents, medical emergencies. That's why fire departments rescue cats in trees. That's why you're seeing things like water rescue units, haz-mat teams, and teams equipped to rappel off cliffs and perform mountain rescues."

"Okay, so maybe we just emphasize that what we're creating is a fire rescue team, and a medical rescue team. What's the difference?"

"We must go back to the belief system principle. Don't forget that it is often the same individuals that are on all these units and teams. Again, the belief says, our job is to come to the rescue, and anything that goes against this is an attack on the American flag. Don't put blinders on, Betty Sue. You're operating from the belief system that says we should do things based on cold hard logic, but perhaps that is a view that isn't universally held."

"Maybe so, but that's why we're in the dark ages in so many areas."

"This may all be true," I said, "but at this point it's too late to win over the firefighters. Our challenge now is with the public. What do we do to inject some rational discussion in the hysteria that's floating around now?"

Max got up and poured himself a cup of coffee. "I propose a forum where these issues can be aired," he said. "We can share the same analysis with the public that we did with the council. Let them see the data for themselves."

"Okay, that's a possibility," I said. "The only problem with it is that people don't like to go to forums to learn things, they like to go to forums to talk, to tell other people what to do."

"Sure, we'll just get mobbed by the Association and their mouth-pieces," Betty Sue said.

"How about this," I said. "We're probably seeing and hearing from the folks on the extreme ends of this issue. I've got to believe there's a large block of people in the middle, who may have some questions and concerns, but generally have an open mind. We'll never get them to a forum, but if we mail them some information, they may actually read it."

"I don't know," Betty Sue said. "Nine out of ten of them will just throw it out with the other junk mail."

"Right, but at least we've reached the one person out of ten."

Max shrugged.

*   *   *

I met with Matt Monroe at a Shari's restaurant near the Portland Airport. His company, City/County Fire Services, served as the contract fire department for Las Vegas and several other cities in the southwest. From what I knew of them, they claimed to be more efficient than city fire departments because they "operated like a business." But I wondered if it really had something to do with the relative lack of union strength in their part of the country. And it seemed they had independently come to the same conclusion as Betty Sue on the separation of fire and medical services. A former colleague of mine—the assistant city manager of Reno—served as a volunteer firefighter for City/County, and I knew he dealt with fires only, and never responded to medical calls.

The temperature was mild, by our standards, but Monroe had been wearing an overcoat when I picked him up at the airport. He had high cheekbones and hawk-like eyes. We ordered bowls of chowder and talked about the weather and the quality of Oregon microbrews and the UNLV basketball season, before getting down to business.

"So Ben, you're probably wondering why I came out here."

"Yes, I'm mildly curious."

"Well, part of it is that I just want to find out what's going on with your city—I've heard a lot of rumors, but I'd like to get it from the horse's mouth, if you'll pardon the expression."

"Actually, it's a pleasant change to be associated with that part of a horse's anatomy," I said. "I've been called a lot worse." He laughed.

I described our budget challenge, and the analysis that Betty Sue had done. Monroe nodded, occasionally jotting a note in a planner he carried.

"It does make a lot of sense," Monroe said. "But I can see why the union is fighting it so hard. You know what they say about the fire service. 'Two hundred years of tradition unfettered by progress.'"

I chuckled. "That's about it."

"And the ambulance company—Oregon Ambulance Service, did you say?—turned you down?"

"Yep."

"Hmm." Monroe picked up a salt shaker and turned it in the air, watching the light shine through the facets cut in the glass. I gave him time.

"When you first talked to OAS," Monroe asked, "did you talk at all about ambulance service and the revenue that brings in?"

"No, at least I don't think so. My assistant, Betty Sue, handled the discussions. What's the issue there?"

"Well, here's how I see it. You were on the right track with OAS, but the contract you would have had with them—if they had had the courage to carry through with it—would have cost you more than it needed to. See, here's a little secret of the trade. The ambulance service—transporting people to a hospital—is a profit center, and cities are crazy for not getting a piece of that."

"Some do, actually."

"Yes, but not very many. And the ones that do always have a lower net cost for their fire department, because for a change they actually have something they can bill insurance companies for. Matter of fact, if a transport is involved, the ambulance fees can cover the whole response cost."

"Yes, but not everyone has insurance, or the right kind of coverage. Not every transport is going to bring in money. And a lot of emergency medical responses don't result in a transport, either."

"True, but how much are you billing for now? You're making medical house calls for a lot of people who are well off, and for people who have plenty of medical insurance. What kind of sense does that make?"

"So what do you propose we do?"

"Well, here's the angle I'm looking at. Now, understand I'm just exploring it, and can't make any commitments until we can take a closer look at it. But if City/County can provide your EMS service, and if you throw ambulance service in with it, I think we can do it at a fraction of the cost you're paying now."

"And this is because you're netting out the billings to insurance companies."

"Right. Plus, we do operate very efficiently."

"Well, let's talk about that. The way we've got it now, our crews often beat the ambulance company to an accident. But people have come to expect a quick response, and in fact, that's something we've pledged in the reconfiguration of the fire department. Does your higher efficiency really translate into less service?"

"No, not at all. Response time is simply a matter of having the right resources at the right place at the right time. We can configure our service to any response time you specify. True, the higher the service, the more it costs, but I think you'll find that we can beat anyone on cost."

"Would you be able to offer jobs to our firefighters?"

rse, we make a point of doing that. It would be at the pay and benefits we set, though."

Meaning less pay and benefits, no doubt. "So that's part of the secret to your efficiency?"

"Some, but a smaller part than you might think. Sure, the entry level is lower, but most of our management positions are occupied by people who were previously in the municipal fire service, and I can assure you that they're very satisfied with their situation. And all of our staff participates in our gain-sharing program, where they receive bonuses based on the financial performance of the company. These bonuses can be very substantial, and this creates a tremendous incentive for efficiency."

I thought about Max's observation about belief systems. Maybe it took one set of beliefs about capitalism and profit to trump another set of beliefs about doing things the way they had always been done. If so, it wasn't a card I had to play, but City/County might be able to pull it off.

"Okay," I said, "but how about this problem. We're going through enough turmoil in attempting to reduce the number of fire crews. Turning the whole medical area over to a private company might be just too big of a leap."

"You were facing that issue with the OAS contract, right?"

"Yes, and frankly, I didn't know how it would play out. But of course it ended up being a moot issue."

"All I can say is, come to the communities we're in now. When you see a pumper or rescue rig roll down the streets of Springfield, it looks exactly like a City of Springfield rig, and when the staff jump out of it, their uniform says City of Springfield Fire & Rescue. Think of it as a unit within your own organization. True, it may operate by a slightly different set of rules, but I think you will find that we fit in very well with your government and your community."

Something he said sent off a warning bell. "You said 'Fire & Rescue.' You're not looking for the fire contract too, are you?"

"No. To tell you the truth, I'm intrigued by the experiment you've got going here, and I want to see how it turns out. Contracting that out would just muddy the waters. But I also know that, over time, you and the community will become very supportive of our EMS service. In the future, contracting for fire suppression will be a very different question than it is now, and I would just as soon wait until then before even bringing it up. I don't like controversial issues any more than you do. That's probably why I got out of city management in the first place."

"Oh? You were a city manager?"

"Yes, for a small town in Utah."

"For how long?"

"Six years."

"Well I'll be. So how did you like it?"

Monroe paused and took a long drink of his water. I tried to remember if I had ever seen his name mentioned in the city management newsletter.

He carefully put down his glass. "I did enjoy it, for the most part. It was interesting—maybe too interesting. The council members hated each other. In a meeting, the mayor publicly referred to one of his colleagues as the worst specimen of humanity he had seen outside an institution. We had to put two armed cops up there, one on each end of the council bench, to keep them from going at each other. The council had a sheet of steel installed into the front of the bench, in case someone brought a gun into the meeting. And they had me put a phone at the staff table, with a direct connection to the police dispatch desk."

"You're kidding."

"No. At some point in the town's history a guy had come into city hall, waving a gun around and saying he was going to liberate the city."

I laughed. "So I'm not the only one who gets to deal with kooks, huh?"

"No. And that wasn't half of it. We had a police officer—a woman— who was in line for promotion to sergeant. She was married to a firefighter. Just before he promoted her, the police chief caught wind that she was having an affair with one of the police officers—one of the officers that she would end up supervising as sergeant. So the chief told her she would have to knock it off if she wanted the promotion. She agreed, but a year later the chief discovered she was still shacking up with the officer. He busted her to corporal, and then she informed him that she had gone to the human resources director for advice, and he had told her that the chief didn't have any grounds for a nepotism policy if the people involved weren't married to each other and if the policy wasn't in writing. Last I heard, the court cases are still dragging out over that one."

I just shook my head.

"Wait, that's not all," he said. "The cops wanted us to buy into a new, expensive state pension plan. And, of course, they wanted a healthy raise at the same time. The council said they could have one or the other, but not both. The cops said, 'Fine, we'll strike.' The council said, 'Well, y'all go right ahead.' So they did, but the council stuck to their guns. The cops finally came back to work and settled for a raise but no new pension system. The whole thing had dragged out so long that we were back into the next contract negotiations in three months. I was amazed when they brought the pension issue up again. 'Are you crazy?' I asked them. 'You just took a strike over it and lost.' So they said, 'Yeah, but this time we've got three more council votes.' I asked them how they had managed that, not believing a word of it, and they said, 'Sure, we got three of them to commit to it in exchange for our endorsement in the election. You wanna see the videotape?'"

"The videotape?" I asked, not sure I had heard him right.

"Yep. Apparently the police union guys told the council candidates that, since the officers worked different shifts, some of the other guys wanted to be at the meeting but couldn't, so they wanted to watch it on a videotape. The amazing thing is *the council candidates agreed.*"

"So the cops got their pension?"

"Yeah. After the election. The new council members were even worse than the old ones. They had run on the promise of shaking things up at city hall, and they did—before I knew it, I was out on the street. You know what they say—I left the same way I came: fired with enthusiasm."

I chuckled and shook my head "Yeah, that's rough. Happens all the time, though."

"Sure. And it turned out all right in the end. I did some consulting for a while, then City/County offered me a job, and I haven't looked back. In fact, I started there about the same time that your Max Oakley did."

"What?"

"Yeah, I started with them about fourteen years ago. Oakley was hired just after me, at the headquarters in Tempe. He left after a couple of years though."

"Hmm." I hadn't remembered that, but Oakley was already fire chief when I started with the City of Trillium, and he had never talked much about his past.

Monroe glanced up, piercing me with his eyes. "You know, if we start up an operation out here, we'll need someone to manage our northwest region. You might want to give that some thought."

"Hmm." Was it a serious offer, or just a plum to dangle in front of my eyes? "Well, I appreciate it, but I'm doing all right where I am. There are still a lot of other projects I want to see happen."

"Well, keep it in mind."

When I got back to the office, I told Betty Sue about the conversation with Monroe, and the possibility of entering into a contract with City/County.

"I gave him a copy of our budget document," I said, "but he'll probably need more information before he can give us a proposal."

"Okay," she said quietly.

"You might want to forward him the analysis you did on the fire and EMS calls."

"All right."

"So, what do you think about this turn of events?"

"It sounds fine," she said, without enthusiasm.

I looked at her for a moment. "Okay, I'm pretty dense about things like this, but it seems that something is bothering you."

"No."

I waited.

"Is that all?" she asked.

"You tell me."

She sighed. "Okay. Maybe it's just that you caught me by surprise. But here I've been in the middle of this from the beginning, it was even my idea in the first place. You let me negotiate the deal with Oregon Ambulance, and I've been slaving away on the PR stuff for you. And then you go and set up a secret meeting that you never tell me about, and don't even invite me to join you. How would that make you feel?"

I didn't know what to say. I could have told her that it would have been difficult to include her without including Max, and I had a vague suspicion that it had been Max who soured the deal with Oregon Ambulance. I could have said that it was Monroe who set up the meeting, and I didn't have any idea what would come of it. Maybe earlier in my career I would have tried one of those excuses.

"You know, Betty Sue, you're right. I just wasn't thinking, and that was pretty inconsiderate of me."

"Well, it's okay."

I studied her eyes. "No, it's not. You should have been in the meeting, not only to keep on top of the issue, but to ask the questions that I didn't think of."

"Well, I'm sure I'll get a chance to talk to this Monroe guy soon. It's no big deal."

*   *   *

In contrast with Rob Titus, Seth Rosenberg didn't hang around city hall, and in fact rarely participated in issues and events that were outside the normal city business. So I had to go to his office to seek his wisdom.

The Trillium Business Leadership Committee continued to put out publicity on their phone referendum on whether I should be fired because of my support for Nova's housing project. They had made arrangements with a real estate office to use their bank of phones, and claimed they had recruited twenty volunteers to take the calls on the day of the big event.

Seth told me not to worry about it. He said the council wasn't going to get bullied into any rash decisions, particularly when the source was the TBLC.

"So you already think their phone poll will come out negative?" I asked.

"You've got to admit there's a good chance. Who's going to call in? People who were satisfied by the city's decision on the housing project? People who weren't even paying attention to the issue? No, they'll attract negative responses like fly paper."

"Great. Thanks for your encouraging prediction."

Seth laughed. "Like I said, don't worry about it. It's irrelevant."

The small meeting table in his office was piled high with files, glossy brochures with pictures of saws and mill equipment. Seth had pushed a stack aside to clear a space for me at the table. The top half of the pile looked like it wanted to slide onto the floor. I kept an eye on it.

"Well, here's another hot topic that you may get to deal with." I told him about the possible option of contracting with City/County.

Seth pulled at his beard for a few moments. "That wouldn't be a bad alternative at all."

"You really think so? It's rough enough with the firefighters association on our case; this will get Oregon Ambulance to jump into the fray too."

"You're right, and they were an important source of my campaign funding."

I looked at him in surprise.

"Just kidding," Seth said. I figured so. Except for a few yard signs, council candidates didn't spend much on campaigns, and instead relied on the press and statements in the voters' pamphlet. People didn't always realize that there wasn't much money involved in council campaigns, or council salaries, for that matter. State and national elections revolved around money, but people forgot that that too was a relatively recent phenomenon, and that even national elections were fairly low budget affairs before Lyndon Johnson's congressional campaign.

"So you think it's okay to pursue this?" I asked.

"Sure. We need to keep all our options open. We've got to do what makes most financial sense, even if it means taking some flak. How does the saying go? You can't see where you're going if you spend all the time with your ear to the ground? Besides, you don't even know yet if City/County is going to make a proposal. Let's stay in the game and see what cards we draw."

The pile of papers started to slide. I caught it and straightened the stack a little. "How come you don't get someone to file this stuff?"

"Then how would I know where it is?" Seth said, smiling. "Besides, if I let it sit here long enough, we never have to file it at all—I can just chuck it."

"Are you getting many irate calls on the fire issue?"

"No, not really. Maggie and Rob seem to be magnets for that kind of thing. For whatever reason, people leave me alone. That's fine with me."

*　　　　　*　　　　　*

The foundation was being poured for Nova's factory, and the utilities were being buried in trenches that generally followed the street right-of-way. We had had a pre-application meeting with Nova's housing development arm, and for a change, things seemed to be working smoothly.

It didn't last long, though.

"Listen, Ben, we really need to get our expansion area into the urban growth boundary," John Collins said on the phone. He reminded me of the jobs that would be produced on the current site, and the potential for more that an expansion would yield.

"That's right, John. But that's exactly why you're safe holding off until later. The state economic development folks will make sure you get the approvals, when the time comes." Unless, of course, the state government finally figures out that job growth is fueling the population growth that the state's residents are starting to rebel against.

"Well, you and I may believe that, but the corporation doesn't like to take those kind of chances." He paused for a moment. "Look, the head of our land acquisition group wants to fly out from Toledo to talk to you about it."

I agreed, and let Terri set up the details.

We met a few days later in the city council's conference room. Anthony Costoso had arrived with John Collins and Ken Ishido. His handshake was a little too firm, and the two massive gold rings on his right hand pinched my fingers. He was a few years younger than I was, with jet black hair combed straight back. He wore an expensive wool suit with a handkerchief carefully folded in the breast pocket, and his argyle socks matched the colors in his tie.

I checked for Bess Wilson's reaction, but if she was impressed or intimidated, she didn't show it.

"With all of Nova's property in California, what the hell are you doing living in Toledo?" Bess asked.

"It's not such a bad town, and I got family there," Costoso said. "Besides, we do property work for other companies in addition to Nova, and do a lot of deals on the east coast. So it's centrally located, see?"

John Collins summarized their situation, which we all knew already. I asked him what they wanted from us specifically.

"I don't know too much about Oregon land use law," Costoso said, "but I understand that if your land is outside the urban growth boundary, it isn't worth jack shit."

Bess looked at me for an answer. "Well, it can still have value as farm land or forest land," I said, "but in terms of higher intensity development, you're basically right. That doesn't mean somebody might not pay a higher value, on the assumption that it will eventually come within the boundary, but that's purely speculative."

Costoso looked at me for a moment "Okay, so here's how we need your help," he said, leaning forward. "I assume you—the city—has a lot of influence in this, so we need you to move the urban growth boundary so our expansion property is in it. We'll pay for any studies, surveys, whatever it takes, but we need your support."

"You know, Tony, it isn't that simple," Bess said. "Our support and two dollars will buy you a cup of coffee these days. Any change in the urban growth boundary has to be approved by the Department of Land Conservation and Development. If we already have a twenty year supply of vacant land inside the boundary, they're not going to allow a change. Especially if there's any opposition at all."

"No, I just don't buy that," Costoso said. "You're the city, and it's your urban growth boundary. From what I hear, you've made things happen like this before. Don't worry about the state-we've got connections to the Governor's Office. They'll play along. But you've got to carry the ball for us here."

"Bess is right," I said. "You're over-estimating our influence on this. Besides, it's got to go through our own planning commission. They know the criteria for a boundary change, so you'll have to have an argument with more substance than just a vague need to avoid uncertainty for your future plans."

"We can do that."

"How? Do you plan to expand on the property in the next five years?"

"Yeah, that's possible. Depends on the market, but it could happen."

That would be their angle, then. Hold out an ambitious expansion plan with hundreds of new jobs, and when the expansion never materializes, blame the economy.

"No, it just doesn't make sense," I said. "Come to us when you're ready to pull a permit for a second plant. That will change the whole picture. Moving the boundary will be simple then."

"Can you guarantee that? What if someone comes in on the other side of town and beats us to it? What about this movement-what the hell's it called, voter annexation? If your so-called business leaders keep their heads up their ass about Nova, they could jump on that bandwagon and run a campaign against us. There are just too many things that could go wrong. We can't risk it. And you owe us this, Ben. Nova has done a lot for your town."

"We OWE you??" Bess stared at Costoso. "What do mean, we owe you? We got the access road for your plant, we approved your plans for the plant in record time, and the city manager is facing a public vote of no confidence over your housing project. Don't give me that 'we owe you' crap, Tony."

John Collins leaned forward. "No, we do appreciate that. Don't get us wrong. But what Anthony is saying is that Nova took a chance with the location here, and we are investing a lot in your community. We depend on your support, though, to make this project a success."

There was a silent moment. From the twinkle in her eye, I guessed that Bess was helping with the "good cop/bad cop" role play. It worked for me.

"Listen, here's what we can do," I said. "We can enter into an agreement—a memorandum of understanding, or something like that—that states that when your current site is built out, we will recommend an extension of the urban growth boundary to accommodate your plant's expansion. We might need to run it by the Planning Commission, but that's probably a good thing, since the current commission members are still enthusiastic about your manufacturing facility. The same goes for the state folks."

Costoso's eyes narrowed. "When the current property is built out? How do you define that? Do we have to build on every square inch of the thing?"

"I don't know," I said. "We can allow a certain percentage of the site to be landscaped. It can be pretty liberal—a lot more than our minimum setback requirements—to keep the campus look that you want. We can negotiate it."

"Hmm." Costoso reached into his inside coat pocket for a case. He opened it and took out a cigar.

"Uh, this is a no-smoking building," I said. "Part of the Oregon Clean Indoor Air Law requirements."

"Yeah, sure," Costoso said. He proceeded to pull a solid gold lighter out of his side pocket.

"Well, Anthony, you can light it if you want," I said, "but it may turn into a very expensive cigar." Ken Ishido watched, motionless. Bess rolled her eyes.

"Look, how about we go outside for a smoke," Collins said. "We need to caucus on this anyway."

Costoso paused. "Yeah, let's do that."

The three of them left. Bess was silent for a moment.

"You know what's odd about this?" she said.

"The fact that they haven't talked about a comp plan amendment?"

"Exactly."

The land that Nova was looking at for expansion was shown as having a future commercial—not industrial—zone in our comprehensive plan. Getting that changed would be every bit as hard as moving the urban growth boundary.

"Maybe they figure that the prospect of new jobs and a good looking campus would make a zone change easy" I said.

"Or maybe they don't have any intention of expanding their plant, but just want to cash in on the higher valued commercial property."

"Could be."

"And they need the UGB change now, since people aren't going to be nearly as excited about the potential job creation of a Wal-Mart."

"Possible," I said. "But let's not read too much into it."

After another five minutes the three Nova men returned.

"Listen Ben, we still want the boundary moved," Costoso said. "I guarantee you, it will be worth your while."

"Well, you're free to try," I said. "Submit an application to the Planning Commission, and give it your best shot."

"So is your staff recommendation going to be to support it?"

I hesitated. "No, not until your existing land is built out. It just wouldn't pass the straight face test."

Costoso stared at me. Bess slouched in her chair, waiting to see what happened.

"Okay," Costoso finally said, "I guess we'll have to fall back on your proposal for a written agreement. I'm disappointed that you're not behind us on this, but we have to take what we can get. We'll have our attorney work up a draft and send it over to you. But we want to move fast on this—the price of the land is locked in, but only for another month."

Land deals always seemed to be urgent. We weren't always able to move quickly when land use issues were involved, but when we did, more often than not nothing happened with the property for years. "Hurry up and wait," they said in the Army. And in this case I had a hard time thinking of anyone else who might make an offer on Nova's property. So what was the urgency?

"Do you want to include the comprehensive plan amendment in the agreement?" I asked, innocently.

"How's that?"

"Do you want to get the land use designation changed from commercial to industrial?" Bess said.

Costoso looked briefly at Ishido. "We've been working under the assumption that that will be a fairly simple thing to do," he said. "People go nuts when you talk about different kinds of housing, but they don't give a shit about commercial or light industrial. I guess its all the same to them."

"So do you want that in the agreement or not?" I said.

"No, we don't want to make it too complicated. Let's stick to the UGB issue, and cross that bridge when we get to it." Costoso stood up, and the rest of us followed. "Say, we're going out to see some show playing at the Schnitz tonight. You two want to join us?"

"Sorry, got other plans," Bess said.

"Same here. But thanks anyway," I said.

They left. The air smelled of cologne and cigars.

17

I awoke from a vivid dream. In it, Kate and I had been somewhere in Montana at an isolated cabin by a mountain lake. We cooked dinner and sat on the floor and drank wine in the candlelight. We slept curled up under blankets in the cool nights of early spring. We went for a walk by the lake, and were caught by a downpour. We ran to the cabin, and took a steaming shower and kissed under the water. We huddled under a blanket in front of the fire and let ourselves be mesmerized by the dancing of the flames.

The images were so strong that they stuck in my head for days, and I started to think that it was a recurrence of a dream I had had years ago. I debated with myself about writing to Kate about it. I had a hard time putting it into words, but I finally tried, partly to re-live the experience. Kate said she read the message twenty times on the day she got it, in the hope that she could launch herself into the same dream that night.

*   *   *

The Trillium Business Leadership Committee used our cable public access channel to televise their call-in poll. It looked like a low-budget version of a Jerry Lewis telethon. Every few minutes they ran the results on the bottom of the screen. "Should City Manager Ben Cromarty be fired? Yes-38 No-25" In the background, Todd Pritchard and his friends were busy answering phones in the crowded office of the Walter Mitty Real Estate Headquarters.

I switched the channel to catch one of the games in the NBA playoffs, but during commercials I found myself getting drawn back to the public access channel. The results stayed pretty much the same—there wasn't an overwhelming number of calls, but the ones that came in were about four to three in favor of getting rid of the city manager. I remembered Seth's advice, and tried to distance myself from it, but I couldn't.

The camera zoomed in on Pritchard. He held the microphone like Mick Jagger and told the viewers how the citizens had clearly lost their confidence in the city administration over the Nova housing issue.

"Why don't you just turn it off?" Mary asked.

"Morbid curiosity, I suppose."

"Well, it's awful. Don't pay any attention to it. Go back to your basket-ball game and forget about it."

I sneaked a peak when the ball game ended, but the coverage was over. The headline in the *Oregonian* the next morning read, "Straw Poll Calls For Firing Cromarty." In the article, mayor McTavish characterized the phone poll as merely a vendetta by some disgruntled business owners, and she pointed out that the final decision on the Nova housing project was made by the planning commission and the city council, not the city man-ager. Rob Titus was quoted too, saying that the city manager was appointed, not elected, and the straw poll would be one of many things the council would look at when the next performance evaluation came up.

I made it into the office that morning, without much enthusiasm. The staff were supportive, but the first few hours were awkward, as if I had my fly open and no one wanted to mention it. Eventually, though, the press of routine business drove the whole thing out of my mind, mostly.

I was in the middle of a phone call when Betty Sue came in, holding a dozen faxed sheets of paper. She paced near my window until I was fin-ished with my conversation.

"City/County came through with a proposal," she said. Her eyes were sparkling. "Check this out." She perched on the edge of my side chair. I scanned the papers until I found the cost quote. I whistled. "Not bad, huh?" Betty Sue said. "It's half of what Oregon Ambulance was talking about."

"Maybe they just low-balled it to get us hooked," I said. "How long is the proposal for?"

"Five years, with a firm price. They propose a fudge factor for inflation and increases in calls for service, but it's still a smokin' deal."

"Did you look it over pretty carefully? Anything that might come back to bite us if we sit down to negotiate a contract."

"Yes. I mean, I read the proposal a couple of times. It looks straightforward enough to me."

"So…what do you think we should do with it?"

"Easy. Take it to the city council. This is too good an opportunity to pass up."

I thought about it for a while. I noticed the ring wasn't on her finger any more.

"If the fire union's hot now, this will really get them going," I said.

"Yeah, but how can it get any worse?" Betty Sue asked. "Our contract negotiations are still tied in knots. We spent hours last week arguing about why the captains get personal chauffeurs."

"How's that?"

"Didn't Ken tell you? It turns out that for the last few years, the fire captains haven't driven anywhere—the rookie firefighters are assigned to drive them. They pick them up at home in the morning, take them to meetings and drive them home. It's a cushy deal. The captains are supposed to be management anyway—how did they ever get into the union in the first place?"

"Past bargaining, I suppose." All the management positions—except the chief—were members of the union. For obvious reasons, the brass were glad to join, and once they were in, the concept of management rights became a joke. "You're thinking you took up the wrong profession, I'll bet."

"No kidding," she said. "I had to go through six years of college, and I still don't have a personal chauffeur. How about changing my title to captain?"

"Captain what?"

"Uh, just management captain. Or maybe captain fantastic. That wouldn't be too presumptuous, would it?"

I laughed. I was going to ask her about the ring, but changed my mind. None of my business.

"So you think we ought to go ahead with this?" I asked.

"Definitely."

"What about Max?"

"Oh." She leaned back in her chair. "I forgot about him. He's not going to be too thrilled with this, is he?"

"Nope."

"But if he had better control over his staff, we wouldn't even be looking at it. He's got to live with the consequences of a renegade department."

I looked at her for a moment. "Don't be too hard on him. I don't think any of us could manage that department."

Betty Sue gathered up the fax papers. "Well, it isn't the end of the world for him. He could still be the public safety director, with both police and fire. Do you think the loss of EMS will be that big a deal?"

"Yep. But we'll see."

*　　　　*　　　　*

Later, Sabrina Chan called to say she wanted to talk to me. I assumed it was a follow up interview on the TLBC straw poll. It wasn't something I was looking forward to. But when she showed up in my office, she surprised me by not pulling out her notepad; instead, she simply asked me how I was doing.

"Fine, considering," I said. "Why?"

"What the TLBC did—that was a crummy thing. You didn't deserve it."

What kind of interview was this? It was a side to Sabrina I didn't see very often.

I shrugged. "Just goes with the job."

Her fingers worried a strand of her black hair. "Listen," she said, "I'm going to tell you something, but—this is weird for me to say—it's got to be off the record. Okay?"

"Sure."

"Last night…Walter Mitty's real estate place…they had caller I.D. on their phones."

"Oh yeah?" Not too surprising, come to think of it. A lot of businesses had it.

"Yeah. So here's the thing. Apparently the TBLC boys were taking down names, especially the ones that had it in for you. I guess they reckoned they could build up a mailing list of people with similar views, maybe use it for fund raising or political action, that sort of thing."

"Hmm. So much for an anonymous poll, huh?"

"Really. So anyway, I got a hold of the list—"

"You're kidding!"

"No, and don't ask how I did it. I got the list, and started going through the names. A few of them rang a bell, especially after I saw them listed a few times."

"How's that?"

"Think about it," she said. "Didn't it occur to you that a few people might want to jack up the numbers by calling more than once?"

"Oh, of course." It hadn't.

"Anyway, a lot of the names were from your fire department. I didn't have much time to dig into it, but I pulled out a voter registration list, and got some of the maiden names of the wives of the firefighters. Sure enough, there were some of those names too."

I leaned back in my chair. Sabrina sat quietly.

"So they organized a call-in campaign, huh? They had plenty of time to do it. But the poll was about the Nova housing project. I wouldn't have figured they would care that much about affordable housing and zoning issues…but that wasn't the motivation at all, was it?" She just looked at me. "I'll be darned…"

"If it's any consolation," she said, "when I took out the names that I could connect to the fire union, the poll actually turned out in your favor."

"Great." I searched Sabrina's eyes. "What are you going to do with this information? Use it in a story?"

"No." She smiled wistfully. "I can't. It would put my source in an awkward position, and I can't afford to lose it. But as you might guess, it'll be great for background information as the issue unfolds."

"Mmm." She was right—it sure didn't hurt to have a reporter who was at least a little sympathetic. "Thanks, Sabrina. I do appreciate it."

"Sure. And good luck, Ben."

*   *   *

My strategic goal was clear—I had to get the council to make a decision on the City/County proposal, and quickly. But the tactical situation was more complicated. I went to Ken Longstreet for advice.

"Here's the deal," I said. "I can't spring it on them cold. We need time to brief them on it, and let them think about it—"

"But you know that as soon as you talk to Rob and Maggie, the word will leak out, right?"

"Exactly. It might not be intentional, but we can't expect five people not to talk to somebody about it."

"And then," Ken said, "the Fire Association picks up on it, and all hell breaks loose."

"Uh huh. In hindsight, if we could have had some calm, rational community discussion on this whole thing, that would have been the way to go. But we're past the point of no return —there's no way we're going to have anything like a civil dialogue on it now."

Ken rubbed his forehead. "Let me think about this." He took a pen out of his shirt pocket and doodled on a pad of paper.

"How about this," he said after a few moments. "Get Pete to brief them on the proposal in executive session, as a contractual issue. He could remind them that it's illegal to divulge the executive session discussion."

"Yeah, I thought about that, but it really doesn't qualify under the state law. It would probably make things worse—a council member or two would leak it anyway, and the press would accuse us of violating the open meeting law."

"Umm, you're probably right." Ken drew a series of small boxes on his paper. "City/County offered to hire any of our paramedics who would be laid off, right? So no one's going to be out of a job here."

"Yes."

"Okay then. Maybe the best defense is a good offense. Just go public with the thing. Put it on the council agenda, but circulate copies of the staff report to as many people and groups as you can think of. Give it to Gallagher, and to the Rotary Club and even the Business Leadership Committee. Present it as a logical next step in the city's mandate to provide services at less cost, to operate the city like a business, to encourage privatization. Hit as many hot buttons as you can. Make as many arguments for accepting the proposal as you can. But anticipate every argument anyone can make, and state them up-front, along with counter-arguments. You know, you can mention that the paramedics may see lower pay and benefits at first, but they would have more long-term career opportunities, that sort of thing. That way, the Association will be stuck in a defensive position. They'll have to scramble to re-gain the initiative."

I thought about it. Ken stopped doodling and waited for a reaction.

"It might work," I said. "But there are some negative consequences to the contract that we just don't have good answers to."

"Like what?"

"Well, for one, it isn't a reversible decision. Once we lose our staff and rescue equipment, it would be pretty hard to get back into the business. And Oregon Ambulance has served us well for years, and they would be a casualty in all this."

Ken tapped his pen. "Maybe that's not so bad. Just admit there's a downside to it, like there is in any major decision. Acknowledge the downside risk, but emphasize that on balance, it's a good deal for the community. Take possession of the whole decision, both the good and the bad sides of it."

I laughed. "This is a good one. I've got our chief negotiator—the master of intrigue and secret strategies—advising me to be totally open and honest about our strengths and weaknesses."

He smiled. "Yeah, I wouldn't recommend it very often. But sometimes you've got do what you've got do."

I never knew if the tactic was the best one, since I didn't get the chance to try anything else. Betty Sue and I spent a day writing and refining our cover staff report. I called Matt Monroe at City/County a couple of times to clarify details of their proposal, and faxed him our draft staff report. It was a pleasure to deal with him—perhaps because he was still trying to gain our approval, but I sensed it was just the way he did business.

My meeting with Max Oakley had been as difficult as I had anticipated it it would be. I assured him that the City/County proposal had been unsolicited, which was the truth, but I didn't tell him that I had known it was coming.

"Are you seriously going to consider this?" Max had asked, with an edge to his normally controlled voice.

"Of course. It looks like too good a deal for the city and the taxpayers to ignore."

"It may look like that in the short term, but you're ignoring the tremendous cost to the community due to the turmoil this will cause. It would be an irresponsible thing to do."

"Max." I tried to sound as sympathetic as I could. "Don't personalize this. We've got to step back from it, and do what's really best for the city. I realize that this would be a major change to your department, but it isn't the taxpayers' duty to maintain our organizational structures. Sometimes we just have to adapt."

"Perhaps, but this just goes too far."

"Does it? But we were ready to consider it when we negotiated with Oregon Ambulance."

Max was silent.

"Look," I said, "it's still a council decision. If they go with it, you'll still have plenty to do in making the transition, and it could really make your life easier, in the long run. All I ask is that you keep an open mind."

"Ben, that's awfully easy for you to say, but it isn't your department that's being decimated here."

"Yes, Max, it is. It's as much my department as yours, and it isn't a decision I take lightly. But ultimately I'm the one who makes the staff recommendation, and the council makes the decision. You knew that's the way it works when you took this job."

Max reached for a stack of papers, as if to dismiss me. "Well," he said, "don't say I didn't warn you."

*   *   *

One of our police officers hand-delivered the proposals, along with the regular council agenda packets, to the city council members' homes. We simultaneously delivered them to Brian Gallagher and the rest of the union officers, and to everyone else on Ken's list. I steeled myself, and stayed close to the phone. I didn't have to wait long.

The first call was from Gallagher.

"Well, Ben, I just got a coy of a staff report from you, and I have just one question: what exactly is this shit?"

"It's just what it looks like; read it, Brian."

"Don't be cute. You're never going to get away with this, and you know it. You may think that the threat of a private contract will beat us into submission, but I guarantee it, it's going to do just the opposite. You better be brushing off your resume."

"You're still a member of my staff, Brian. This is sounding a lot like insubordination. Keep it up, and I'm going to have to get Terri on the line to make a transcript of this call."

The line was silent for a moment.

"What really pisses me off," he said, "is that you didn't even bother to talk to us about this before suddenly springing it on us. What happened to the great labor/management communication that you keep talking about?"

"Don't give me that crap, Brian. I offered that to you from the beginning. I handed it to you on a silver platter, and you refused it. You flat out told me you would fight it and didn't want to have anything to do with the decisions."

"I never said anything of the sort. I have always insisted that the rank and file have a full say in any...decisions."

"What were you going to say? A full say in management decisions? That's ridiculous, but that's exactly what I offered, and you refused."

"Bullshit."

"Okay, I'm not going to debate you on it. Did you actually call with a question, or did you just want to get into a pissing contest?"

He ignored the question. "All I got to say is this time you've gone too far. From here on out, you better watch your back."

"All right, Brian." I hung up.

I told myself I was calm and collected, but I could tell that my face was hot and my pulse was pounding. I found myself in the conference room and got a glass of water from the sink.. When I got back to my desk, the phone was ringing again. This time it was Joe Secomb from Oregon Ambulance Service.

"Ben, this is your decision, but I must say I am disappointed that you would consider contracting with an out-of-state company."

"Yeah, I tried to contract with a local company, but it didn't work out."

"Touche. But have you looked into our franchise provisions? My understanding is that the franchise has another eight years."

"Yes, we did check into it. You've got a non-exclusive franchise, and we're not doing anything to change that. You would still be free to do business in Trillium, and you can transport private patients. But if we go ahead with this, it does mean that when we get a 911 call, we'll dispatch City/County, not you."

"That will have a major impact on our business."

"In Trillium, maybe, but we're small potatoes in the overall metro area. Look at it this way: you'll be able to shift resources into the other communities that you're so concerned about."

He chuckled. "Okay, Ben, don't rub my nose in it. And I'm not going to give you a hard time about it—my guess is that you'll have your hands full anyway."

"No kidding."

"Well, good luck to you, whichever way it goes."

"Thanks, Joe."

I couldn't wait much longer to talk to the council members, but I didn't want to be far from my phone. I switched on my cell phone and forwarded my calls to it, and got a car out of the city hall motor pool.

Hank Arnold wasn't home, but Maggie Henderson was. She was surprised to see me. She hadn't opened her packet yet. I briefly explained the City/County proposal. I emphasized that there were disadvantages as well as advantages, but to my amazement, she was supportive.

"We have to do what's best for the people," she said.

"I agree, but you realize the firefighters are going to be upset."

"That's all right, they already are anyway," she said. "I don't see how it could get any worse. I kind of resent some of the things they have been doing, so I—"

My cell phone rang. Maggie started skimming through the rest of the council packet, so I flipped open the phone.

"Interesting report, Ben," Sabrina Chan said. "So what's the bottom line—how much of the fire department would you lose under this proposal?"

"About two thirds of them," I said. "But don't forget that they could transition to City/County. They'd be doing the same job and wearing the same uniform; they would just get a paycheck from a different organization."

"Sure, but the paycheck would probably be smaller."

"That would be between them and City/County."

"Yes, I can see why that would appeal to you. What did Brian Gallagher have to say about it?"

Had Brian told her about our conversation, or was she just guessing? "We did discuss it, but I can't comment on the specifics of what we said."

She laughed. "I can imagine the conversation, though. I would have liked to have been a fly on the wall. What about the mayor and council?"

"Actually, I'm talking to you from a cell phone at councilor Henderson's home. The council got the proposal at the same time you did. Feel free to talk to them directly about their reaction. In any case, we'll have a full open discussion of it at the council meeting. What you see in the staff report is the full picture—there really isn't any behind-the-scenes maneuvering on this one."

"Is that so? Well, it's going to make a good story. How can I reach somebody at City/County?"

"Call Betty Sue and get the number for Matt Monroe. I don't have it with me."

"Okay. Thanks Ben."

Maggie asked if there was anything else interesting on the agenda. I said no. As if the City/County proposal wasn't enough for one night.

Over the next three hours I managed to track down Hank Arnold and Rob Titus. Hank ushered me into his kitchen and had me sit at a small breakfast table. A pot of spaghetti sauce was burbling on the stove, making me hungry. I had forgotten about lunch. Two small grandchildren were scurrying around on the floor. Hank and Gretchen were taking care of them while their son was off on a construction job somewhere.

Hank was noncommittal about the proposal, but he was pleased to have another option, and without looking at the staff report, he had pinpointed most of the pros and cons that we had included in it. He talked about it cheerfully, while gently scolding the kids and stirring the spaghetti sauce.

Rob was harder to read. I sat in a small chair in his office. It felt like it was several inches lower than the massive executive chair behind his desk.

He skimmed the staff report and proposal, occasionally asking questions. When he was done, he simply put it down and thanked me for bringing it by. He said I would have to excuse him because he expected a client in a few minutes.

"Actually, you might be interested to know that it's John Collins. They've asked me to research the name 'Nova Corporate Park' to make sure it hasn't been trademarked somewhere."

Warning bells were going off in my head. It was an obvious conflict of interest, especially if any more hot decisions reached the council. And why hadn't Nova used it's own lawyers? I thought about it and realized they probably already had—they wouldn't have gone ahead with their marketing effort if there had been a legal question about the name. Clearly they were just throwing Rob a bone. I couldn't figure out why.

"You know, you'll have to declare it if the council ever has any quasi-judicial proceedings involving Nova."

"Sure," he said. "No problem."

It was getting late by the time I got back to my office. I had fielded a few more calls on my cell phone, but had let the voice mail take them when I had been talking to Hank Arnold and Rob Titus. I replayed the messages. Most were related to the City/County proposal, but a few were on completely different topics. It reminded me that, in spite of the conflict and tension of the moment, life goes on.

The sixth call was a brief message from an anonymous muffled voice. "You don't know who I am, Ben Cromarty, but I'm warnin' ya, you're takin' a dangerous path. It ain't gonna be healthy for you and your family." There was a pause and some unintelligible sounds. "...so I gotta tell you, you better watch yourself."

I saved the message and called Simon Garret.

"It probably doesn't mean anything, but I just got what sounded like a threat." I described it to him.

"Yeah, you're right to take it seriously. I'm heading home in a minute—let me stop by and listen to it."

When he got there, Simon pulled a small dictation machine out of his coat pocket and held it against the earpiece of the phone as I replayed the message. Low tech, but it seemed to work.

"Probably just some jerk who's messing with your mind." Simon wrote a few words in a note pad. "Let me know if you get anything else like this, okay?"

"Sure."

He looked at me for a moment. "Say, do you want to stop for a beer?"

I sagged in my chair. It sounded good, but I was anxious to see Mary too. What the heck. I called her and told her I'd be late for dinner. She said that was fine; she had worked late, and it looked like we'd be eating out.

Simon and I took a back booth at the Plow and Harrow pub, and ordered a plate of calamari with hot sauce and two pints of Haystack Rock Hefeweizen.

"So how's it going?" he said. I unloaded it on him, describing my conversations with Oakley and Gallagher and the other members of my fan club who had called. I didn't though, mention Sabrina's revelation about the TBLC phone poll. Simon and his staff had to work too closely with the firefighters to risk building more barriers there.

"That's rough," he said when I finished. "I guess that's why you get the big bucks."

I laughed, without much humor. "If that was all there was to it, I should be playing the stock market or selling real estate. But you know, Simon, as messy as this is getting, I still get some perverse pleasure out of it."

"You just like danger. You should be a cop."

"No, taking verbal shots is enough for me."

Simon swirled a piece of calamari around in some red sauce. "This stuff really squid? It tastes sort of like onion rings."

"Maybe that's what it is. They figure if we have enough beer we won't know the difference." The owner of the Plow and Harrow was from a town called Camden—New South Wales, not New Jersey. He had a great Australian accent and an outgoing personality that made up for the quality of the food. I never figured out what a harrow was—something to do with a farm and plows, I guessed.

I watched the after-work crowd mingle by the bar. Most were at least a decade younger than us, flirting and rubbing against each other. A brief image of Kate in a Montana mountain cabin flew through my mind.

Simon's voice broke through my reverie. "Damndest thing happened last night," he said. "I was working late, and one of our reserves came in. One of the greener kids. He had his sidearm on; I found out later he hadn't had a hell of a lot of experience with it. Anyway, he goes to sit down at a spare desk to write a report. He's got his radio and his gun on his belt, and has a hard time getting it all to fit between the arms of his chair. So he goes to pull the gun out of his holster. Caught it by the trigger, and the damn thing goes off. I flew out of my office to see what the hell was going on. Damn bullet hit the floor and bounced through the wall into the rec center next door."

"You're kidding." There must have been a report on this in my in-basket that I had been too preoccupied to read.

"Nope. There was an aerobics class going on in there, but they had a boom box going and didn't hear a thing. The bullet just stuck itself into the ceiling."

I whistled. "What'd you do?"

Simon chuckled. "I asked the kid if I could take a look at his gun. Then I just took the bullets out and handed it back to him. He was a little shaken—must have wondered at first if he shot his dick off."

"Ha. But thank God it didn't hit anybody."

"Damn straight. I had a few words with Ramos about our firearms training. I can't for the life of me figure out what the guy was doing with the safety off. He said he thought it was on. That's the kind of stunt one of our snot-nosed gang wannabes would pull—makes me a little nervous seeing it happen with one of our own guys."

The talk of gunfire reminded me of something.

"Say, Simon, whatever happened with the Seven Eleven murder? They ever catch the guy?"

About a year ago, a hold-up at a convenience store had resulted in the shooting death of a young female clerk. Our police were the first on the scene under our mutual-aid agreement, but the store was outside the city limits, so the sheriff's office took the lead on the investigation. They had, through several eyewitnesses, come up with a strong suspect, and plastered the Portland area with the man's picture, but he had apparently disappeared into thin air.

"No, they never caught him." Simon eyed me for a second, then leaned forward. "But the guys and me, we've got a theory about it."

"Oh?"

"Yeah. See, a couple of our guys know the father of the little gal that got killed. He's real handy with guns, a top notch hunter. Plus, we guessed from the beginning that this dad knew where the suspect hung out. A few weeks into the case, and he sort of cools off on prosecuting it—almost like he didn't care."

"Really? How come?"

"Cause he took care of it himself. Just went out and thumped the asshole. That's our theory, anyway. Body's probably buried deep in a ravine in the woods somewhere, and we'll never know for sure."

I whistled. Justice in the wild west.

We sat for a few more minutes and watched the crowd. As usual, Simon wasn't in uniform and didn't attract any attention, even with the service revolver tucked under its Velcro strap on his side. The waitress knew who he was though, and flirted with him. "I just don't get to see you enough, honey," she said.

Simon put an arm around her waist. "Aw, that's just 'cuz the missus found out about us."

"Speaking of which, I've got to head out," I said.

"All right. Take care of yourself, Ben, okay?"

"Sure. Thanks, Simon."

         *   *   *

Trixie was at a friend's house, so Mary and I had a nice candlelight dinner at an Italian restaurant. We spent most of the time talking about school politics, and the friction that was building between the principal and a few of the teachers. Both sides saw Mary as a neutral third party to be won over to their side, and she was caught in the middle. To me, the issues almost sounded trivial. I had to remind myself that, from a cosmic perspective, my struggles were just as insignificant: a flash in the pan. I was too tired to talk much about them anyway.

         *   *   *

The week moved slowly. There wasn't much more I could do about the fire situation, but I was too preoccupied with it to do much else. It gave me an opportunity to talk to a lot of people about it—both supporters and fence-sitters—and that was therapeutic, if not otherwise useful. I was feeling some relief at not getting any more threats, until I checked my messages after lunch one day.

"You better back off from the City/County contract," a woman's voice said, "if you don't want the world to find out about your correspondence with Kate." The message clicked off and my heart froze. For a minute, the building went silent—I couldn't hear the sound of the heating system or the traffic below. Then a thousand thoughts crashed into my head. Who knew about Kate? What did they know? Did they have copies of our e-mail? I tried to think how incriminating it would be. No matter how I looked at it, the situation was no good.

It had to be an inside job. I had always been careful to delete Kate's messages as soon as I read them, and I had disabled the gizmo that automatically saved sent messages. But that didn't mean that some computer geek couldn't have dug around on my hard drive and spirited them out.

But how had they got to my computer? I had an open-door policy, but we did lock the office up at night, and there were too many people around to get at it unnoticed during the day.

Then it occurred to me that the network would have let anyone get onto my machine. But it had to be a city hall staff person; the fire department was on a completely separate network, and we had a pretty good firewall to protect against access through the Internet. Who in city hall would do it? A few names popped into my head, but there would be no way I could find out for sure. I could ask Ken for help from our information technology department, but I would have to explain the problem, and that wouldn't get me anywhere.

And what should I do? Try a pre-emptive strike, and tell Mary all about it? But that would only—maybe—avoid a disaster on the home front; there would be no way to keep from being a runaway issue in the community. As sympathetic as she might be, Sabrina would smell a great story. And really, that would only be the beginning of my problems. Someone once said that you can't enjoy writing if you're worrying about how your parents would react, but the fact was, there were a lot of people whose opinion I valued, and I would be mortified if any of them saw some of the notes I had sent to Kate. I figured that Bill Clinton had more on his mind than just Hillary and the presidency when Monica made her oral report.

"What's wrong, Ben?" Terri Knox had started to come in to re-load my inbox, but stopped at the doorway.

"Oh. Uh, nothing. Just more of the same. Come on in."

"You sure? Have you caught my morning sickness?"

So she was pregnant. "Maybe that's it," I said. "What's the cure?"

"Ha. It's worse than the disease. Go out and get some fresh air or something. You look awful, no offense."

"Good advice." I had to walk and clear my head. The hard part was that there was no one I could talk to, except maybe Kate, and I was afraid to send a message. Should I risk a phone call and warn her? Or was I the only target?

I found myself heading for the fire station and stopped walking. It wouldn't do to step foot in there right now.

I found a bench that wasn't too wet, and just sat down.

*   *   *

Twenty four hours passed, and nothing happened. I felt powerless, but I couldn't think of anything I could do. I just waited for the shoe to drop.

Brian Gallagher called, but I couldn't tell if there was any question. He had cooled down, at least compared to our earlier conversation, and simply asked if I had re-considered my position. I told him no, I hadn't, but it was still a council decision. It sounded chicken, but it was the truth. All he said was, "Okay, just checking."

In the middle of it, I got a long message from Kate. I was afraid someone else was reading it, and I wasn't thrilled to see it—a thought that provoked some guilt. But there was nothing I could think of to stop her. She talked about the progress of her business expansion, and her frustrations with her boys, and she concluded with a few hot paragraphs that caused a rise, in spite of myself. She was getting quite adept at turning me on without touching me, which made me wonder how she had acquired that talent.

I deleted the message, wondering what kind of trail it was leaving. On an impulse, I sent a reply.

> Kate, hold off on the messages for a while. Somebody over here is intercepting them. I've discovered who it is, and will deal with it, but the city attorney said it would take a couple of days to start the prosecution. You and I both know that our correspondence has been innocent fun, but someone with an axe to grind could make something of it. I'll get in touch soon.
>
> —Ben

I intentionally misspelled her user name, knowing that the message would eventually get bounced back by the Internet without reaching her. No sense in dragging Kate into this unless I had to—at least not yet. My subterfuge may have been fairly transparent, but if someone was eaves-dropping, it might give them some food for thought.

In the meantime, Trillium was causing a stir in the Portland area. Our fire issue made the front page of the *Oregonian*. Sabrina had done a good job with the lead story, although I felt she had too many quotes from peo-ple who were whining that we had just sprung this on the community. Sabrina's article was accompanied by contributions from other writers, who didn't normally cover our beat. One covered the union reaction, which was pretty universal. The teachers, teamsters, food handlers, and pipe fitters all came out in vocal opposition to it. Their arguments seemed more grounded in emotion than logic, but the effect was the same. There was a story from a guest writer from the Nevada Plain Dealer that gave the full history of City/County Fire Services, including some time-warn rumors that the company had got some of their seed money from the Las Vegas mob connections. The same reputation had dogged the big national solid waste companies, but I had discounted it as mere bellyaching by smaller companies that weren't able to compete.

I called Max to set up a meeting with him and Matt Monroe, but his secretary said he was out for the day; she didn't know where, but she offered to page him. I wondered where he was; I hadn't remembered him talking about taking a day off, but then again he had a habit of taking off for week-long vacations or conferences without bothering to let me know.

By the next morning, I was starting to think that nothing was going to come of the threat about revealing my correspondence with Kate. When I got to the office I made a routine check of my internal mail and my Internet messages. There was nothing from Kate, and I disgusted myself for feeling relieved. But there was a message from an unknown sender under the subject "Pay Attention."

Ben Cromarty: You may be biding your time, but so are we. Our request is simple and reasonable. Rescind your recommendation on the City/County contract at the council meeting, and your secret will remain safe with us. But if you don't, we have plenty of material that will end your career in Trillium. Is that simple enough? Go ahead and show this to your city attorney, and explain to him about Kate. It will serve our purpose no matter how your sordid affair goes public.

I checked the sender's Internet tag, but neither the name nor the server were familiar to me. Whoever did it must have known their way around cyberspace—my guess was that if I knew how to trace it back, the message would appear to come from some innocent and unaware engineer's account in a large corporation. There were maybe a couple of staff in city hall that might have that kind of knowledge, but I couldn't connect any of them with the fire issue. Of course, I had no idea what most of the staff did in their spare time—we could have a few hackers on the payroll without me knowing it. People who appeared unable to learn the basics of our planning databases occasionally surprised me with their stories of buying cars through the Internet or playing sophisticated cyber games of dungeons and dragons.

But it didn't matter who it was—they had me checkmated. As hard as I tried, I couldn't find any way out of the mess. I could cave in at the council meeting—if I was smart, I could come up with some fatal flaw in the proposed contract—but there would be no guarantee that that would be the end of it. The fire union—assuming that was who was behind it—would have me by the neck, and they could control any issue that came up.

1 8

It was small consolation, but blackmail was only one of my problems. Betty Sue was standing in my office, talking about another personnel problem in the utility billing department, when a call came through from Sabrina Chan.

"Ben, a bunch of the fire union guys just left our offices here. Do you know what they were here for?"

"No, but I can think of a few things. What is it now?"

"The union just took a vote of no confidence in the chief."

"Great. That's all we need."

"So it's news to you?"

"Yes."

"I was afraid so." Sabrina paused, and I could hear the sounds of the southwest bureau in the background. "Well, can you make any comment about it?"

"No. I would need to see the specifics of their charges first. Can you give me the gist of what they told you?"

"Oh, the usual stuff. They say that Oakley is aloof and has poor interpersonal skills. He has provided inconsistent leadership, and doesn't support his staff. Let's see, what else…. Oh yeah, he's too competitive."

"Too competitive?"

"That's what it says."

"Well, I'll have to talk to Gallagher before I can give you any comments."

"It wasn't just Gallagher. Red Rogalsky was here too. Plus a group of firefighters, but they didn't do any of the talking."

"Is that right? Hmm."

"It's a big deal, huh?"

"I don't know. We'll see. Thanks for the heads up, though."

"Sure. Call me as soon as you can make a comment."

"When's your deadline?"

"Three thirty. I'll call you by three if I haven't heard from you."

"Okay."

Betty Sue looked at me quizzically.

"Sabrina said the firefighters have taken a vote of no confidence against the chief," I said.

Betty Sue struggled to hide a mixture of emotions. I guessed she would take some pleasure in seeing Max squirm a little, but she knew this wouldn't help us with the decision to contract out the medical service. She sat down at my meeting table.

"They went to the paper first?"

"Yes," I said. "It's a typical strategy, but if they really want me to do something about Max, it's a bonehead move."

"Why's that?"

"Think about it."

Betty Sue frowned. "It paints you into a corner, right? If you took any disciplinary action against Max now, it would make you look like you were just bending to the will of the union."

"Exactly. If it was really Max they were after, they should have come to me privately, with the threat of public action only if I didn't respond."

"So they're just throwing one more grenade into the mix, aren't they? But I wonder if the strategy is going to backfire on them. What if the public realizes the timing is a little too suspicious, and sees the union as a bunch of whiners?"

"I don't know," I said. "The charges that Sabrina mentioned—that Max is aloof and has poor interpersonal skills—are certainly believable, even though they could apply to a lot of the managers in the private sector too. Maybe they're figuring that the public will see this as just one more example of management beating up on the hard working and downtrodden rank and file firefighters. And maybe it doesn't matter so much now what the public thinks, but what *the council* thinks the public thinks."

Betty Sue chewed the end of her pen. I noticed the ring again. How long had it been back on? "Do you suppose Max knows?" she asked.

"No, my guess would be that he's getting a call from Sabrina too, right about now."

She nodded, and thought for a moment. "Is there anything I can do on this?"

"Uh, let me get a better handle on what's going on. But you can do one thing. The same sort of thing happened to Rudy Marx in Corvallis. How about giving him a call to see how they handled it?"

"Will do."

As it turned out, I never did hear directly from Brian Gallagher. Instead, a copy of a press release appeared in our office fax machine. It was only a single page, even with the obligatory quotes—"Our men and women have reached the breaking point, and we are demanding a change in management," said Firefighters Association President Brian Gallagher. I called Max Oakley.

"Life continues to be interesting, eh Max?"

"Yes, you could say that."

"Could you come over here to talk about it?"

Max paused. "Ben, I'd prefer to discuss anything we need to discuss over the phone. I want to give the staff the impression of business as usual, as far as I'm concerned. I believe they're just sitting here waiting for me to get called into the city manager's office."

"Okay, good point. Did you have any inkling that this was coming?"

"No, not directly. Gallagher has made some veiled threats from time to time. But the assistant chiefs have most of the day-to-day contact with the troops, not me."

That could be part of the problem, I thought. "Well, in any case, their allegations were pretty light on specifics."

"Yes, they are totally groundless."

"Say, what's this 'too competitive' business? Did you beat Gallagher at handball or something?

"No. It is difficult to imagine. Perhaps it is because I purchased my Ferrari just after one of the battalion chiefs bought his Porsche. I don't know."

"Well, you know the union did you a favor by going public instead of talking to me, right?"

"It may seem that way from your perspective, but I still have my reputation and career to maintain. The damage they are doing to me goes beyond Trillium."

That hadn't occurred to me. Max needed his prestige and standing more than he needed his paycheck. "Yes, I see. Well, as much as I hate to do it, we're going to have to make some kind of response. Like, bringing in a counselor to help you and the firefighters deal with your differences, something like that."

"Then you're not going to support me."

"I didn't say that at all, Max. The quote from Gallagher seems to imply they want you fired. I will absolutely refuse to discuss that, or even any sort of disciplinary action that they might demand. As far as I'm concerned, I'll treat the allegations as poor communication on the fire union's part, as much as any fault of yours. But they've put the turd in our pocket. We've got to do something."

Max was silent.

"We'll get through this, Max. Hang in there, okay."

"Yes, there is no need to worry about me. There are ways to fight back."

I wasn't sure what he meant, but I let it go.

I put in a call to Brian Gallagher, trying to get more specifics about the union's charges. The conversation was tense, and he was mostly evasive. I asked him why he hadn't come to me first.

"We knew nothing would happen if we did," Gallagher said. "Besides, we have nothing to hide, and prefer to be open with the public."

"Open with the public? Was the meeting where you took the no confidence vote open to the public? I'd like a copy of the tape, then. And while you're at it, put me on the mailing list for your future meetings."

"Yeah, right," he said.

I had to call the council members too, before they got the news through the media. Seth Rosenberg laughed, Diane McTavish shrugged it off, and

Hank Arnold wasn't surprised—the vote of no confidence was a tactic he was familiar with—but he was concerned that it would put me in a defensive position. Rob Titus was with a client and couldn't come to the phone, so I left a message with his secretary. Maggie Henderson couldn't believe that the union was just playing games.

"The firemen may have grounds for their complaint," she said. "I myself often feel that Chief Oakley speaks down to me, that he seems aloof. I don't like it when he treats me like I'm stupid or something. Have you noticed that he does that?"

How was I supposed to answer that? "Well, Max does have his own conversational style, but I think that's just the way he is. He doesn't mean any harm by it. And it really isn't a good reason to get rid of him—all people have strengths and weaknesses, and Max has never been a back-slapping Rotarian."

"Now Ben, you will have to investigate this. I don't think a person can be a good supervisor if he doesn't have the respect of his employees, do you?"

"Maybe, but I would take this a lot more seriously if the timing wasn't so convenient. Max hasn't changed—they could have made these allegations months ago, and didn't. It just seems fishy."

"I see. But I wonder if it's a good idea to use that as an excuse to avoid your management responsibility in this area."

"Yes, I'll look into it. I don't have any choice, since I'm sure the union will get as much publicity out of this as possible. I'll let you know if there's anything to it besides a superficial complaint about how Max speaks."

Betty Sue had talked to Rudy Marx. In the case of Corvallis, it had been the police chief, but otherwise the situation was similar. Rudy's advice was to respond quickly with a press conference, stating that the complaints and allegations would be thoroughly investigated. No matter how it turned out, the public and media would lose interest long before an investigation was completed.

"That's not all," Betty Sue said.

"Oh? What else do you have?"

"I talked to Ken, to see if he had any contacts in the union negotiation world who had dealt with this before. He gave me a few names, and I managed to make contact with one of them."

"Really? Who?"

"Duke Blitzen, a labor negotiator in northern California. Have you heard of him?"

"The name sounds vaguely familiar. So what did he say?"

"Well, for one thing, this vote of no confidence thing doesn't have any official standing. It's always used as a PR ploy, and it almost always creates a really sticky situation for the city. So the good news is that we don't have to make any response to the union. But we can pretend that it *is* an official act, sort of like a grievance procedure, and we can take the public stance that we are involved in a dialogue with the union, and that it's confidential."

"Okay, but then we have to follow through with it. If we didn't, the union would make it known soon enough."

"True, but like any labor negotiations, it can drag out a long time. Remember Ben, it's a PR ploy, so the sooner we get it out of the public arena, the better."

"Yeah. You're right. Nice work, Betty Sue, and good thinking. You need to be managing your own city, not that I want to lose you."

She grinned. "Thanks, but no thanks. I'd rather give my advice and then go home and forget about it. You can have the manager job—at least for the time being."

Betty Sue worked up a press release, and it was about ready to go out when Sabrina Chan called. I summarized our response, and she said she would keep an eye on her fax machine for our official statement. I had decided a press conference wasn't necessary. It might have worked for Corvallis, but Trillium rarely warranted coverage by the radio and TV stations—we were usually too small to get noticed in the overall Portland noise.

*   *   *

I was wrong. When I got home, I turned on the evening news, and caught the middle of an interview with Brian Gallagher. The young reporter looked serious and concerned. Gallagher tried to match his expression.

"The situation with the Chief has become untenable," Gallagher was saying. "We are demanding his immediate removal. He has proven himself to be incompetent, aloof, and completely unfit for leadership. Based on our own investigation, he has shown the same pattern in the previous agencies he has worked for. We also have found evidence of ethical issues."

"Can you be more specific, Mr. Gallagher?"

"No, not at this time. We have laid these issues out for the city manager, and it is up to him to respond to them."

It was a complete lie, but how was the TV reporter going to know it?

In the morning, I opened the Metro section of the paper and groaned.

"What's the matter, Dad? Did the Mariners lose again?" Trixie asked.

"No. Well, probably, but I haven't hit that section yet. One of the council members is quoted in here, and he isn't going to make my job any easier."

"Who?" Mary asked.

"Rob Titus. Apparently the *Oregonian* picked up on the union's allegations of 'ethical issues' involving Max. They must have asked Rob if he knew what they were talking about. So here's what he said.

"This causes me grave concern," said Trillium city council member Robert Titus. "I believe the unethical conduct is related to sexual harassment, and it is something I do not tolerate. This will put an end to Mr. Oakley's career with the fire service, and justifiably so."

Mary handed the paper back to me. "Is any of that true? I think Max is kind of a jerk, but he doesn't strike me as an unethical person."

"No, there isn't any basis for it at all. I don't know who's feeding Rob this garbage. Well, on second thought, I could make a pretty good guess, but I wonder why he's letting himself get dragged into it."

A crew from Channel 7 was waiting for me when I got to city hall. I summarized our official statement for them, but it wasn't enough.

"How are you going to respond to the charges of unethical conduct and sexual harassment?"

"Let's be clear about that," I said. "Those issues weren't mentioned in the document I received from the fire union. We have a good process for responding to sexual harassment complaints, and it is available to every city employee. No such complaint has ever been filed against Max Oakley, and I have seen no evidence of unethical conduct whatsoever."

"But what about the statement from councilor Titus?"

"I haven't had a chance to talk to him about that, so I can't comment on it."

The media kept the issue alive for three days. Brian Gallagher and some of the other union leaders added more fuel to the fire, hinting at a variety of indiscretions that were supposedly under discussion. It made me even less interested in taking the vote of no confidence seriously, but Ken Longstreet lined up a counselor who could come in and make a show of patching up communications between the chief and his staff.

*   *   *

I pushed my spoon through the layer of cheese in a bowl of French onion soup. Max had requested the lunch meeting, but all he was having was a plate of salad and coffee. He seemed a little on edge, but I wasn't surprised by that. When I had expressed my sympathy over what he had been going through, he just shrugged.

We ate our lunch and talked about other things—mostly the City/County contract and how the council would respond to it. Then Max put down his fork and leaned forward.

"Ben, the reason I wanted to talk to you is I need you to convey some information to a few individuals."

"Oh? What's that?"

"I have been in contact with an attorney in Los Angeles. After considering his advice, this is what I'm going to do. I am going to personally sue Brian Gallagher for one million dollars. I am going to sue the firefighters association for five million dollars. Further, I am going to sue Rob Titus for one million dollars. Now, my attorney specializes in cases like this. In the last year, he has won a court verdict for five million dollars, and he has settled out of court for two cases involving several million dollars each. He informs me that the facts are on my side on this, and we have a very good chance of winning."

"Really? As public officials, we're expected to take a lot of flack from folks—they can even lie about us and we can't sue them for libel."

"That may be true in general, but when false statements cause material damages in an individual's career or earning potential, there is still legal responsibility. But here's the point I want to make. I don't need the money. I'm not interested in the money. What I am interested in is taking them down. If I go down, they are going down with me. I will bury them so deep in attorneys' fees that they will lose their houses, their cars, and everything else they have in their name. I'm serious about this, and I will pursue it for as long as it takes. This isn't a city issue—it's my issue, personally, and I will make it be their personal issue too."

Max leaned back and watched something out the window. In an earlier era, he would have pulled out a cigarette case and a gold lighter. But we had other vices now, and Max just sat and waited for my reaction. I had no doubt that he was serious.

"So what do you want me to do?"

"Just tell them what I've told you."

"And what do you want from them?"

He was silent for a moment. Then he leaned forward again.

"They must cease and desist from slandering me and tarnishing my reputation. Gallagher and Titus must retract their libelous statements. And as for the union, there are a few more things I will insist upon, but I will discuss them later, after you have conveyed the initial message."

"Okay. But why do you need me in the middle of this? Why not have your lawyer contact them?"

"Ben, I am asking for your help as a friend. If the parties will agree to the terms of my settlement, then we can all put this behind us. I also believe it is in your best interest to see the union silenced on this matter."

"You're right about that."

"You also have credibility with them."

"Are you kidding? Credibility with Gallagher and the union?"

"Yes. They might not like you much, but they see you as a force to be reckoned with. Don't discount that."

"Hmm. Well, it would give me a certain amount of pleasure to be the bearer of this news. I'll do it." Max nodded with satisfaction, and reached for his cup of coffee.

"Say, Max, I've been meaning to ask you about something. Matt Monroe told me that you used to work for City/County. That true?"

The coffee mug froze in midair, just for an instant. "Well—"

"Excuse me." Our waiter had suddenly appeared. "Is one of you Ben Cromarty?"

"Yes, I am. Why? Did my credit card bounce?"

"Sorry, sir. We just got a call from Legacy Hospital. They said they have just admitted your daughter, who was involved in a car accident."

"What? Are they still on the line? What kind of accident?"

"I don't know sir—it sounded like they were in a hurry, but they said your office said you might be here so they left the message just in case."

The room spun. I held the edge of the table and tried to stand up.

"Ben, I'll drive you," Max said. "Let's go."

I followed numbly. In the car a chill came over me, and I felt perspiration break out on my forehead. I had to do something to keep focused. I fished in my suit pocket for my cell phone and tried to remember Mary's work number. I watched as my fingers pushed the keys.

"Good afternoon. Trillium School District Administrative Office, this is Cherie."

"Uh, Cherie, this is Ben. Ben Cromarty. Is Mary there?"

"Well, I can—"

"It's an emergency. Please."

"Okay, okay."

After a long minute, Mary came on the line. "What is it Ben?"

"I just got a call from Legacy Hospital. They said that Trixie has been in some kind of car accident. I'm on my way there."

"Oh no! What…is she all right?"

"I don't know. All I know is what the message said. I can meet you at the hospital if you can get away."

"Oh Ben! Yes, I'll be there right away. Oh no…" The line went dead.

I was thrown against the side of the car as Max took a corner too fast. The traffic must have been light but to me it seemed that the road was strewn with obstacles.

We finally got to the hospital. Max dropped me at the main entrance and went to find a parking space. I made my way to the admissions counter.

"Excuse me, my name is Ben Cromarty. My daughter Trixie was admitted to the emergency room. Could you tell me where she is?"

"Yes, sir." She punched some keys on her computer. "Please spell the last name."

I did, and her fingers flew over the keyboard. She frowned and continued to type. It was taking too long.

"What's the problem?" I asked, trying to keep the panic out of my voice.

"There is no record of her being admitted."

Of course, I thought, with a wave of dread washing over me. If she had been unconscious, the hospital wouldn't be able to identify her.

"Where's the emergency room?"

"It's the next building over. You can use the connecting walk way to your right, or the sidewalk outside. You'll see—"

I left her in mid sentence and hurried to the entrance doors. Outside I saw Max walking casually from the parking lot. The E.R. was in the opposite direction and I broke into a run. After a few paces I began thinking more clearly, and spun around to intercept Max.

"They don't have a record of her being admitted," I said, trying to catch my breath. "I'm going to the emergency room. Stay at the main entrance and watch for Mary."

"No problem."

A half dozen people sat in chairs along two walls of the waiting area. A young woman holding a baby paced back and forth. None of them looked like they were from Trixie's school. The nurses' station was empty, and I could hear the sound of a child crying down the hall. I was going to follow the noise when a man in hospital scrubs moved behind the counter.

"Can I help you?" he said.

"I'm looking for my daughter. Trixie Cromarty. She was in a car accident."

"Well, let's see…" He looked through a stack of forms in a tray. After he got to the bottom one, he looked up. "What does she look like?"

"Blond hair, about this long. Brown eyes. Eleven years old."

"Okay. Hold on."

He disappeared down the hall and was gone for a long time. Another nurse walked behind the counter and asked me if I had been helped. I told her, and hoped she would find out what was taking her colleague so long. Instead, she picked up a form and called out a name. She led a man in his eighties down the hall.

Finally, the male nurse reappeared. "I'm sorry," he said, shaking his head. My heart skipped a beat and my legs started to buckle. I was too late, and she was already dead.

"I've checked out all our patients," I heard him saying through the pounding in my ears, "and she isn't one of them. We haven't had any young girls in a car accident yet today. Are you sure she was brought here?"

I stood, mute.

"Are you all right, sir?"

"Yes, yes I am," I said, regaining my composure. "She was supposed to be here, but maybe I got the message wrong. Do you have numbers for the other hospitals in Portland?"

"Sure." A piece of paper was tacked to the wall. He removed the tack and handed it to me.

"How about a phone?"

"We need to keep this one available for ER staff. There's a pay phone near the doors. Please be sure to bring that list back to me."

"I will. Thanks."

I hurried to the phone, thinking about how much time I had wasted coming to the wrong hospital and picturing Trixie in a room somewhere surrounded by doctors and surgical equipment, wondering where we were. I fished in my pocket for change, then remembered I still had the cell phone in my coat. I called the first hospital on the list, and was on hold when Mary and Max burst through the doors.

"Ben! Where is she?" Mary's face was pale and her eyes were moist. I put an arm around her waist and held her close.

"I don't know. Not here, apparently, so I'm trying—"

A voice cut in on the line, saying that they had no record of Trixie being admitted. I punched in the number for the next hospital on the list. Mary watched me, looking dazed and worried. Max went over to the waiting room and picked up a magazine. After being passed from one staff member to another, I drew a blank again. I was about to call the third number on the list when Max walked back, looking a little impatient.

"What about the school?" he asked.

"What school?"

"The one your daughter attends. This is a school day, isn't it? If she were involved in a car accident, I would imagine that they might know something about it."

Maybe he thought more clearly than I did because he was practiced at dealing with emergencies. On the other hand, it wasn't his child we were talking about.

"Good point. I'll call."

Mary rang her office to get the number, then passed the phone back to me. I punched the keys and waited for an answer.

"Hello, Trillium Middle School."

"Yes, this is Ben Cromarty, Trixie Cromarty's father. I got a call saying Trixie was involved in a car accident. I want to know if you can give me any more information."

"My goodness. Trixie Cromarty? Hold on."

I listened to the tinny sound of a country music station. Why was it taking them so long?

"Hello, Mr. Cromarty? This is Mel Zimmer, the school principal. I'm sorry, but we don't have any information about a car accident. We're checking into it, but so far—hold on."

He must have cupped his hand over the mouthpiece. I could hear voices, faintly.

"Hello Daddy!"

"Trixie?"

"Yup."

I took a deep breath. "Are you all right? What happened?"

"I scraped my knee in PE. Except for that it's been a pretty boring day. My knee is okay though. They put a band aid on it."

I slumped against the wall.

"Dad? Are you still there? What's up?"

"Oh, it's okay sweetie. There was some kind of mix-up in a message I got. Don't worry about it. I'll let you get back to your class. I love you."

"Love you too, pop. Bye."

Relief filled Mary's face. Max glanced at me with an arched brow.

"Trixie is fine," I said. "Either some hospital got screwed up, or somebody is playing a pretty sick joke."

"Oh. Thank God," Mary said, and collapsed into my arms. I felt her sob. Max moved to a discreet distance.

"Do you think someone could have done this on purpose?" Mary asked, her voice catching.

"I don't know," I said. "There are enough wackos out there, it's possible. But the important thing is that Trixie is all right. Sorry for putting you through this."

"It's not your fault." She stood back for a moment, then leaned into my arms again. We held each other for a few minutes. I tried to comfort Mary, but my mind was racing. I had always dreaded the possibility that my job would spill over into my family's life, and I felt nothing but guilt.

Max walked back toward us. "I called Simon," he said. "He's sending a detective over to the restaurant to get some more details about the phone message. He said to tell you that he will find 'the son of a bitch that done this.' His words."

"Huh. Well, we can still hope that it's some kind of miscommunication."

Max shrugged.

"Yeah, it doesn't seem likely, does it?" I said.

Mary glanced at the entrance doors. "Well, I better get back to work," she said, drying her eyes with a tissue.

"Yes. Me too."

*   *   *

Mary was quiet over dinner. She wanted to stay and play a card game with Trixie and me, but she had made a commitment to attend a meeting at the church—something about a fund raiser for some missionaries in China. I finished up the dishes and paced around the house. Trixie was watching a show where young adults in their twenties seemed do nothing but sit around and talk. I went back to the kitchen and made a phone call.

"Hello?"

"Hi Kate. It's Ben."

"Well, hello there. I was just thinking of you."

"Oh? I'm flattered," I said, trying to sound like it was a joke.

"Yeah, well the reason is, I'm sitting here trying to sort out all this paperwork for my SBA loan, and wondering why you government types make life so difficult."

"Oh."

"But I know you're not like that, right?"

I laughed. "I wonder. I'm not into forms and red tape, but I suppose I make life difficult enough for some folks."

"Is Mary there?"

"No, she's at a meeting. Trixie's watching TV."

I told her about the phone threat, the one telling me I better watch myself, and the call from the hospital.

"That's pretty creepy, Ben. You think it's connected to this fire department stuff?"

"Chances are pretty good."

"Mary must have been spooked by it. Think I should talk to her about it?"

"Yes, she would appreciate that," I said, "but—"

"I'll tell her that I called to see how you guys were doing, and you told me the story."

"Okay. And there's another thing, Kate."

"What's that?"

"Things are getting strange enough that I'm concerned about somebody trying to break into my e-mail account. I'm probably just paranoid…."

"So you think I should hold off on sending any messages, right?"

"Yes. At least for a few days, until I set up a new account or something. Is that okay?"

"Well…it's going to be hard. I've come to depend on those little notes, more than you can know."

"Yeah, me too. I'll work something out. How's everything else going?"

"Well, Gordon is in the den, buried in some kind of database software. Just before you called, I heard Luke yelling at Joshua. He said something like, 'Josh, if you have a booger and you don't want to wipe it on your clothes and you don't want to eat it, then just leave it in your nose.' That's about the level of my intellectual stimulation these days." She giggled.

"It's good talking to you, Kate."

"Mmm. You too."

The line was silent for a few moments.

"Well, I'll let you know if we get any more excitement here," I said.

"Yeah, keep in touch. I'll call Mary."

"Good night, Kate."

"See ya."

19

Jake Wildavsky came ambling into my office and folded himself into my side chair.

"So did you hear the one about the Englishman, the Scotsman, and the Irishman in the bar?" he said.

"Uh, no."

"Well, you see, they're sitting there drinking their beer, and a fly drops into the Englishman's glass. So he pushes his glass away in disgust. A while later, a fly drops into the Scotsman's beer. So he sticks his finger in and flicks it out, and keeps on drinking. After a while a fly lands in the Irishman's drink. He reaches in, picks it up, holds it over his beer, and starts hitting it. 'Ah, spit it out, ya beggar, spit it out,' he says. Pretty good, huh?"

I laughed. Jake did a fairly decent Irish accent for a Polish guy.

"You want to hear the latest?" he said.

"I'm not sure. Is it good news for a change?"

"Of course not. When do you ever hear good news from me?"

"Got a point there," I agreed.

"Well, Dyson's giving me a hard time about this privatization deal."

Frank Dyson was a crew leader for the public works staff in field operations, and the shop steward for their union.

"Why does he care?" I asked. "They haven't been that sympathetic with the fire department in the past." In fact, several of the public works staff had told me privately that they thought the firefighters were acting like a bunch of prima donnas.

"Yeah, well apparently they're getting spooked that we might do the same thing in public works. And I think they're getting a lot of pressure from the OPEU."

I tried to clear my head. The Oregon Public Employees Union wasn't affiliated in any way with the Firefighters Association, but they would certainly be sympathetic, and support the cause of union solidarity.

"There isn't much threat," I said. "We've already privatized about as much as we can there. We contract out for all major improvements, street sweeping, meter reading, the works. The only thing that's left is the small stuff like maintenance and pothole patching. So what's the problem?"

"Think about it. Suppose you were in their shoes, and someone came up to you and said, 'You know, there are a lot of private companies that do maintenance work, and they have next to zero pension costs.' How would you feel?"

"I guess you're right," I said. "So assure them that we have no intention of doing that. Tell them that we're proud of their efficiency and hard work, and we know there's no private company that could beat that."

Jake cracked his knuckles. "Okay, I guess I could. But it would be better coming from you."

"You mean they can never tell if you're being serious?"

"Aw shucks, Ben. I'm always serious. I'm a really serious guy. I'm hurt that you don't know that about me."

I smiled. "Jake, as long as we're being serious here, how's your daughter doing?"

He was silent for a moment, then sat up in the chair. "Up and down. The chemo was working and the leukemia was in remission, but now she's sliding back again. I guess the statistics are pretty good—the recovery rate is decent—but it isn't 100 percent. I just hope she isn't on the losing side of the percentages."

He took off his glasses and polished them on his shirt sleeve. "Well, we're all praying for her," I said.

"Well, thanks. I do appreciate it. Sue and I are doing a lot of that ourselves."

*　　　　　*　　　　　*

Brian Gallagher and Red Rogalsky looked wary. I had called them into my office—no reason to look for neutral ground for this meeting. I didn't bother with small talk.

"Chief Oakley has asked me to convey some information to you. Briefly put, you've pushed him too far on this no-confidence issue. So this is what he told me he's going to do. Brian, he intends to sue you personally for a million dollars. And he intends to sue the fire association for five million dollars."

"He can't do that," Gallagher said. "He doesn't have a case."

"Oh, I don't know about that. Max says he has a hotshot attorney from LA. One who specializes in cases like this, and who has a great track record. Apparently this attorney smells blood and is eager to file."

"Doesn't matter. We've got attorneys too. We'll call his bluff."

"Well, you might want to think about it. Max told me he doesn't care about whether he wins or not. He said he plans to bury you so deep in attorneys fees that you will be personally bankrupt, and the union will be bled dry. He said he doesn't need the money, he's got plenty."

"Aw, shit, he's just blowing smoke. Tell him to screw himself."

"Hold on, Brian," Rogalski said. "What is it that Oakley wants?"

"He wants all allegations and insinuations about his character and management ability to stop. He wants you to publicly refute your prior statements. There may be some other terms, but those are the ones I know about."

"I see. Of course, we stand behind our statements."

"Of course." I tried to keep the sarcasm out of my voice.

"This is crap," Gallagher said. "Forget about it."

"This isn't coming from me, Brian. I'm just passing this on from Max. Do what you want."

"We'll have to think about it," Rogalski said. "I'll call you tomorrow."

I gave the same message to Rob Titus, in his office. It was a little more awkward, since I had to avoid the appearance of threatening one of my own bosses.

"He can't do that," Rob said. "He's one of my employees. He can't sue me."

"Well, Rob, you're the attorney, not me. But apparently Max's lawyer said that being a council member doesn't give you protection for making personal attacks. I don't know. From what Max says, this lawyer has a pretty good track record. I checked with Pete too, and he said you should take the issue seriously. You might want to talk to him."

Rob chewed on his fingernail. "What does he want?"

"Just some public acknowledgement that there isn't any grounds for the comments about his management ability, and particularly about the sexual harassment thing."

"Well, I didn't make that up," Rob protested. "It was something I heard."

I didn't say anything.

"Okay," Rob said. "That's easy enough. I was obviously given erroneous information. I can say that. Tell Max I'm sorry for any misunderstanding."

*　　　　*　　　　*

Simon's detective work didn't yield any results on the hospital crank call. The message at the restaurant had been from a man, probably the same one who had called the office a few minutes earlier. Most of the hospital admissions staff were women, and in any case, there was only a slim chance the call had originated from the hospital. Simon was convinced it was a firefighter—probably one from another city—or a relative of a firefighter, but of course he had no proof.

I didn't have to wait for a call back from Red Rogalsky. The day after I talked to him, Max stopped by my office to tell me that he had already reached a settlement with the union and Gallagher, and that he was pleased with the outcome. That evening, a press release went out, stating that the union had completely resolved it's issues with the chief, and was looking forward to a positive continuing working relationship. There was more to the agreement between the union and Max, but I never discovered what it was.

Rob Titus was quoted in the paper the next day, stating that he had been misinformed about the sexual harassment allegations, and that he had personally apologized to the chief about them. I knew the last part was a lie—Rob had never talked to the chief—but I also knew that Max didn't care. He had gotten what he wanted.

*   *   *

We had had a rare stretch of warm and clear weather. After months of rain, the lawns of Trillium seemed to be growing an inch a day. I tried to get home early enough to mow ours before it got too tall for my lawnmower. Even though the ground was relatively dry, the grass seemed filled with green juice, and Trixie followed me around with a wheelbarrow and helped me empty the grass bag. As small as our yard was, we managed to nearly fill the compost bin on the back of the shed. The sweet smell of the freshly cut grass made me think that spring was here, and that summer was around the corner. It was an illusion: native Oregonians knew that anything resembling summer didn't appear until after Independence Day.

Just before I had left the office, I had replayed another phone threat. Again, it was a muffled male voice. "Back off of the county city deal if you know what's best for you" was all the message said. Simon would scold me, but I just erased the message and tried to put it out of my mind—without much success.

Trixie went bike riding with Nathan in the remaining daylight, and invited him for dinner. They talked and giggled about things that had happened in school, and their open innocence was therapeutic for me.

"You know what mittens does?" Trixie asked me.

"Mittens?"

"That's my cat it's his cat," Nathan and Trixie said simultaneously.

"No, what?"

"He keeps bringing body parts onto my front porch," Nathan said.

"Huh?"

"Yeah, his Mom said, 'What's that green thing on your shoe?' when Nathan walked in the house. He said 'I think it's a spleen!'"

"No, a gallbladder," Nathan said.

"Whatever," Trixie said. "It was stuck to his shoe! And he was walking around with it flapping like a piece of gum!"

They cackled in laughter.

"Yeah, Mittens put it there," Nathan said. "She catches mice and takes them apart and leaves the pieces on our porch. It drives my Mom nuts—"

"But I think it's pretty neat," Trixie said. "Me and Nathan, we try to figure out what the parts are. Maybe we should take them to our science class, huh?"

"Yes, I'm sure your teacher would appreciate that," Mary said. "There's a few dozen slugs in our garden you can take too."

"Naw, they're not as much fun," Nathan said, with a serious expression. "They don't have as many parts."

Mary and I did the dishes together. We talked about the small things that seem trivial, but make up the fabric of life. In the middle, Mary put down her drying towel and gave me a hug. I squeezed her back with my forearms, trying not to get her wet with my soapy hands.

"Thanks," I said. "What prompted that?"

"You haven't said much about work, but I can tell it's getting to you. I worry about you, honey."

I muttered something stoical, but I realized how much I needed her.

I sorted through some papers in my briefcase, and Mary quietly played the piano. She got out the music for a Bach sonata that sounded familiar at first, but then I noticed she gently switched to a minor chord and eased into a jazz tempo. I paused from my reading and watched her play. Her hair looked like honey in the soft light. Her head was bowed and I guessed her eyes were closed as she let her fingers feel their way over the keys. Her right hand worked a repetitive pattern while her left hand walked up and down the keyboard in a complex bass line, building from a soft murmur to a powerful crescendo, and switching at the last moment back to a series of major chords that ended in a surprise key change. She sat silently for a moment with her head still bowed, and then must have sensed I was watching her. She turned and asked if she was breaking my concentration. I told her no, keep playing, but she was too self-conscious and contented herself with some simple exercises.

On the way to the kitchen to refill my coffee mug, I paused and rubbed her shoulders, then lifted her hair and kissed her on the nape of her neck.

Before putting Trixie to bed, I read to her from Orson Scott Card's *Ender's Game*. She was old enough to read it herself, but it was a routine that we had started when she was an infant, and neither of us wanted it to end. She hugged me when I tucked her in, and I thought about how much I needed to count my blessings.

But as with most nights lately, I had a hard time getting to sleep. I finally drifted off around one o'clock.

The muffled explosion must have become part of a dream I was having. I didn't wake up until I heard the piercing scream of the smoke alarm. The sound and a faint smell of smoke started my heart racing, and I bounded down the hallway to find the source. By instinct, I pulled open Trixie's bedroom door.

Smoke poured out. I took a deep breath and plunged in and cradled Trixie in my arms. I ran out and closed the door behind me with my foot.

Mary was behind me. "Call 911," I shouted. I carried Trixie downstairs and into the living room and laid her on the couch. A second smoke alarm went off. Trixie's eyes fluttered open, and she sat up, coughing.

"What happ—" She was hit with another spasm of coughing.

"Just lie down for a minute, baby," I said. Mary came through the doorway, her face white.

"I called—they're on their way," she yelled over the noise of the smoke alarms. "Do you know what's on fire?"

I shook my head. "Stay with Trixie." I ran up to the bedroom and pulled on a pair of jeans. I looked into Trixie's room, but couldn't see any flames. The window, though, was glowing red and orange. I flew downstairs and ran out the door and around the side of the house.

The shed was fully consumed, and it looked like the back wall was about to fall in. The fire was intense enough that it had ignited the house siding, and flames were licking under Trixie's open bedroom window. I went for the garden hose, but it was on the other side of the shed, and the heat was too intense for me to run to it. I jumped the fence into the neighbor's yard, giving the burning shed a wide berth, and jumped back into my yard. I yanked the hose out of the reel and twisted open the faucet. The water turned to steam as it hit the fire but I could barely hear the hissing over the roar of the flames. I had to shield my face with my arm, and hoped that the spray was going in the right general direction.

I heard a shout. On the other side of the shed, a figure in yellow turnout gear and a helmet was waving me away. The heated air between us made him shimmer like a ghost. I dropped the hose and made my way around the back side of the house, stumbling in the dark.

"We'll take over from here, Ben," Captain Phil Tucker said.

I nodded. After the heat of the fire, the cold night air made me shiver. Tucker reached into his command vehicle and pulled out a spare coat.

"Here, this'll warm you up."

"Thanks."

In a practiced series of movements, the firefighters quickly and calmly began their attack on the fire. A line was run to the hydrant and coupled. At the same time a pair of firefighters ran out with a hose from the pumper, getting into position, one in front on the nozzle and the second a few feet behind, ready to absorb the recoil from the pressure. Using only hand signals, the firefighter on the hydrant opened the valve, while the engineer operated some controls on the side of the pumper and the two firefighters on the end of the line braced themselves. The engine growled under the load and a blast of water smashed into what was left of the shed.

Mary was huddled on the front steps under a blanket, watching as two paramedics bent over Trixie.

"How come you came out here?" I said. "Too smoky in the house?"

"No, I had to get away from the smoke alarms," she said.

"You know, they probably saved your lives and your house," one of the paramedics said.

"How is she?" I asked.

"Just fine," he said. "I'm going to give her a little oxygen to clear out her lungs, but it looks like you got her out in time."

I could see the fear in Trixie's eyes, and I bent over her and stroked her forehead.

"It's going to be okay, sweetie," I said.

"What happened, Dad?"

"I don't know, hon. It's just the shed—it caught on fire somehow."

The paramedic slipped the oxygen mask over her face. I held her hand. Mary squeezed her shoulder.

The houses on our street were washed in a red strobe light from the sweeping beams on top of the vehicles. I became aware that all our neighbors were on their porches or driveways, watching the commotion. They stood in clumps, talking to each other and shaking their heads.

There wasn't much left to see; the fire was out in minutes, and the firefighters were digging around in the wet ashes, looking for any remaining embers. Captain Tucker and another firefighter went up the stairs and into the house. After a few moments, the smoke alarms went silent.

The paramedics checked Trixie's vital signs, and removed the mask. They tucked her into her blanket and quietly started packing up their equipment.

Tucker rejoined us on the porch. "We're airing out the house," he said. "Doesn't look like you have any smoke damage, but it may take a few days for the smell to completely clear out. No damage inside, and it looks like we got it before it got past the siding on the outside."

"Good."

"We've got the fire marshal and arson investigator coming out; they should be here in a minute."

"Arson?"

"Don't worry, it's routine when it isn't obvious how a fire starts. You don't have any ideas, do you?"

"No."

With smooth precision, the firefighters rewound the hose and began putting away their gear. Before getting back into the pumper and rescue truck, a few came up the steps to offer their condolences.

"Thanks, guys," I said.

An hour after they arrived, only the command vehicle was left in front of the house, and the neighbors had gone back to bed. The fire marshal pulled up, followed within minutes by a police vehicle. They huddled with Phil Tucker for a few minutes, and started sorting through the remains of the shed. Tucker set up a portable light for them, then signaled a firefighter and the two of them drove off in the command vehicle. A few minutes later they returned, and Tucker carried two cups of coffee in Starbucks containers up the stairs for Mary and me. "Hope you like it black," he said.

"Hey, thanks Phil."

He sat down on the stairs next to me.

"You know, Ben," he said quietly, "there've been rumors floating around the station about people making threats against you."

I just shrugged.

"Well, chances are this was just an accident, a coincidence. But you need to know I think those threats are completely uncalled for, and most of the men are disgusted that that kind of thing is happening. We know you've got a job to do, just like everyone else, and part of your job is making tough decisions."

Mary looked over at him, silently.

"Thanks Phil, I appreciate that."

"Listen, if there's anything you need, let me know, okay."

"Sure."

He put a hand on my shoulder, and stood up. The fire marshal appeared around the corner of the house and she beckoned the captain over. He talked to her for a few moments, then got in the command vehicle and left. Bernice Jenkins walked over to us, carrying a large notepad.

"Hey Ben, it's been quite a night for y'all, hasn't it?"

"Yes. You find anything over there?" I was almost afraid of the answer.

"Naw, things were pretty well burned up. But say, there was a mound of something on the back of the shed—what was that?"

"Compost pile."

"Looks like that's where the fire started. You put any fresh grass in there lately?"

"Yeah, just today, I guess it was technically yesterday now."

"Hmm. Not enough time for spontaneous combustion to do its thing. Grass pretty wet?"

"Yeah, and there was already a bunch from last week. I saw it steaming a little, but I figured that was healthy, just the bugs going to work."

She made some notes. "Yep, that could be it. The new stuff coulda just put a lid on it, and started cooking the side of your shed. Shouldn't have it so close, you know."

"Yeah, I guess so."

"You have some gas or something in the shed?"

"I don't know. There was a five gallon jug that didn't have much in it, and whatever was left in the lawnmower."

"Uh huh," she nodded.

Police Detective Larry Footen ambled over toward us. One of his areas of special training was arson investigation. He and Bernice made a good team—she specialized in the fire scene forensics, and Larry took the lead on interviews with witnesses and suspects.

"So what about arson?" I asked.

"If it was, they either knew what they were doing, or the fire obliterated any evidence. Don't you think so, Bernice?"

"Yep." She ran a hand through her short curls. "The only thing that makes me wonder is the timing. It's hard to see how it could go from an overheated compost pile to flashover in eight hours without a little help. But heck, it's possible. I've seen a lot stranger things happen."

"I'll talk to your neighbors when it gets light out," Larry said. "I doubt any of them would be looking out their windows in the middle of the night, but maybe they heard something."

Trixie shivered under her blanket.

"Say, if you folks want to come over to my place, I'll fix you up some breakfast," Bernice said.

I looked at Mary. "Thanks, but I think we'll just head back to bed. What time is it?"

Bernice looked at her watch. "Four."

"Sorry to get you two out of bed in the middle of the night like this," I said. They were both on a regular eight-to-five day shift.

"Hey, no problem—it's part of the job," Bernice said.

Inside the house, the smell of smoke was already faint. We put Trixie to bed in the guest room, and Mary and I tried to catch some sleep. After a few minutes, I felt Mary relax and her breathing fell into a steady rhythm.

I couldn't sleep. I felt my way in the dark to the living room, turned on a reading lamp and reached for a Bible on the coffee table. It seemed like my life was crashing down on me—the threats, the fire, the conflicts at work, the thought of losing my connection with Kate. The Bible fell open to the words, "I lie awake; I have become like a bird alone on a roof. All day long my enemies taunt me; those who rail against me use my name as a curse." Great. I looked for a familiar passage, and found it. "And surely I am with you always, to the very end of the age." That helped.

I tuned into a late night music station, turned off the light, and lay down on the floor. I buried my head in my arms. Jackson Browne was singing, "Doctor, my eyes have seen the years and the slow parade of tears, without crying…"

2 0

We let Trixie sleep in for a while and I drove her to school, then stopped by our insurance agent's office to go over the process for repairing the fire damage. I had taken a look at the side of the house—in the morning light, it didn't look as bad. Just some blackened siding, a mound of ash and charred metal where the shed had been, and a wide circle of burnt grass.

The staff in the office hadn't heard about the fire yet, which was fine with me since I really didn't want to talk about it. I made it through my appointments and paperwork in a dull stupor—lack of sleep, I supposed.

Later in the afternoon, I came into the office reception area, and interrupted Mrs. Dunwoody, who was in the process of giving Terri Knox a severe lecture.

"The airborne vehicles are the reason you are pregnant," she said, her voice shrill. "Their rays are everywhere and they impregnate young girls like you, and nobody does anything about it."

Mrs. Dunwoody was wearing a yellow raincoat with a hood, and yellow rubber boots, even though it was dry outside. She looked like a duckling. Terri, trying to ignore her, was typing something into her computer, occasionally looking up and saying, "Uh huh."

Mrs. Dunwoody paused and looked at me for a long moment. "What you need to do, mister," she said to me, "is find out the name of Brian Gallagher's wife."

Gallagher's wife? I had met her once, and although I didn't remember what her name was, it wasn't unusual and I couldn't see how it was relevant to her lecture on airborne vehicles.

"Yes ma'am," I muttered, and ducked into my office.

Max Oakley stopped by later. "I'm sorry you had to have a first-hand experience with our service," he said.

"Me too, but I'm glad they were there," I said. "Do you know if Larry has made any progress interviewing the neighbors?"

"Don't know. Do you think there might be a connection with the threats?"

"No, I guess I'm just getting spooked."

Max stood and looked out my window with his hands clasped behind his back. "There may be some complications with a contract with City/County," he said.

"Oh? How's that?"

"For one, our union contract calls for reductions in force to be done by strict seniority."

"Yeah, I know."

"Well, it makes no distinction between levels of training. Of course, the least senior will have generally lower levels of training, but as we go deeper in layoffs, we may be losing personnel with more extensive fire training, and retaining personnel with more extensive EMS training. This is opposite from what we would need to transition staff to City/County. We want to keep the personnel who know how to fight fires."

"But doesn't it sort of average out? I mean, over time, don't most of your staff get training in both areas?"

"Yes, but we start with the fire training."

It didn't seem like a big problem to me. Some of the staff with more advanced paramedic training could even volunteer to move to City/County to take advantage of a possible promotion.

"That's the way it goes," I said. "Hey—our union negotiations are still open. Let's just propose a change to the contract. Think they'll go for it?"

Max turned to look at me and chuckled. "Not very likely."

"Say, this is off the subject, but what is Brian Gallagher's wife's name?"

"Shirley. Why?"

"No particular reason, just curious."

Max raised his eyebrows, but didn't comment. He sat down at my round table and stroked his moustache.

"Ben, I hope you're keeping an open mind about this City/County proposal."

"Yes, of course." Now what?

He thought for a moment, as if choosing his words carefully. "It's too early to tell, but I may have an additional alternative for the council to consider."

Why didn't he say, for *me* to consider? The council made the ultimate policy decisions, but any staff proposals theoretically went through me.

"Oh? What's that?" I asked.

"Like I said, it's too early to tell, and I have to do more research before I'm prepared to present it. But I wanted to ascertain that you would be receptive."

"I'm willing to listen to anything," I said.

*   *   *

Max had just left when Marie called from the main reception counter downstairs.

"Ben, there's someone here to see you."

"All right. Who is it?"

"She just said her name is Scarlet. I tried to keep her here, but she headed straight for the stairs."

I groaned. "Okay. Thanks Marie."

She appeared in my office door, breathing hard. I couldn't keep from looking behind her to see if she was carrying something. She was, to my relief, empty-handed.

"Hello, Scarlet. How can I help you today?"

"You can start by firing your lousy public works department."

"Oh?"

"Yeah. See, I'm at the end of the water line or something, and I keep getting this orange stuff in the water. My boyfriend, he says it's 'cause the line needs to be flushed or something. I keep complaining about it, but they never do nothing." She paused for a breath. "So finally I tell 'em I've had enough, that my damn bathtub has an orange ring around it, and that they better do something about it. So finally they give me this stuff to rub on it, they say that'll just take care of the problem. Like hell. I put the stuff on like they said. You know what happened? Took the damn porcelain right off the tub. I went to get in, sat down in the tub, and it was like sittin' on sandpaper. Gave me a rash all over my butt. Here, look."

I sat, paralyzed with a kind of morbid fascination as she proceeded to unzip her jeans. Her belly started to spill out of it and I recovered.

"Hold it, Scarlet. Please don't show me, I'll take your word for it."

She gave me a cold look, breathed in deeply to give her jeans some slack, and slowly pulled the zipper back up. Outside my office, Terri was craning over her desk to get a better look. This would make a good story.

"So. What're you going to do about it?" she demanded.

I thought quickly. "How about this? I'll get our utility supervisory to take a look at the bathtub. If he doesn't think it can be fixed, we'll buy you a new one. How's that sound?"

"Sounds to me like you're pretty stupid to be a city manager. How in hell do you suppose you're going to get a new tub through the door? It's a big tub—pretty old maybe, but definitely big."

I sighed. "We'll figure it out. Maybe through the window, I don't know. Let's just leave that part up to the field staff—that's what they're good at. What do you say?"

"Well…" She clenched her jaw. "Well, all right. But if it isn't fixed in a week one way or the other, you're going to hear from me again, and next time I won't be as polite." She marched out before I could say anything.

*   *   *

Somehow I found Scarlet's visit stressful, so I wandered down to the employee lunch room to take a break and read the Metro section of the *Oregonian*. I saw Sabrina Chan's byline, and remembered she had said something about checking out the names of firefighters' spouses. She had been looking for maiden names. What had she used to get to them?

I went back upstairs to the city clerk's office.

"Say, Twila, do you have a printout of registered voters?"

Twila Bettle was in her late fifties, and had been City Clerk forever. She wasn't much for small talk, but she could put her fingers on almost any document in the city.

"Yes, of course. I assume, by the way, that you mean Trillium voters. I don't have any other ones."

"Yes, I think that will do."

"What order do you want, alpha, street, or doorbelling?"

"Huh?"

She sighed. "Alpha is by voter name, street is alphabetical by street name, and doorbelling is ordered the way a person would use to canvass the city."

"Wouldn't street and doorbell be about the same?"

"No, of course not." You fool, her expression said. "Under street order, Ash Street is right next to Atlas Street, but they're on opposite sides of town. You wouldn't want to go door-to-door that way, would you?"

"No, I guess you're right. But anyway, I need the alpha order."

"Don't have one sitting around, but I can print it out. It'll be about 100 pages. Take some time."

"Oh." I hadn't wanted to reveal who I was looking for, but it seemed to be a waste to print the whole thing.

"Okay," I said. "Can you bring individual names up on the computer?"

"Certainly." She waited for me to say something. "Okay, who do you want to look up?" she said.

"Uh, Brian Gallagher," I said.

She looked at me over her reading glasses, then began typing on her keyboard. She turned the monitor toward me, wordlessly. I saw the entrance giving first, middle and last names, residence, date of birth, and which of the last 15 elections he had voted in. To my surprise, he was a spotty voter—only cast a ballot on one out of every five elections.

"This is all public information, isn't it?"

"Yes."

"What about Shirley Gallagher?" I asked.

Again, she paused and gave me a schoolteacher look, then shrugged and brought up the information.

Shirley Singleship Gallagher. 15344 Lupine Drive, Trillium. DOB 4/15/48.

Her voting record was actually better than her husband's, for whatever that was worth. I thanked Twila—she said nothing, shrugged again, and returned to her work.

I wasn't sure where this was taking me. The name Singleship rang a bell—it was unusual enough that it might have been more than a coincidence, but I wasn't able to place it.

Mary called to tell me she was leaving work early—she was too tired to get much work done. I told her I felt the same way, but had a couple more hours of issues that had to be dealt with. The city council meeting was going to be on the following evening, and we still had some details to work out.

I checked my e-mail and didn't see anything from Kate. I wasn't surprised, but just the same, I was disappointed. I needed contact with her.

Something was nagging at my mind as I scanned the messages. On a whim, I opened my archived messages, and ordered them by sender. I scrolled down several pages, until I came to it. A year and a half ago, I had received a brief message from Mason Singleship informing me that the e-mail server would be down between midnight and two a.m. for an upgrade to the modem lines. Mason Singleship was, apparently, a Technical Specialist with WillVallNet, our Internet Service Provider.

I sat back and let the information sink in. My brain still felt foggy, but even so, some of the pieces were falling together. There was a good chance that Mason was related to Shirley—brother and sister, probably. Althought the e-mail was supposedly private, it was a fair assumption that the technicians on the host computer could get into it somehow.

Way to go, Mrs. Dunwoody, I thought. What didn't fit was her connection with all this—I had always assumed she was completely looney—but this whole deal was taking on an unreal quality anyway.

I paced in front of my window for a few minutes, sorting things out, then looked up a number in my business cards file.

"WillVallNet, to whom may I direct your call?"

"Steve Jackson, please. This is Ben Cromarty with the City of Trillium."

"Hold on while I transfer you."

I sat through their on-hold music, which was actually an ad for some local car dealer, and then the phone rang a few times.

"Hello Ben, How are you doing?"

"Fine, just fine."

"How can I help you?"

I paused for a second. "Steve, we've been customers of yours since you got into the business. All our e-mail accounts are with you now."

"Yes, and we do appreciate your business." His voice raised slightly, making it into a question.

"So here's the problem. We have reason to believe that one of your employees has been sharing the contents of some of our e-mail messages with people who shouldn't be seeing them."

There was silence on the line. Jackson was thinking through the implications of this. If word got out that they had a leak in the mail server, it could end their business as an ISP.

"What makes you think that?" he asked carefully.

"I can't go into the details, but to make a long story short, information has come back around to us that could only have come from someone who had access to our mail."

"How do you know it was on this end? It's possible that someone could get into the downloaded messages on your end."

"I thought about that, but some of the messages were deleted on this end as soon as they were read. And we stumbled onto a connection with one of your staff just today."

"Who?"

"I can't say. We don't have any hard proof, and due to the sensitivity of the information, I don't want to raise a hue and cry over it."

"Yeah, I know you've had your fill of controversial issues the last few months."

"Here's all I ask, Steve. Please pass the word to your staff as quickly as possible. Tell them what I just told you—that the City of Trillium has reason to believe someone is opening private e-mail, and that we have an idea of who it might be. I suspect you'll want to add your own comments, too, but that's the gist of it. My guess is that the problem will stop there, but if not, we can get more specific about our suspicions. How's that sound?"

"Good, but are you sure you don't want to pursue it now? This is pretty serious, and frankly, if I found evidence of this kind of thing going on, I'd fire whoever it is on the spot."

"No, it may be an isolated indiscretion. Let's ride it out, okay?"

"Fair enough."

I thought about calling Brian Gallagher and warning him that I knew about his brother-in-law or whoever it was, but decided against it. The call to WillVallNet would be enough, and I didn't have any hard evidence that Gallagher was directly involved.

While I worked on some correspondence, I kept my computer busy downloading the software for one of the free e-mail services. When it was done, I set up a new account for user name bencromarty. The password was, of course, "kate."

*   *   *

We were in the middle of another staff meeting, pulling together the pieces for the council agenda. Bess Wilson came striding in, twenty minutes late as usual. I looked up to say something, but was caught short by her grim expression.

"What's up?" I said.

"How much of this do I have to take?" Bess asked.

"What?"

"Just when things seem to be running smoothly, things go to hell in a handbasket."

She held a pen in both hands, like she was going to break it in half, and glared at the table. I waited.

"So here's what happened, as far as I can piece it together," she said. "Nova's contractor is working on the site, putting in the roads and that kind of stuff. One of the conditions we put on them is they keep the row of birch trees along the street, as a buffer for the Hemlock Creek neighborhood. It was a big deal for them. You know those folks—they created the Citizens for Good Planning group, what a load of crap. Anyway, they must have got their kids sucked into it too. Apparently, for the past week or so, this gang of teenage shitheads would stand across the road and hassle the contractors—"

"How?" Betty Sue asked.

"Oh, the usual stuff for snotnoses like that. Yelling at them, mooning them, whatever. So today they're doing the same thing. The foreman drives up in his pickup truck, and these miscreants start yelling and giving him the finger, then they start lobbing rocks at him. He said one hit his window."

"Break it?" I asked.

"No, I don't know. But I guess they pushed him too far. He gets out of his truck, see, and reaches in the back and pulls out a chain saw, and then one by one, he starts to cut down every damn one of the birch trees along the road. It made a helluva noise, probably scared the shit out of the kids, and before you know it, the houses on that side of Hemlock Creek empty out and these insane residents are yelling and swearing at the contractor. He just ignores them and keeps on cutting. They call the cops, but by the time they get there, the trees are lying in a heap on the ground and their main job is to keep the kids and their parents from beating the crap out of the contractor. What a friggin' fubar."

"Huh?" Betty Sue said.

Bess gave her a level look. "It's a military term, honey."

"Oh."

"How did you hear about it?" I asked.

"Well, not all the parents were out there trying to mix it up with the foreman. A dozen of them were on their phones at the same time, trying to call me and my staff. I heard the same story from all of them. Well, at least when I tried to sort the hysteria out of it. They're calling for a stop work order on the Nova project, demanding that we throw the contractor in jail, and suing the city for good measure. Or so they say."

"Great." I stared at Bess for a moment. This really was turning into the project from hell.

"Well, what can we do?" I asked.

Simon tried to be helpful. "I doubt there's any criminal problem, since it was their own land to begin with," he said. "Matter of fact, if there was any criminal act, it was the kids throwing rocks at the worker. We could cite 'em for assault."

"Sure, throw some more fuel on the fire," I said. "But there's a civil case against the contractor, since the buffer was a planning commission requirement, right Pete?"

"True," the attorney said. "But we can't push it too hard, since we were out on a limb with that requirement to begin with. There's nothing in the development code that requires it."

"Yeah, I know," Bess said. "But Nova's problem isn't what we're going to do, it's the public relations mess they're in now. I think they'll expect us to hit them with a fine, and require that they re-plant some trees. And the contractor will probably tell the public that they disciplined the foreman."

"Hardly seems fair," Jake Wildavsky said. "I probably would have done the same thing in his place."

"Oh? Do you know how to run a chain saw?" Simon asked.

"Well, good point."

"Don't worry about him," Bess said. "The contractor will probably just shift him to another job. But *we* still have a problem. I'm just waiting for the Citizens for Mob Rule Planning to march on city hall."

"Hmm. We'll just have to ride it out," I said. "So…where were we?"

"Oh yeah. Sorry for the interruption," Bess said.

"We were discussing background material," Max said.

"Right. What do you have in writing from the Willamette Fire folks?" Bess continued to seethe, and the staff meeting went on.

*   *   *

When the time for the council meeting finally arrived, I had an uneasy feeling that Betty Sue and I hadn't done all we could to give the City/County proposal a fair hearing. Should we have done more reference checking in other cities? Should we have included a few more scenarios based on future increases in calls for service or inflation? Should we have worked harder to spring some sort of trap on the arguments that would inevitably come from the Firefighters Association?

But in the end, I tried to tell myself that the council members were adults and free to sift and weigh the information themselves. They were, after all, ultimately responsible for this decision, and I would live with whatever decision they made.

Fifteen minutes before the meeting, I looked out my window. The city hall visitor parking lot was already almost full. Great. It was going to be another one of those nights. I entered the council chambers from the side door and saw the expected fire fighters and their groupies. But there was also a row of middle-aged residents. Some of them held feather dusters in their hands. When I got closer, I discovered what they were really holding: boughs from dead birch trees.

Mayor McTavish opened the meeting on time. She moved the fire issue to the front, out of consideration for the crowd that had shown up to speak on it. She started by asking for the staff report.

I carefully went over the arguments, both pro and con, that we had included in our written material. Betty Sue occasionally added comments and clarification based on a script we had worked out before the meeting. For most of the council members, this was redundant information, but I felt compelled to present it, if nothing else for the benefit of the viewing audience on our cable channel. The crowd in the room looked bored or impatient.

Matt Monroe had flown up from Las Vegas, and the mayor called on him to stand at the lectern and answer questions from the council on their proposal. Rob Titus began.

"What I want to know is, why aren't any other Oregon communities using your services?"

Monroe responded formally, "Madam mayor, councilor Titus, that's a good question. A large part of the answer is that, until now, our company hasn't expanded into the Pacific Northwest, and it is only in the last few—"

"Why weren't you interested in the Northwest?" Rob said.

"It wasn't a lack of interest, it was more a case that we didn't want to grow too quickly and spread ourselves too thin. As I was going to say, over the past five years we have built up our staff and management resources to the point where we can establish a Northwest presence. The timing is just right, both for us, and for Trillium."

Maggie raised her hand, and McTavish nodded at her.

"People have told me they're concerned about the response time with your company," Maggie said. "How are you going to handle that?"

Mayor McTavish answered before Monroe could speak. "It's all there, in the proposal. They said they would guarantee the same response time we have now, and adjust staffing levels based on the statistics."

"You're right, mayor," Monroe said, astutely keeping Maggie in eye contact as he spoke. "And we don't control or compile the response time stats—those are done independently by your dispatch center. If we don't meet your standards, you cancel the contract. It's as simple as that. But I'm not concerned about it—we've studied your call patterns very carefully, and based on the physical layout of Trillium, we're confident we can meet or exceed your present average response time."

There were a few other questions, mostly to clarify points in the proposal, but I could tell that the mayor was anxious to get on with the meeting.

"Okay," she said, "this isn't a formal public hearing, like we have for land use issues, but we're certainly going to take your comments. Tell us what you think about this proposal, either pro or con, but try not to repeat things that others say. Okay, who's first?"

Brian Gallagher sprang to his feet. To keep his status with the union, he would have to be the primary gladiator. He gave me a dark look on the way to the lectern. If he had been part of the blackmail scheme, he would know by now that I was calling their bluff. But I had no idea if it would work.

Gallagher unfolded a prepared speech, gripped both sides of the lectern, and leaned into the microphone.

"Members of the city council, my name is Brian Gallagher and I reside at 15344 Lupine Drive, Trillium. I am an eighteen-year veteran of the Trillium Fire Department and for the past five years I have been honored to serve as the president of the Firefighters Association Local 255.

"On behalf of the loyal and hard-working staff of your fire department, we're very disturbed that we even need to be here tonight to speak on this issue. It is such an outrage that it is almost inconceivable that the City of Trillium would even consider such an irresponsible action.

"What you are considering is the tearing apart, piece by piece, of your fire department, and replacing it with a for-profit business that has absolutely no experience with our community, and no long-term commitment to our families and businesses.

"We see this as a slap in the face to the men and women who have risked their lives for the protection of Trillium.

"This is a slap in the face for the Firefighters Association, which has been negotiating in good faith for a fair extension of our contract, but which has been blocked—" he looked at me "—at every turn by management.

"This is a slap in the face of the citizens of Trillium, who expect and deserve the best level of safety protection possible, not the cheapest public safety that can add to some private business' bottom line.

"And finally, this a slap in the face for our ambulance company, OAS, which has served us well for many years, and which supports dozens of community organizations and events throughout the year, including sponsorship of last year's state champion Little League team, the Trillium Tigers.

"The recent election conducted by the Trillium Business Leadership Committee resulted in a resounding vote of no confidence against the city manager. That he would seriously propose and recommend this kind of scheme is further evidence of how hopelessly out of touch your administration is with the needs and wishes of the people of our community.

"We ask that you as the elected representatives of the people of Trillium do the right thing and make a strong show of faith and support for the men and women who daily risk their lives saving other peoples' lives in our great city of Trillium. Thank you."

The room burst into applause. I watched the council members. Diane McTavish looked grim. She didn't want the meeting to turn into a circus, but she was reluctant to gavel it to order. Maggie nodded sympathetically, Rob Titus and Hank Arnold folded their arms impassively. Seth Rosenberg's eyes sparkled in quiet amusement.

A small army of firefighters, friends, and family trooped up to the lectern to echo Gallagher's comments. Not one of them addressed the actual merits of the decision, but I had to admit to myself that their trotting out of the "America, motherhood, and apple pie" argument was pretty effective.

There were a few people—mostly business owners—who had the courage to speak in favor of the proposal. One of them, a longtime resident and owner of a jewelry business, had the wits to revise his speech to turn the "apple pie" argument around.

"You have heard the employees portray this as a decision for or against the firefighters," he said, "but this isn't the case at all. City/County has committed to retaining all existing employees, so the only thing that is changing is the management. And the union spokesmen have criticized—unfairly, in my opinion—the current management, so it is hard to see how they would fail to prefer a management that specializes in the provision of emergency services. And they speak with pride of their well-deserved reputation of service to Trillium's businesses, but in the same breath, they turn around and cast aspersions on businesses because they exist to make a profit. Isn't that what free enterprise in America is all about? I don't know about you, but those are the kind of values that my parents raised me with."

There was another string of opponents, this time recruited from neighborhood associations and other groups. Not one to miss an opportunity, Todd Pritchard got up to speak, and with a smug smile, began a rambling discourse on how the Trillium Business Leadership Committee supported their fire department and that they were opposed to any change. It seemed to me that he had sung a different tune a few months ago when the fire department had proposed increasing the fees for commercial fire inspections, but I really didn't care. In the middle of his speech I leaned over to Betty Sue and whispered, "This is getting long, I gotta take a leak." She stifled a laugh.

When I got back to my seat, a stooped gray-haired lady shuffled to the lectern. I had seen her here before. Years ago she had refused to pay her water bill, so we eventually cut off her meter. For months, she dragged a five-gallon bucket down the sidewalk, bumming water off her neighbors. Eventually, her brother agreed to pay the bill, but then she even managed to get him mad, and he quit doing it. Last I knew, the water was off again. But that wasn't why she was here tonight. She bellowed into the microphone with a surprisingly strong voice.

"I want to go back to the question asked by Mr. Tight Ass—"

"That's 'Titus,' the mayor said, with a hint of a smile. Ron Titus clenched his teeth.

"Whatever. The question is, how come we never seen this outfit before? How come we never heard of them before? And you're asking us to put our lives in their hands," she said, smacking the lectern. That got another round of applause. Government, Jerry Springer style.

Finally, the crowd wore down both themselves and the council. There was nothing left but for the council members to deliberate. I leaned forward in my seat—I couldn't afford to miss anything here.

The mayor looked around. I knew she wanted to say something—the emotional appeals probably turned her stomach, although she'd done a good job maintaining a poker face. "Who wants to start?" she asked. "Seth?…"

He leaned into his microphone to make sure he had the floor, but took a few moments to collect his thoughts.

"First," he said, "we have heard many reminders of how effective our fire department has been, and that point is well-taken. We have an excellent department—possibly the best in the state—nobody has disputed that. The very fact that City/County has committed to the same high standard of service is a tribute to the quality that our department has aspired to.

"Second, we have been urged to yield to the will of the people. But the message from the people has been very clear—we must make do with less money. Trillium voters, you remember, passed Measure 5-47 with a 3 to 1 vote. So this proposal is precisely a way to respond to the wishes of the people of Trillium.

"Third, this proposal has been criticized because it might harm our current employees. Yes, it is true that our department would see a large reduction in force, but each and every one of our employees can be transitioned to the new service provider. This kind of transfer occurs in the private sector every day, with corporate mergers and takeovers, and there is no reason that public employees should be protected from it at the expense of the taxpayer. But I believe that this can be a smooth transition, one that has apparently been successful in many other communities.

"So, on balance, I believe this is a good and fair proposal, and we would be negligent if we didn't give it serious consideration. I believe we should direct the staff to negotiate a service contract for us to consider.

Mayor McTavish nodded slowly, letting Seth's words sink in for a while. Then she looked around for another potential ally. "Hank?"

I saw the blurred images of his eyes blinking behind his thick glasses. "This is a difficult one for me."

No kidding, I thought. This whole issue probably looked like deja vu from the perspective of his former union leadership days—the plumbers union was constantly fighting efforts to out-source work to firms in the southeast and Mexico. But he was on the other side now, and over the years he had probably become a little disillusioned with the union hard line.

"I'm very concerned with the impact on our employees," he continued. "I would want to be absolutely sure they were kept whole. But on the other hand, we can't ignore the cost. We have a duty to make our city as efficient as possible. I guess what I want to say is it merits further consideration. I'm not ready to plunge into it, but I'm certainly not ready to dismiss it out of hand."

"Okay," McTavish said. "Maggie? Rob?"

Rob Titus remained uncharacteristically silent. Maggie looked around for a while, then acted like she was surprised it was her turn to speak.

"Well, I just don't know. This is an awful lot to absorb, and the people tonight have made some very good comments. I guess if I had to make a decision, I would say, let some other city try this first, then we can learn from their mistakes."

The mayor couldn't contain herself any longer. "But dozens of cities HAVE tried it."

"Oh? Well, none in Oregon, that's what I meant. Let another Oregon city try it."

"All right. Rob? Any comments?"

He continued to lean far back in his chair. "Yes!" he boomed. Even though he was a few feet from the microphone, his voice—and spit—had no trouble reaching it.

"There is an obvious and simple solution to this. As I have said previously, I am becoming concerned about the reliability of the advice that we are receiving from our city manager." He looked at Gallagher for approval. "The straw poll on the Nova housing project clearly shows the staff is out of touch with the people."

I hadn't shared with the council members Sabrina Chan's revelation about the poll—mostly out of respect for her request to protect her source, but partly because I didn't think it was necessary. I never put much stock in unscientific polls, so the fact that the results had actually come out in my favor—as far as the housing issue was concerned, anyway— wasn't anything to crow about. But I had to bite my tongue when Titus started waving the poll results around.

"That wasn't a poll or even a scientific sample," Mayor McTavish said, to my surprise. I wondered if Sabrina had talked to her too. "Get to the point, Rob."

"The point is this. A decision like this is just too important to make on our own. I say, let the people decide. Let's put it to a vote. It's that simple." He folded his arms and looked around the room. The audience stirred.

McTavish stared levelly at Titus. "What happened to your speeches about the need to take a leadership position, to make the tough decisions? Is this the way to do that?"

Councilor Titus simply nodded. "Yes, in this case, it is."

A voice came from the crowd. "Listen to him. Put it to the people!" Another wave of applause.

McTavish looked at the audience. The temperature of the room was getting high, both physically and emotionally. At a hundred watts per body, I figured we had a fifteen kilowatt heater going there.

"All right," she said. "What Rob has suggested is a valid alternative. But I have to tell you that I don't think the results of that kind of election will be as obvious as some of the speakers tonight would have us believe. There are a lot of folks out there who *do* want the city to be run like a business."

That was received with some hooting and harsh laughter. McTavish tapped her gavel lightly and waited patiently for silence.

"My own feeling is that this proposal is the wave of the future, and that sooner or later all cities are going to have to look at something like it. I have relatives in Nevada and Arizona, and they swear by City/County Fire Service. We've never been afraid to be on the cutting edge, and this shouldn't be any different. Granted, we owe our firefighters and para-medics the best treatment in how a transition is done, and we should make that be a priority. But it can't be the only thing we look at. I say, let's draw up a contract and have a look at it. Ben—how long will that take?"

"Well, you've got a draft in your packet, so all we need to do is make some changes based on tonight's comments. We can have it on the next agenda."

More noise from the audience. The natives were restless.

"Okay," McTavish said. "Do I have a motion?" Councilor Rosenberg immediately leaned forward. "Yes, I move that we accept this proposal, and direct staff to return to us in two weeks with a contract."

"Second?" Silence. Finally councilor Arnold leaned forward. "Yes, I'll second it to get it on the table."

"Discussion?" More silence.

"Well, I'm going to vote yes, and this is why," councilor Arnold said. "It isn't a final decision until we approve a contract. I said we need to give this due consideration, and we can't do that if we shut the door on it tonight."

McTavish looked around the table. "All right, I'll ask the clerk for a roll call vote."

Twila leaned forward. "Councilor Titus."

"No."

"Councilor Arnold."

"Aye."

"Councilor Henderson."

"I don't know. My mind isn't cast in concrete. But I guess I vote no."

"Councilor Rosenberg."

"Yes."

"Mayor McTavish."

"Yes. The motion passes, three to two. I'm going to call a five minute recess for a powder room break."

*　　　　　*　　　　　*

When the council re-convened, they still had to contend with the Hemlock Creek neighborhood association. Bess traded places with Max in the seat to my left, and gave a surprisingly calm rendition of the events from the week before. None of it was news to the council members. We had shot out an e-mail message to them, and the *Oregonian* had run a ten inch article to accompany their color picture of a knot of neighbors standing in the middle of the downed trees.

"We are levying a fine of $20,000, or a thousand dollars for each tree that was removed," the city attorney said. "We are also requiring that the contractor replace the trees immediately with trees of at least eight inches in diameter, and submit a bond for their maintenance for the next five years."

It wasn't enough, apparently. A pale woman with thin blond hair and a down vest marched up to the lectern.

"This is the last straw," she said. "We're sick and tired of this development that you people have crammed down our throats."

She paused for the applause. Nova owned the property, and they had been forced to submit to a lot of conditions that were initiated by the Hemlock Creek neighbors. I wondered who was doing the cramming.

She continued, "We are demanding an immediate stop to the project, to assess the damage they have done."

Hank Arnold adjusted his glasses. "Assess the damage?" he said. "Looks pretty clear to me—a worker got frustrated and cut down some trees."

"Oh? We didn't come down here to put up with your...your cavalier attitude, councilor Arnold."

Hank raised his eyebrows, but didn't say anything.

Diane McTavish looked at Pete Koenig. "Is there anything else we can do, legally?" she asked, knowing the answer.

"No, I don't think so, mayor," he said. "There aren't any grounds for criminal charges, and the civil penalty we're levying is the maximum that our code provides. We can't put a stop work order on the contract, because there's no connection with that and the loss of the trees."

"We'll have them re-plant with elms," Bess added. "These will probably be better street trees than the birches anyway. They were always breaking apart in the ice storms."

"Yeah, a lot of good that will do," the woman said. "It will be years before the new trees grow enough to be any buffer at all. Until then, we're the ones who are going to have to stare into this ugly mixed up use development that you've allowed. It's easy for you to sit up there and tell us how you're solving our problem, but we're the ones that live there."

McTavish sighed. "I'm sorry, ma'am, but we're doing what we can. There's not much more I can tell you."

"Well, it's not enough. You haven't heard the last from us."

"Yes, I'm sure—" the mayor caught herself. "I'm sure this is upsetting for you and your neighbors. You have our sympathy."

2 1

We were immediately hit with a sequence of events that, in hindsight, might have been predictable.

First, the Fire Association, with the encouragement of the Citizens for Good Planning, circulated a petition for the recall of mayor McTavish and councilors Rosenberg and Arnold. The petition listed as the basis for the recall "an overall inability to reflect the will of the people," and cited the Nova housing and fire privatization issues as the only specific examples. The recalled council members would be replaced by a slate of three candidates—one of which was Todd Pritchard—with the first order of business being to terminate the city manager's contract.

Second, a petition began circulating that would amend the city's charter to prevent the city council from ever contracting out any aspect of fire or emergency medical services.

Third, Oregon Ambulance Services filed suit against the city, claiming a violation of their franchise agreement.

Mayor McTavish was seething. She paced back and forth in my office hurling a string of curses into the air. I could only mutter out a few words of sympathy before the next onslaught began. Finally, she just leaned her head against the wall and moaned, "goddamn it anyway…"

I stood up and walked around, ostensibly to get a cup of coffee. If this was going to be an aerobic meeting, I didn't want to feel like a slacker. I filled my mug and leaned against the windowsill, waiting.

McTavish gave me an absent look, then flopped into one of the conference chairs, her eyes focused somewhere in the distance. A small bead of sweat gathered on her forehead.

Suddenly, she snapped out of it and pulled herself together. I quietly slipped into a chair and opened my notepad.

"It isn't that I'm worried about my job, you know," she said. "I'd be more than glad to give up this twenty to forty hour a week thankless chore that doesn't pay a dime in order to spend more time with my family."

She scrunched up her eyebrows and looked at me. "Matter of fact, you're the one that needs to be worried about the job, since you're the one that gets paid. Sorry, didn't mean to rub it in."

I shrugged.

"No, what really rips me is their arrogance. What if every unpopular decision got slapped with a recall, a charter amendment, and a lawsuit? The city council would be a revolving door without any latitude to make decisions and the lawyers would run the place. What kind of future is that?"

I figured it was a rhetorical question.

"Oh hell." She picked at a thread in the cuff of her blouse. The seam started to unravel by the time she realized what she was doing.

"You know," she said, more quietly this time, "that this is going to mean a change in our strategy, don't you?"

"You mean a preemptive strike?"

She gave me a quick glance.

"Yeah, but go on, tell me what you have in mind."

"Okay," I said. "We can't afford to let that charter amendment get on the ballot. We've got to get something there before then. And I'm afraid that it will have to be something like what Rob Titus proposed—an advisory vote on the fire contract. There's a big risk there, but I would rather lose the battle than the war."

She nodded pensively. "I'm afraid so, much as I hate to admit it. When's the next special election date?"

"May 10."

"Then time is on our side. They'll never get enough signatures to put their measure on the ballot by then, but all we have to do is pass a resolution at the next council meeting. That still would give us time to file with county elections, wouldn't it?"

"Yes, I already checked with Twila on that."

She smiled, then turned serious again. "You think we're just playing into their hands?"

"Maybe. But look at it this way. Taking it to the people isn't the end of the world. We'll just have to lay out all the arguments, the same ones the council looked at. I'm sure City/County Fire will put a few bucks into the campaign. The vote could well come out the same way it did for the council."

"You think so, huh?"

"Well, it's possible. When I took economics in graduate school, one of the key assumptions that economic theory is built on is that people make rational decisions: if faced with two choices, they will make the choice that makes the most economic sense."

McTavish snorted. "Yeah, but in the real world, the voters aren't encumbered by concepts of economic rationality."

I shrugged. Maybe she was right. She had hung on her office wall a framed cartoon that was signed by Scott Adams. In it, Dilbert asks, "Do you think love is the strongest force in the universe?" Dogbert replies, "No, I'd have to go with stupidity. Followed closely by its cousin: ignorance. Then you've got selfishness, lust, fear, money and luck." "But love is in the top ten, right?" Dilbert asks. "It's fourteenth, right after foolish optimism."

We sat in silence for a few moments. McTavish rubbed her eyes.

"What about the lawsuit?" she asked.

"Pete says there's nothing to worry about—they're just blowing smoke. He reckons they were talked into filing it by the Firefighters Association just to put more pressure on you."

"Uh huh, figured as much. We'll have to call their bluff, but it pisses me off that we have to incur legal expenses on it."

"Me too, but that's the way it goes."

"Where's Max in all this?"

"Still on our side, at least on the surface, but to tell the truth, I really don't know."

*   *   *

I found out soon enough. Oakley called and asked if I could come over to his office. I agreed, but with some apprehension. I hadn't been in the fire station for a while.

As I walked up to the building, a half dozen firefighters were polishing the chrome on a pair of American Lafrance pumpers. They paused and looked at me in silence.

Oakley closed his office door behind me, and motioned me over to his meeting table.

He skipped any attempt at small talk. "I have a proposal that I believe you should consider."

"Okay, shoot."

He polished the crystal of his Rolex with his sleeve, and carefully began.

"I have been approached by Willamette Valley Fire about the possibility of annexing the City of Trillium into their district. Our existing department would be merged into theirs, and the city would be relieved of the financial burden of the entire fire department."

I sat back, stunned. The Willamette Valley Fire District was huge. It had started out as a simple rural fire district, but they had picked up a lot of urban assessed value before the State of Oregon tried to close the door on sprawl. One by one, many of the suburban cities had annexed themselves to the district, or contracted for its services. Because they had gained so much industrial and commercial land—which pumped in enormous tax revenues but had next to no demand for medical service—they were able to undercut most city fire departments. Their employees were the highest paid in the Portland area, and most firefighters were eager to be assimilated.

"I didn't think they came out this far," I said. "Where does their boundary end?"

"About eight miles away. But I have researched this issue, and ascertained that we don't need to be contiguous. They can have separate islands of territory in their district. In fact, there's a district in Deschutes County that's done the same thing."

"It would mean an election."

He nodded. I scratched my head, thinking through the implications.

"What's their tax rate now?"

"About $2.50."

"So most residents would see a tax increase of three to five hundred dollars a year."

"Yes."

"What do they get for that?"

"They get their lives saved," he said, without smiling.

"Maybe we should hold the election in a revival tent."

"Revival tent?"

"Never mind. How about your staff—how would it affect them?"

"Willamette Valley has had extensive experience in this. The employees are transferred straight across, and they take with them their seniority, and accrued vacation and sick leave. But they are moved to higher pay ranges, and they have more promotion opportunities. I think you will find that the staff are very supportive of this."

"Oh? Do they know about it?"

"No. Not from me, at least."

"And how about you? How do you fare in this kind of deal?"

"I would lose my status as chief. They have talked about creating a position responsible for strategic planning. But my interests are secondary to finding a solution that is best for the department and for Trillium."

A charitable sentiment, but I would put money on the fact that his position with Willamette Valley would pay more than his current position—and that he would still be called "chief." The district had at least a dozen assistant, deputy, and battalion chiefs, and they all went by "chief" for short. Sort of like bank vice presidents.

I thought about my conversation with mayor McTavish, and wondered how much of it I should share with Max.

"You know, with the threat of this charter change initiative, the council might be more willing to put the City/County proposal on the ballot."

"Why do that? Why not abandon the privatization scheme, and simply put our efforts behind annexation to Willamette Valley Fire? If that passed, it would certainly address your budgetary concerns. The privatization issue would just cause confusion."

I found a loose paper clip on his table and started unbending it. "I'll tell you why, Max. As a resident and taxpayer myself, I think being part of Willamette Fire would be an absolute rip-off. If contracting out doesn't get the support of the voters, maybe we could look into it, but I personally think it's nuts."

"I see."

"Besides, the fire district can't get involved in an election. Who would come up with the bucks for a campaign?"

He smiled. "I think that could be arranged."

The Association's war chest again, no doubt. Indirectly funded by the taxpayers through the union dues that were withheld from the payroll.

The paper clip bent one too many times and broke. I let the pieces fall on his table. "Well, Max, I want you to drop that idea for now. I don't want any more complications over this issue than we've already got. Okay?"

He looked me in the eye, but didn't say anything.

*   *   *

I started coaching another season of Trixie's softball team. It was a safety valve from the problems at work. But I couldn't completely escape them. I watched Trixie laughing with her friends, and wondered if she would have to find a new set of friends next school year. If the recall passed, I'd be out of a job, and in the city management profession, that almost always meant moving to another town. It didn't seem fair to put her—and Mary—in jeopardy for something they didn't have anything to do with. But there wasn't much I could do about it.

The insurance company cleared the paperwork quickly, and a contractor was already at work repairing the siding on our house. Filing the claim for the shed was more difficult. With the years' accumulation of junk, it was hard for Mary and me to remember what all we had in there. If nothing else, it looked like I was going to get a new lawnmower out of the deal. The issue of arson was still an open question, but it didn't seem to be affecting the insurance claim. The threats had ended—at least for the moment, but I still had the uneasy feeling that at any moment the other shoe was going to drop.

*   *   *

The day after my conversation with Max, our office fax picked up an urgent message from the League of Oregon Cities. Our own representative, Lynn Pennington, had, in the final days of the session, introduced a bill to prevent cities from contracting out "essential" services like police and fire. The deadline for new bills had passed, but she used the venerable "gut and stuff" procedure where the entire contents of an existing—and dead—bill were replaced by the new language.

By doing so, she had clearly picked sides in our struggle with the fire union, so there was no way I was going to talk her into withdrawing the bill. On a whim, I got in my car to see if Bo French had as much influence with her as he had claimed. Stranger things had happened lately.

I didn't see him sitting outside his camp, so I wandered into the plant office.

"Hi Cap. Have you guys seen Bo lately?"

"Nope. Not for a while. Why?"

"Just need to talk to him about something. No big deal."

"Well, it's not like he carries a cell phone or anything, so you'll have to track him down if you want to talk to him. Or just take a whiff of the air."

"Easy for you to say in the middle of a sewer plant."

"Hey, it smells sweet to us."

I walked back to the camp and called out. No answer. I hesitated a minute, then ducked under a tree branch to get to Bo's lean-to. I gingerly pushed aside the flap of an old army surplus tarp and looked inside. Bo was asleep inside, peaceful as an angel. I decided to just let him be.

There was a cup of minestrone soup outside the flap door. I felt the metal cup. It was cold. I called Bo's name, softly at first, then louder. Nothing. I took a breath, then stepped in and shook him by the shoulder. His body was stiff.

I stood there. Maybe it was all I had gone through, or maybe I really did care for the guy, but whatever the reason, my eyes welled. Bo French had been dead for a while and nobody had even noticed.

After a few minutes, I shook myself out of it. I wiped my eyes with my shirtsleeve and trudged over to tell the plant operators. They would have to deal with tracking down Bo's sister and figuring out what to do with the body. Part of the "other duties as assigned" in their job description, I supposed.

*   *   *

The one piece of good news was that the Nova plant was well under construction, in spite of the chain saw incident. I walked through the shell of the factory with Bess Wilson and one of our building inspectors. It was enormous, and the construction contract alone was already making a difference in our economy.

The inspector poked a flashlight at some tags hanging off a fire sprinkler pipe. Bess spun around and took in the scene as if she owned the place.

"Bitchin', huh?" she said. "Isn't it great?"

"Yeah, chips on the whole block."

"Huh? Is that some kind of pun? Besides, they don't make chips, they make high tech ceramic stuff. Here, check out the airlocks for the clean room."

She led me through some stainless steel and glass doorways with unfinished air ducts hanging from the ceiling. The inspector caught up with us.

"How's it look, Tom?" Bess asked.

"Fine, so far," he said. "They still got a lot of finish work to do, though. It's moving so fast it takes one of us out here pretty much full time."

"Don't sweat it, the building permit alone was eighty grand," she said.

We continued the tour. I felt some of the same excitement as Bess. It was Nova's plant, but I felt some small sense of ownership in getting it there.

"Any more word from that guy, Costoso?" I asked.

"Nope. I heard a rumor about a Walmart looking at the property, but I called John Collins to see if there was any truth to it, and he said it was news to him. I don't know, but I think I believe him. Then again, Costoso and the boys in Japan could be keeping him in the dark."

"If they are, they're smart. If people thought there really was a Walmart going out in that farmland, they'd go ape. And it wouldn't have much connection with this factory, except the workers would have a place to go and buy their caramel popcorn."

Bess laughed. "By the way, I've been meaning to congratulate you on finessing the fire union deal."

"How so?"

"By getting Willamette Valley Fire into the mix. Either way—private contract or annexation to the district—you win. No more ass-biting pygmies to deal with."

"Where did you get that information?" I asked, trying to hide the concern in my voice. "About Willamette Valley Fire, I mean."

"Oh, I don't know. I heard it from someone, don't remember who. They said the city was looking into getting annexed to the district."

"Well, there's nothing to it. Just a rumor, that's all."

"Hey, but it would make your life easier."

"Maybe, but do you really think my motivation for doing things is just to make my life easier? If that's the case, I've really screwed up over the last year, haven't I?"

"Ha. Good point. I still think you planted the idea in Max's head."

I let the comment pass.

2 2

Trixie had carried the flu home from school, and I was feverish, but I had to go to the meeting. I should have let Betty Sue handle the staff support, but with as much as I had invested in the issue, I couldn't just lie at home and watch it unfold on cable TV.

As I expected, the council members unanimously voted to place the City/County contract on the ballot for the voters to decide. It seemed to be a small victory for the opposition, but it wasn't enough to avert another speech from Todd Pritchard.

"We see this as a transparent attempt to undercut our charter change initiative," he said. "Your scheme won't work, because we will continue our signature drive, even if it means placing the measure on the September ballot. You may have come to your senses on this, but what's to stop future councils from going down the same path? We need to put a stop to it."

I felt like my body was on fire, and all I wanted to do was go home and crawl into bed, but Pritchard droned on.

"Other petitions are circulating, and they take a lot less signatures, so don't be surprised if you see them on the May ballot. This council and staff have been reckless in pursuing courses that would endanger the lives and quality of life of Trillium citizens, and we can't let that go unchallenged. You have made the right decision to place these issues before the voters, but it is one of the few good decisions I have seen you make."

Mayor McTavish had put on her reading glasses and was skimming through a stack of correspondence as Pritchard spoke. She let the silence hang until he had got back to his seat, then slowly took off her glasses and looked up. "Thank you Mr. Pritchard," she said, without expression. "Any other comments from the audience? Okay then, next item."

"Excuse me, madam mayor," Rob Titus blurted out, "but I have an issue to bring up related to this, and we must discuss it in executive session."

McTavish gave him a skeptical look. He had clearly taken her by surprise. She rubbed her temples.

"All right. But I hope you've got a good reason for doing this."

"Yes, you will see that I do."

The mayor announced that the next part of the meeting would be closed to the public. There was an awkward pause as the council waited for the audience to file out. Reporters were allowed to remain, along with staff who were involved in the issue being discussed, but everyone else had to leave the room. I noticed Rob Titus whispering to the mayor. She in turn motioned for the city attorney to come up and talk to her. After a couple minutes of conversation, Pete Koenig returned to the staff desk. "Uh, this is sort of strange, but apparently the council doesn't want you to be in the executive session."

"Huh?" The only time I had ever been excluded was when they were discussing my performance review. That wasn't scheduled for another six months.

"Yes," Pete said. "I'm not sure why. But that's the way it looks."

"Okay," I said, trying to sound stoical but in fact feeling like an outcast. I looked at the mayor, but she was studiously avoiding me. I pulled together my files and notebook. "I'll be in my office," I told Betty Sue on my way out.

In fact, my fever was raging and I would have rather gone home, but I had the feeling that something worse than the flu was about to happen to me. I went upstairs to my office, trying to avoid the looks of the crowd in the lobby, and started to read one of my professional journals, but I couldn't concentrate. I drank a glass of water and loosened my tie. My shirt was damp with sweat.

The executive session seemed to take forever. I thought about going back downstairs to see if they had somehow started the regular meeting without me, but I didn't want to have to face the public. I just sat at my desk with my head in my hands.

I heard the elevator doors open and sat up, pretending to be reading a memo. Diane McTavish and Seth Rosenberg walked in. They pulled up chairs gingerly, like they had arrived late for a funeral service.

McTavish pressed her lips into a thin line. "Ben, this is very difficult for me to say, but I suppose someone has to. Titus told us about the deal that Oakley has been working out with the Willamette Valley Fire District. He said that it should have been brought to us as an option, and that you intentionally withheld the information. He was pretty adamant about it, actually. Chief Oakley confirmed that he had shared the information with you and that you directed him to sit on it."

She paused, looking uncomfortable. She clenched her jaw and continued. "I guess I'm not allowed to give the specifics of what took place in the session, but the upshot was that the council voted to put you on administrative leave, effective immediately."

She squirmed a little in her chair, but met my eyes.

"It was a three-two vote, for what it's worth," Seth said softly.

I was speechless. I could feel that my face was red, and not just from the fever.

"How could you take a vote in executive session?"

"Okay, it was a straw poll," McTavish said.

"And my contract doesn't have any provision for 'administrative leave.' Where did that come from?"

"It was a compromise, actually. Your contract does have a termination clause. Do you want to push the issue?"

I couldn't think of anything to say.

"I'm sorry to have to give you this news," Seth said. "It really is a rotten deal for you. You may feel you're being made a scapegoat, and I don't think you would be far from the mark on that. But it's just the way it goes, I guess."

McTavish stood up, towering over me for a moment until she stepped back. "We've got to get back to the meeting," she said. "I'll try to make this as painless as possible for you. Take some time off, maybe get away for a few days. It might be good for you to get out of the hot seat for a while."

Seth put his hand on my shoulder. "Hang in there, Ben."

*   *   *

The hardest person to face was Mary. I knew she would mirror and amplify all the emotions that I was feeling, and I really didn't want to deal with that.

"Short meeting?" she asked when I dragged myself into the living room.

"No. They threw me out."

"What?!"

I slumped onto the couch next to her and explained, trying to make it sound like an every day occurrence. It was, after all, something almost all city managers faced eventually. But Mary grew more agitated the more I said, so I finally stopped talking.

"How could they do this?" she demanded.

"Sshh. Don't wake up Trixie."

"I can't help it. I'm...I'm pissed, that's what I am." She stood up and started pacing.

"Seth said it was a close vote. Three to two."

"Oh?" She wheeled around, her blond hair flying. " So who voted against you?"

"Titus and Maggie, I'm sure. I don't know about the third. I know it wasn't Seth, so it was either Hank or the mayor."

"Well, I think you should make them take action in a regular meeting. Make them be up front about their...chicken actions. You know that they can't do that kind of thing in a closed session."

"No, I'm not going to make a scene. I'll just say I'm taking a leave of absence. I've got to stay professional about it."

"But Ben, the word will get out. Think of how much Todd Pritchard is going to gloat. The kids at school will ask Trixie all sorts of questions. It'll be—"

I stood up. "No, Trixie's friends don't have a clue what I do for a living. We'll get through it. But I need you to give me support, not hysterics."

I regretted it as soon as the words were out of my mouth. A tear came to Mary's eye. "I'm sorry," she whispered. She put her hand to my forehead. "You're burning up! We've got to get you to bed."

*　　　　　　*　　　　　　*

I slept in the next morning, telling myself that I needed to take it easy to get over the flu. In fact, there was some psychological relief in being sick. I couldn't go back to the office anyway, and it seemed to give me a different reason for staying home.

Over the next few days, I began to feel better physically but not emotionally. The house was quiet with Mary at work and Trixie at school, and I didn't feel motivated to do anything. In the morning I sat in my bathrobe reading the newspaper and doing the crossword puzzle. I made a halfhearted attempt to check the web for job openings in other cities, but none held any interest. I questioned whether I really still wanted to be in that business anyway.

Betty Sue stopped by on the excuse that she needed to get my signature on a few contracts, but I think she really just wanted to console me. It worked both ways. The council had named Ken Longstreet as acting city manager instead of her. I knew she couldn't express any disappointment over that—it would have been like complaining about the inheritance while the corpse was still warm—but I could tell it upset her. She had never had line authority over any of the department heads, and I could understand why the council didn't want to take a chance with that now. But I had often left the city in her hands when I was out of town, and I felt she was up to the task.

And she was genuinely bitter over the council's treatment of me. She told me that if she had had any idea that would be the result when she first brought up her idea about the fire department, she would have dropped it right away like I had told her to. I reassured her that it wasn't her fault, and that the real issue with the council had been my failure to inform them of the Willamette Valley Fire District proposal—a decision that had been mine alone. She didn't stay long—I sensed she felt awkward being alone in the house with me, and in spite of my effort to be cheery, I was depressing company.

I thought about sneaking into city hall on a Saturday to gather my personal effects—framed photos of the family, the college textbooks that I kept on a shelf and never opened, my coffee mug—but decided not to. I didn't want to face anyone who happened to be working, and it seemed like clearing out my desk would be a sign of surrender.

A few other Oregon city managers called me with words of encouragement. I appreciated it, but I felt some obligation to explain the circumstances of my downfall, and each time in the telling, I thought of more ways I should have avoided it. I should have spent more time with the council members, I should have at least tried to win Todd Pritchard and his followers over to my side, and above all, I should never have stirred up the fire union. I tried not to wallow in self-pity, but I couldn't escape the fact that ten years of work had pretty much ended in failure.

At least I had provided plenty of material for the newspaper. Sabrina Chan had sat through the executive session when the council decided to remove me, and although she couldn't report directly from it, she knew exactly what was going on. She might have been personally sympathetic, but the realities of modern journalism compelled her to get some juicy quotes from Rob Titus, who emphasized the key role he played in making tough personnel decisions as the protector and champion of the taxpaying public. Todd Pritchard could barely contain his glee, and he stated that now that I had been fired, it was time to switch to a strong mayor form of government. I'm sure he imagined himself in that role, which filled me with revulsion. Diane McTavish had been a more effective leader of our community than most of the buffoons that I'd seen elected under the strong mayor/weak council form of government in other cities. The stupidity of his position made me especially concerned, since in the depths of my cynicism and bitterness, I figured that was the one criterion that would make his suggestion appealing to the voters.

Brian Gallagher had declined to comment on my demise, in spite of repeated attempts to provoke a statement by both the press and the TV stations. That puzzled me at first, but then it occurred to me that as long as I was no longer in a position to cause him any trouble, there was no reason for him to antagonize me. I caught myself admiring his professionalism, as much as I was angry about the dirty tricks he had played during the campaign.

The council had, of course, placed the Willamette Valley Fire annexation measure on the ballot, along with the City/County contract. They had washed their hands of the issue, willing to just stand by and let the public do the job that elected representatives were supposed to do. It gave me some satisfaction to see that Seth Rosenberg and Diane McTavish had voted against it, citing the unjustifiable cost to the taxpayers. I suspected that the mayor was astute enough to have counted the votes before she took her stand, knowing that the measure was going to go on the ballot anyway.

As much as I hated going out in the public, I couldn't avoid it. One evening, Mary and I had a parent-teacher conference at Trixie's school. When I entered Trixie's homeroom, her teacher gave me an icy look. I was taken aback, then remembered that her fiancée—husband, now—had been one of my firefighters. I wondered what kind of line she'd been fed, but steered clear of the subject.

To fill my days, I started taking on more of the domestic chores. I tried to time my trips to the supermarket so that I would run into as few people as possible. I kept an eye out for familiar faces, and if I saw someone I knew coming down an aisle, I would steer my shopping cart in the opposite direction. It made buying groceries a lengthy process, but time was something I now had in abundance.

This fact hadn't escaped some of the men I knew at my church, and they kept urging me to join them at their weekly early morning Bible study group. I finally ran out of excuses and found myself eating donuts and drinking coffee with a group of people that I really didn't know very well. But it was good therapy—they seemed to give me unconditional acceptance, and their frank sharing of their own experiences reminded me that, in the big picture, my own struggles were fairly insignificant. One of them was caring for a dying parent, another had gotten laid off after a twenty-five year career in a metal fabrication shop, and another had been accused of sexual harassment by a female co-worker. They amazed me in their ability to shrug off their problems and dive cheerfully into the scripture study.

In one of the sessions, the discussion drifted to the topic of adultery. One of the women in the congregation, rumor had it, had caught her husband in an affair. When she confronted him, he had wanted to have it both ways—to stay with his wife but still see his lover from time to time. According to the story, he couldn't understand why she didn't go for that proposal. One of the wags in our group noted that Solomon had had plenty of concubines, and monogamy was probably no more natural for humans than it was for other primates. Another said that it was an inevitable result of our throw-away society: if nothing was permanent and people were encouraged to buy a new house and car every few years, who could blame them for going through a few mates in their lifetime? They were joking, but the conversation made me uncomfortable, even though I knew it didn't apply to me.

Every day in the middle of the morning I would go for a jog through our neighborhood and compose in my mind long notes to Kate. I had realized that I could get to my new e-mail account through our home computer, and in my long hours of solitude and despair she had become a lifeline. She asked me to tell her everything about the events and politics that were taking place in Trillium, and her acerbic wit and occasional flashes of warmth were like a balm for my soul. We could even sneak in a few phone conversations, and as I ran under the trees that lined our street I could hear her sweet voice in my head and replay the sound of her carefree laughter.

At the same time, there was a potential problem with our relationship that I really didn't want to face. We had achieved a kind of intimacy that I hardly thought was possible, but the relationship was platonic. I also knew it could take a different turn if Kate and I actually got together.

Mary had started talking about summer vacation plans with the Andersons and I didn't know how to respond. Spending a week close to Kate would be awkward for me no matter what happened, but I was like a moth drawn to a flame. I fed myself an illusion that I could just enjoy her company without any physical tension tugging at me. But at the same time, I thought about taking a shower with her in my dream, and sliding the bar of soap over her body, and I knew that that scene would be pretty easy to arrange if our families spent a week together in a couple of vacation cabins. I should have talked to Kate herself about it, but I didn't—maybe because it was a problem I really didn't want to resolve.

2 3

As much as I wanted to detach myself from them, I couldn't ignore the events that were going on around me. The six weeks before the election brought out the worst in our community. People were polarized. To some, what the city was doing amounted to an attack on truth, justice, and the American way. To others, the issue boiled down to a greedy union exploiting the taxpaying public. The rhetoric only inflamed the situation.

Even Betty Sue Castle, I learned, came under attack. Ken Longstreet told me that he had walked into her office, and found her staring vacantly at the screen saver on her computer. He asked her what the problem was, and she wordlessly handed him a sheet of typewritten paper. It had come in the mail, anonymously. It was shocking, Ken said, one of the most spiteful examples of personal invective that he had ever seen. He told her it was terrible, that she didn't deserve it, and that he would have Simon investigate it. She had just nodded silently when Ken took the sheet, and he said that a tear had rolled down her cheek.

Hundreds of signs appeared in front of the homes of Trillium. One set, painted in stark red letters, urged "VOTE YES FOR PUBLIC SAFETY." Another set, in red, white, and blue, was emblazoned with the words, "YES FOR EFFICIENCY IN CITY GOVERNMENT." They both had their respective ballot measure numbers printed in small type, but I wondered if people would really know which was which.

Red Rogalsky leased some space in a storefront office for the International Association of Firefighters. The windows were covered with banners and posters, exhorting the proletariat to break the chains of the bourgeoisie. They used the office as the headquarters for their PR campaign, and in the evenings it was filled with volunteers getting their marching orders for the door-to-door campaign. Rogalsky held a series of press conferences out on the sidewalk, but the business owners across the street observed that fewer and fewer reporters were showing up. The message probably wasn't changing much.

I noticed with a sort of dull detachment that there wasn't any local backlash against the outside intervention in the campaign. In other issues, the voters had resented it when outside forces attempted to influence local elections. The city council had seized on that fact when a Washington D.C.-based group came in and pushed a city anti-tax measure. It wasn't a secret that Rogalsky and his minions were part of a national organization with no long term ties to Trillium. But it didn't seem to matter—maybe people just bought into the concept of the "brotherhood" of firefighters, like they were boy scouts or something.

The other odd thing was that, as hard as they tried, the City/County Fire Service folks couldn't get people excited about the cost of annexing to the Willamette Valley Fire & Rescue district. A few of the bigger businesses caught on, and in a panic, raised the issue. But the fire union just shrugged it off. "People are willing to pay for what's important to them," they said. "To us, there is nothing more important than saving the life of a neighbor or loved one."

Two weeks before the election, I walked to the end of our driveway to pick up the mail, and found a glossy brochure that had been sent by the City of Trillium. It was an attractive piece—I could see Betty Sue's handiwork—but the bizarre restrictions imposed by the State Elections Commission prevented the city from providing much useful information. There were some bland columns of numbers, and even I had a hard time concentrating on them.

The "Concerned Citizens for Good Government" had just managed to meet the deadline for the council recall petitions, and there was some campaigning for those measures too, although there didn't appear to be as much money behind them. McTavish, Seth, and Hank didn't appear to acknowledge the recall petitions and came across in the press as being utterly indifferent. But they were only human, and I suspected that the statements against them in the voter pamphlet and in the letters to the editor must have weighed heavily on them.

The election wasn't the only arena for a good fight—Pete Koenig called me at home to give me the sordid details. Oregon Ambulance Service was pressing on with its complaint about contract violations, and Pete was afraid that the city might be vulnerable. Even though our own franchise agreement was non-exclusive, the state legislature had slipped in a bill that allowed a city to have only one ambulance company at a time and even prevented a city from providing the service itself without buying out the remainder of the contract. I asked Pete how that had gotten through a Republican-controlled legislature, and he just laughed and said that the 'whereas' clauses in the bill played up the safety of the public. If the legislators have been consistent in anything, he said, it's protecting us against ourselves.

But that wasn't the worst of the news. Although the Business Leadership Committee had apparently lost interest in Nova, they had one more shot to fire at me. Pritchard's attorney had called Pete to say they were going to sue me personally for violation of the open meetings law. They were claiming that I had met privately with the council on the City/County contract, which was true, but I had met with them individually, not as a group. There was nothing legally wrong with that. Pete agreed, but informed me soberly that he expected that they would run me through all the steps of discovery and depositions, if only to make my life as miserable as they possibly could.

I speculated that, while the TBLC was no doubt glad to be out front in suing me, it was probably Fire Association money that was paying for Terry Judd's legal fees. Pete commented dryly that the union would want to keep their involvement quiet—they would want to be seen as the good guys in the election. Their PR machine was nothing if not pragmatic.

* * *

At the same time that my city seemed to be showing its ugliest, most dysfunctional side, something else was going on that I watched with more than passing interest. People in the community—many of them strangers I had never met—were coming out in support of me.

It started with a few letters to the editor expressing outrage that the city council would discipline me for just doing my job. Sabrina Chan had picked up on it, and started running a series of interviews with people who echoed this sentiment. The president of the chamber of commerce said she was mystified as to why the council would throw away a decade of solid progress in building up relations with the business community. A disabled veteran said he had met me at Memorial Day ceremony and felt it was unfair for me to take the bullet for the council. A community college professor stated that if the city ever needed strong executive management skills, it was now, and that it was suicidal for the city to be without a CEO.

Rob Titus had tried to force the issue, and the rumors were that he wanted the council to convert my administrative leave to full termination. In a perverse way, I almost hoped he was successful, since the administrative leave was a form of purgatory with no clear end in sight. My contract provided six months severance pay if the council fired me, so I would at least know what I was dealing with.

The rumors inevitably leaked into the open, and the escalation of the issue kicked the TV stations into gear again. It gave me some guilty pleasure to know that Titus faced a barrage of criticism when he turned on the evening news. The chamber president commented that she was disappointed that it was too late to get Titus' name on the recall ballot along with the others.

The council made a hasty retreat and convened another executive session. Seth called me afterwards and said that the consensus of the council was to reinstate me, but they couldn't figure out a way of doing it and still save face. In the end, they decided to let the election settle the issue. I agreed with Seth that it wouldn't be worth coming back anyway if he and the other two were recalled. It would take a few months to schedule a special election to pick replacements, but Pritchard had let it be known that he and his slate were the only real alternatives. He was probably right, as much as the thought disgusted me.

2 4

We had pulled four tables together in the lounge of the Plow and Harrow. All the council members were there, except Rob Titus, and so were most of my department heads. I hadn't seen most of them for six weeks, and the situation at first felt awkward. But Seth had insisted I join them, and I figured it was as good a time as any to come out of exile, even if it might be only for one night.

Normally the big screen TV was used for sporting events, but Jake Wildavsky had talked the owner into switching to the feed from our local cable TV operator. There weren't many other people there on a Tuesday evening, anyway.

It was an off-election year, so there were no state primaries. The only issues on the ballot were local ones—mostly money measures.

"So Jake, you think the county road levy has a chance?" Diane McTavish asked, looking for a way to make small talk.

"Nope. The potholes are still small enough that you can drive around them. They've got to let them get big enough to swallow a small car before folks will spend money on roads."

"I don't know," Simon Garrett said. "The way everyone's buying these four wheel drive pickups and sport utilities, they probably figure they don't need roads anymore. Let's just go back to dirt."

"Are you suggesting I actually take my truck off-road? But I might get it dusty," Jake said.

"Well, that's true." Simon popped a greasy French fry into his mouth. "We do spend a lot of time pulling Eddie Bauer Explorers out of ditches because the owners don't know how to deal with ice—or even rain."

Seth Rosenberg had disappeared a few minutes ago, and then came back with two more pitchers of beer.

"That'll get you a good tip," McTavish said.

"Well, it got me through college."

I filled my glass and sat back. Will Smith and Bess Wilson were deep in conversation, leaning over a paper napkin that Bess was drawing on. I suspected they were cooking up some scheme to get a community park out of one of the developments Bess was working on. Max Oakley sat erect at a corner of the table, watching the TV screen. It wasn't eight yet, and not much was happening. A political science professor from the community college was summarizing the local ballot measures, and making his predictions. We were probably his only viewers.

Betty Sue had been glancing at the door. Suddenly her eyes brightened. Lavar Washington pulled up a chair between Betty Sue and Ken Longstreet.

"So this is the political hot spot," he said. "Where's the cigar smoke? I thought these meetings always took place in smoke-filled rooms."

"No, only in the movies," Betty Sue said. "Now we would get thrown out for violating the clean indoor air act."

"Aw, what's the world coming to?"

Hank Arnold squinted at the TV screen. "I know that guy," he said.

"How?" I asked, seeing a safe place to enter into the conversation.

"I was on the faculty of the college, did you know that? Yes, I was."

"That right? So what did you teach?"

"Aeronautics. Okay, it was a course on building experimental aircraft. No big deal, but it paid for a new set of tires for my truck."

I nodded toward the talking head on the screen. "That was probably a lot more useful than what Wallace there teaches. What do you suppose someone does with an AA in political science?"

"That's more qualification than you need to run for county sheriff," Jake broke in. "Or county treasurer, or judge—"

"Or governor, for that matter," McTavish said.

"Or city councilor," Seth said quietly. "But hey, if we're all out of jobs tonight, maybe we can run for county commissioner or something. The pay would be better, at least."

The others laughed. I felt better about being there—I realized that I had missed them all over the past weeks.

The room suddenly got quiet. The early election returns were flashing on the screen. It had been a mail-in ballot, so the results would be counted quickly.

The county road measure came up. Jake was right, of course. It was failing, 13,555 to 2,989. A neighboring town had an anti-growth measure that would sharply restrict the number of building permits issued. It was passing by a two-to-one margin, but it would probably be pre-empted by the state the next time the legislature was in session.

Finally, our measures appeared on the screen. With a third of the ballots counted, the City/County contract measure was failing, but with forty percent voting in favor. Seth shook his head.

We waited. In a minute, the Wilammette Valley Fire annexation results popped up. It was passing, with seventy five percent voting in favor.

There was silence as the implications soaked in. Seth stroked his beard. "Notice anything odd about these results?"

I thought a second. "Yeah, some people are voting for both measures."

"How do you figure that?" Maggie Henderson asked.

"The percentages add up to more than a hundred," Seth said. The only way that can happen is if at least fifteen percent of the people are voting for both measures. But they are so different, I can't imagine why they would."

McTavish had a cold look in her eye. She was waiting for the recall election results. But instead of the rest of the Trillium results, the program went back to the commentary from the political science professor.

"Hey, where are the council results?" Maggie asked.

Seth shrugged. "Maybe they haven't counted them yet."

The screen switched to a public service announcement on the county's solid waste recycling program. Our eyes stayed glued to the set.

"You know, I just don't get it," McTavish said. "Going to the private sector for our emergency medical just makes so much sense. How can that measure be failing, and the fire district annexation measure be passing?

Are people that stupid? It'll just cost them a lot more money, for a service that hardly any of them will ever need." She shook her head.

"I don't know," Seth said. "But I don't think it's an accident—people really want it that way. And you know, they have the right to choose things that don't make any sense. It happens more often than we realize. The folks in Seattle voted to extend the monorail, when even the public transit zealots said it didn't make financial sense. We still follow an agricultural calendar for schools, even though it's a hardship for working parents, but people just want it that way. Voters approve huge subsidies for sports stadiums, even though their teams have absolutely no loyalty to their host cities. County governments and county boundaries are a throwback to the days when you rode a horse to the county seat, and picked the best gunslinger as your sheriff, but the people insist on keeping them that way even when they're given alternatives that are much more efficient. The list is endless."

"So, don't confuse me with the facts, just give me what I want, huh?" McTavish snorted in disgust.

"Maybe. But on the other hand, some of the best achievements of civilization are things that don't make much financial sense. Like Notre Dame cathedral in Paris, or the Sydney Opera House, or Toronto's public transit system, or landing on the moon, or sailing single handed around the world, or beating the four-minute mile."

"What does that have to do with voting for an over-staffed, over-priced empire-building fire district?"

Seth laughed. "Not much. But I guess people have to have the right to make choices that may seem frivolous or whimsical or even irresponsible—the world would be a much duller place without them."

"Sometimes I would like it to be duller, you know," Hank Arnold said. "Speaking of which, what happened to Todd Pritchard's campaign? I haven't seen much from that guy in the last couple of weeks."

Simon looked around the table. "It's been pretty quiet," he said, "but the word is that he and the missus split up. She kicked him out of the house. The old man took back the business and Pritchard skipped town to avoid alimony."

"You're kidding," McTavish said. She smiled. "Maybe there's some justice after all."

"We'll see," Hank said. "We haven't seen the results yet. He could still get elected as a government in exile." He laughed at his own joke.

"Well, there will only be an election if some of the recall measures pass. When the word gets out, I doubt anyone would vote for him."

"Don't be so sure," McTavish said. "When Bunny Copper got indicted for income tax evasion, she withdrew her name from the county treasurer ballot, and got elected anyway."

"Yes, there is that," Hank said.

"More beer?" Bess asked. "Or how about a pitcher of margaritas?"

"Works for me," Jake said.

A woman in skin tight jeans and a tank top was feeding quarters into a video poker machine. Betty Sue and Lavar had wandered over and put a few coins in the machine next to hers. They came back to the table. "We can't keep up with her," Betty Sue said quietly. "She must have dropped eighty bucks in the last half hour."

"Well, it's keeping our state government solvent." I looked at Betty Sue, to see how she was taking this. All her work, and all her carefully thought-out analysis, were getting flushed down the toilet. On the outside, she would be philosophical about it, but it had to hurt. At the same time, she was probably relieved just to be done with it. She caught my eye and must have read my thoughts. She gave me small smile and shrugged.

Mary came in and sat next to me. She had been at a PTA meeting. I hugged her shoulder and she rubbed my knee. I noticed that she avoided eye contact with the council members.

"So what's happening?" she said.

"Too early to tell," I said. "The Willamette Valley deal is passing, the City/County contract is failing, but they've only counted a third of the ballots."

She raised her eyebrows. Those weren't the issues she was worried about.

"No results on the recall measures yet," I said. "Don't know why, though. Want some of Bess' margaritas?"

I got up to get her a glass. Will Smith was leaning at the bar, drinking a Coke and talking to the waitress.

Finally, another set of results started appearing on the screen. The room got quiet as the group waited for the Trillium results.

"Oh well," McTavish said when the fire issues came up. With two-thirds counted, the results hadn't changed much.

Suddenly the recall measures came up. "Recall—Mayor D. McTavish. Yes 2,455. No 15,888. Recall—Councilor S. Rosenberg. Yes 3,066. No 14,750. Recall—Councilor H. Arnold. Yes 1,905. No 16,250."

McTavish let out a hoot. Seth raised his glass in a toast. They were beaming. My staff was supposed to be immune from politics, but the relief was apparent in their faces.

"Go figure," McTavish said. "They don't like our ideas but they keep us in government anyway."

"No, I think the voters expect us to make decisions, even if they don't always agree with them," Hank said. "They don't blame us for putting choices on the ballot. We're just doing our job."

Bess laughed. "No offense, but the voters don't know shit. That's fine with me, though—I'd just as soon keep working for y'all."

Mary reached under the table and squeezed my hand. I caught her eye and winked. Bess and her colleagues were interested enough in the results of the recall election, but for Mary and me, it meant that I had my job back—at least for the time being.

25

The Boeing 767 climbed, heading west over the Columbia River. It was a clear morning, and I could see the Cascade peaks—Mt. Hood, Jefferson, the Three Sisters—from my window seat. After a few minutes, the plane banked sharply to the right, and I got a good view of the volcanic crater of Mt. St. Helens, and Mt. Rainer to the north. Mt. Adams began to appear from under the wing.

I pulled my briefcase out from under the seat and went through some papers. We had less than six weeks left to complete the assimilation of our fire department by the Willamette Valley Fire District. It could have been complicated, but the district had done it enough times that they had the process down pat. The union had already worked out the staff transition details, which was potentially the stickiest part. There were some remaining issues involving the assumption of the city's debt for fire equipment, and transfer of assets like the fire stations themselves, but they were down to minor details.

The sudden removal of $4 million in expenses from the city's budget was like a mid-year Christmas present. We had already assumed $800,000 in savings from the City/County contract, but this still left over $3 million. The council had restored all the programs they had cut in the past year, and still had money left over. It was an odd situation to be in, and the interesting thing was that it didn't make my job much easier. The competition between the departments for the extra money was creating more tension than the cutting process had. But it was keeping me busy, and the new set of challenges almost made me forget what I had gone through before the election.

With Pritchard's departure, the Trillium Business Leadership Committee had faded into oblivion. It did give me some satisfaction, but I knew I shouldn't gloat about it—some other group of malcontents would take their place soon enough.

I couldn't keep my thoughts on work, though. Just after the election, I had read my last e-mail from Kate. She had written that she was thinking of leaving Gordon. In vain, I had sent her a string of messages, imploring her not to go through with it, to seek counseling or some other alternative. I told myself I was looking out for her well-being, but I was tormented by guilt over the possibility that I had driven her away from her husband.

She hadn't responded to my messages, and in desperation, I finally called her. She was cheerful enough on the phone, but when I asked her why she was ignoring my e-mails, she had simply told me she couldn't talk about it. I didn't want to push her, but I wanted desperately to connect to her.

I couldn't get much work done on the flight, and finally passed the time by reading a novel. I changed planes in Chicago, and got stuck on a full 727 for the flight into DC National. I was travelling light, and carried my bag to the Metro station. The evening commute was in full force and I had to thread my way through the crowd to make the transfer at L'Enfant Plaza. I stood for the three stops it took to get to the hotel.

My meeting with the ICMA Committee on Public Safety wasn't scheduled until the next morning, so I had some time to kill. I wondered around in downtown Washington, looking for a grocery store, and finally found a high-priced convenience store that would sell me an apple and a small block of cheese. I carried it down to the capitol mall and sat on a bench, watching a group of bureaucrats play a late evening game of softball on the grass.

I took a few laps in the hotel pool, then returned to my room for what I knew would be a difficult time going to sleep. It wasn't just the time change. I tried to picture Kate sleeping next to me, and realized with some surprise and relief that it was Mary who I really wanted there. I latched onto anything I could find to ease my guilt. I called Mary, but didn't have much to say except that the trip had been uneventful so far.

I finally fell asleep during the commercials near the end of Letterman's show, and woke up a few hours later with a wake up call from the hotel operator. I showered and put on a navy suit and a conservative striped tie, vaguely wondering who I was trying to impress. I would be meeting with a bunch of city managers, and it really didn't matter what they thought about me.

I caught the Metro to the offices of the International City Management Association. The receptionist directed me to the meeting room. I looked for a familiar face, and found none.

A man in his mid-fifties with a bit of a paunch saw my hesitation and made his way over to me.

"Hi, I'm Art Lebanon, chairman of the Public Safety Committee."

"Hi Art, I'm Ben Cromarty from Trillium. Hey, I thought your name would be Robespierre."

"Why's that?"

"You know, public safety committee? Never mind, it's a bad joke. So what do you have in mind for me here?"

"Well, just tell us the whole story about your experiences with the fire issue, from the beginning to the end. Take your time—we've blocked the whole morning out for it. I know the other committee members will be fascinated by it. We've been exploring a lot of ways to make fire service more efficient, but from what I hear, you've taken it farther than most cities."

"Yeah, but it was pretty much a disaster. I wouldn't want to wish it on anyone."

"Doesn't matter. Give us all the details, including the union issues and the politicking. You never know, maybe your story will inspire enough other cities that somebody will finally be able to pull it off."

We shared a few war stories as the committee members filed in. Most were city managers, but there were a few assistants, and a couple of police and fire chiefs. About a third of the members were women, a much higher ratio than when I entered the profession.

I had prepared a few notes, but I made my presentation from memory. I had some handouts to keep the committee members' hands occupied. I supposed I should have enjoyed being in the spotlight, but the truth was that I had had enough of the whole issue and didn't particularly like revisiting it. Near the end of my presentation, as I described being cut loose on administrative leave, my audience was spellbound. I was humble enough to realize it wasn't my speaking prowess. They were all sitting there thinking, "but for the grace of God go I…"

The staff had sent for box lunches, and we ate them in the meeting room. I sat next to June Rosencruz, the city manager of Traverse City, Michigan. I had known her earlier, when we were both working in other cities, and we talked about the turns our careers had taken. She had gotten divorced a few years earlier, and I caught her when she glanced at my wedding ring.

After lunch, the committee's attention turned to the latest developments in community oriented policing. I excused myself, and descended underground again to take the Metro to the capitol. I hoped to catch our congressman, Al Disdera, in his office, but he was off in some meeting. I did manage to see his chief legislative aide, Anna Golden, and we sat in her small, wood-paneled office, drinking coffee and catching up on issues in Trillium and on Capitol Hill.

She asked why I was in DC, and I told her.

"That reminds me," she said. "I was surprised you folks opposed the National League of Cities on the OSHA issue."

"What issue is that?"

"The bill that OSHA is pushing that would require four-man fire crews as a safety issue. The League was pretty adamant that it would cause a huge increase in costs without a demonstrated improvement in safety. I think they're right—the safety record for firefighters is actually better than for a lot of outdoor professions."

"And you say Trillium opposed that position?"

"Sure. Your fire chief—what's his name?"

"Max Oakley."

"Right. He spoke to the subcommittee on occupational safety and health, urging them to adopt the four-man requirement. He was really pretty eloquent, I hear. The bill has a good chance of passing."

"When was this?"

"About a month ago." She squinted at me, making some of the freckles on her forehead move. "This is news to you, isn't it?"

"Yep. But it doesn't really surprise me. Max can be a loose canon sometimes. It is ironic, isn't it? Here we're paying a few thousand dollars in dues for the League to represent our interests, and at the same time footing the bill for Oakley to fly out here and oppose the League."

"Maybe you didn't foot the bill. The Firefighters Association could well have sponsored his trip."

"You may be right. I can find out easily enough. But you know, it doesn't matter any more—at least to Trillium."

"Yeah, I guess not."

Anna had ignored a half dozen phone calls, but I didn't want to take any more of her time. I invited her to stop by city hall the next time she was back home in Oregon.

It was only mid afternoon, so I strolled over to the National Air and Space Museum. Summer vacation must have already started for some schools, since the place was full of families with children. I was overdressed in my suit, but no one seemed to notice. The exhibits held as much fascination for me as they did for the school kids.

I finally walked back to the hotel. I passed couples on the sidewalk, arm in arm, heading for happy hour. The prospect of dinner alone in the hotel's coffee shop didn't seem very appealing. to me.

I watched some news, and was thinking about ordering a sandwich from room service when the phone rang.

"Hello, Ben?"

It was a high, sweet voice.

"Kate! Hi! I've been dying to hear from you. How're you doing?"

"Oh, fine, just fine."

It was an unusually clear connection.

"Where are you?"

"Well, actually, I'm down here in the lobby of your hotel."

I froze, speechless.

2 6

"Ben? Are you still there?"

I sat down on the bed and struggled for words. "Yes. Sorry. You caught me off guard. Do you want to come up?"

"No... Could you come down here?"

"Uh...sure. Just give me a second."

I paced around the room and checked myself in the mirror. On my way out I almost latched the door before I remembered to get my room key. I watched through the glass walls of the elevator, looking for Kate, but didn't see her until the doors opened. She was wearing a long tropical-looking skirt, and a simple white blouse. She smiled shyly.

"Hi Ben. It's good to see you."

She came close and hugged me. I wrapped my arms around her back. For a long moment she nuzzled her face into my neck. Then she gently pushed back.

"What...uh, why...." I wasn't impressing myself with my conversational skills.

"What am I doing here?" she said. "I came to see you, silly. Actually, I was in Philadephia working on some details with my SBA loan—don't ask, it's a long story—and decided I needed to talk to you."

"Oh. Well, I'm glad you did."

"Can we go somewhere? Like to dinner or something?"

"Uh, yeah." The sounds of the lobby seeped back into my consciousness. I thought of room service again, but decided not to bring it up. "You know, there's a good place in Georgetown. A French restaurant that I went to a few years ago. How does that sound?"

"Fine."

"Do you have a suitcase?"

"No, just this."

She patted the purse that hung over her shoulder.

"Well, let's get a cab."

The driver had never heard of L'Auberge des Pays, but he got us to Georgetown and I managed to navigate us to the restaurant. There was a half hour wait for a table, so we sipped on Perrier water in the bar.

"So. Here we are," I said.

Kate laughed. "Sounds like a honeymoon."

"Hmm. But I won't go there. So…."

"You have a lot of questions, but you don't know where to start, right?"

I smiled. "You've had more time to think about this conversation, Kate."

"Not that much. I kind of got on the plane on impulse. And I really don't know what to say, except I decided it wasn't fair to leave you hanging. We've shared too much, and I value your friendship too much for that."

Friendship? "Okay. Start with the easy parts. How's your new business venture coming?"

"It's hard to describe. In one way, I'm loving it—there's so many new things to do, you know? And my customers are being great about it, except the ones that are total jerks and don't like change. I wish you and Mary could see the things we've done to the place."

"You're pretty proud of it, huh?"

"Yeah. But it takes up so much time. The boys are having all of their end-of-school activities and all that, and I just can't give it the time I need to. But I guess that's the story of my life."

"Have you been able to hire any staff yet to take some of the load off?"

"One person, yeah, but she's sort of a ditz, and I have to spend my time training her. I can't afford to hire anybody else until we start making more money." She grinned. "I don't know why I let you talk me into that deal in the first place."

I laughed. Her dress had a slit in it, up past her knees, and my eyes strayed to her legs. They were smooth and tan, like I remembered them, but I guessed that was from her nylons. Somewhere in the restaurant, a violinist played a Mozart sonata. We talked about our jobs until we were summoned to our table, taking plenty of time to re-connect. In spite of our intimacy, the e-mail correspondence had provided some emotional distance. Kate's physical presence was now making me re-learn how to talk to a woman I had fallen in love with.

We ordered the seven-course meal that the chef recommended, wanting to make it last as long as possible. My French was rusty, and I didn't have a clue what was coming.

The waiter brought our salads. Kate dug into hers like she hadn't eaten all day. She finished before me and put down her fork.

"And you're probably wondering about me and Gordon…"

"Yeah, I was sort of guessing you might get around to that."

"Mmm. Well, before I tell you, you do know there's no way for us to be together, don't you?"

"'You mean you and me, or you and Gordon?"

"You and me. Right? You have thought about it, haven't you?"

"Sure. I guess you're right, as much as I don't want to admit it. We probably couldn't live together, anyway—we'd drive each other crazy."

She laughed and I felt her knee push against mine. "Yeah, I know what you mean." She looked at me for a moment, and I thought I saw her blink a tear away.

"Anyway, I did a lot of soul searching, and decided the only thing that made sense was to really try to patch things up with Gordon."

"You make it sound like an intellectual exercise."

She raised her eyes at me. "Are you teasing me? Don't do that—this is hard enough already."

"No hon, I'm sorry. And I know you're right. I tried to tell you that. Did you read any of my messages?"

"Of course. I read them all. They helped, really. I just couldn't write back—I had to work this all out myself."

The violin player came over to our table and we stopped talking. Our legs were intertwined, and as we listened, Kate put her hand over mine. I wondered if we were supposed to tip him, but then decided that in a classy place like that, we were simply expected to leave a huge tip at the end of the meal.

I squeezed Kate's hand. We were both wearing wedding rings, and I didn't care if people thought we were married. We didn't speak again until the violinist moved on to another table.

"So what will you do to rebuild your marriage?"

"Well… someone said that God brings us together, but creeping separateness drives us apart. I think that's been our problem. So the obvious answer is to make more time for each other, and to work on doing things together that we both enjoy. We agreed we wouldn't spend as much time on work, even if it comes down to selling our businesses. Anyway, that's the general plan."

The waiter brought another course, and said something in French. Kate poked at her plate with her fork.

"What do you suppose this is?"

I shrugged. "Snails? Who knows."

We ate in silence for a few moments.

"You know what we even did last weekend?" she said.

"No, what?" I started to picture a romantic weekend retreat, and decided maybe I didn't want to hear the details.

"We went to church."

"You're kidding. I mean, that's good, but what made you decide to do it?"

"Our counselor recommended it. And I've been thinking it wouldn't hurt Luke and Josh either. You know? They're around so much negative stuff at school, a lot of their friends are pretty screwed up, or at least their parents are…it just seemed like they could use some positive examples."

"Where did you go?"

"A big place. Community Church of the Rockies, I think it was called. Seemed all right—better than I thought it would be."

"You didn't have to sing too many old hymns, eh?"

"Yeah—none at all, in fact. Anyway, we'll give it a try for a while. Maybe there's hope for a wretch like me."

"Yep, that's how the song goes." I filled her wine glass. "I admire you, Kate. I hope you stick with it, even if sometimes it's tough. I used to think that church potlucks were designed to shape us up by giving us a taste of hell. You know, sitting on uncomfortable chairs, talking to people you don't know very well, eating a plateful of Jell-O and mystery casseroles, and worrying about who you're going to offend because you didn't sample their hamburger helper surprise."

Her laugh was a sound that I lived for. In all the months of writing to each other, it was something I missed. That, and seeing her eyes. In the candlelight I discovered that they were actually pale blue with a halo of darker opal. I watched her and sighed.

"What are you thinking?" she said.

"I probably shouldn't say."

"Oh go ahead."

"Well, I was just thinking how much I love you. I don't want to change your mind or anything, but I just can't help it."

She leaned so close that her forehead almost touched mine. "I feel the same way, Ben, and that's probably something that will never change—at least I hope not. The last few weeks went better for me, thinking about you being there. You know?"

"Yeah."

My butt was going to sleep, but I didn't want to untangle my legs from hers.

"It's been the same for me," I said. "With all the insanity at the city, I don't know what I would have done without you."

The courses continued to come, and we ate without hurrying. It was after midnight when we finished our coffee and dessert. We were the last couple left in the place. Kate insisted on splitting the bill—she said it would make it less complicated when I filled out my expense account. I told her that it didn't matter, that the bill was too steep to have the city pay for it, but she insisted anyway.

When we stood up, Kate swayed and leaned against me. Maybe the bottle of wine, I thought, or just sitting too long.

Outside, the night was warm—at least compared to what both of us were used to.

"Where do you want to go?" I asked.

"I better be getting back."

"To Philadelphia?"

"Yes."

"You're not going to find a flight at this hour. Besides, I don't want you to go."

For the first time in my life, I kissed her. Instead of resisting, she pushed her body against mine. Her taste and the feel of her heat were intoxicating. I slid my hand along her side and felt her tremble.

She pushed away, leaving her hands on my shoulders.

"This probably isn't a real good idea," she said breathlessly.

"I guess not. But I liked it, Kate."

"Me too." Her eyes were moist in the lamplight. "Let's walk."

"Sure."

We wandered aimlessly along the streets of Georgetown, holding hands and talking. We eventually made our way into a nightclub that had a live band, but we really weren't interested in drinking much, and the music was too loud.

Back on the streets, we slowly made our way back toward the capitol. Even the hookers and drug dealers were disappearing, and there was a faint hint of light to the east. I suppose we should have been concerned about getting mugged, but we were oblivious to the risk.

Kate said, "What about you and Mary? Don't you think our secret life has had some effect on you two?"

"I don't know. I tell myself it hasn't, and that in some ways our relationship is stronger than ever. But then I wonder, when I think of you and write love notes to you, am I taking something away from her? Would I be doing that with Mary instead? But it isn't that simple." We stepped over the legs of a wino sleeping on the sidewalk, his top half covered in a cardboard box. "Sometimes when I came up with something good to write to you, I used it in a note to Mary too. She was pleased, I think—said it seemed like I was courting her again. Does that make you jealous?"

"No, not really. I've been close to Mary more years than I've known you."

A breeze blowing between the buildings chilled me. Her hand felt warm in mine. "Well anyway, sometimes I even forgot which one of you I said something to. Like, did I ever send you the words to the 7th chapter of the Song of Solomon? You know, Your rounded thighs are like jewels, your two breasts are like two fawns, that sort of thing?"

"No. Wish you had though."

"See? I must have left that in a note to Mary, some place where she would discover it at work. Of course, maybe I was doing all that to ease my guilt about being so crazy about you. I just don't know."

We ended up at the reflecting pond in front of the capitol building. The sun lit up the top of the Washington Monument. I took off my shoes and socks and dangled my feet in the water. After so much walking, it was refreshing. Kate checked to make sure no one else was around, then hiked up her skirt so she could roll off her pantyhose. She put them in her purse and eased her feet into the pond.

"So what're we going to do?" I said.

Kate was silent for a long moment.

"We can't go on this way," she said. "I think we have to end our secret correspondence, much as I hate to say it."

The buildings on the west end of the mall were bathed in red. I looked at Kate's face in the reflected glow.

"But," she said, "we could still send an occasional message to each other, as long as we sent it to the whole family. You know what I mean? Just nothing secret or spicy."

"Yeah. It wouldn't be the same, but it would be something." I knew it wouldn't work.

"It's better this way. We have enough secrets between us that we can never tell anyone. We're better off not making more."

A flock of geese flew over, honking.

"You're a strong person, Kate. I'm impressed."

"Don't be. I'm just saying what we *should* do. We haven't put it to the test yet. I tell myself I'm going to be strict with Luke, but then I let him get away with murder. Josh doesn't give me any trouble, but Luke pushes me when he knows I'm out of energy or willpower. So I'm not that strong. This will only work because you are."

"I am what?"

"Strong. If you tell yourself this is what we need to do, you're the one that can make it happen."

"Gee, thanks. It's going to take some prayer, though. Now that you're a church-goer, you can understand that."

"I guess so."

We let our feet dry in the cool air, our shoulders touching as we sat on the granite side of the reflecting pond. We finally put our shoes back on, and walked arm in arm to Pennsylvania Avenue. The traffic was picking up. I flagged down a cab.

We held each other for as long as we could. Then I watched helplessly as the taxi took Kate away.

2 7

Every year, it seemed the airlines squeezed the seats a few inches closer together, and took out another of the plane's restrooms. I figured the airlines should just skip the pretense about comfort and administer a drug before every flight to put the passengers into a deep stupor. I didn't need it though: I slept hard on the first leg of my flight back to Portland.

As the plane taxied into the gate at Denver, I thought about my night with Kate, replaying it in my mind. I could still see her in the candlelight, in the moonlight, in the light of the reflecting pond. I savored the images, knowing they would fade over the next few months.

Then my mind drifted to the coming week at work, forcing a hard reality check. Betty Sue had sent a fax to my hotel room, giving me an update. The public works union was insisting on some major increases for standby pay and shift differentials—they knew the fire department was freeing up a lot of money, and they didn't want to miss the gravy train. All the lawsuits against the city had been dropped, except one: the personal suit against me for the alleged violation of the open meetings law. A parting shot from the Fire Association, which had taken over the case from the now-defunct TBLC. Depositions were scheduled for next Wednesday. But, on the positive side, the Fly Creek Fire Board had suddenly dropped its opposition to the golf course project, under pressure from their own volunteer firefighters. It appeared that a lot of them hoped to get hired by Willamette Fire.

I made my connection, and got a window seat. We took off to the south and climbed to get over the Rockies. I tried to find Kate's house below, but the city was too far away. I pushed the thought from my mind, and pulled a novel out of my briefcase. When the plane leveled off, a steward pushed a cart down the narrow aisle, passing out containers with cold salads and packets of imitation food. I washed mine down with a ginger ale. When the steward came by again, I started to ask for coffee, but changed my mind when I saw the line for the restroom.

I drifted in and out of sleep. We seemed to be flying through clear skies all the way from Denver, but we hit clouds when the plane crossed the Cascades. It was a climate pattern that I had become accustomed to. The plane descended into the white blanket, and I couldn't see anything until the Columbia appeared in the gloom.

I found my carry-on bag and joined the herd moving up the jetway. I saw Mary waiting for me at the gate, alone in the crowd of people. Her hair fell on her white T-shirt in a cascade of gold. She grinned and moved forward to hug me. It was good being home.

*   *   *

I had been back in the office for two days when Simon Garrett called. "There's something we need to talk about," he said cryptically. It wasn't unusual; he was good about keeping me informed about cases in progress. But when I asked if he wanted to meet at his usual booth at the Fir Away Café, he said that it would be better to meet in his office. This piqued my curiosity.

I hadn't spent much time in Simon's office. Neither had he, for that matter. He was more likely to be in the squad room, skimming over his officers' reports, or riding with one of the sergeants or officers, or sitting at his table at the café, smoking his pipe. In contrast to the luxurious mahogany of Max Oakley's office, the walls of Simon's office were finished in rough hewn cedar planks that he had nailed up himself one weekend eight years ago. Commendations, photos of officers and relatives, and yellowing cartoons cut from newspapers were tacked haphazardly on the wood. Simon's wooden swivel chair creaked when he leaned back. I pushed aside some papers on his desk to rest my coffee cup, and sat in a red vinyl chair, its padding poking out from a small tear in the front corner. I waited, knowing that Simon wouldn't be rushed when telling a story.

"Here's one I thought you would enjoy." He pulled a typed report out of a stack and fished around for his reading glasses. "Yeah, here it is.

Howlett wrote it when he arrested a drunk driver. It goes, 'When the subject got out of the car, I informed him that he was under arrest and to get on the ground. The subject responded with a raised middle finger and matching expletive. I then pulled out my pepper spray and warned the subject to get on the ground or he would be sprayed. The subject refused. I sprayed him and administered several blows to the wrist with my sap. Subject finally went to his knees, at which time I was able to cuff him.'" Simon glanced at me over his glasses. "Now get this," he said. "Howlett writes, 'I noted that he had a moderate odor of alcohol and slurred his expletives.' How do like that? 'He slurred his expletives!'" Simon took off his glasses and guffawed.

"Good job. The prosecutor and a judge will get a kick out of that." I pictured them sitting in the judge's chambers, imitating some choice slurred expletives.

"Yeah. Most of the guys hate writing these things, but a few of them are creative." Simon rubbed his chin, then abruptly got up and closed his office door—a first in the ten years I had known him. He sat back down and propped his elbows on the desk, peering into the bottom of his empty coffee cup. "I've got a, uh, delicate situation. It involves Max Oakley," he said.

"Oh?"

"Uh huh. Remember when you mentioned that he once worked for City/County Fire?" I nodded, although I really didn't remember telling Simon about it. "Well, it got me to thinking. I've been here longer than him, so I reckoned I would have known about it. And what really got me curious was why it never showed up on his resume."

"You've got a copy of his resume?" I asked, surprised. Simon never struck me as someone who would keep that kind of thing.

"Yeah, well, your secretary sort of let me into his personnel file."

"Really?"

"Yes. I assured her it was official police business. And that she couldn't tell anyone. Anyway, there wasn't any mention of it, so I went ahead and talked to some of the folks down there in Arizona, and started figuring out why it never showed up in his file."

Simon leaned back in his chair, still serious but relishing his role as storyteller. I raised my eyebrows, willing him to continue.

"See," he said, "it turns out that old Max was there all right. Only a couple of years, but that was enough, I guess. He was put in charge of equipment specs and procurement when they were expanding into some of the New Mexico and Nevada markets. They were buying half million dollar pumpers like they were goin' out of style, mostly from American LaFrance, but from other companies too."

With a feeling of morbid fascination, I started to guess where this was heading. "And some of the funds turned up missing, huh?"

"Yep. One of their auditors stumbled onto it when they tried to match invoices to purchase orders and payments. There were duplicate payments to vendors, and payments on a few invoices that the companies denied they had ever submitted. Somebody had to have forged signatures when they deposited the checks, but they never did figure out who did it."

"How's that?" I asked. "*Your* guys have always managed to solve embezzlement cases." It was true: Kimberly Phelps—one of our detectives—was a genius at sorting through stacks of accounting records and seeing the patterns that led to arrests and convictions.

"Yeah, but they didn't bring in the cops. I guess they figured that, on balance, the bad PR would outweigh the loss. They depended on their reputation as a well-run, efficient business. Compared to the value of their new contracts, a couple of million bucks wasn't that big a deal. 'Course, they had to do something. Old Max wasn't directly implicated, but at best, he was guilty of mismanagement. Since it happened on his watch, he took the fall for it, and moved to Roseburg."

"How'd he cover the gap in his resume?" I asked. I may have looked at it once, but if so, it had been a decade ago.

"It just said he was working on his master's degree at ASU. Which is true; he was doing that, but only part time."

"Okay. So?...." There had to be more to the story.

Simon leaned forward. "You know Max is sort of a type A guy? Pretty meticulous?" I nodded; compared to Simon, Oakley was downright compulsive. "Well," he continued, "it turns out that he kept detailed records on the whole thing—how he set up the accounts, where he deposited the funds, and where he moved the money to when the audit caught up with him."

I was speechless. Simon let the silence hang, his jaw set but with a flash of amusement in his eyes. I could hear the muffled sound of telephones ringing behind his office door, and the ticking of a cuckoo clock on the wall behind me.

"What, he had all this stuff just sitting in a file in his office?" I finally said.

"No. It is—or was—buried with a bunch of tax stuff in a desk in his house."

"Okay. So how did you get it?"

"Got a search warrant, and just found it."

I shook my head. "I may have been preoccupied the last few weeks, but I can't believe all this happened without me knowing it. I mean, if nothing else, Max would have been in my office, pounding on my desk and telling me to keep you off his back."

"Yeah, but he didn't know about the search warrant. We just happened to get it when he was out of town somewhere. DC or someplace like that. Gave us plenty of time for a really thorough search."

It seemed fitting. Simon had always been critical of Oakley's out-of-town conferences. "He still doesn't know?"

"Oh, he knows now. We had to leave a copy of the search warrant on his kitchen table. Pesky state law, you know. It kind of tickles me picturing him sitting there waiting for the shoe to drop. City/County seems a lot more interested in prosecuting, and the Maricopa County D.A. is eager for us to send him back there. So I'm ready to make the arrest. But I wanted to, uh, talk to you first."

Talk to me? I wondered if he was just extending a professional courtesy, or feeling me out to see if he should follow through with it. I thought about Max's quiet and comforting presence as we raced to the hospital on the prank call about Trixie. And the way I had publicly defended him after the union's no-confidence vote. Then another image formed: Max sitting in a coffee shop somewhere, telling Rob Titus about the Willamette Valley Fire District proposal and making broad hints that I had instructed him to keep the information from the city council.

"You've gotta do what you gotta do," I said.

"Of course. But I just wanted to let you know before the shit hit the fan."

It would be a mess, but I couldn't say I didn't look forward to it. I could at least give Sabrina Chan a heads up—I owed her that much.

"So, is there anything to the inheritance story, or is this how he really got his money?"

"No, that was the first thing I checked, because I could do it on my own. I dug around in probate records here and in Arizona and everywhere else he's lived, and couldn't find anything about an inheritance like that. And when he worked at Roseburg, nobody figured he was independently wealthy then. It's what got me suspicious. He must have concocted that story here, when he wanted to start using the money."

I thought about Max's lifestyle and the extra income someone would have if they invested two or three million dollars. It seemed to fit. "You must have put a lot of time into this, Simon."

"Yeah. It was worth it. See, he came in one day, all friendly like, but all he was really interested in was my retirement plans. That sort of pissed me off."

I didn't tell Simon that I had been the one to put that idea into Oakley's head. Unwittingly—or maybe subconsciously—I had put the investigation into motion. "Who else knows?" I asked.

"Only Sgt. Ramos and Detective Phelps. But I have to move fast on the arrest, or word will get out somehow. The City/County boys have got to know by now that I have something on this."

"Yeah, you're right." I started to get up. It wouldn't have been right for me to be anywhere near when Simon made the trip to Oakley's office.

"One more thing, Ben." Simon leaned back and waited for me to sit down.

"What's that?"

"You know that fire out at your house?"

"Yeah....?" He had my full attention again.

"After it happened, one of the firefighters mentioned that a couple of gallons of kerosene seemed to be missing from the training tower. They wouldn't have noticed it, except they had to do an inventory for the annual audit."

"So?"

"So when I was out at Oakley's place, I thought I saw a couple of those cans in his garage. I didn't pay too much attention to them at the time, since I wasn't looking for any connections with the fire, but I'm pretty sure I saw them."

"Well, why don't you send somebody out there to check it out?"

"I did. Well, it was me, actually. Last weekend, when I knew that Oakley and the missus were at a retirement banquet. It was dark and I had to use a flashlight through a side window. The shelf was empty."

"Really?" I pictured Simon lurking around in the dark in Max's neighborhood. The high cedar fences would have given him plenty of cover. "Well, that's not much to go on."

"Right. But it got me to thinking. Tell me this: did you ask Max directly if he had ever worked for City/County?"

"Yeah, I think so. I don't remember what he said, though."

"Okay. When, exactly, was this?"

I tried playing back our conversations, connecting them with events. But too much had been happening to keep it all straight. "Let me see. I wanted to ask him about it, but then that vote of no-confidence issue came up. We had a meeting in a restaurant, and I might have brought it up then." It seemed so long ago, but it wasn't, really. "It could be that I asked, but then the call from the hospital came in and I forgot about it. I just don't know."

"Was that before the fire?"

"Yes." Those events were still clear in my memory, as much as I wanted to forget them.

"Hmmm." Simon absently tapped a pencil against the side of his coffee cup.

"What are you thinking?"

He looked up. "I don't really have anything that will stick. But it might be something I can use if Max gets, uh, uncooperative."

A thought occurred to me. "Are you sure you're going to be able to track him down? I heard he was already moving some of his stuff into his new office in the Willamette Fire headquarters."

Simon grinned. "I'll find him. He was in his Station One office when you got here." He turned serious. "Ben, I'll do this as discreetly as I can. We can do the booking down at the county jail, and avoid stirring stuff up here. But we can't keep it quiet."

"Yes, I know." The rest of my day would have to be spent in calls to Council members, a carefully worded press release, and fielding questions. I could get Betty Sue to help with some of the behind-the-scenes work, and I smiled when I thought of how much she would relish the task. "What about having the D.A. and County Sheriff handle all the press and public contacts?" I asked. "I don't want this to seem like a personal grudge."

"Makes sense. That's how we've handled internal situations in the past."

Once more, I got up to leave. "Hey Simon, thanks for your work on this. You're a good man."

"It's my pleasure. Really."

*   *   *

When I got home, Mary listened to the news with wide-eyed amazement. She wasn't one to let resentment fester, and I was often impressed with her ability to forgive people. But she was unusually cheerful at dinner, as if her sense of balance and justice was restored.

Before she went to bed I read to Trixie from T.H. White's *The Once and Future King*. I had read it years earlier, but I couldn't remember the details. Did Lancelot keep his love secret from Guinevere? Or if she was aware of it, did she and the hapless knight summon sheer willpower to keep from expressing their attraction, out of their love and respect for Arthur? Or was Lancelot doomed to give in to his feelings for the Queen and incur a reluctant banishment by the King? I supposed that, being a legend, it could accommodate any of the variations. The one that I knew would never work, though, was for Lancelot and Guinevere to live happily ever after. The once and future conundrum.

After a chapter, I tucked Trixie in, then sat next to Mary on the living room couch. I handed her an envelope.

"What's this?" she asked.

"Tickets for a four-day weekend at Cabo San Lucas."

"Really? When?"

"The weekend after next. I figured you could get away easier once classes were out."

"Sure, and Trixie too."

"No, just the two of us. I made arrangements for Trixie to stay with Abbie while we're gone."

"Ah," she murmured. "A romantic getaway, huh?"

"Yep. That okay with you?"

Instead of answering, she just hugged me and pressed her cheek to my chest.

*   *   *

A month later, I found myself back in Fire Station One, having been invited to attend the celebration of the handover of our fire department to the Willamette Valley Fire District. It was in the middle of the day, to avoid paying overtime to the assistant chiefs and others on a five-day work week. I hadn't looked forward to it, and thought that I would, at best, feel awkward surrounded by individuals who had only months earlier tried to get me fired. But they were all cordial, greeting me warmly and acting like nothing had happened.

I wandered through the crowd, holding a plate of meatballs on sticks. A callout was signaled on a loudspeaker, dozens of pagers sounded, and four of the firefighters hustled out of the room with self-important expressions on their faces. I looked around, but didn't see any sign of Brian Gallagher. I approached Phil Tucker, who had been a captain with our department, and was now a battalion chief with Willamette Valley. I hadn't seen him since he had lent me his coat and fetched a hot cup of coffee as we sat on the porch after the fire.

"Hey Phil, congratulations on your promotion."

"Thanks, Ben. It was good of you to come over for this."

I shrugged. "It's no problem." We talked about the changes that the fire district was making, and how it had affected some of our mutual acquaintances. We were standing by a window, and out of the corner of my eye I could see the fire truck returning to the station. Must have been a false alarm. "So where's Gallagher?" I asked.

Tucker glanced at my eyes, trying to gauge if it was just an innocent question. "Didn't you hear? He's in California. Or, he will be in a month or two. He got a job as a contract negotiator for a bunch of the bargaining units in the Bay area."

"Is that so?" I said. "I would have thought he would have wanted to stay through the transition."

"Uh, I'm not sure he was offered a job with Willamette," Tucker said quietly.

I considered that for a moment. The fire district was completely dominated by current and former firefighters, from the entry-level recruits to the chairman of the fire board itself. But the executive staff wouldn't be any more enthusiastic about union strife than I was. It made sense that they would want to keep him off the payroll.

"Well, I'll be darned," I said.

"Yeah. You've probably figured this out, but the troops will often push a guy like Gallagher to the front and let him do their battle for them. Then they just stand back and watch. It's entertainment for them, like watching a gladiator fight. Most of them are sort of—what's the word?—appalled by the tactics their fighter uses, but hey, if they all make out better in the end, they're glad to put up with it. For Gallagher, though, it was a suicide mission."

"Hmm. Can't say I'm too sympathetic, though."

"Yeah, and the funny thing is, Gallagher didn't really care much either. He lives for the fight, and he probably reckoned that things were going to get pretty dull around here." Tucker scanned the crowd and spotted one of the Willamette Valley assistant chiefs. "Well, it's been good talking to you, Ben, but I've got to go over there and suck up for a while."

I laughed. "Good luck to you, Phil."

The speeches were mercifully brief and I was able to leave the party soon after. It occurred to me as I walked back to city hall that Max Oakley's name had never come up. The arrest had stirred things up enough, but Oakley was out on bail, waiting for a grand jury hearing. There hadn't been much more juice for conversation in a while. The sun warmed me as I walked, and I took off my coat and slung it over my shoulder. Mt. Hood dominated the eastern horizon, its snow cover retreating to the glaciers.

I returned a few calls, and had just put the phone down when my intercom buzzed. It was Marie in the downstairs lobby.

"Ben, there's someone heading up to your office to see you."

"Oh? Who?"

"Scarlet!"

I groaned. "Great." For an instant I thought of hiding. "Was she carrying anything?"

"Yeah, but I couldn't see it too clearly. Looked like maybe a dead goldfish in a jar or something. Oh, and there's a guy with her."

"You're kidding. Who?"

"Lenny Fiala, and he looked just as mad as the last time he came storming in here."

"Oh, man. Thanks for the warning, Marie." I moved as quickly as I could into the reception area, shutting my door behind me. I leaned on Terri's desk, and waited.

About the Author

Scott Lazenby has over twenty years experience in city management. He has degrees in physics and public management, and is the author of several nonfiction articles on government challenges. He and his wife Sandy live in the town of Sandy, Oregon, where he serves as city manager.

Made in the USA
Middletown, DE
30 January 2023

23508012R00236